"I hope yore ﾠ the phone, instantlﾠ ﾠ ﾠ ﾠ ﾠ ﾠ ﾠ ﾠ joy's eyes and blanketing her in panic.

"I'm *lying* down," she said, checking the bedside clock. "I do that at two thirty-seven in the morning."

"I know what time it is," Quida Raye snapped. "I just thought you might like to know Doyle's in jail and it's a miracle I'm not, too."

Joy sprang up in bed. Doyle was in jail? Had they run over someone? It was her worst fear, the thought of her mother hurtling through the night, a tawny, heat-seeking missile shot from charred, mangled metal. If there *had* been a wreck, Joy realized with some degree of relief, at least she was still alive.

"*What happened?*"

"They got him for grand theft," her mother said.

"*What?*" Joy heard a quick gulp of breath, nicotine nerves rushing to neurons near and far. Not even that steadied her mother's voice when she spoke again.

"Joy Faye, you know full well that truck we've been drivin' is stolen property."

She said this as if stating actual fact, as if stealing an eighteen-wheeler was a minor maternal detail that had simply slipped her daughter's mind. Joy Savoy knew what brand of beanie weenies her mother preferred. She was pretty sure, even jolted from a sound sleep, she would have recalled some mention of a snatched semi.

Praise for Kathy Des Jardins

"After joining The Alexandria (LA) Daily Town Talk, Kathy Des Jardins quickly became the 'star' of a staff of 50 talented journalists. Her regular column, laced with the sense of humor reflected in her first novel, and feature stories won a number of state, regional and national awards. Yet the enduring work was a remarkable investigative series focusing on domestic abuse. Des Jardins brings both her creative talent and her journalism skills to her debut novel."

~Jim Butler, former executive editor of The Alexandria Daily Town Talk and night editor of the Gulfport (MS) Sun Herald, winner of the 2006 Pulitzer Prize for Public Service for Hurricane Katrina coverage

~*~

"Kathy Des Jardins' storytelling is bright, funny, touching, and, most of all, authentic. Her boundless curiosity and compassion make her one of the South's best listeners, and she remembers every tale she has heard or lived. Her fiction reimagines this treasure chest of human experience and emotion for all of us to enjoy, to laugh and cry over, and to nod repeatedly at the truths we all recognize."

~Bruce C. Steele, author

~*~

"As an editor Kathy took chances, all in service of making tired writing sit upright in its coffin. As a writer, she appears to be leaping off the high dive."

~Herb Benham, Bakersfield Californian columnist and author

Mama Tried

by

Kathy Des Jardins

Kathy Des Jardins

Mama Tried

Cover Art by *The Wild Rose Press, Inc.*

The Wild Rose Press, Inc.
PO Box 708
Adams Basin, NY 14410-0708
Visit us at www.thewildrosepress.com

Publishing History
First Edition, 2022
Trade Paperback ISBN 978-1-5092-3966-5
Digital ISBN 978-1-5092-3967-2

Published in the United States of America

Dedication

For Will, Luke, and Jack.
If I could introduce you to your grandmother,
she might look a little like this.

My boundless thanks to:

My fairy godmother, Marilyn Baron, and the wish-granting team at The Wild Rose Press, particularly Nan Swanson, editor extraordinaire.

Angela Wendell Hayes for ghost stories I'll always believe and a rare friendship I'll forever cherish. Alice B. Thomas Story for unparalleled editing and four decades of fortitude. The incomparable Tracy Bedell, who shaped this entire story. My early readers, both friends and family—Yvonne Irby, the late Hope J. Norman, and retired Police Sergeant Marlene Bearden.

Roylee Erwin for invaluable radio tutelage, some of which I retained. All errors and liberties taken are my own. Dr. Stephen Norman for charity hospital and pecan input, the late Dr. Thomas Norman for cowboy hat advisement, and Mike and Leslie Elliott-Smith for vegetation consultation.

All who tolerated years of tedious book updates, chiefly the unrivaled Rick Bentley, co-worker at three of four newspapers charitable enough to hire me, including *The Alexandria Daily Town Talk*, where some of the flights of fancy herein first fluttered. Jeanne Marvine, Margaret Cohen, Lynn Easley, and retired Army Colonel Michael Eyre also get gold stars for help and endurance.

Those indomitable Lancaster boys—Jimmy for Harleys and heart, Ray for stories and soul, Uncle Larry for truck talk and grave tending, and Uncle Robert, leader of the pack that left too soon.

My husband, Ron Cioffi, for decades of patience and tireless support. All my sons, my all in all. And my mother, Lora Dale Lancaster Vinson Phillips, who is no doubt scootin' through stardust not so very far away.

Prologue
"Leaving Louisiana in the Broad Daylight"

Nashville, Tennessee, July 7, 2022

"Mother was ornery as a knot and tougher than gristle, but love could have saved her." Nodding at the engineer who would be running the board for however long this retrospective took, Joy Savoy paused to adjust the mic and consider her story. Not much had changed in all the time she'd been taping occasional guest spots regarding her long-ago life as Small Market Syndicated DJ of the Year. Hers was a simple tale of loves, lunacy, and lives lived between the lyrics of classic country songs. She knew it by heart and was always happy to share—mainly to hear the old tunes again.

"While love might have saved my mother," Joy continued, "a pair of stolen eighteen-wheelers, conversely, could not. Idling on either side of the three-year period during which her hijinks became the toast of a few towns, thanks to my ragtag radio show, those filched semis bookended—in long-haul, fume-choked fashion—the time I spent as the most popular country disc jockey in our small part of the world.

"But even though I got the glory, Quida Raye Perkins was always the story. And now she can be again, thanks to the fine folks here at *American Country Radio Revisited*," Joy said, giving the engineer a thumbs-up.

"They say all I've gotta do is play some songs and tell some stories about those years, in the middle of nowhere Louisiana, when my life became an open book with a soundtrack provided by country classics from the sixties, seventies, and eighties. As glad as I am that my hosts see value in such a gig, I learned long ago that the real service is in the sweet serenade. How, when I stop yakking and the old hits play again, you and I can be transported, free of charge, back to a time and place some of us would pay anything to visit again. If there's a better way to time travel than with a stack of oldie goldies, I've yet to find it. And I've been looking a while now.

"Back when I first mentioned my mother on air, women of a certain age seemed to relate to her sorry luck with men, those liars, cheats, and/or felonious thieves who always caught her eye. Then there were daughters who likely felt an uneasy kinship with DJ me—sullen, grumpy, and a good fifteen pounds on the far side of fine. In other words, not much of an improvement over the men. And not much of a problem for Mother's fan club, either.

"From that May morning in 1983, when she appeared at my door like a Cat Five hurricane and blew a man out of my bed, folks ate up everything Quida Raye Perkins did. They couldn't get enough of her big-haired, starched-jeans self, making her somewhat dated, slightly faded 'Yesterday's Wine' way toward a dance floor, hell-bent on scooting through sawdust across a hardwood memory.

"In no time, my radio show turned her into the consummate country music fan in the hearts of thousands. The collective sentiment seemed to suggest that, while country stars sang the songs, Quida Raye Perkins had *lived* them. Men and motherhood might have let my mama down, but the music never did. People who listen to country radio respond to plain truths like that.

"They also evidently have a soft spot for truck-driving, chain-smoking, sun-tanning, law-breaking, cola-guzzling know-it-alls. This became clear the first day I griped about Mother over twenty thousand watts and the phone lines lit up like propane cars in a train wreck. Everyone wanted to tell me what mule-headed moms they had, too. The more I bellyached, the higher my ratings climbed, till I was soon contractually obligated to make Quida Raye Perkins the bull's-eye in the middle of the best classic country forty-fives ever tossed on a turntable.

"As I ramble on about the most cantankerous one-two punch to come out of Kentucky since Muhammad Ali, the rare listener from long ago will know I'm only doing what I started the Monday after Mother's Day in 1983, when a slow-going truck delivered a fast-moving woman to my—till then—sorrowfully stalled world."

As usual at that point in her soliloquy, Joy Savoy felt a strong urge to fall silent. Forever. Then she considered the paycheck at taping's end and, sighing, forged on.

"Returning to that first day, I see how she inescapably shaped the last. And because I've long since learned I'm hardly alone in tangling with a pistol of a parent, or in loving hard and losing large, I suppose it's a story that bears repeating as much as the music that serenaded our every rowdy step.

"In those rich old melodies, I hear one of the few things my mother and I had in common. I hear yesterday. It's a catchy little tune as timeless as regret. And like the open book with its own soundtrack that my life used to be, I still know all the words by heart.

"Feel free to wrap your own recollections around the old honky-tonk hits I'm about to play. I'll do the same and, in the end, I promise we will have remembered well and been serenaded even better."

Chapter 1
"Roll On, Big Mama"

Avalon, Louisiana, May 9, 1983

"Need me to show you where the gas pedal is, Grandma?" Those were the first words Quida Raye Perkins had bothered with in twelve hours and the last she intended to waste on the man to her left. Doyle Ricketts knew she wanted to make good time getting to Joy Faye's so she could have her big surprise. But they may as well have been parked in the dern road the way he'd poked along from the bottom of Kentucky to the middle of Louisiana.

Scowling at the truck's clock, wondering if they'd arrive before her daughter's alarm went off, she reached for her cigarette pouch, flicked the lighter, and tried not to bite her unfiltered smoke in two. There were few things in life Quida Raye enjoyed more than showing up at someone's door without a word of warning. This was not news to Doyle. Just the day before, he had already gassed up the truck and was sitting in it, waiting, while she called Joy Faye to say she'd gotten her Mother's Day card. Then she made that off-handed comment about going to Kentucky Lake in the morning. Of course she and Doyle were no more headed thirty minutes down the road to Kentucky Lake than they were bound for Timbuktu. Their destination was on page forty-four of the atlas that was already in the semi, wedged alongside a thermos of black coffee and a full night's worth of honeybuns and donut holes.

"Happy Mother's Day," Joy Faye had said before hanging up.

Smirking, Quida Raye knew it was about to get *real* happy. Truth was, Doyle had a load of gazing globes to deliver in west Texas, and since he was on her last nerve anyway, she was sending him on alone so she could spend a few days giving Joy Faye's shack a much-needed scrubbing. If Joy Faye wasn't piled on a couch with her face stuck in a book, she was slouched over a table, shoveling food into it while the house fell down around her ears. Which didn't bother Quida Raye Perkins in the least. She enjoyed cleaning almost as much as she liked turning up unannounced at front doors.

Picturing how furious her surly daughter would be after getting barged in on before dawn the morning after Mother's Day was the only fun she'd had in six hundred agitating miles. Not counting the honeybuns. She and Sugar Pie had polished off half a box, though Sugar Pie probably ought to lay off the sweets. Situating the pudgy Pekingese atop a lap she liked to think of as lean even though her daughter called it "bony" brought a bigger lap to mind and a wider grin to her tanned face. If Joy Faye ever went on a dang diet, maybe she'd learn a thing or two about "bony."

"Almost there," Doyle said, sounding happier than he had in days. She swung her head around and glared at him, face as hard as her orb of teased and shellacked hair. While she would have preferred not to admit it just then, Doyle Ricketts, long-haul trucker for thirty-plus years, wasn't too far from movie-star material. If only the movie wasn't *Smokey and the Bandit*.

Frowning, Quida Raye checked the truck's side mirror, relieved yet again to see only a trace of her own reflection, dimly lit by the dashboard lights—a heart-shaped smudge surrounded by a big brown ball, the finer details burnished to near invisibility by the darkness and what her pasty daughter called "extreme" tanning.

Doyle glanced over and noticed she had the back of her head to him again, never a good sign. Taking a stab at one of a million reasons she stayed teed off, he cleared his throat and offered his usual defense for going less than the speed of sound. "If I've told you once, I've told you a thousand times," he said in a singsong that only aggravated her more, "I'm not goin' one mile over the speed limit. You know all I've gotta do is get stopped and we'll have every state trooper in a hundred miles all over our asses."

All over *yore* ass, buddy, she thought. I'm just along for the ride. Squinting out the window through her own reflection, it occurred to Quida Raye Perkins that she had pretty much been along for one ride or another with one joker after the next for the last twenty-five years, all of which had been every bit as bumpy as these last few. As Doyle hit another pothole and 40,000 pounds of gazing globes jostled in back, she reckoned no year had truly been smooth sailing since about 1957, something her daughter—born in 1958—was only too fond of pointing out.

Instead of being a less-than-hearty endorsement of motherhood, 1957 simply stood in her mind as the last year she had looked her level best. It was a notion she knew Joy Faye, with her stringy-tail hair and big white face, would never understand. Appearances mattered. And, back in 1957, Quida Raye could not be beat. Eighteen years old and decked out in the cutest outfits her carhop money could buy, she kept her bow lips red, her tight legs bronzed, and everything in between positively shipshape. Which was easy since she danced her way through 1957—"Little Darlin'," "Whole Lotta Shakin' Goin' On," "All Shook Up." Day after day, she wiggled and jiggled, whirled and swirled off to the drive-in, a sassy storm of pretty pastels, white bobby socks, and long, brown hair yanked into a bouncy ponytail. GIs from the nearby Army base routinely beat each other to bloody pulps behind the Double Dip because of her, thrilling her to no end. Until the waistbands on her poodle skirts got tight and—"Oh, Joy!" as her daughter would later crack—the happy songs came to an end.

She had listened to country pretty much nonstop since then. She liked to think every song told some part of her unique story, like the one on the radio just then. Grinning, she reached over and cranked up "A Lesson in Leavin' " so she could send Doyle a message. She was constantly sending Doyle messages via the radio, not a single one of which he ever appeared to have received.

Eyeballing his blank, frustrating face, she sighed and settled on the less annoying sight of Sugar Pie's front paws. They were situated atop the creases the dry cleaners had put in her pink jeans, which she had paired with a pink shell top and a pink-and-white-striped overshirt. Doyle, going five miles an hour two feet away, completed the ensemble with a pink cotton/poly shirt she had pressed and laid out for him the day before.

For what it was worth, Joy Faye approved of Doyle. "And not because he lets you dress him, either," she liked to say. She claimed Doyle was a nice change because he was "stoic" and "oblivious" to being bossed around, unlike her mother's two ex-husbands. Whatever that meant. Bottom line was, Doyle would do for now. So what if his pet name for her was "Grump," a handle that never failed to trigger hoots of hilarity from her daughter. Quida Raye knew the only thing worse than having a man around was not having one at all. And she tried to remind herself of that fact on the rare occasions her daughter managed to drag home an even more sloppily dressed specimen than the last.

As the big rig crawled along the last bit of bayou lane leading to Joy Faye's shack, her mind played a familiar cruel trick. In wondering just how long it had been since her daughter dated the last mismatched loser, Quida Raye again tripped across the moment— two and a half years earlier—that stabbed her heart with pain so deep she must have made a sound.

"You okay, Grump?" Doyle asked. But she didn't answer. Didn't feel the road inching by under eighteen wheels. Didn't feel anything at all except bottomless despair. She had been on total disability for five years, since an inept Kentucky doctor had taken half her stomach—without asking—in 1977. But that was nothing compared to what she had lost two and a half years later.

Moving Sugar Pie aside, she reached for the bottle of caffeinated, capsulated pain relievers in her purse. Shaking out several, she screwed the top off a soda, knocked the tablets back with a long slug, took a ragged drag off her cigarette, and stared out at the endless dark. She had never, not once, talked about that night. And she wasn't about to start now. By the time she finally exhaled, blanketing Sugar Pie in a cloud of secondhand sorrow, they were at Joy Faye's ditch-straddled driveway.

"We're here," Doyle gaily announced, dimming the lights. "Happy?"

Blinking herself back to the familiar—and welcomed—vexation of the moment, she screwed the top back on the soda and scowled out her window, not anywhere near happy. No, she hadn't been happy for two and a half years. But she *was* satisfied that he'd managed to get her to Joy Faye's house before Thanksgiving.

In the process of presenting Doyle once again with the back of her hairdo, however, something caught Quida Raye's eye. Something about the front of this last dump her daughter had rented. Days of petty frustrations evaporated in the thick Louisiana predawn as she turned her beady brown stare back to the front door. It was standing wide open. Nothing but screen stood where solid wood should have been, knowing her fraidy-cat daughter. Ever since all those nurses were murdered in Chicago when she was a girl, Joy Faye had been terrified to go to bed at night.

There were only two explanations for that front door standing wide open a full hour before Joy Faye got up for her radio station job. Maybe someone really had broken in and attacked her in her sleep, a possibility Quida Raye immediately rejected since any burglar would have tripped over mountains of junk in the dark and broken his neck first. The other scenario thrilled her even more than the prospect of appearing at that very door when she was supposed to be six hundred miles away—the only time Joy Faye thought she was safe from the lunatics outside was when she had invited one *inside*.

Reaching over to clap Doyle cheerfully on the thigh, causing him to jump and goose the gas for the first time since Vidalia, she whooped and said, "Looks like we've got comp'ny!"

Sugar Pie popped up on all fours. Together, dog and woman gaped at the dark door and, off to the side, the shape of some weird little car. While Sugar Pie's teeth were bared, Quida Raye Perkins would have sworn she herself was only smiling.

Chapter 2
"Delta Dawn"

Joy **Savoy** was engaged in the high point of her life—dreaming. At the moment, she was driving across a bridge, going up, up, up, until blue sky turned gray and the bridge went down, down, down, into crashing waves. Then she realized she had something else to worry about, a *blam, blam, blam* that indicated she also had a flat tire. The blamming got louder and the water got deeper until Joy floated into consciousness. Her first thought was what a lousy way to start the day, with that bridge dream again. Her second was she still had a flat tire.

Blam, blam, blam!

Then understanding dawned with a jolt that rocked the bed. That was no flat tire. Either a serial killer was at the door, or it was her mother again.

Blam, blam, blam!

Taut as a drawn bow, Joy clutched the sheet, boggled by the incomprehensible recollection of what she'd done hours earlier, when she and the new guy at work rolled in from the bar and, in a calculated show of hillbilly bravado, she had left the front door wide open. Although she had been a country disc jockey most of her unremarkable career, her roots were in rock, so she was always trying to appear more good-ol'-gal-like than she actually was. And carrying on behind a flimsy screen door had struck her as just the kind of hellcat thing some rowdy country siren might do. But now her thoughts ran wildly to the White Album and the Manson family, and Joy **Savoy** knew, in death as in the studio, she was doomed to be exposed as nothing but a fraud.

Blam, blam, blam!

She stared through the dark bedroom, across the small living room, eyes frozen on the black rectangle that was her screen door. She could no more tell if it *was* a serial killer, knocking before slicing through the screen, or if indeed it was her mother. Which, in some ways, could be worse.

"Don't thank I cain't see you," her mother hollered. And Joy groaned as the springs behind her regrettably squeaked.

"Whuh?" Nick mumbled, sitting up.

"Lay back down," she hissed, which he lamentably did. Too late, she realized she had just provided her mother with the first piece of evidence she would hold against him—he was far too compliant a man. Hearing a snort come from the door, she said, "Or sit back up. Whatever."

"Who's here?" Nick whispered in a trembly quiver. To keep him from wobbling out any more anemic words that would only further inflame her mother's rigid sense of acceptable male attributes, she tipped over and said, "The good news is it's not Son of Sam. But that's sort of the bad news, too."

She glanced at Nick and, even in the dark, could tell their first date wasn't ending in a fashion that might precipitate a second. And, after two and a half years, Joy **Savoy** felt she might finally be up for a second date.

The thought no sooner crossed her mind than her eyes and nose began stinging.

Rolling on her side again, she moistly glared through the dark at the skinny nightmare she could now see standing ramrod straight on her front porch, backlit by a big rig's running lights. The lump at her mother's feet, she knew, was Sugar Pie, the only member of that entourage she was ever happy to see at her front door before dawn.

Lifting himself on an elbow and squinting at the door, Nick said, "Is that your *mother*?"

"And her little dog, too," Joy cackled, an ill-planned witticism that only mobilized her overnight guest. Up Nick sprang, frantically patting around the foot of the bed for his clothes, which Joy vaguely recalled getting kicked to the floor fairly early in the evening's festivities, such as they were.

"It's not like I'm sixteen," she said, sitting up and making a leisurely show of gathering the top sheet around her. Not quite as blasé, Nick fell to the floor and proceeded to throw into doubt the entire subject of future canoodling. Joy watched him leaping about and patting around in the dark like a great ape—or maybe not even that, a lesser ape perhaps, a wan gibbon still in search of a single item he had worn into her house. As if that wasn't unfortunate enough, she remembered the empty ice cream containers and paper plates crusted with days-old smears of ketchup and gravy he might also encounter.

"Be careful," she cautioned. "I, uh, haven't tidied up in a while."

A hoot came from the front door. "She ain't *'tidied up'* a day in her life," her mother squalled, which only served to accelerate the action on the ground. Joy's bra flew across the room, followed by that month's *Cosmo*.

"Shit!" Nick said.

"Yep, I wouldn't be surprised if there wudn't some of *that* down there, too," her mother dryly noted. The ransacking came to a timid pause.

"Do you have a *dog* or something?" Nick faintly asked.

Joy groaned, wishing she had known what a gullible, humorless sort he was before she brought him home. It was a thought that made her even angrier at her mother, whose presence had historically done little more than shine a white-hot spotlight on every shortcoming in any male Joy had found attractive. She looked at Nick, hunkered atop the dark floor fluffy with dirty clothes, and decided her mother wasn't winning this time. Besides, he was KLME's newest hire. For more reasons than he *or* her mother could possibly guess, it simply would not do to leave him with tales of a one-night stand from hell.

"No dog, no worries," she glibly said, adding quietly, "You're the only animal here. Well, except for Sugar Pie now." Some animal, she thought, recalling a modest assortment of tolerable fumblings. Still, with her mother at the door telepathically beaming female disapproval her way, Joy was determined to see only the best in Nick's every jerky move, hunched over and Curious George-like though he was at the moment. "Whatcha say we pick up where we left off tonight? At your place?"

"Sure," he muttered and, as she had hoped it would, the promise of another round of tussling soon paid off in the happy discovery of his underwear.

"Any day now," her mother called, jiggling the screen door. Satisfied that, no matter how the next few minutes might go, she would have the last word later at Nick's, Joy climbed out of bed and, sheet encased, flounced through the living room to flip the latch with as much pique as she could muster at 4:05 a.m.

"Kentucky Lake, huh?" she crabbed, glowering at her mother.

Quida Raye just shrugged and stared back, taking in her daughter's smeary polecat eyes and stringy wild hair, all wrapped up in a sheet that barely made it around. It was a miracle she got any man to come home with her, even whatever was flopping around on the bedroom floor.

"Yore gettin' as big as a dern barn," Quida Raye announced. "And I thank you might be goin' deaf, too."

"And good morning to you, too," Joy grumbled, feeling like she'd missed half her mother's conversation, as usual.

"Good mornin' my foot," her mother shot back. "I've been standin' here five full minutes knockin' hard enough to drive a ten-penny nail through the wall. I coulda woke the dead."

"I was *asleep*, like most normal people at this hour," Joy exclaimed, though her mother twisted her mouth and looked away, as if the truth of what she'd really been doing was floating off in the dark somewhere.

Little did Joy know that Quida Raye Perkins was searching for the spurt of hope she'd lost somewhere between the truck and the porch, after she spied that wide-open front door and realized her surprise appearance would shortly flush out a beau or maybe even her second son-in-law. But listening to soft sounds mewling from the bedroom and picturing some fool on all fours wrenching his drawers away from the dust bunnies—hell, the dust *jack rabbits*—all she saw in the waning night were agitations lining up one after another, and some strange little car.

Joy glanced at her mother's profile, as stern and disapproving as a statue of Jefferson Davis, then leaned around her globular do to watch Doyle unpack bag after bag of no telling what. Her mother always had about twenty different projects going and seldom traveled without all the necessary supplies—yarn, calico fabric, ratchet sets, hacksaws. Half of everything Joy owned her mother had bought and the other half she'd made. It was a crafty collection that, in the immediate vicinity alone, included a spool top coffee table, wheel rim stools, two braided pantyhose rugs and a soda-case organizer. Joy couldn't throw away a pop top without her mother fishing it from the trash for some masterpiece.

Shifting her attention back to her mother's rigid profile, it occurred to her that chiseling allure out of that stony facade had been a similar, ongoing enterprise. From the self-satisfied lilt of her aggressively plucked brows to the smart tilt of her fiercely teased ball of hair, the look her mother had spent years perfecting—cool, critical, strenuously unimpressed—held a strong appeal for men like Doyle. Men partial to dirt tracks and malt liquor, drug-store aftershave, and hard-box smokes. Joy had had occasion to feel sorry for plenty of them. It seemed like her lot in life, as the dull daughter of a pretty woman. Though, at the moment, her mother simply looked big-haired and bad as she turned and grudgingly marched two steps through the door, tugging her dog behind her.

"Don't eat nussin' off this filthy-tail floor, Sugar Pie. God only knows what woo'll find, and Mom dudn't have money for a vet bill." Then, steering her tone from baby talk to bad-ass, Quida Raye lifted her voice and aimed it like a spear toward the bedroom.

"Let me know when yore decent in there," she barked at Nick in the dark. "I haven't seen the inside of a bathroom since Hernando, Mississippi."

Just then something fell, and a strained male voice said, "Oops."

Satisfied that her first words to him had resulted in some form of destruction she could sulk about for days, she said, "I hope that wudn't that nice chicken bucket lamp I made you last time I was here."

"If it was, it'd be your own fault, blowing in here like Ma Barker." Joy shuddered. Making a mental note to nail the front door shut should hell freeze over and another man come home with her, Joy called toward the bedroom, "That's all right, Nick. Just leave it. I'll pick it up later."

Quida Raye snickered, knowing a tree could have fallen in there and her daughter wouldn't have touched so much as a dang leaf. "You do still have electricity, don't you? Let's see if this helps." Clicking on a light, she turned her attention to the wreck that was the living room and, off to the side, the teetotal disaster of a kitchen.

"I'd be ashamed of myself," she said, though in truth, nothing thrilled Quida Raye Perkins more than the sight of an ungodly mess she could make *Good*

18

Housekeeping-worthy in the time it took her daughter to work a single shift.

Bending down to scratch Sugar Pie's head, Joy caught a whiff of the trash can and decided her place *could* use a good cleaning. Standing back up and resituating the sheet, she sized up her high-handed maid, figuring she'd lost another pound or two just since April. Knowing hours of housecleaning would only contribute to her ongoing calorie deficit, a chronic condition for people with half a stomach, Joy once again considered the active role she had always played in ruining her mother's life. Indignation gave way to feeling like a heel, which was the usual chain of emotional events where Quida Raye Perkins was concerned.

"You don't always have to ambush me, you know. You could just call and say, 'Hey, I'm coming to visit,' and who knows, I might clean up a little. Why don't you give that a whirl sometime?"

"I gotcher '*give it a whirl*,' " Quida Raye said, rolling her eyes toward the bedroom.

"Right," Joy replied, understanding her mother wouldn't be entertaining even a hint of conciliation— not now, maybe not ever. It was no accident that her signature coiffure had grown over the years to resemble a massive walnut propped atop her shoulders. Quida Raye was quite literally a hard nut to crack. So Joy moved on to the next best thing—antagonizing her. "To continue a theme, then, you might be interested in knowing I *am* giving it another 'whirl.' I've already made plans to see Nick again later."

"Well, that right there's enough for me," her mother said, motioning with the last half-inch of her cigarette toward the bedroom door, past which Nick and his tightie-whities had just lurched.

"Can we talk about something else so the poor man can get dressed in peace? Is that a new top?"

"Five dollars on clearance," her mother jauntily said, adjusting the Peter Pan collar.

"Let me guess," Joy began, peering around Quida Raye's bowl of hair to wave at the eighteen-wheeler backing none too swiftly out of her driveway, getting a friendly toot in return. "Doyle's wearing a pink shirt, too, isn't he?"

Her mother, the very embodiment of the case against color coordinating among couples as far as Joy was concerned, turned toward the truck. "Could be," she hazily said. "And I'll bet that one in there comes out sportin' a rainbow poncho."

Then she shoved the screen door open, and Joy's heart leapt. Maybe she was going to dart off and flag Doyle down. Maybe Joy could lock her out again. But, alas, all Quida Raye did was flick her cigarette into the yard and let the door pop shut. Snapping on the porch light, she fished a fleck of tobacco forward with her tongue and grimly nibbled it.

"I've got a sick headache, and it looks like a bumb went off in this place," she declared. "If you'd move, I could get busy."

Joy stepped to her right, toward the kitchen and the trash she could vividly smell now, and watched her mother march past, snatching Sugar Pie's leash like she was restraining a pit bull instead of a tubby Pekingese. Sweeping into the bedroom and scooping up laundry as she went, Quida Raye stomped up to the bed, ripped off the bottom sheet, emptied the pillowcases, shoved what was on the floor into a pile, and quickly sorted darks and lights on the bare mattress. She was popping dust off the vanity with a sock when Joy reluctantly swished in and noticed Nick zipping his jeans as quietly as possible in the far corner.

"Um," he said, "do you mind…" His sentence trailed off as he leaned toward the bathroom and buttoned what Joy noted with a twinge of relief was a plain, white shirt.

Still holding the sock in one hand and a rancid, petrified dishrag in the other, Quida Raye turned to finally behold her daughter's overnight guest. He was tall, she'd give him that. And not half-bad looking. But otherwise she wasn't impressed. He'd been hiding in the corner far too long for her to think anything other than, "Here we go again. Another dud."

"Be my guest," she said, forlornly waving the dishrag toward the bathroom. "I've waited this long." Tossing the rag on the bleach pile, she reached down to unsnap Sugar Pie's leash. "Don't mind her. She dudn't bite."

"I don't think it's the dog he's worried about," Joy observed, shuffling up to the bed and digging something out of the darks—a vast muumuu-looking red number. Sniffing it to make sure it hadn't been wadded up with the dishrag, she pulled the flouncy shift over her head and discreetly dropped the sheet. It wasn't until she turned to find some fresh underthings in the dresser that she noticed Nick and her mother were still in something of a standoff.

Facing each other, he with his hand on the bathroom doorknob, she holding a stiff, mildewy towel, Nick seemed to sense this scary little woman wasn't finished with him yet. And, as dawn made its first, pinking inroads on what would be a blazing May day, Joy could tell that was true. As she dug around in her underwear drawer, Joy watched her mother's expression settle into another of her favorites—slave driver. It was a look invariably triggered by a man or her daughter, the latter of whom waited for the direct order she knew was imminent.

"I'd bet my bottom dollar Joy Faye dudn't have a drop of co-cola anywhere in this filthy-tail rat hole of hers," her mother said in the pleasant trill she reserved for strangers. "When yore finished in there, why doncha run go pick me up a six-pack."

"Yes, ma'am, Mrs. **Savoy**," Nick exclaimed, disappearing into the bathroom. Joy winced, but her mother just grinned, relief washing over her tanned, tired face. That "Mrs. **Savoy**" told her everything she cared to know. This wasn't her next son-in-law or even a beau. Why, Slick or Flick or whatever his dumb name was hardly even knew her daughter.

"Did woo hear dat, Sugar Pie?" her mother asked her dog. "Dat boy called Mom Miz *Savoy*. Dat boy hadn't been around here too wong, has he?" Anything of substance Quida Raye had to say, she generally said to her dog.

"That 'boy' is twenty-seven years old," Joy said, throwing a pair of underwear at her mother, who tossed them straight on the bleach pile. Still grinning, she scooped up the darks and stalked off toward the kitchen and the washer-dryer combo.

"You don't have to go to the store for her," Joy yelled toward the bathroom door. Rooting around for a belt and finding none, she shoved the drawer closed.

"And, not that it matters, but her last name's not Savoy. It's Perkins."

The toilet flushed and the bathroom door flew open as Nick bolted through the house. "Sorry," he called. "Is regular cola okay, Mrs. Perkins?"

"Do they make any other kind?" Quida Raye innocently asked, dark eyes drifting toward the bedroom and her daughter's big tent dress. "Oh, that's right. They *do* make diet, don't they?" Smiling, she said, "No, regular'll be just fine for me, thanks."

****

Joy sat on the edge of the tub and waited until she heard Nick's car whining back down the bayou road. The less she had to interact with her mother, the better she knew her radio shift would go later. Stealing one last look in the mirror, wishing she had taken time to wash her hair, she trudged on into the living room to gather her purse and keys. The washing machine was running, dishes were soaking, and throw rugs were piled by the door, beside which her mother had propped herself in a chair, striking her usual pose. Knees up to her chin, chewing a fingernail on one hand while the other held a smoldering cigarette, she was as thin and angled as a praying mantis, aimed toward Nick pulling into the driveway.

"You know I don't want you smoking in here," Joy said.

"That's why I'm sittin' by the door. Shoo," her mother said, batting at the cloud around her head. "Git."

"You're sitting there so you can agitate Nick some more," Joy said, yanking the screen door open and letting it slam behind her. Turning her attention to the glorious world outside her smoky shack, she stood on the porch and filled her lungs with sweet, fresh air, watching Nick park and get out. As if reconsidering the entire arrangement, he came to an abrupt stop beside his bumper, holding the soda away from him like a six-pack of snapping turtles.

"I see you bought the new radioactive formula," she said, chuckling. Morning was just flirting with the far tree line, lending the slightest lavender blush to the bits of bayou Joy could see from her porch, between the brush and the weeping willows clotting the bank. It was a rapturous scene well worth the rent on an old sharecropper's shack, though she could tell it was currently lost on Nick. Nick seemed focused only on calculating the shortest course for a misty six-pack to travel while providing him the greatest possible distance from her mother.

"Just don't hurl them through a window." Joy laughed again, feeling oddly lighthearted when she knew she should have been embarrassed, given the morning's raid. But she just stood there and smiled in her enormous crimson dress, waiting for Nick to either hand her the drinks or leave them on the steps and run. He was still befuddled, the amber porch light spreading a regrettable yellow glow across his face, when a shrill voice came shooting through the screen.

"Good God in heaven, boy. Just set 'em down, and I'll get 'em later!"

The bottles were deposited and the subcompact was spraying gravel back down the drive as Joy skipped down the stairs, knowing it could have been worse. The screen door could have been unhooked. And Nick could have been someone she'd miss if their next date failed to materialize.

Collecting the many folds of her queen-sized kimono, she climbed into her car, decided against running over the sacks of her mother's stuff Doyle had lined up down the driveway, and hurried to catch up to Nick, heading for the blurry flush that was Avalon just waking. As she drove, her mind turned the glow of Central Louisiana's lone city into what it had really been every morning for the previous **two and a half** years—something of a halo over the wavy black head of the man who truly had her heart. The man Nick didn't have a chance of replacing and, best of all, the man her mother didn't even know existed. Ira Everhart.

Ira Everhart was KLME's news director, reporter of all that was evil, criminal, or, in one particular case, simply too horrific to believe. That story, which took Ira thirty seconds to deliver **two and a half** years earlier, nevertheless summed up a heartache that would stretch across all eternity. Just how the man she first saw the night her entire world fell apart had become her dark obsession was as much a mystery as it was a torment. Her best friend Tanya, a part-time college student and full-time floozy, called it a classic case of transference.

Joy considered it a classic case of utter futility. Because, in addition to being inextricably tied to the unspeakable event that had cleaved her world in two, Ira Everhart was also married.

Given her matrimonial history, not to mention that of her mother, marriage was an institution her head was determined to honor even if her heart could not. Though her ex had been fond of saying, "A ring don't plug no holes," it wasn't until Ira came along that Joy thought kindly at all of that odd axiom. Only, the hole was in her heart, and nothing but sad, secret desire oozed out like black oil down a cracked driveway.

Forcing herself to focus on something other than a fantasy for a change, she followed Nick down the road that set in stone the sway of the bayou to their left, concentrating on his taillights sidewinding like snake eyes through the curvy darkness. Past planed cotton fields and bleached-out, boarded-up fruit stands they went, ruffling that low-slung river town's outskirts until they reached the first of Avalon's two traffic circles. Since Nick wasn't due at the station for hours, he kept circling, heading for his apartment on the new side of town. She took the road less traveled at 4:55 a.m., the one cutting through the historic heart of Avalon.

It was the route that, with one small detour, took her by Ira and his thin wife's duplex every morning. She eased past their front door that fateful day, dress flowing out around her like the mighty Red River. Then she frumpily went on to work, humming a little ditty that just popped into her head.

Chapter 3
"Mama Tried"

Joy **Savoy** was pulling into the radio station's parking lot when she realized she'd left home without a belt for her fire-engine-red fat-lady frock. And now she was at the only place she could always count on seeing Ira Everhart. The solution—running back to the house—was viable, given how early she was. It was also the last thing on earth she felt like doing, farther down the list even than billowing up in front of Ira like the Hindenburg aflame. Picturing her mother snapping on the radio and settling in with Mr. Clean, the only male she always found agreeable, Joy trudged on inside. With any luck, Ira would be off on assignment, covering some shooting or hostage situation that required his undivided attention.

"What are you doing here already?" Boo-Boo asked, glancing at his wrist. "It's only two hairs past a freckle."

Joy smiled at KLME's program director and, after Tanya, her best friend in the world. Robert Bailey—Boo-Boo to his oldest pals—was striking his usual pose, languidly tipped back in a rolling chair alongside whatever DJ happened to be on the air, which, at the moment, was WildDog. A big, burly teddy bear, Boo-Boo had been like a brother to Joy since she was in ninth grade and he was in eleventh, working the after-school shift at the little 5,000-watt station in Pitts. Even after he went off to college and started climbing career ladders near and far, Boo-Boo managed to have a hand in practically every radio job she eventually landed, up to and including her current position. Joy gazed upon his fuzzy face—a sweet, smoochable mug he never managed to get clean shaven years before the scraggly look was in—and smiled at an old buddy who required nothing more than a moany-groany bit of verbal shorthand to grasp the morning's high points so far.

"Guess who showed up at my front door again."

Boo-Boo's grin widened, whiskers prickling with perception. "Without a word of warning?"

"The exact opposite, as usual," Joy replied, collapsing into the nearest chair from the sheer weight of the injustices she had already suffered, and it wasn't even 5:15. "I was on the phone with her just yesterday, and she clearly said she was headed to the lake today. *Kentucky* Lake. I should know better by now."

"Yes, you should. How's Sugar Pie?"

"Short."

"How's the hair?"

"Tall."

"So all's still right in the world." Turning to WildDog, Boo-Boo said, "Joy's mother goes for the look your more big-haired groupies embrace. 'Stand by Your Man' meets 'Harper Valley PTA' with a little mid-sixties high-class style thrown in." WildDog nodded, setting four inches of trendy strands swaying beneath his baseball cap. The subject of hair was near and dear to WildDog's heart as, from the rim of his cap on up, he was bald as Elmer Fudd, something only Boo-Boo was supposed to know. As Boo-Boo had of course told Joy, WildDog's hair had already begun thinning when he went to Woodstock at seventeen and was little more than a horseshoe-shaped ring several years later, when he was back down South, hovering along the fringes of Nashville's Outlaw movement. To WildDog's eternal relief, his particular brand of male-pattern baldness could pass as a full head of hair with the simple application of a cap or hat, and he was never without one or the other. For years a fan favorite in Central Louisiana, WildDog was long and lean, with a deep, smoky drawl that drew throngs of adoring females. Those who went home with him—and legions did—often gushed that WildDog could do *anything* with a backwards baseball cap on his head.

"Yep, she waltzed in like she owned the place," Joy continued, "and let's just say I wasn't the only one she blasted out of a sound sleep this time." WildDog grinned and gave her two thumbs up. Boo-Boo only nodded.

"Let me guess," Boo-Boo said. "Nick."

"How'd you know?" she demanded, blushing.

"Never underestimate the power of a card-carrying member of Mensa," he answered, a pat reference he could work into any conversation. "That and the fact that I saw both of your cars outside Ship O'Hoyt's on my way home last night. Correction, I saw *your* car and *his* tricycle."

She laughed and punched him. "I bet it gets better gas mileage than your honking pickup truck."

Boo-Boo grinned and rubbed his shoulder. "No doubt. At the expense of every shred of male dignity. Just ask Quida Raye."

"That would require speaking to her, something I

don't plan on doing anytime soon. Get this—after she scared Nick half to death, she made him run to the store and get her some sodas."

Boo-Boo snickered. "Must have taken forever to pedal there. Ouch." Lifting a booted toe, he shoved his pugilist friend and her rolling chair across the room. "You might go faster if Nick loaned you his training wheels."

Joy threw a cartridge at him just as Ruthie walked in. "Good catch," she said, handing Boo-Boo some messages. Ruthie was the happiest, sweetest soul Joy had met since coming to KLME six months earlier. And it didn't hurt that Ruthie's Uncle Vernon was the station manager.

"What are you doing here so early?" Ruthie asked. "Nice dress."

"Nice? Maybe for Mama Cass Elliot," Joy protested, momentarily forgetting her new friend's complete inability to grasp most rock references. Ruthie came from a long line of ultra-evangelical Pentecostals for whom famous hippie-dippie female artists began and ended with Judy Collins and "Amazing Grace." Nevertheless, Pentecostalism was an affiliation Joy deemed negotiable in Ruthie's case, since she had managed to lure her to Ship O'Hoyt's occasionally. At twenty-nine, Ruthie was the oldest virgin Joy had ever met, owing either to her zealous clan or a nose that struck Joy as oddly off-center somehow. With any luck and all Ship O' Hoyt's sway, her friend's chasteness was a condition Joy hoped to see rectified by the time Ruthie turned thirty.

"Let's just pray she doesn't start speaking in tongues at your favorite biker bar," Boo-Boo had opined before their last excursion. "That might put the kibosh on any matchmaking you have in mind with guys named Killer or Skull."

That morning, as Ruthie turned with a swish and headed for the door, Boo-Boo gestured at her long, flowing skirt and hair, then devoutly clasped his hands.

"It's a pretty color at least," she sweetly said over her shoulder. "I like red."

"Well I sure won't be wearing it to Ship O'Hoyt's next time we go," Joy replied, ignoring **Boo-Boo**. "Speaking of, maybe we can see if that new guy, Nick, wants to meet us there. He's actually sort of the reason I'm in early."

"Be sure to give him a head start with that little trike of his," Boo-Boo said. While he and WildDog collapsed in snorting fits and Joy threw more carts at them, Ruthie made her bewildered way through the door.

"I'm going back to my nice, quiet desk now," she said. "Come see me later and tell me all about Nick. Ship O'Hoyt's sounds fun."

"Fun," Boo-Boo silently mouthed, shooting an A-OK sign as the door closed. Joy wheeled around in her chair, intent on studying the rack of records she was now facing. Rolling to her left, she flipped through the H's till she found the tune she'd been humming on the way to work. Then she selected more songs for her first hour or two. Who needed Boo-Boo Bailey anyway?

****

Outside of town, Quida Raye Perkins gave the old sharecropper's shack a lick and a promise, then stood back to admire her handiwork. All four rooms were fairly straight, though no one in their right mind would call them clean. Before she could get down to business, however, she needed to pick up some supplies from the country store she'd sent what's-his-name to earlier. After checking to make sure the liquid shoe polish she'd dabbed on her white tennies was dry, she slipped them on, hooked her purse on her arm, and headed out the door, down the drive, and up the road, marching like a little tin soldier all in pink. By the time she made it to Pud's Bait & Goods, she had produced a light sweat and a long shopping list.

"Gonna be a hot one," Pud said in greeting.

"Shore is," she replied. "I'll be working on my tan later, after I pick up a few thangs."

"Heard dat. Let me know if you need help, Miz Quida."

Though she smiled cordially, in stores, as in life, Quida Raye Perkins rarely needed any assistance whatsoever. She had, however, come to appreciate good customer service in her forty-four years, the gainfully employed portion of which had been spent largely in retail. Pud's, lately her first stop when she visited Joy Faye, was occasionally her only stop, too. He had everything a body could want—from fresh bread to horse manure, and good service to boot. He also wasn't too hard on the eyes. If only he wasn't married and she wasn't expecting Doyle to rumble back through. Slowly but surely.

Commandeering a buggy, Quida Raye headed down the first aisle, occasionally erupting into fits of giggles at the memory of Joy Faye's furious face and that doofus overnight date of hers running around in nothing but his dang drawers. By the time she made it to the register, she was pushing one buggy and pulling another.

"Looks like you're gonna need a ride back to your daughter's house," Pud said, turning to smack the boy slouched on a stool beside him. "Quit fiddlin' with the radio and go get the truck." Pud started ringing her up, toe just a-tapping. "That there's one of my favorites. I sure do love me some old Hag. Doncha wish they'd play more of them oldie goldies?"

"Shore do," Quida Raye said, placing her treasures on the counter.

"They got more rock-and-roll oldie stations than you can shake a stick at," Pud continued, popping open a new sack. "But you hardly ever hear country classics like this one anymore."

Checking the clock on the wall, Quida Raye knew her daughter's shift had already begun. Joy Faye's old friend Robert Bailey picked most of her records, and Robert liked fresh hits and new acts. She did, too. In fact, she hoped they'd play something from that sharp new mother-daughter duo from Kentucky soon. Quida Raye smiled and bobbed her head along as mama tried one last time. With any luck, Joy Faye would say something now so she could grin at Pud and stand a little taller.

"KLME, Call Me Country," Joy said, and in a small store eight miles away, all the short hairs on her mother's arms stood straight up. "Thanks for tuning us in this Monday after Mother's Day. 'Mama Tried' wraps up three back-to-back. I did some wrapping up myself this morning when *my* mama tried to pay me and my, uh, *friend* a surprise visit."

Pud lifted a brow and pointed at her. Quida Raye felt a warm tingle start at her collar and prickle all the way to the top of her scalp. She put a loaf of processed cheese and a pack of clothespins on the counter, numbly reaching in the buggy for more. "Yep, she roared down from Kentucky with a big ten-four breaker. In more ways than one, and apologies in advance for any rhymes that might spring to mind, but I suppose you could say she's something of a *mother trucker*."

Pud threw his head back and guffawed. "I'll be blame!"

Aside from having her name read out loud at two divorce proceedings, Quida Raye Perkins had never been the subject of public discourse before. Standing in Pud's Bait & Goods, a can of Vienna sausages in one hand and a chew toy in the other, she couldn't believe her ears.

"I guess she thinks the Hatfields were gettin' boring," Joy continued. "So if you know any real McCoys who might keep a certain gun-totin', hell-raisin' livewire from driving me nuts and my overnight guests off, just give me a call."

As the airwaves swelled with a used-car-commercial and various and sundry grocery items seemed to take flight and swirl around her head, Quida Raye Perkins stood stock still in her snow-white tennies, listening to Pud hee-haw. She figured this must be what it felt like to get crowned Miss America.

"Holy moly," Pud bawled. "You're a star!" He finished checking her out with another few chuckles, throwing in a free stick of beef jerky for good measure. "Tell Junior I said to carry your groceries inside. Maybe Joy'll put in a good word for us some day, too."

****

"Where did *that* come from?" Boo-Boo exclaimed.

"Why?" Joy asked, instantly abashed. "Was it too racy? Off color? Am I in trouble?"

"Yes. No. Maybe. I don't know," Boo-Boo said, grinning and worrying Joy even more. "But I think I liked it."

"I loved it," WildDog whooped, adjusting his baseball cap. "The phone sure is lighting up."

"Oh, Lord," Boo-Boo groaned, glancing at the blinking buttons. "Here, play this, and I'll deal with the callers."

Joy's hand trembled as she reached for the turntable. But call after call ended with Boo-Boo laughing and saying, "Thanks! I'll tell her."

"What?" she kept asking. "What?"

"Here's what," he finally said. "Don't stop talking about your crazy mother. Folks love it!"

So she didn't.

From "Hello Walls"—"This one's for Mother, who's home sayin' hello to my walls, my floors, my fridge, and every other filthy thing with an arsenal of scrub brushes and noxious chemicals. Wonder what she's gonna use on those dirty movies I've got hidden behind the TV. Har har. Just kiddin', Ma,"—to the song she ended every shift with, "Leaving Louisiana in the Broad Daylight," Joy talked about little more than her mother that Monday after Mother's Day in 1983.

Never had she had such an amazing day on air. She didn't notice when WildDog left. She didn't take a single bathroom break. And it wasn't until she turned the show over to Warren Piece and was standing up, fluffing out her Mrs. Claus clothes, that she realized hours had passed without a single thought of Ira

35

Everhart. Then, with enough crimson flowing out
around her to rival Antietam, she slowly turned toward
the big glass window into the newsroom. Sure enough,
there he sat, going over something with **Boo-Boo**. She
felt the way she did every time she saw that man—like
she'd poked a bobby pin into a wall socket. Like
jumper cables had been clamped to her left and right
ventricles, red for want, black for need.

Though he was over six feet tall and dusky as a
good roux, Ira wasn't what most women would call
handsome. All the years he'd spent covering car wrecks
and deadly shootings, first in his native New Orleans
then later at KLME, had furrowed his stern face,
scrunched his black hair, turned down the corners of his
thin, Crescent City lips. There was nothing sweet or
soft about him, nothing gentle or smooth. Ira had what
was, for Joy **Savoy**, the most toxic combination of
manly traits: a bad attitude, a good mind, and a great
body. Then there was the unspeakable event of two and
a half years earlier.

Joy could barely look at Ira Everhart and breathe at
the same time. She did, however, manage to nod. He
nodded back in an indifferent, married-man way that
only reinforced what an idiot she was. Spinning around,
she hove into the front office, big as Red China, feeling
not at all like she'd just had her first, and probably last,
stellar day on air.

"You sure hit a nerve with that mother routine,"
Ruthie said. "Uncle Vernon's gotten at least fifteen
phone calls from folks wondering where he got you
from." Gathering her yards of cardinal crinkle-cloth
material around her, Joy decided it was nice to hear
people were calling because they liked something for a

change. But it was also irritating to have worked at that radio station six whole months, not to mention the years she'd slaved away at turntables elsewhere, without anyone noticing until she poked fun at her mother every few minutes.

"Tell Boo-Boo I'm cutting out early," Joy said. "I'll make it up tomorrow." Dragging back into the studio for her purse, the oscillating fan in the corner blew her magenta muumuu far and wide. Feeling like a big red bull's-eye, she turned and slumped on home to her mother.

She was past the south traffic circle when it occurred to her that she may have made the worst possible devil's bargain—a great day on air for hell to pay when she got home. Except, when she got home, hell didn't appear to want anything more than her culinary opinion.

"Eat this and see if it's got a wang taste," her mother said, jabbing at her with half a sandwich. "I thank yore mayonnaise has turned on you."

Joy took a bite. "Tastes fine to me."

"Good. Putcher purse down, then, and let's eat."

Joy looked around, amazed as always by how much her mother could accomplish when she wanted to get back in someone's good graces. Their lunch, for example, featured some of Joy's favorites: pimento-cheese sandwiches, homemade vegetable soup, cornbread, sliced cantaloupe, and tea so sweet it made your teeth sing, nary an ingredient for any of which had been in her dusty kitchen when she'd nearly slammed the screen door off its hinges that morning.

Her mother had furthermore found time to rearrange the living room, wash, dry, and fold three loads of clothes, plant some coleus and caladiums out by the porch, and scrub the entire harvest-gold kitchen down to sunburst yellow. Calculating the costs of Quida Raye's, as usual, mute apologies, Joy knew they reached far beyond financial, though that certainly couldn't be discounted. Her mother received a modest disability check every month, which she had been known to blow on a single trip to Pud's. And if she happened to be broke when Joy wanted anything the rest of the month—a special supper, say, or a new book—she had two white-gold diamond rings she regularly pawned for quick cash.

Checking to make sure those rings were still on her hands, and they were, Joy pulled out a chair and decided her mother wouldn't have to hike to the store and slave away in her sweatbox-with-a-stove just to *imply* she was sorry if she was capable of actually *saying* the words. It was a form of emotional math she frequently engaged in during these visits—subtracting her mother's physical efforts from her own psychological sufferings. It was her way of rendering the two of them equal in their opposite approaches to putting up with each other for however long it took Doyle to get back with that damn truck. Her mother would make life miserable and work like a dog as compensation. And Joy would grit her teeth and eat every scrap of food she prepared and ooh and aah over everything she bought or made, just to show the apology was accepted. Even-steven.

Taking a seat and scooting up to the table, a chair leg hooked on the hem of Joy's flouncy red dress, which loudly ripped.

"There's another one for the rag bag," Quida Raye

announced.

"And not a minute too soon," Joy muttered, watching her mother at the stove, chiseling cornbread out of the cast iron like gum from a keyhole.

"Shoulda used more bacon grease," she said, chunks flying. "I bet you'll have a field day with this tomorra." A playful smile smushed her face sideways as she deposited a plate of golden crumbs in front of Joy, who gathered she was being provided with cornbread *and* fresh ammo for her show.

"I take it you were listening," Joy said, ladling soup into a bowl.

"Couldn't get away from it. I about died when I was checkin' out and you called me a dern *mother trucker* for Pud 'n' the whole world to hear."

"Well, you *are* a mother," Joy pointed out, looking up to make sure she was still grinning. "And you *do* ride in a truck. 'Maternal transit figure,' just doesn't have the same ring."

" 'Maternal transit figure' my foot," Quida Raye huffed. But this was not a censure. In fact, the way she was bouncing around the kitchen, it seemed more like a blanket invitation to talk about her till the cows—or Doyle—came home. Joy slid a pile of cornbread chunks onto her plate and decided that might not be such a bad career move, assuming Boo-Boo approved.

Pinching off some pimento-cheese sandwich for Sugar Pie, her mother mumbled, "Dirty movies, my word." Then she popped the rest of the triangle in her mouth, happier than Joy had seen her in two and a half years.

After lunch, Quida Raye pulled on a one-piece bathing suit, headed outside, yanked the electric lawn mower and coils of orange extension cord out from underneath the porch, and went to town on her daughter's yard. Joy knew she would have a deeper tan and most of Happenstance Plantation's front forty mown before dark.

Where Joy had one true love—Ira—her mother had four: nicotine, caffeine, over-the-counter painkillers, and hard-core tanning. When she wasn't riding shotgun in an eighteen-wheeler, she could generally be found flat on her back on a folding chaise lawn chair, wallowing with all four, thinking thoughts she shared only with her true soul mate, the sun. Since she never flipped over, she always looked like a slim slice of chocolate meringue pie—half brown, half white. What strangers didn't understand, of course, was Joy's mother lived for the moment, caring only what you thought when you laid eyes on her rich mahogany face, before she passed you by like last winter's driven snow.

She was not, however, about to get prone anywhere near a tall stand of grass. Other than men her daughter dated, the only creatures Quida Raye Perkins gave a wider berth to were mice. And, to her eyes, the scraggly fields around that sharecropper shack were high enough to accommodate either. So there she was in Joy's back yard, bush-hogging every hiding place for any rat, whatever his species, just so she could lay out.

Joy stood on the back porch dripping sweat, swatting gnats, and watching her mother tearing through the weeds, the lawn mower whipping wood chips and small rocks into shrapnel.

"Watch out," Quida Raye yelled. "You'll lose an eye!"

Freed then from her only role in most manual

labor—obligatory bystander—Joy trudged back inside and was in the middle of a nice nap when the phone rang.

"So my favorite mother's blown in again," cackled Tanya, her rarely-too-supportive best friend.

"Why, yes, she has," Joy said, trying to sound awake. "I guess that means you were listening this morning, too. Don't you ever go to class?"

"Are you kidding? My professors wouldn't know what to do if I actually showed up. Besides, I'm too busy waging mortal combat here in Pitts with my own dear maternal unit."

"What's Lynda done now?" Joy said. *Besides have the patience of Job with you*, she didn't say.

"Nothing more than bitch and moan nonstop about my weight. Happy Mother's Day to Medea herself. Finally, I told her, 'Fine! Just take my *fat ass* to Gran D.'s so you don't have to look at it anymore.' But, on the way there, damned if she didn't start in about dieting again. So I opened the car door and jumped out."

"While she was *driving*?" Shocked as she was, Joy could easily picture her impetuous best friend flinging herself from a moving vehicle, white legs flopping, red hair flying.

"Not fast," Tanya said, laughing. "Ten, fifteen tops. But at least it shut her up. She turned around and got me and didn't say another word all the way to town. I still haven't spoken to her. Haven't been able to concentrate on a single assignment, either. So I decided to stay in Pitts another day or two."

"Uh-huh," Joy said. "Gran D. had Ethelene make one of her famous hummingbird cakes for Mother's

Day, didn't she?"

"Yep. And a key lime pie, too. I exercised restraint and gave myself an additional day to polish them off," Tanya said with a big belly laugh. "Anyway, if the well runs dry on this mother tear you're on, feel free to use my story. Who knows, it might get other mothers off their daughters' backs."

"Or send Pitts Family Services flying up to Lynda's door," Joy noted. Between her headstrong best friend and the ever-oppressed Lynda, Joy usually sided with Tanya's mom. Which made them even since Tanya was invariably of whatever deranged opinion Joy's own obstinate mother embraced.

Sensing they had once again reached the point where their parental sympathies split, Tanya began updating Joy instead on her love life, always a long, drawn-out affair. Lushly arranged at five foot eight and 179 pounds, Tanya attracted more men than Monday night football, thanks in large part to a jovial come-one-come-all glamour-puss quality that had clung like static to her since puberty. A loud, jolly gal with a lighthearted love-'em-and-leave-'em attitude, Tanya at twenty-one took on more men in a year than Joe Louis did his entire career.

But all Joy saw when she looked at her was the nine-year-old she used to babysit, a big-boned little girl who, under Joy's inadequate supervision and Pitts' verdant conditions, developed as fast as a common cold. And now, against all odds, she had her first full-blown boyfriend, poor guy. When they weren't locked in Tanya's favorite pastime, she and Lonnie Luneau were engaged in her second favorite—fighting like North and South Koreans. As the mowing droned on outside, Tanya rattled on about her latest clash with Lonnie, a skirmish culminating in the stabbing of his perfectly good set of truck stereo speakers.

"I just know in my heart some other woman gave him those speakers," she wailed, though the distant sound of Ethelene calling "Suppertime!" put a momentary end to her misery. "Gotta go. I'll call and finish the story later."

Can't wait, Joy thought dully, hanging up as the mowing likewise ended. Looking out the window, she watched her mother roll up the orange extension cord, stashing it and the mower back under the porch, obviously satisfied with the rat-free tan zone she had so far carved out of the field. As she turned and whitely headed for her lawn chair, the phone rang again. It was Nick, calling with directions to his apartment. Joy halfheartedly mentioned he could come back out to her place, but dead air communicated the fact that, having narrowly survived meeting her mother mere hours earlier, Nick had clearly had enough for one day.

"Maybe this weekend," he offered, "if the coast is clear. Besides, I'd like you to see my new digs."

Changing out of her big red tent, Joy glanced one last time out the window to see the late afternoon sun had had its usual effect on her mother. Stretched out flat on her back on the chaise lawn chair, cigarette case, lighter, and pop bottle in the short grass beside her, she was sound asleep, as evidenced by the jaw that was never slack any other time. Scribbling a note and patting Sugar Pie, Joy dashed out the door.

Later, in Nick's fancy new apartment, chilled to a glorious sixty-eight degrees, she was somewhat surprised when all they did was eat the burgers she had picked up and watch an episode of *A-Team*. At least she was well-rested Tuesday when she showed up to work and found it hadn't all been a dream—listeners were still calling in.

"Just don't stop talking about your mother," Boo-Boo advised. WildDog nodded, and the two of them set about spending Tuesday much as they would the entire week—answering phones and cueing up songs so Joy could tell her mother stories.

Like how her mother collected two things—green stamps and speeding tickets. "But she's never figured out that she can lick one and not the other."

And how her mother had one recipe for all vegetables. "Take a can of veggies, add a stick of butter, two tablespoons sugar, some salt and pepper, boil for an hour, peel from the pot, slice and serve."

And how annoying it was that her mother was so skinny. "I'd have to amputate both legs just to fit in her jeans. On second thought, considering the tree trunks I walk around on, I think the term would be 'slash-and-burn.' "

Nick called later to say he'd love to meet her and Ruthie at Ship O'Hoyt's but he was still setting up his apartment and needed to spend the night unpacking.

Wednesday's high point, other than more mother gags, was the breakfast Quida Raye fixed for supper, after which Nick called to report he was in for the night again. Stuck paying bills. "No fun," he said.

Thursday, in a grocery store across town, Quida Raye Perkins was in line, listening to the cashier laugh at her big-mouth daughter on a radio beside the register. Nodding toward the FM dial, she amiably said, "I'm gonna wring that girl's neck when she gets home."

"You know her?" the checker asked.

"I'm afraid I do. It pains my soul to admit it, but that's my dern daughter."

"Lady Bug's your daughter?" the clerk screaked. Then, "You mean that's *you* she's been talking about?" Quida Raye Perkins didn't have to say a word. She just fake frowned as a small crowd gathered around her pork 'n' beans, four for ninety-nine cents. There she was, in the Piggly Wiggly, famous. She nearly wet all over herself.

By the time the taxi dropped her back off at Joy Faye's, she had made up her mind to let Doyle deliver another load without her. She was having far more fun being the butt of on-air jokes than she'd ever had dragging along some bumpy road next to his slowpoke self. Besides, she wanted to head to Pitts the next day and spend the weekend bar-hopping with her buddies. She'd heard from most of them, and they'd all been glued to their radios, too. Doyle could pick her up the next week, assuming she was in a good enough mood to look at his irksome face again.

None of which she bothered mentioning when Joy Faye dashed home and wolfed down some pinto beans and cornbread before disappearing into the bathroom for her second bath of the day. Whatever promising suspicions Quida Raye had nursed since Monday night, after Joy Faye drooped home trailing a hint of french fries and a heaping helping of frustration, then had sat sulled up in the house with her the next two nights, had clearly been wrong. Vick, or Mick, or whatever his stupid name was, must still be in the picture. She stacked up the supper dishes while Joy Faye dug around in her purse for her keys.

"I'm meeting Nick at Ship O'Hoyt's," she said as the phone rang and she jogged over to answer it. It was the fastest her mother had seen her move since she'd stood in a red-ant pile that Easter.

"Hello," Joy breathily said, only to hear Doyle's familiar, "Grump there?" over a crackly connection.

"Yep, hold on." Thrusting the phone toward her mother, who was already reaching for her cigarette pouch, Joy slung her purse over her shoulder and went to sit with a couple of chartreuse lizards sunning themselves on the porch. They were all ears.

"You go on to Cincinatta without me," they heard her say through the screen door. "I've got some thangs to take care of here. You wouldn't *believe* the mess I walked in on the other mornin'." With that, Joy got up and slouched off to her car. So much for sleeping somewhere other than the couch for a while. Not to mention any hope of weekend entertaining.

****

Friday morning at work, raring to go after another eight hours of sleep—Nick had called it a night after just one drink—Joy collected a stack of songs that perfectly complimented the little mother jabs she had planned for the day.

Shuffling through them, Boo-Boo shook his head. "Just when I thought I'd left Pitts far behind, you keep dragging me back." Holding the records up for WildDog's entertainment—"Ballad of the Green Berets," "The Fightin' Side of Me," "Soldier's Last Letter"—he said, "You ever been to Pitts, Dawg?"

"Fort Dewey a couple of times," WildDog said.

"One and the same," Boo-Boo said.

"You and Joy grew up there, right?"

"We did," Boo-Boo replied, leaning back in his chair, settling in for storytime. "Alongside water moccasins, rattlesnakes, alligators, scorpions, fire ants, snapping turtles, black bears, and bobcats." Pausing to comically inhale, he continued. "Not to mention ticks, chiggers, roaches, wild boar, coral snakes, mountain lions, panthers, and coyotes, as well as a fabled beast of lore—wampus cats. You name it, and if it bit, stung, snapped, or attacked, Pitts, 'Home of Fort Dewey,' had it. Including drill sergeants like Joy's father…"

"Probable *step*father," Joy interjected. "Or, as I like to refer to him in the most intentional sense possible, Father *Number Two*."

"Clarification," Boo-Boo said, glancing at the clock, "the father who raised her, though we'll discuss *that* another day. Suffice it to say the only creatures that didn't always flourish in **Fort Dewey's** jungle-like conditions were the humans sentenced there by the U.S. Army. While the most endangered species were various wives and children of enlisted men," he said, motioning to himself and Joy, "running a close second were the hordes of recently drafted buzz-headed boys. Since Fort Dewey was so much like Southeast Asia, over one million of them drifted through Pitts during the sixties and early seventies."

"Interesting," Wild Dog said.

"Don't encourage him," Joy warned, though she always enjoyed it when Boo-Boo got on a roll.

"Which means the town that claimed the best years of yon Joy's life was a lot like Phnom Penh. Only with more friendly fire."

"Are you done?" Joy asked.

"Quite," Boo-Boo replied, grinning.

"Good, 'cause the sergeant here wants to put some silver wings on his son's chest, if you don't mind."

****

After work, Joy drove home, shoved the screen door open, caught the unmistakable stench of her mother's lunch—fried Spam sandwiches—and staggered back outside for air, instantly agitated. The weekend had officially arrived, but Nick had barely pecked her on the cheek since her mother's oh-so-rude arrival four days earlier.

Twenty feet away, Joy saw her sprawled across her chaise lawn chair, merrily giving herself second-degree burns with baby oil and iodine. Acres of freshly mown soybean fields arrowed out around her.

"I didn't expect you home so early," she said as Joy stomped up. "Why aren't you off with that boy? Finally come to yore senses?" Joy could have been dating Grandpa Jones and he'd still be "that boy" to her mother, which was beside the point.

"If you mean *Nick,*" she snapped, glaring down at her, "I haven't heard from him today, so I'm guessing he's not home. Which, unfortunately, is more than I can say for *some people*."

Taking a drag off her cigarette and a swig from her soda, Quida Raye Perkins turned and squinted ferociously into the sun. While she believed any pursuit that didn't hurt enough to peel your skin away in sheaths, like full-time tanning, couldn't be good for a body, Joy knew spiteful words were in an altogether different category. Tossing bon mots at her on air was one thing. But sticking it to her in private—with no audience and no loftier goal than sheer hatefulness—was something else entirely.

48

As regret beaded up in rueful drops across Joy's forehead, she realized she was standing close enough to detect, somewhere beneath her mother's sweaty Spam bouquet, the coconut-cookie scent of Quida Raye's flesh baking, her fury building. Which reminded Joy of eating cookies. Which reminded her of the trainloads of them she had inhaled. Which reminded her why she was killing time with drippy Nick instead of magnificent Ira, who would never in a million years leave his slender wife for a cookie-snorting Bertha Butt like her. Joy's enthusiasm for an argument fizzled. She was immediately sorry for suggesting her mother had worn out her welcome.

Scrambling for an apology, eyes fixed on her mother's spread-eagled, blistered carcass, it occurred to her that the poses for tanning and full-frontal assault were quite similar. With her appendages arranged so as not to crimp any skin and all ten toes splayed, Quida Raye looked like one of those howling tree monkeys that fly tree to tree. Only she was lying completely still. She didn't intend to move a thing except her sharp tongue, which she hadn't planned on tanning anyway.

Joy was opening her mouth to make amends when her mother leveled her with a steely glare. "Don't you worry," she said. "I'll be outta yore hair soon enough. And mark my word, yore gonna miss me when I'm gone."

This was classic doom-and-gloom Mother, the kind of spirit-lacerating comment she occasionally made to remind Joy that (a) Despite her fractious ways, she wasn't in the best of health, hadn't been for years, and (b) Boyfriend aside, she was a divorced woman whose only child was a real jerk. Clearly, there was nothing left for Joy to do except turn around, get back in her car, and go surprise Nick, assuming he was home and had simply forgotten to call.

Besides a final glimpse of her mother stewing in her own juices on the chaise lawn chair, one additional sight would be burned into Joy's brain that fateful Friday afternoon. It materialized shortly after she eased Nick's front door open and crept through his apartment. Deciding to take a page from her mother's playbook, she intended to surprise him with a big "Boo!" Only what she heard herself yelping before stumbling out of that cushy love nest forever was a rather loud and exceedingly clear, "Boo*B!*"

"Wait," Nick called, not even bothering to get out of bed. "She's just a groupie!"

But Joy kept going. And during the time she spent aimlessly driving around, seeing the double yellow lines through her mother's eyes for once, she choked up a bit even though she knew all she would really miss about Nick was the central air conditioning in his swanky new apartment. Thinking about that glorious chill, those snazzy rooms, she suddenly understood how he could afford such a nice place—he was getting paid more than she was. The revelation dried her eyes and turned her irate mind toward other disparities she had personally experienced between men and women in radio. All these years, Joy Savoy fumed, and *I've* never had a groupie. How is *any* of this fair?

****

A quick Louisiana rain soon blew up, sending hard drops plinking like pennies against her windshield. Just as the sky opened, Joy pulled into a drive-through for a couple of sacks of hurt-be-gone, then drearily headed home, woefully crinkling through the screen door.

"Just set mine on the stove," her mother called. Judging from the drinking song on the stereo and the fragrant clouds billowing from the bathroom, Quida Raye had plans for the evening. Which makes one of us, Joy thought, eyeballing the table and that day's conciliatory gesture—three Spam cans glued together with five-minute epoxy and spray painted in fast-drying enamel—purple and green, Joy's two favorite colors. The conglomeration was a "carefree organizer" according to the book *Treasures from Trash*, which her mother had conveniently left open next to her creation. Collections of barrettes and bobby pins were clustered in each can.

A minute later, her mother emerged long enough to eat only those items with the nutritional content of cotton candy. The rest she gave to Sugar Pie. Quida Raye Perkins, a veteran not only of two bad marriages but the ulcers they had caused and a couple of loosely related surgeries, preferred to reserve the half a stomach she had left for cherry pies and strawberry shakes and the like, most of which she overate and lost anyway. It didn't take much to top off half a stomach.

"At least you can keep track of all yore hair thangs now," she said, nudging the organizer.

"Thanks," Joy mumbled.

"'Cept for the Spam, all I bought was the paint. Seventy-nine cents a can," she bragged.

"Nice," Joy said.

After nudging her handiwork again, Quida Raye padded back to the bathroom. "I'm takin' yore car to Pitts tonight, if you don't mind," she called over her shoulder. "Why doncha come with me? That'll perk you up." Sweet, musty plumes of smoky perfume were once again drifting out of the bathroom before Joy realized she hadn't uttered a word about the trouble with Nick. She supposed the sacks of burgers had said it all.

As Joy Savoy began preparing for a rare night out on the town with her mother, it occurred to her that they made quite the pair. There she was, dead set on finding someone to take Nick's place, which—even adjusted for romantic inflation—she knew could be accomplished with little more than a chummy hug. And there her mother was, doing a shuffle to "Whiskey Bent and Hell Bound." On the bed lay her size six jeans, fresh from the cleaners where they'd gotten enough extra starch to look like a pair of denim two-by-fours. Directly below sat her red dancing shoes. Blasting one last coat of hair spray across her brown balloon of a do, she skittered toward the bed in full makeup, red shirt, white vest, pink bloomers, and suntan knee-highs. It had been days since she had scooted around with anything other than an electric lawn mower, and she was ready to hit a dance floor, and hit it hard.

"Shake a leg if yore goin'," she said, reaching for her jeans.

"It's shakin'," Joy replied, right leg waggling.

"Stupe," her mother said, grinning. "I wish you'd act like you've got good sense for once."

"Oh, but if I had good sense I wouldn't be going to Pitts tonight, now would I?" Then, slipping on a freshly washed and, therefore, shrunken pair of jeans, she stretched out flat on the bed so she could snap and zip herself in.

Ten minutes later, after a quick call to Tanya, they

were headed south in Sally, Joy's name for her worn-out fastback pony car with rear-window louvers. While her mother attempted to set a new land speed record behind poor Sally's wheel, Joy stared out the passenger window, reflecting on Boo-Boo's diatribe about Fort Dewey and Pitts—and the rest of the story he'd left out. How, by the time the Vietnam war ended, and retired Army First Sergeant Dick Perkins had dragged his drunk ass back to Missouri where he belonged, it was too late for Joy and her newly divorced mother. Pitts and dozens of Pittsvillians had become as much a part of their lives as some of their own shiftless Kentucky family. Throw in Uncle Sam and her mother, Joy thought all those years later, headed back "home," and she was about familied out.

But on they zoomed that momentous Friday after Mother's Day in 1983, toward an Army town's star saloon where the *most* treacherous creatures in Pitts that bit, stung, snapped, and attacked would soon be on full, heart-stopping display.

Chapter 4
"Ruby, Don't Take Your Love to Town"

With special sauce on their breath and partying on their minds, Quida Raye and Joy Faye shot through Avalon and onto the Pitts Highway in record time.

"You know who's at the Wagon Wheel tonight, doncha?" Quida Raye asked, white-knuckling the steering wheel. "Gary Ferris and the Giddyups."

"Hmph," Joy said, which was about all she could muster any time she was her mother's passenger, or, considering the clip they were going, copilot. Eyes locked on the road ahead for signs of potential speed traps, she squinted into the setting sun, which was making it difficult to tell patrol cars from the usual brand of civilian vehicles headed away from Pitts. The latter generally had mattresses or out-of-season deer roped to the roofs, which, from a distance, often looked to Joy like racks of official lights. Nevertheless, when her mother dropped her cigarette and veered into the other lane while digging around for it, there soon was no doubt what she had run off the road.

"Not again," Joy groaned, glancing over her shoulder at the swirling blue lights flying up behind them. She glared at her mother, whose pointy jaw had far too felonious a set to it. Could she seriously be considering making a run for it in a seven-year-old V-6 in dire need of a full set of sparkplugs? "You *are* planning to pull over, right?"

Heaving a sigh and checking her watch to see just how late this nuisance was going to throw them, Quida Raye took her foot off the gas and aimed for a pebbly stretch of shoulder so she could hit the brakes and spray gravel across the marked unit on their tail.

"Good move," Joy observed. "I'm sure a state police car's windshield is in your budget. As is everything else you're about to get hit with." Figuring that might include the usual array of infractions, from careless and reckless smoking to improper use of a floor mat, Joy watched as her mother slammed the gearshift into park and fished around in her purse for her wallet. Snapping it open and sliding out her license, she reached in the compartment holding her folding money for a ploy she'd had plenty of historical success with on the speed-trap straightaways between Pitts and Fort Dewey. Finally ready, she rolled down the window and, as the scorching May afternoon boiled in, scowled up at the white-faced patrolman who, as a precautionary move, had unsnapped his holster.

"What? Ya'll shoot folks for tryin' to get the hell outta Roshto Parish these days?" she brusquely inquired, poking her arm out the window.

Trooper First Class Donis Wayne Broussard, a six-year Troop Q veteran, observed the woman's balled-up brown fist. In addition to a half-smoked unfiltered cigarette, it appeared to also be clutching a Kentucky driver's license around which a couple of twenties were wrapped. Broussard's heart, nearly back to the excellent resting rate of a well-trained athlete, skipped a happy beat at the thought of scoring a felony that dreary May day. Maybe two, if he threw in endangering a peace

officer. He was cheerily flipping his ticket book open to
a fresh page when his gaze drifted over to the woman's
passenger. Long brown hair. Big brown eyes. Smiling
apologetically as she mouthed the words "I'm sorry"
and dug around in the glove compartment for
registration and proof of insurance. Probably her
daughter, he guessed. The vehicle did have Louisiana
tags.

Something about those big brown eyes and the
nearly filled ticket book he was now smacking against
his palm reminded Broussard he was rolling off shift
shortly. As soon as he finished here, in fact.

"I just need your license, ma'am," he reluctantly
said, handing the twenties back and leveling a flinty
squint at her over his mirrored field glasses, cockeyed
on his head. "You *are* aware that you just ran me off
the road, correct?"

Quida Raye Perkins stared up him with a look
intended to instill some confidence in the man. "Don't
tell me you couldn't see me comin'," she said. "I
thought they taught you fellers better defensive drivin'
skills than that." Then she snatched the money back
while simultaneously attempting to graze his hand with
the business end of what in very short order would be a
$238 cigarette, sizzling from the last drops of rain that
would fall that unforgettable Friday. "If yore gonna
scribble something in that little pad a yores, can you
make it snappy? Gary Ferris and the Giddyups are
playin' where we're goin'. And it's ladies' night."

Joy glared at the heat squiggles radiating off the
slick asphalt yawning in front of them, thinking her
mother had always known when to turn on the charm.
Wondering where Boo-Boo was and if he might be free

to meet them at the jail, Joy reconciled herself to getting fired from yet another radio job. As if the field hadn't proven unstable enough, what with constant ratings, now Joy had to factor her mother into the prickly twin subjects of workplace volatility and her own unrelenting mediocrity. Flipping through her mental file for all the radio stations in a fifty-mile radius, their formats, and who was currently on air that a minimally talented parolee might replace, Joy worked herself to the heart of the matter—leaving the only place she could count on seeing Ira Everhart—and was near tears by the time the trooper walked back up, tapped on the window, and handed her impudent mother a stack of tickets.

"Today's your lucky day, ladies," he said. "Nothing but misdemeanor traffic citations."

"I guess I'll be seein' you in court then," her mother announced, which is what she always said when she couldn't bribe her way out of a ticket. Of course, Quida Raye Perkins never challenged a moving violation in her life, lest she be thrown *under* the courthouse should she dare walk back into one.

The state trooper just tipped his Smokey the Bear hat and stepped back. "Slow down and maintain your lane, please." Looking over at Joy, he added, "Good day, Miz Savoy." Then her mother rolled up the window, blasted the AC, and laid rubber.

****

For the rest of their journey, Joy telegraphed ardent disapproval through her window to the scrub pines flying past, until they were in Morrow Parish and at the trailer of her mother's weekend host and boon companion, Harvey. In the same vein as "A Boy

Named Sue," her mother had a girlfriend named Harvey. Harvey Guy, no less. Harvey functioned as the leader of a group of big-haired, dickey-wearing, girdle-gripped gals Joy's mother had palled around with since they moved from Germany to Pitts in the mid-sixties. One of many peculiarities the women had in common was the fact that all were products of fathers who had wanted sons, which is how those accidental daughters got saddled with popular boy names from the 1930s: Billie, Bobbie, Tommie, Ronnie, and any other handle that might prettily precede Sue or Lou or Jean or June, middle names they all dropped for expediency's sake once they started writing checks. Joy's own mother—a third child but the second girl in a row—received a male middle name with a feminized spelling. Harvey and, consequently, everyone else in Pitts called her Raye.

That Friday, Joy sat in the passenger seat of her own car, gaze irately aimed out the window until they pulled up to Harvey's swaybacked, mildew-streaked trailer and a pack of dogs flew out from under the porch, improving her mood considerably. As her mother swung the door open, sending traffic tickets fluttering to the floorboard, Joy also got out and started petting five or six friendly cur mixes. A couple farther back scampered around the car, only to elicit her mother's usual *"Git!"* when approached by any creature over calf high. It had cost three dollars to have those jeans dry cleaned, and the last thing she needed was a big old drooly-mouthed muddy mongrel jumping up on them. *"Git,"* she yelped again, reaching into the back seat for the paper bag holding her dancing shoes and a couple of hangers' worth of starched, color-coordinated clubbing clothes.

Satisfied that she had everything and the dogs weren't going to leap all over her, she said, "See you and Tanya at the Wagon Wheel," then turned toward Harvey's trailer. For the umpteenth time, she considered what a good power washing would do for that moldy old thang, not to mention a bird bath, some concrete statues, and maybe a nice, white picket fence. Knowing Harvey had about as much gumption in the decorating department as her own dang daughter, she just sighed and headed for the grungy door, out of which Harvey's ginger head was poked, yelling at the dogs and hollering a happy hello.

"Hey," Joy yelled back.

"Hope it cools off," Harvey called. "At least till me and Raye arrive to get things cookin'."

Joy laughed and agreed, continuing on around the car with the dogs. "Go on now," she told the friendliest of the bunch, a blue-eyed Catahoula cur who looked like she'd just had puppies. Wondering how old they were and if Harvey might bring her one when she drove her mother back to Avalon, Joy got in and aimed all the vents at her face. Then she turned and watched as a pair of snow-white tennies did a dainty *pas de deux* around the dog poop and crawdad chimneys that constituted Harvey's front yard. When her mother finally made it to the top step of the sagging porch and turned to wave, Joy waved back and thought, why, she looks like Harvey's kid sister standing there. She knew Miss Finicky wouldn't eat a bite of anything Harvey fixed in that dump of a trailer. But she figured a night or two of conviviality might do her cranky little self more good than a steady infusion of calories. Pulling away and taking care not to run over any dogs, Joy bounced her way back toward the highway, happy to be alone for the fifteen minutes it would take to reach her next mind-rending distraction.

Feeling her spirits ebb, Joy headed into town, past the "Welcome to Pitts, Louisiana, Home of Fort Dewey" billboard she had spent her entire childhood rebranding into "Welcome to *The* Pitts, Lousy-anna, Home of Fort Screwy." While her best friend frequently elicited similar juvenile musings, it was also true that Tanya functioned as an excellent diversion. At the moment, Joy was steering her thoughts away from Nick and his groupie and toward Tanya and her grandparents, the gentle giant Boss-man and his bride of forty-five years, glamorous Gran D. Having long since decided her tree-hugging mother was too much like Joy to live with, Tanya stayed with her grandparents when she was in from college. Joy relished staying there, too. Between Gran D. and Ethelene, the big white house in the middle of town served the best food around.

****

Gran D. listened for a car heading up her driveway and considered the distressing situation testing her mettle in a most unusual fashion. While she and her only daughter had their differences, she had to admit Lynda had a point now—Tanya Lynn, light of her life, *could* stand to lose a few pounds. Though she loved all her grandchildren equally, in her heart of hearts, Gran D. was most sentimental about this one, the feisty redhead who reminded her of her own younger, sassy self. If only Tanya were a size or two smaller. Of course, Gran D. knew some of the blame fell at her own feet. She and Ethelene had practically raised the girl, so it was Ethelene's rice and gravy, and homemade rolls, and chicken 'n' dumplings, and bread pudding that Tanya had grown up on. Grown up and *out* on, Gran D. reminded herself, watching through the beveled glass of her mahogany double door as one of her honorary granddaughters started up the circular drive.

"That strangy-haired girl here yet?" Ethelene asked, wiping her hands on her apron and coming to stand beside the only employer she had ever had, the woman her no-count kids called her white twin. Together, they watched the familiar black rattletrap pull up and braced themselves for the sound of Tanya thundering down the stairs. It had not been the most peaceful afternoon at the Fitzgerald residence. "Don't know why you think *she's* gonna help us. She ain't exactly no twig herself."

"Well, she's the last hope we have to keep Tanya on track today," Gran D. said, reaching for the door. "You ready?" Ethelene forlornly shook the gallon zip-top bag she had just filled and together they stepped out on the porch, all smiles.

"Girl, you just in time for Whirl War Three," Ethelene called as Joy rolled down her passenger-side window.

"Nothing new there, I'm afraid," Gran D. said with an uneasy smile. Patting her crisp, beauty-parlor curls, she took the plastic bag from Ethelene and said, "Joy, sugar, come get this nice sack of carrots and celery sticks that Ethelene fixed you girls. I won't even *say* what Tanya Lynn told us to do with it." The two women cut their eyes at each other and pursed their prim lips. Gran D. waggled the bag, jostling the orange and green bits inside.

Joy had one leg out the door when Tanya burst through the gate at the side of the house and screamed, *"Get back in that car!"*

"Snuck out the back," Ethelene muttered, shaking her head.

"Probably snatched some of those snickerdoodles you've got cooling on the counter, too," Gran D. added, sighing.

Just like countless times before, Joy stared at Tanya in utter wonder. It was a perfectly reasonable reaction to one so alternately stunning and startling. Tanya had a unique approach to making up her face, which—even furious—was lovely in a big-boned, satanically silky way. Each Halloween, she'd buy pots of fright mask to use as foundation the rest of the year. Then she highlighted the resulting pearly palette with blue eye shadow and black eyeliner. While Joy thought the finished product looked like it had gotten up and walked out of a morgue, Tanya's unusual combination of pale makeup, double-D cup, and easy ways struck most males as something like a life-sized porcelain doll in heat. There had never been a guy she had wanted to "cavort around with," as she put it, who hadn't returned the compliment. Between Fort Dewey and the campus of Northeastern Louisiana College, where Tanya was concluding her junior year in fits and starts, there had been much cavorting, Joy well knew.

Wheeling around to her grandmother and the housekeeper who had raised her, Tanya roared, "I already told you two I'm not eating any more of that damned rabbit food." Then she yanked Sally's door open and hurled herself inside. Turning to Joy, she sucked her front teeth over her blood-red lower lip, smacked once or twice and said, "What's up, Doc?"

Slamming the door hard enough to jam the lock, she yanked the window up and said, "I'll tell you what the hell's up here. That pair of Tooney Loons over there are about to drive me freaking insane. Thanks, as always, to my mother."

"What's Lynda done now?" Joy said, pulling away. *Except grin and bear it for twenty-one long, hard years,* she didn't say.

"Nothing more than stir up a hornets' nest with this damn diet kick she's on. Speaking of, want some snickerdoodles?" Pulling a paper dinner napkin out of her purse, she unwrapped a mound of cookies, filling the car with sugary cinnamon temptation.

"Thanks, but I just had a bite," Joy said. "Besides, I could barely zip these dern jeans."

"Suit yourself." Tanya shrugged and said, "So what's going on with the new guy at work?" For the time it took them to travel through Pitts, Tanya munched and listened sympathetically. When she had nearly finished the snickerdoodles, however, she was likewise approaching her last scraps of conciliatory goodwill.

She could listen to Joy bellyache just so long before her attention strayed, and it invariably wandered all the way back to the beginning, when her grandmother hired Joy to babysit during Thursday bridge games at the Pitts Country Club. Not only did Tanya think she was old enough at nine or ten to be trusted at the pool by herself, it also galled her to no end that her babysitter was a know-it-all who never admitted when she was wrong.

And she was wrong a lot. Case in point, Joy made her sit out of the water for a full hour after eating, an edict that condemned Tanya to entire afternoons frying poolside on the sizzling concrete while her beach towel grew fluffy from candy bar wrappers and potato chip bags stuffed under it. Everyone knew it was *meals* you weren't supposed to swim after. Not *snacks*.

But Joy never admitted she was wrong, splashing around in the deep end, laughing her fake laugh with all her fake friends. Where were those so-called friends now? Certainly not in some beat-up old clunker, listening to her snivel about yet another loser. Scratching a suspicious-looking spot on her forearm, probably a precursor to the skin cancer for which Joy would be completely to blame, Tanya inched around and, using her favorite childhood nickname, decided to nip this little diatribe in the bud.

"Well, Killjoy, it sounds like you should have listened to your mother. He *is* a loser. Don't look at me like that. You know she's an excellent judge of character."

"Yeah, right. Give me some of those cookies," Joy snapped, cranking up the air. "If my mother's such an excellent judge of character, what happened with both of the men she married?"

"Can't say," Tanya replied, narrowing her heavily lined eyes and placing the last two snickerdoodles on the center console. "But she sure wasn't far off on the one *you* walked down the aisle with." The last person Joy wanted to think about in The Pitts, party central for all her post-pubescent dementia, was Sonny Savoy.

"Thanks for the reminder," Joy grumped, shoving both cookies in her mouth.

"I'm just making a point. I think it goes without saying that you haven't always been the best judge of men. It's one of *many* subjects you've been wrong about," Tanya said, scratching her arm again. "If you can't listen to your mother, at least listen to me."

Joy couldn't help but laugh, spewing a bit of snickerdoodles. "And what pearls of wisdom might *you* have to impart? Sleep with everything on two legs?"

"While that would certainly take the pressure off the occasional poor soul you *do* end up with, we both know that's about as likely as MTV calling and inviting you to be a VJ." Joy groaned, but Tanya kept jabbering. "So my first suggestion would be to stop dating guys you work with. Name one radio personality who hasn't had a trillion groupies. With the exception of Boo-Boo, of course. Boo-Boo's too hung up on *you* to notice anyone else is alive, poor guy."

"You are officially rude *and* insane," Joy said, some version of which had been her standard response any time Tanya had dusted off that rusty notion during the last ten years.

"And second of all, you should listen to your mother when she tells you what she thinks about men."

Joy's eyes goggled at the very idea. "Maybe we'll get lucky, then, and Lonnie will be at the Wagon Wheel so she can size *him* up." Though she had known Lonnie since high school and always enjoyed seeing his long, tall, sexy self, Joy couldn't imagine a worse possible end to a totally hideous day, what with Tanya about one assault shy of a restraining order.

"If Lonnie knows what's good for him," Tanya calmly said, "the Wagon Wheel will be the last place he'll be. As far as he knows, I'm still at school. We haven't talked since I stabbed his stupid truck stereo speakers. Which, again, I'm sure some other woman gave him." Joy drove on as Tanya wadded the napkin into a hard little ball and shoved it under the seat. Yanking the visor down to reapply her lipstick, she turned her big white face toward Joy, fluffed her flame-red hair, batted her black-rimmed eyes, and grinned, lips dark as death.

"Because, if you think this is scary, you ain't seen na-na-na-nuthin' yet if Lonnie Luneau shows up at the Wagon Wheel tonight looking for love." Then she laughed till tears glistened in her crazy eyes.

Chapter 5
"Older Women"

The sun was setting in a tangerine blaze when they pulled into the Wagon Wheel's parking lot. Joy spied Harvey's car on the front row, an old full-sized four-door with enough headroom to accommodate six hairdos the size, shape, and general density of bowling balls cast in earth tones. Red Ginger. Black. Blue-black. Flame. Nordic Blonde. Joy knew Pud saved all his boxes of Moonlit Brown just for her mother.

Strutting past a row of men waiting to pay cover, Tanya and Joy entered the equivalent of a smoky high-school reunion staged on a weekly basis at every dive joint around Pitts. As they made their slow, convivial way through the club, they passed table after table of old friends whose life stories were as familiar as if they'd been first cousins. Girls Joy had sleepovers with in elementary school. Boys she'd played spin-the-bottle with in junior high. Representatives of both sexes she'd ridden ruts into the roads around Pitts alongside, throbbing with high-school hope and tie-dyed optimism. Until Sonny Savoy had come along to change everything.

Since thinking about Sonny twice in one day exceeded her quota on such atrocities, Joy turned her attention instead to the warm-up tape, amused to hear "Red Neckin' Love Makin' Night" juking away. While she had come to the genre gradually, distracted by the rock'n'roll of her viperous youth, she knew the transition had been more abrupt for most of The Pitts. When the Vietnam War ended and Fort Dewey's official status switched from trainees to an older, permanent-duty demographic, bars that blasted acid rock and oozed black lights didn't close. They just redecorated.

As far as country music and Pitts were concerned, Saigon couldn't have fallen at a more opportune time. When "Wanted: The Outlaws" became the first album produced in Nashville to go platinum in 1976, Fort Dewey's population had just aged ten or fifteen country-appreciating years. Checking out the crowd, Joy could tell GIs were still coming to the Wagon Wheel to remember home. And the locals were still coming to forget it.

"How's this?" Tanya shouted over the music. Looking around for her mother's table and spying it on the far side of the big-box bar, Joy nodded and hooked her purse on a chair. While Tanya proceeded to hold court with a stream of old beaus and minor flings, Joy ordered a Tom Collins and glanced back at her mother's table.

In a sea of feathered or crew-cut silhouettes, Quida Raye and her round-haired cohorts sported a six-pack of true country western coiffures. And Joy knew everything else about them had been similarly shaped by the distant, twangy strains of a sad fiddle song, an age-old mountain melody that molded as surely as it haunted.

There wasn't a woman at her mother's table who didn't have stretch marks by the time the Country

Music Association was founded. And there wouldn't be a person in the Wagon Wheel that night, no matter how white his hat or how shiny his boots, who would have a clearer claim on the music than those six, sweet-smelling, hard-living women with high hair and he-man names. Each of them had been beaten on and cheated on, had been taken for granted as often as they'd been taken for a ride. About the only thing none of them had been taken for was a fool, though Joy knew they'd be the first to admit they'd all married one or two.

Across a dark bar, through the smoke, in two-part harmony, there was no doubt country music had left its mark on Joy's mother and her pals as surely as if it were a ten-pound breech birth. They might not have made the music, but they certainly had lived it. And there was no measuring the effect a lifetime steeped in country lyrics had had on that particular band of merrymakers, each of whom had her own favorite recipe for coping with it. Quida Raye's was a brick-colored swirl of beer and tomato juice. Squinting through the smoke, Joy saw three little tomato juice cans lined up in front of her. Four and she would be popping out her partial and snapping it at people. Joy wasn't going anywhere near that table all night.

"Tell me if you see Lonnie," Tanya yelled during a brief lull in old flames.

"Okay," Joy said. *During my next life*, she didn't say. Setting her sights back on her mother's crew, she saw the full moons had paired off and were gaily orbiting their table to what would be the last song on the warm-up tape, the throbbing, prophetic "Someone Could Lose a Heart Tonight." When the song ended, Gary Ferris and the Giddyups came on stage to a din of wolf whistles and Rebel battle cries. In May 1983, Gary Ferris had hit the charts once, barely making it to the Top Twenty. But you would have thought he was the CMA's Entertainer of the Year the way the crowd carried on.

"Isn't that bass player a doll," Tanya bellowed, shimmying to the music and setting her ample assets a-sway in a fashion that had never failed to get any man's attention. It definitely got the bass player's. As was the case with anyone laying eyes on her for the first time, a shock wave rippled across the man's face. Then Tanya did what she had done to half the guys in that joint— shot pheromone bullets through his eyeballs or something—and he was hooked. After several more songs, once it became clear the bass player was indeed serenading only Tanya, Joy glanced longingly toward the door and the red "Exit" sign. Experience had shown that, once Tanya got a bead on any man, Joy's chauffeur services would no longer be required. Squinting at the clock above the door, she figured she might get home in time to catch the next-to-last episode of "Taxi."

It was at that moment, as she was reaching for her purse and leaning toward Tanya to say she was leaving, that her gaze snagged on a familiar feather. It was sticking up from the cowboy hat of Lonnie Luneau. The hat, one of Tanya's countless love gifts made possible by Gran D.'s tabs across town, was a top-of-the-line Triple X. And Joy could tell, even through the crowd and the smoke and the snickerdoodles suddenly making their way back up, that it was a twin to the smaller Triple X snugged beneath Lonnie's handsome, square jaw.

Chapter 6
"Fist City"

"Uh-oh," Joy heard herself say.

"Where?" Tanya roared, pivoting from the bass player to the door, following the trajectory of Joy's regretful glare. Instantly, she targeted the he's-here arrow of Lonnie's feather and the she's-here plumage sideswiping his nose. Then she was gone, as invisible as propane hissing toward a spark. Fumbling for both of their purses, Joy watched as the bigger feather flipped into the air, then flew Roadrunner fast through the door, closely followed by Lonnie's bare head.

Thinking she could catch up with Tanya and whisk her to the car before the police got called, Joy picked up her pace, vaguely aware the bass player had jumped off the stage behind her. But neither of them saw Tanya again until they made it to the parking lot, where the main event was just beginning.

"You two-timing, no good, son-of-a-cheating-dog-bitch," Tanya shrieked. Everyone in the small crowd already gathered looked confidently from the feather on the hat Tanya was holding behind her head, well away from Lonnie's lunges, to the feather on the hat of the sharp little number standing forlornly off to the side.

As Lonnie jabbed the air in vain for his hat, Joy inched closer, past old friends, Tanya's former flings, and GIs already three sheets to the wind. The more

Tanya heaped flaming curses atop Lonnie's hatless head, the more revelers poured out of the club, including six Joy saw emerge from the side door. As Quida Raye and her teased and sprayed comrades coolly leaned against the far wall, looking from a distance like a clutch of deputy sheriffs in parti-colored bowler hats, Joy scanned the faces closest to hers, hoping to spy a mediator in the antsy mob. But all she saw was amused relief that all hell was about to break loose on someone other than themselves for a change. Then again, she knew no one short of Gran D. could stop Tanya now.

Inside, Gary Ferris and the rest of his Giddyups were wrapping up their first set. Outside, Joy was preparing to step forward just as Tanya snarled, "Oh, is *this* what you want?" Then, while everyone groaned in anticipation, she flung Lonnie's pricey cowboy hat to the puddled pavement and began yowling and squalling and jumping up and down on it with all the fury a hundred seventy-nine pounds could muster.

"Good Lord," someone said.

"The girl's got spunk," the bass player observed.

As Lonnie's hat became a doomed trampoline, Joy glanced over at the familiar face beneath a previously matching and, for the moment at least, still intact hat. Missy Williams hadn't changed a bit since high school. From her late-'70s feathered hair to the rest of her poster-worthy self, lovely Missy was just the spark to blow Tanya off Lonnie's felt launchpad and clear to the moon. The last Joy had heard, Missy was working as a cocktail waitress. And, judging from her skimpy outfit, she'd come straight from work. Checking to see which arm held her purse, Joy began digging for her keys just as Missy unfortunately emitted a dainty squeak of a sneeze. "'Scuse me," she said to no one in particular.

Tanya came to a complete standstill and swiveled her head, hoot-owl like, to behold a brassy blonde poured into blue-jean short shorts, falling out of a tank top, and wearing a damn little wide-brimmed hat exactly like the one currently underfoot. Everyone around Missy took several giant steps backward.

Trembling now with rage, Tanya turned back to behold the lying whoremonger who'd wasted two months of her time and untold amounts of Gran D.'s credit. "You bought that hat for her, didn't you? To match the one *I gave you*?" As white-hot fury all but blotted Lonnie from view, Tanya couldn't name a single thing he'd given *her* except perfectly good reasons never to believe one damn word he said.

Wrongly accused yet again, Lonnie's chest indignantly swelled with the truth—Missy had been wearing the hat that afternoon, when he laid eyes on her for the first time since 1974. After dropping his truck off at the car audio shop downtown and walking across the street to wait at the Pink Kitty Cat, there Missy was, waiting tables in a cowboy hat that was a twin to his. He considered it a sign—as if a set of stabbed truck stereo speakers hadn't been—and was opening his mouth to say as much just as Tanya decided she had heard enough.

"*Shut your filthy, cheating, man-whore hole,*" she roared. Then she decided to do it for him. But with what? Her purse would have worked, but she guessed Joy was off playing mother hen with it somewhere. Her fist was another option, though she knew from experience that would hurt and quite possibly require stitches. Spinning back around to Lonnie's cute little thing and her pretty little hat, Tanya knew exactly what she could cram down the bastard's throat. Reaching over and palming the hat's crown, she yanked. Then she yanked again. Both times, the Triple X came only as far as the fragrant neck beneath it would stretch, giving Tanya the strangest impression that it was glued to the woman's dumb blonde head.

"Ow!" Missy yelled, lamenting her old habit of using an entire slip of gold-toned bobby pins to effectively nail her hat to her head when she went dancing.

As spectators clotted around in eager anticipation of a girl fight, always a top attraction in the bar parking lots around Pitts, Joy held a purse in the crook of each arm, balancing herself against the swell of onlookers gathering to pick sides. The women gravitated toward the underdog, currently in a ninety-degree angle to the slippery asphalt. The men were evenly split between Tanya and Missy. But everyone seemed to agree that, no matter what happened to Lonnie, he'd be getting what his dumb ass deserved since he so far hadn't done a blessed thing other than watch his cowboy hat get squashed. Pitts bar-fight patrons expected more involvement from all embattled parties, as evidenced by helpful suggestions coming from Lonnie's former teammates in the crowd, like, "Come on, man. Don't be such a pussy."

But Lonnie just stood there, utterly bewildered. His hat was a goner, and it was looking like Missy soon would be, too. Nothing short of manhandling Tanya would change things now. Assuming he *could* manhandle her. Lonnie had yet to score a clear decision in any clash they'd had, which was how his speakers got stabbed in the first place. The thought of Tanya sending him down for the count in front of half the town paralyzed him, arms limp by his side and mouth hung open, begging the question among female bystanders as to what either Tanya or Missy had seen in him anyway.

Joy glanced from the flaccid O of Lonnie's gape to Tanya's clenched jaw and saw the trajectory Missy's hat would travel once it was wrenched free, which Tanya accomplished with a final demonic grunt and yank. Immediately, she and Missy both tumbled backward as the hat popped off with a sickening slurp. Missy shrieked and the crowd gasped in horror as Tanya glanced at her trophy before slamming it into Lonnie's face, but with a puzzled jolt saw what appeared to be a live creature that had been hiding beneath it somehow and now dangled free in untold hairy scariness. Screeching, Tanya hurled the hat and its bushy beast into the crowd, which erupted into mayhem.

There was not a female in Pitts who hadn't been dragged off on snipe hunts or tormented by trick mongoose cages during their frequently traumatized early years. When Tanya slung Missy's hairy hat into their midst, all the women promptly experienced PTSD moments and squealed like a parking lot full of loose serpentine belts. And the men weren't any better. While most relished the opportunity to kill anything that was either in season or at war with the U.S. government, identification was key in any strike. And, for the first few seconds, no one knew what the hell this shaggy critter was that had landed, hat-up, on the wet pavement. The women grabbed each other and kept screaming, while the men looked as inept as Lonnie. Finally, Peanut Sibley, first team all-state his senior year, shuffled over to kick the hat, sending it flying several feet before it toppled over to reveal a neat rim of blonde locks bobby-pinned around the brim. Lonnie looked from the hat, lifeless on the ground, back to Missy, who was clutching her head with both hands and still shrieking.

"I didn't know you wear a *wig*," he said, confused.

"I don't," Missy wailed, confusing Lonnie further because, it was true, she still had hair. Maybe a little less of it. But certainly enough that she wouldn't have required the services of a hairpiece. Perhaps the hat had been one of those jokes that come with glued-on hair, though he couldn't imagine why she had worn such a thing on their first date. Suddenly relieved that Tanya would likely ensure this would be their last date—hell, the rate Tanya was going, she might cure Lonnie from looking at another woman the rest of his godforsaken life—he lifted his eyes toward the edge of the parking lot. His truck was waiting there, along with his rods, reels, tackle box, and all the stink bait he would need for some night fishing out at Lake Morrow. He was imagining the catfish he could catch and how his mother might fry them up with some nice hushpuppies and coleslaw on the side when the thick kitten heel of a size eleven shoe hit him square in the upper lip.

Tanya, teetering on one foot, was drawing back to smack the still hollering tart with the same shoe when the crowd parted for a big-haired woman plowing through. Seeing it was Harvey Guy and realizing she was reaching a protective arm around Lonnie's keening date, Tanya dropped the shoe to her side.

"I know her mother," Harvey announced with authority. "She's a friend of mine. So get me this girl's hat and step aside."

Peanut bent down and obliged, shaking some of the rainwater off the blonde ring of hair. "Here you go, Miz Harvey." Then the crowd parted for the woman who had served as room mom or team mom or second mom to just about everyone there except the GIs, watching as she led Missy past her poufy-haired compatriots still standing by the Wagon Wheel's side door.

"I'll be back soon," Harvey called to them, gently steering Missy toward her big sedan. "She don't live far."

Lonnie was happily thinking he was now free to head straight out to the lake when the thick kitten heel hit him a second time in the exact same spot.

"Fuck!" he yelled, fingertips flying up to his lip and the gush of hot blood spurting out. He didn't think a tooth was chipped, but then again, he couldn't feel much from his nose down. It had been such a damn big shoe.

Tanya, still tottering on one heel atop the uneven pile of Lonnie's ruined hat, was rearing back again when Lonnie finally reached out a meaty arm, snatched the shoe away, and hurled it to the far end of the parking lot. "Touchdown!" someone yelled.

Unfortunately, Tanya lost her balance while losing the shoe. As an arm flung sideways and her head whipped back, her one-night stands farther back in the crowd reached the terrible conclusion that she had been struck instead of merely stumbling off her unsteady felt perch.

Joy doubted if Lonnie knew what hit him next. It could have been one of Tanya's many Lotharios, all of whom were suddenly trying to see if they could cripple Lonnie Luneau for life. It could have been the Wagon Wheel's scrawny little security guard, new on the scene and ever mindful of male customers getting rough with the club's female clientele. Shoot, it could have even been Tanya, though Joy was pretty sure Lonnie was already down before she was all over him again, cubic zirconia-laden fists raising angry red welts across his head and face.

All Joy knew for sure was it must have looked like fun because, in no time, the rest of the onlookers were turning around and taking a few swings too. Spit, snot, buttons, and blood were soon flying through the querulous crowd like Mardi Gras beads on Bourbon Street. When the scrawny little security guard got thrown to the puddled asphalt, Joy knew they had a war on their hands that could finally make Fort Dewey proud.

By the time a mournful steel guitar signaled the first song of the second set, an a cappella number that didn't require the bass player's services, the Louisiana State Police—Troop V, Joy was relieved to see—had nearly dispersed the mob. Other than Lonnie, who was receiving medical attention, and the bass player and troopers who were trying to keep Tanya from knocking Lonnie's stretcher over again, nearly everyone else was back inside.

Wondering if that included Harvey, Joy turned to look for her car. And that was when life as she had known it screeched to a rubber-burning, glass-shattering, world-altering halt.

For standing there, aswirl in a mist rising off assorted bodily fluids puddling the hot pavement, was the last man she expected to see treading the troubled backwater of Pitts, Louisiana—Ira Everhart himself.

Instantly, Joy's mind raced to that starless night when the name Ira Everhart first entered her lexicon of longing. Then, as now, squad-car lights flashed and emergency personnel swarmed. *Jessie. Oh, Jessie.* The awful similarity was so striking that, for a second, Joy thought she, too, would need jump starting by the paramedics working on Lonnie. But she did what she had always done when her thoughts turned, unbidden, to that abominable night. She conjured the face of Ira Everhart. This time it was easy. It was three feet away.

Soon, her heart was beating again, loudly enough, she was sure, to be heard over both Gary Ferris and the bass rumblings of Fort Dewey's perpetual night maneuvers.

"What are you doing here?" she sputtered, trying to wipe the grime of the fight off her face.

"Looking for news," Ira answered. "Seems like I found it." Those three sentences comprised the longest conversation she'd had to date with the man she secretly adored. She just stood there, mute and agape. It was one thing to sit calm and collected behind a mic, catching the occasional glimpse of the star of her most private fantasies. It was quite another to be ambushed by him miles from work, in her own hometown, no less, after her defenses had been sorely compromised by hand-to-hand combat.

"Actually," he said, beginning to smile, "I was down here covering the Pitts City Council meeting. They voted to allow residents to shoot any stray animals on their property, wild or domestic. Dogs. Cats. Woolly mammoths."

"Speaking of woolly mammoths," Joy said, nodding at Tanya, "did they make any provision for berserk women? I'm afraid my friend has once again slipped into that sad category." As she spoke, Tanya darted past the troopers and the bass player and shoved Lonnie off his stretcher. Badges and billy clubs dinged and clacked to his rescue.

"Judging from what I hear on the scanner every day, the Pitts City Council approved the shooting of women years ago." Ira grinned sadly and squinted like he was discovering some deep, hidden truth behind Joy's bangs. Or maybe he was just trying to see past the mud. "If this is the way your friend usually behaves, she's lucky the locals have let her live this long."

"The night's still young," Joy said hopefully.

"That it is," Ira replied with a stare as piercing as if delivered by a pair of black drill bits. "In New Orleans, she'd have her psycho ass in the back of a squad car by now."

"With any luck, that's where they'll cram her in Pitts tonight, too," Joy said.

"Wanna bet?" Ira said, arching his brow. "In case you haven't noticed, it's still the Wild West around here."

"Oh, I've noticed," Joy said. She had also noticed she was being stared at by Ira Everhart for the first time in two and a half years.

"Is it my imagination, or is the ground shaking?" he asked.

"No, it's definitely shaking," she answered. Then, realizing he meant literally, she added, "Oh, um, they're still playing war out at Fort Dewey, and one of the training ranges is just over that ridge. I grew up down the road, and whatever the Army did all night every night shook everything so much it routinely felt like my bed had taken off and was rolling down the highway. Whee!" What am I saying, Joy wondered? And why am I saying so much of it?

"I repeat," Ira said, "the Wild West."

Smiling, Joy had to admit the scene did have a certain O.K. Corral vibe, what with troopers giving Tanya stern warnings, EMTs readying Lonnie for transport, and the security guard hoisting himself up from the spot he had occupied since Tanya laid him out cold. But it was the hot, sticky few inches separating her from Ira that engaged her imagination far more, bringing to mind the last man she'd been this close to— that cheater Nick. Hoping it was Get A Groupie Day for all of KLME's male on-air personalities, Joy's happy speculations were soon interrupted by what she came to realize the guard was shouting.

"You are permanently barred from this establishment!" he was yodeling at Tanya. "Now get in your car and exit the premises immediately!"

Then, as if coming from the clanging gates of hell, Tanya said, "I don't *have* a car. I rode with *her*." Everyone, from troopers to trauma victim, followed the tip of her blood-red nail, aimed straight at Joy.

"Well, she's outta here, too, then," the guard yelled.

What?

Joy had to leave? Just when Ira Everhart was looking back?

"Now!" he bawled.

Tanya, as usual, had something other than obedience in mind, buying herself a short reprieve and Joy a few extra seconds. "I can't exactly go far as long as the fearsome foursome here is threatening to dogpile me," she said with a mock pout. Turning to the state policemen behind her, she batted her raccoon eyes and held out her wrists. "But don't stop now. I've been looking for men who'd handcuff me and show me what a bad girl I've been."

Ira shook his head. "Unless you've got bail money, I suggest you get your whacko friend out of here and let the Wagon Wheel get back to business."

"Don't make me tell you to vacate the premises one more time," the guard bellowed.

It was a tossup who Joy hated more—the guard or her best friend—though she at least had the pleasure of pinching Tanya once the bass player handed her over and she and Ira escorted her to the car, shoved her in, and slammed the door. The only consolation was, while the bass player searched for the gold chains, buttons, and shoe she had lost and Tanya finally sat still and watched him, Ira began walking Joy around to her door. Almost touching, definitely strolling, in Joy's mind they were doing a mambo of the ages, a sort of slow-mo mingling of space and time, seduction and common sense.

Slowly rounding the bumper and easing up along the driver's side, Ira leaned over to get her door. With a small, charged thrill, Joy noticed her shoulder fit beneath his arm, like she always knew it would. Then, as if they were about to kiss, she turned her head, lifted her chin, closed her eyes. And she didn't snap out of it, either, until the car door clicked and she looked up to behold a pair of black eyes she had only dreamed about getting that close to. Joy wasn't sure how long it was before she remembered she was supposed to get *in* the car, but she eventually did, wilting into her seat with the aplomb of a stun-gun victim. Ira eased the door closed, backed away, crossed his arms, and looked at her as if she had uttered something infinitely perplexing. She rolled the window down. He stared a while longer, thoughtfully chewing one side of his mouth.

Finally, he said, "You know this would never work."

Her heart flipped over. "What?"

"Hit the road, miss," the security guard yapped, whacking his club against Joy's back bumper. *Bap bap bap!*

"I'm sorry," she stammered, blindly jabbing at the ignition with her key. "I didn't hear what you just said." Ira shook his head and smiled. "What?" she repeated, but his grin only widened.

"We'll talk at work." *Bap bap bap!* "You'd better go before Buford Pusser back there breaks his big stick."

So she did. She started the car, backed up, and drove away, regrettably missing the guard but thoroughly numbed by the five most amazing minutes of her life. Staring into the rearview mirror all the way to the highway, she memorized Ira standing in the parking lot, watching the ambulance lights flash. And, out of the corner of her eye, she saw something else. A Moonlit Brown hoop of hair wreathed against the Wagon Wheel's side door seconds before it closed.

"I take it that was the famous Ira Everfart," Tanya said, flopping around in her seat, crumpling the traffic tickets on the floor. "If you can rip your eyes away long enough, pull in to the drive-in and park." Pitts' one drive-in theater was located directly across the road from the Wagon Wheel.

"What?" Joy yowled. "Do you really think Lonnie's coming back tonight? Assuming he *survives*?"

"Who cares?" Tanya said with a shrug. "Earl's picking me up there after the show."

"*Earl?*"

"The bass player. He invited me to go on the road with him and Gary." Joy tipped her head sideways. "He said I could obviously use a few days away from this place." Absently picking through her purse for something to hold her gaping blouse together, Tanya paused to dreamily contemplate her prospects. Tears and fury had shifted most of the black outlines on her face a quarter-inch, lending a skewed, out-of-register cast to her wishful delirium. "I've never done it on a bus before. Got any safety pins?"

****

By the time Gary's bus whooshed up and Earl stepped out, Ira had long since driven away without seeing Joy parked across the road, burning holes through the staff car's tinted glass. Tanya had filled the hours by talking her into near paralysis about the glorious new carnal experiences surely awaiting her. And she did so without once putting an anatomically correct name to the body part she'd given more of a workout than the Jaws of Life in a fifty-car pileup. As always, Tanya referred to the whole, roomy lot as her "chewy," just like she had at nine years old.

"A 'chewy,' is something Sugar Pie plays with," Joy said for the thousandth time, only to have Tanya jump out, slam the car door, and kick gravel across Earl's boots while scuttling up to him.

Joy had never been happier to see someone leave, with the exception of her mother a time or two. But Tanya's exit nevertheless left the bucket seat beside her empty. She looked at the stitched red vinyl slowly springing back into place and decided it was fanning out about as forlornly as the rest of that Friday night surely would. With Ira gone and Tanya's foray into the world of country-music groupiedom eliminating Gran D.'s guest bedroom as a lodging option, Joy began the hour-long drive back to Avalon.

Army-green pines surrendered to cypress swamps. Memories merged into expectations. Over and over again she heard Ira's words—"You know this would never work." This what? This car? This life? This crazy fevered dream? With no clue, on she barreled, sliding through the hot May night on nothing more than a slim shot of hope and four mag wheels.

Chapter 7
"Behind Closed Doors"

Monday morning, Joy opened the mic and said, "Mother and I took us a little trip to Pitts Friday. She, of course, was behind the wheel since she'd rather lick the front license plate clean than ride in a car I'm driving. For one thing, it's usually going around fifty-five. For another, I don't assault highway patrolmen quite like she does. Especially when we're headed back home to Pitts. Now that I think about it, home isn't necessarily where the heart is. It's where the Roshto Parish branch of the Louisiana State Police mails your license back to you. Isn't it, Mother?"

"Hey," Vernon said, sticking his head in the studio as Joy kicked on "The Carroll County Accident." "I've got something to talk to you about after your shift today, once Ira gets back from South Louisiana."

Joy's entire torso contracted. What did Ira have to do with anything? Had she crossed some line in the Wagon Wheel's parking lot Friday night? Fantasized out loud? Broken some professional anti-attraction code? And, if so, who had apprised her uptight Pentecostal boss?

"Is everything okay?"

"Sure, sure," Vernon said, checking his watch. "You just keep talking about Mama and everything'll be dandy."

"All right," Joy slowly said. "Except she packed up and left this morning. Took her dog and rode off into the sunrise in a semi bound for Louisville."

Smiling as much for Vernon's benefit as her own, Joy's mind skipped back across a weekend spent in an Ira-infused blur. Saturday, she'd met Boo-Boo for Mexican, to feed the butterflies in her stomach. Sunday was dedicated to making playlists of every cheating song she could think of, till Harvey's car eased into the driveway around dusk.

Holding the screen door open for Sugar Pie to run out, Joy strolled up to Harvey's rolled-down window as her mother dug around the back seat.

"Sorry we only have a one-dog welcome party here," she told Harvey. "You could fix that by bringing me a puppy."

"You need a dang dog like I need another hole in my head," her mother popped up and hollered. Arms full, she kneed the door shut, told Harvey she'd talk to her later, and stomped off toward the house with far more sacks than she'd left with Friday.

"Bye, Raye," Harvey called. Then, quietly to Joy, "You want a boy or a girl?"

"Definitely a girl. And I prefer the runt of a litter."

"Say no more," Harvey declared, shifting into reverse and dropping her voice again. "Make sure your mother eats something. She's barely had a bite since she got to my house. Well, I take that back. After we finished at the mall, we stopped at the Weenie Queen and she did have a slaw dog."

Bubbles of happy, puppy-filled thoughts popped and fizzled in the muggy heat as Joy listened to the screen door slam. "Don't worry, hon," Harvey said, reaching through the window to pat her arm. "Go see what's in them bags. She 'bout broke the bank."

But the bags were nowhere in sight, and her mother was in the bathroom, losing that slaw dog, by the time Joy walked in—and right out again. Sitting on the porch swing till dark fell across the bayou, she listened as the rhythmic, leg-scraping insects that invented zydeco warmed up for their evening concert. Welcoming the racket, she was grateful for the bullfrog-and-cricket choir drowning out the silence now spilling from inside.

Around dawn, Doyle chugged up, and her mother ran out, dog in one arm and paper bags of trucking necessities in the other. Joy rose from her cramped bed on the couch and hummed a happy tune all the way to the bathroom, where she discovered a stack of beautiful new frocks neatly folded on the edge of the glistening tub.

Three hours later, she smoothed the lap of the ruffled forest-green number with a Mandarin collar and smiled again. KLME had a dress code, instituted by the station's ultra-conservative general manager currently standing stock still in the studio's door. Unless they were meeting the public, which wanted its country disc jockeys dressed in jeans, the station's female employees were required to wear dresses or skirts. And, prior to that morning, Joy had five dresses to her name. Four, not counting the ripped red muumuu.

Joy noticed Vernon didn't appear to be on the verge of complimenting her lovely new attire. He actually looked like he might be having a stroke.

"Don't worry," she quickly said. "I'll come up with something else to talk about."

Vernon's crimson flush deepened. "I don't want

something else," he croaked. "I want what sent my salesmen running all over town last week. I want *Mother stories.*" Vernon's normally reedy voice had turned dead flat. It was a tone Joy had heard often enough from other bosses, usually right before they instructed her to box up her personal effects and go home. But she couldn't get fired now. She had a stack of new dresses Ira hadn't seen.

"Mother stories? Why, that's no problem," she insisted, assurance drenching every syllable. "I've got *plenty* of those. Twenty-five *years'* worth."

Vernon weighed this vast archive of promising tales against the only other alternative—Joy's usual vapid banter—and the tendons slowly relaxed in his neck. "I guess that'll have to do," he finally said. "As long as you're sure you aren't gonna run out of cockamamie things that your mama's done."

"Of that I am one hundred percent certain," Joy declared.

"Okay, then," Vernon said. "We'll talk more this afternoon. Say three?"

Joy nodded, and he was gone, leaving her alone with her green ruffles and a slightly sick feeling that something somewhere was reeling out of control. She wasn't sure what. And she couldn't grill Boo-Boo since he was off with WildDog at some grand opening. No Ira, no Boo-Boo, and she hadn't heard from Tanya since Sunday when she'd called to report she was in San Antonio with Gary Ferris and the Giddyups. And that she had indeed "done it" on a bus. After promising to keep Joy updated on any other new erotic locations she might christen, she hung up to answer what was obviously the far more urgent call of country music groupiedom.

****

"I'll just cut to the chase," Vernon said at 3:04. "We're about to make you a statewide sensation, little lady."

To this day, every detail of that meeting hangs in Joy's memory like wisteria tendrils swaying through the mists of her hazy mind. Vernon leaned against the massive oak desk in front of her, Ira in a leather chair to her left, Boo-Boo to the right. And a future blowing up bigger and bigger all around them with every slo-mo word oozing from Vernon's smiling pink lips.

Poi-Son Communications' network of small Bayou-State stations.

Her show.

Simulcast.

Five mornings a week.

A statewide sensation.

Then Vernon stopped talking and laughed.

"Surprised, or just impersonating a largemouth bass?"

With some effort, Joy managed to hoist up her jaw. Shock had obliterated control over all body parts. Good thing she didn't have gas. She didn't even have gasps. She was stunned dumb. Her mediocre show was going to be sent across the entire state? Every weekday? For multitudes to hear?

"What did you think they were gonna let me do?" Vernon asked, grinning. "Keep this gold mine to myself? My phone hasn't stopped ringing since you started all that Mother nonsense last week. Advertising's taken a good little jump. Your numbers'll probably be hotter than a jalapeno. All of which means you, Joy Savoy, are about the best thing I've seen since Dolly Parton bent down to take a bouquet from me on the front row at last year's concert." Glancing at his framed painting of *The Last Supper* behind him, Vernon mumbled, "Forgive me, Lord." Then he crossed his arms and turned back to Joy. "Well? Speak!"

"Good gravy," she spluttered. "Gee willikers."

Ira scribbled something on a pad. "Just say, 'Lady Bug was tickled pink,' or something like that," Vernon suggested. "By the way, let's start calling her Lady Bug, *Mouth of the South*. I think that's got a nice ring to it."

Turning to Joy and Boo-Boo, he said, "Ira came back from Baton Rouge just to announce this on the five o'clock news, then in every broadcast the rest of the week. We're not starting till Monday, so the two of you have time to brainstorm ideas." To Joy he added, "Without interfering with those Mother routines. Which you're sure you've got a stockpile of, right?"

"Right," Joy proclaimed. Of course she wasn't going to stop talking about her mother. She evidently could never stop talking about her mother again. A small jagged lightning bolt ripped behind her eyes.

"You just keep those Mama bits coming, and we'll all be happy. Especially the big brass. As the two of you know," he said, gesturing to Ira and Boo-Boo, "Ray and Jimmy have been wanting the network to have more personality for a while now. But personalities cost money, so they figured they could save a few dimes by experimenting with a show of their own. Joy's mother couldn't have dropped in at a more opportune time."

Joy heard the leather chair squeak as Ira humphed.

"Ray and Jimmy were all set to go with that guy I

told you about in Zwolle, the one who makes farm-animal sounds. Crowing and mooing and oinking and whatnot. They were about to sign him when they decided, 'What the hay, let's give someone already on the payroll a shot first,' " Vernon said. "If it doesn't work out, no harm, no foul, since they've still got the chicken guy." Though Vernon shook as he snickered at his own joke, Joy noticed his dark, heavily lacquered hair, a John Wayne style favored by the men of Brother Stanley's congregation, didn't budge. "So Boo-Boo here will be your producer. Ira's gonna stir up some excitement with newsy clips. And all the other jocks will just keep doing what they've been doing, since this isn't gonna affect any of them anyway. Oh, and Ray and Jimmy want to fly up and meet you soon."

The men who owned Poi-Son Communications wanted to meet her? A statewide sensation? *Her?* As average a know-nothing country DJ as had ever spun a forty-five? And all she had to do was keep talking about her mother? Joy's face hurt, and she wasn't entirely sure it was from grinning ear-to-ear.

"Unless anyone's got any questions," Vernon said, slapping his thighs, "I guess we're good to go."

Ira closed his notebook. "I'll call Ray and Jimmy and get a few quotes," he said, glancing over at Joy. "And I was thinking I'd pull excerpts from some of your recent broadcasts. Like the one where your mother ran your boyfriend out of your bed?"

The blood rushed to Joy's head so fast she was surprised she didn't experience stigmata of the cheeks right there, five feet from Vernon's Christ scene.

"You could also go with something a tad more tame," Vernon said, bucking up from the edge of his desk. "Like that toenail-chewing bit. That just cracked me up, the image of her mama goin' to town on them toenails."

Ira stood up and grinned. "Or that."

"Because everyone loves a toenail-chewing mama, right? Move over, Carol Brady," Boo-Boo said, getting up and stretching. "Sorry to run, but I've got an appointment. And, no, it isn't for a pedicure."

Joy also staggered to her feet. In five short minutes, she had learned her show was about to get beamed to scores of stations. And that Ira Everhart recalled a man had recently been routed from beneath her sheets. Focusing on the lesser of the two life-altering revelations, she turned to Vernon and said, "Wow. Gee. Thanks heaps and gobs. Oodles and bunches. I won't let you down. Uh-uh. No way. Not me."

Spewing a few more inanities for them to slog through on their way out, she was prepared to prattle away on down the long hallway separating Vernon's suite from the rest of KLME's offices. Only she lost two-thirds of her audience when Vernon's phone rang and Boo-Boo dashed off after a congratulatory hug.

As the doors on each end of the long, dimly lit hall clicked shut, Joy stood still and read the immediate future like a steamy novel. She couldn't have been more alone with Ira Everhart than if they'd been buried alive in the same body bag.

"Coming?" Ira said.

"Probably," she said, and instantly wanted to gnaw off her tongue. "I mean, I'm right behind you."

Grinning, he said, "I think it'd work better if you were in front." As she began to swoon, his voice shifted to a casual, impassive tone. "New dress?"

Joy looked down at the white lacy number with tiny pink flowers she had dashed home and chewed the tags off after her shift. "This old thing?"

"Nice," he said. "Come on. We'll take the tour together."

By "the tour," he was referring to an innovative use of the autographed 8-by-10s dropped off by decades of musicians stopping by the station to promote albums or club dates or, in the early days, host their own shows. Vernon's father, then Vernon himself, had framed every photo and hung them side-by-side, row upon row, until smiling, famous faces lined both long walls. It was quite literally a country music hall of fame. Quida Raye could have spent days there. Her daughter could have, too, but for far different reasons.

Slowly, Joy and Ira made their way past hundreds of beaming, approving mugs. Sequins and spangles under glass. A 4-H exhibit of the evolution of Everyman in rhinestone-studded suits and Everywoman in western fringed, appliqued shirts.

Reaching behind her to adjust a crooked frame, it was almost—but not quite—as if Ira were putting his arm around her. Turning toward him to admire an early hillbilly crooner, it was almost—though not exactly—as if they were about to kiss.

Barely moving, ostensibly observing, Ira and Joy inched down the hall, marveling over star after star in a slow, whirling swirl of each other. Back and forth they went, sliding closer with each photo, softly speaking, gently laughing, lightly tapping image after image. Some recalled stories familiar even to Joy, whose wellspring of country wisdom was barely puddle deep. Luckily, many of those muddy recollections were so tragic it seemed entirely appropriate to reach out and touch a hand to Ira's sinewy shoulder, let it lightly drift down his hard arm. Heart attacks, car wrecks, plane crashes. Country music's plentiful calamities had Joy all but weeping in Ira's sturdy embrace as they made it down the hall.

Then there were the wittier inscriptions that had an equally thrilling effect on Joy, when a rumble started deep in Ira's throat and he'd grab her arm, pulling her close. "Look," he'd gruffly say. Once she was near enough to detect his afternoon coffee and, beneath that, a sharp musk layered atop a long day's work, he'd nod to a picture, any picture, and Joy would reluctantly turn and take in nothing but the feel of Ira's big hand around her humerus, its thermal proximity to other body parts on the verge of automatic combustion.

"Mmm," she'd say. And on they went down that storied hall, past a host of superstars on a first-name basis with the world, not to mention scores of other artists Joy would soon be using to serenade tiny outposts up and down that boot-shaped state.

Either to extend the stroll or impress the man, Joy pointed out the performers she had already interviewed. Even in May 1983, the list was impressive, including nearly half the one-name megastars and twice as many other chart-toppers.

"Not bad," Ira said, glancing toward the door at the end of the hall, now mere steps away.

Scrambling for something else to babble on about, anything to delay the inevitable, Joy said, "So you've been in Baton Rouge?"

"I have," he replied, turning toward her. "And you got out of that hell hole alive the other night, I see."

"Uh-huh. As did Tanya."

"Remanded to Angola, one can only hope. Not that being locked up's so bad," he said, nodding back down the hall to an array of famed lawbreakers.

"No such luck." Joy smiled. "The only bars Tanya's gonna see any time soon are the ones Gary Ferris and the Giddyups are playing."

Ira's eyes widened. "How's that?"

"Lonnie wasn't even out of the ER before she'd run off with the band's bass player." Joy watched him throw his head back and laugh, studied his thick neck, the veins striping it, the Adam's apple sliding up and down it, the black hairs curled at the base of it, and got so woozy she nearly knocked a brother band to the floor.

"Oops," she said as Ira reached around her to steady the frame.

Then, flattening his palm against the wall and leaning closer, practically cradling Joy in a one-armed embrace, he said, "Tanya certainly appears to be a woman who gets what she wants. I can see why the two of you are friends." Down went his chin, up went his brows. Joy's move.

"Except I haven't invited state troopers to tie me up and spank me lately," she said, which made him chuckle again. Then he sighed, leaned back and reached for the doorknob. Joy couldn't believe their last seconds of utter privacy were going to be wasted on Tanya.

"You know," she said, "not everything I say on air is exactly true."

"Such as?"

"Such as that wasn't my *boyfriend* my mother ran off with. It was, you know, just a friend."

"Just a friend."

"Uh-huh. Actually, it was that new guy, Nick." Seeing his head do a surprised little jog, she added, "And you might not have heard, but Nick's got a girlfriend. Shoot, they could be getting married, for all I know."

Married! Just like you're married, Ira, remember? Gritting her teeth to keep any more idiotic words from falling out, Joy grimaced, instantly aware she was impersonating a chimpanzee at the very moment Ira's thoughts were surely turning to the decidedly non-simian visage of his lovely wife.

"Here's a word of warning," he began, bending down to whisper in her ear. As molten lava trickled from her lobe to her toes, he said, "It's the married ones you need to watch out for." With that, he opened the door, and Joy stumbled out behind him. Ira turned left and, soaring, she turned right, only to fly straight into Nick.

"There you are," Nick exclaimed. Ruthie and the other secretary looked up while Ira continued on to the newsroom, wagging his head. "I tried to call all weekend." Expecting exactly that, Joy had unplugged the phone. "We need to talk."

"What's there to talk about?" she asked.

"Lots…"

"I'm sorry," she said sweetly. "But did you say '*sluts*?' Because, if you did, I've recently learned everything I care to about that subject." Then, wheeling around, she winked at Ruthie and skipped out of the station.

Chapter 8
"When I Dream"

Already sweating from her time in the hall, Joy walked across the sizzling pavement, got in her cast-iron skillet of a black car, and realized there wasn't a soul she could go home and call with her news, assuming she hadn't imagined it all. Tanya was doing God only knew what with the band in Texas. Boo-Boo's meeting must have been elsewhere, since his truck was gone. Her mother was in an eighteen-wheeler that was surely in Tennessee by now, even with pokey Doyle behind the wheel. Which left Ruthie, who was back inside where she'd just left Nick. Since he wasn't due on for hours, Joy cranked up the AC and circled the block, hoping her car would cool down and Nick would leave, both of which eventually occurred.

"What are you doing back?" Ruthie asked. "Congratulations, by the way. Getting simulcast statewide—that's amazing!"

"Thanks," Joy said, shyly fiddling with the new dress's pearl buttons. So she must not have imagined it all. Or at least the work part. "Hey, it's Harley Davidson Happy Hour at Ship O'Hoyt's tonight. Wanna go celebrate?"

Ruthie seemed to be calculating her odds of getting shot or stabbed while lingering over a friendly drink.

"It'll be fun," Joy insisted. *You might even get laid*

at the ripe old age of twenty-nine, she didn't say.

"Okay," Ruthie grudgingly agreed.

"Great! I've gotta run to the mall, but I'll come pick you up at five."

****

What Joy actually did was drive to the head shop on lower Main to spend the rest of the afternoon in air-conditioned rapture, flipping through albums and forty-fives, her favorite, patchouli-scented pastime. She was probably the only country DJ in town who whiled away hours in a black-light haze, squinting at record labels and album covers by the glimmer of lava lamps and celestial balls.

With oldie bins promising endless tune-fueled time travel and "In-A-Gadda-Da-Vida" thudding through speakers and rhythmically flashing light organs, relics of a bygone bohemian age, it wasn't long before Joy was back in her own flower child days of yore.

Watching a familiar Christmassy spectrum flicker across the C's, she smiled and remembered her mother, the original shopaholic, buying a pair of kaleidoscopic light boxes just like those. It must have been about 1969, she figured, examining a copy of "Born on the Bayou." Sometime around Woodstock, which Joy absolutely refused to concede was closer to Quida Raye's era than her own. It was just one more grudge she held against her mother, who—hardly groovy—had had big hair and starched jeans even then.

Vaguely, through the gauzy veil of time, Joy was eleven or twelve again and seeing her mother alone in the dark once more, immobile on the couch, knees up to her chin, ashtray close, sad songs on. While a scorching damp breeze slipped through cranked-open windows and slow danced the sheers around, that mournful, meditative pose told one truth only—Dick was once again back from Vietnam, but he wasn't back from either the bars or every other delight who made herself available. And many did.

As she had since the fifties, Quida Raye took her troubles to the turntable. Seeking counsel in a twangy four-four beat from countless cheating songs scattering incongruous psychedelic diamonds across the gloom, hers was a jerky light show scored by Countrypolitan sob songs and steel-guitar whines, by every hangdog hymn a young girl would commit to memory from down a trailer's back hall. Because, as much as she liked those cool blinking lights, Joy had learned to keep plenty of distance between herself and the round brown do in the dark, cocked like a rock in a slingshot. As utterly terrifying as Dick ever was, drunk and swinging a steel-riveted Army-issued web pistol belt, not even that matched the unfathomable dread Joy felt when her mother sat, hopeless, in the neon night.

Glancing down and seeing she was holding one of those same cheating songs, she was snapped out of the past and, in very short order, that head shop, too. Joy stuck a shopping bag with two forty-fives in her purse so they wouldn't warp in the car during happy hour, then headed back to the station for Ruthie.

****

If you were a female with "Born To Be Wild" fantasies during the *Flashdance* craze sweeping Avalon in May 1983, Ship O'Hoyt's was the place to be Mondays from five to seven. Judging from the chrome-cluttered parking lot, Joy figured every Harley owner in three parishes was inside enjoying half-priced brewskies. Offering weekly biker-only deals had been a shrewd marketing move on Hoyt's part, she told Ruthie, steering her past a fleet of small sports cars, models favored by Avalon's MTV crowd of edgy young professional women.

"It sure is busy," Ruthie said.

"It's like this every Monday after work," Joy said, reaching for the door. "Between the bikers and the women who think it's safe to ogle them while it's broad daylight outside, we'll be lucky to find a table."

"I'll be lucky if I don't trip and break my neck," Ruthie said as the door swung open and a gust of stale beer rode a low roar pouring out of total blackness. "I can't see a thing."

"Follow me. I know bar Braille," Joy called over a crowd engaged in stiff competition with the jukebox. At the moment, "Maneater" was blasting, as it often did Mondays from five to seven. Expertly fumbling past tables and chairs, boots and heels, she led Ruthie stumbling through the darkness to a roundtop in back, near some leathered-up pool players.

"Here you go," Joy said. "Be right back." Heading to the bar for their drinks, she found her way back by the low, red glow of beer signs.

"Did I miss any cute tattoos?" she asked as the song ended and conversations commenced once more at a low din around them.

"No. But that guy over there nearly knocked my teeth down my throat with his pool cue," Ruthie said. That's all she needed, Joy thought. No teeth *and* a sideways nose. Not even Harley Davidson Happy Hour could help her then.

"Come sit over here," Joy said, patting a stool

farther from the action. Flopping around the table, death grip on her purse, Ruthie plopped down and glared at the bikers as if she were with the Stones at Altamont.

"Here." Joy shoved her Fuzzy Navel across the table. "Drink this." She did and was soon her usual perky self. In spite of her long petticoat and her vaguely wayward nose, Joy noticed several Hells Angels wannabes checking her out.

"So," Ruthie said with a giggle. "How's it feel to be a star?"

"How would I know?" Joy reddened. "It's not happening till Monday and, besides, I doubt if much will change. These *are* the tiniest stations in the state. Plus I'll still live in the same house. Drive the same car. Play the same songs Boo-Boo will still help pick out."

"You're so lucky," Ruthie said, taking another slurp.

"Are you kidding?" Joy had to laugh. "Other than this bolt out of the blue, I assure you luck hasn't knocked on my door too many times in twenty-five years."

"Yeah, but you get to work with Boo-Boo, plus he's been your friend forever. What I wouldn't give," Ruthie gushed with as much wanton desire as a twenty-nine-year-old virgin could muster.

As surprised as she ever was when some female considered her old buddy anything more than cuddly, Joy just patted Ruthie's freckled hand. "Well, don't get your hopes up. I doubt if Boo-Boo's had a date since I had a pet rock. All the man ever does is work. Trust me, it would be a far better use of any romantic impulses you might be experiencing to apply them to any of the fine specimens arranged here for our viewing pleasure,"

Joy said, gesturing with both arms to assorted hunky bikers in varying stages of sobriety all around them.

"What? And get my throat slit?" Ruthie cried, shuddering. "Anyway, have you thought about what you're going to say once you get syndicated?"

She had, in fact, thought of little else. And she had *no screaming idea* what she was going to say come Monday.

"I have no screaming idea what I'm going to say come Monday."

"I'm sure Uncle Vernon's gonna want you to keep telling your mother stories."

"Yes, he is," Joy said. "For what *that's* worth."

"I'd say it's worth a lot." Ruthie sipped her drink and looked around, feeling marginally less terrorized. "Your mother's such a character."

"I believe they said the same about Lizzie Borden." Once again Joy thought about the Faustian bargain she had agreed to that afternoon, the evidently permanent way she had just hooked her work wagon to her mother's dark star. Reaching for her Absolut Tom Collins, which was in quite a tiny glass, she figured she would either have to order an IV line and intravenous vodka her next trip to the bar, or change the subject.

"I'll bet that guy over there hasn't beaten anyone to death this week. Blow him a kiss."

Ruthie just humphed and slurped her Fuzzy Navel. "So, did you hear? Nick gave Uncle Vernon notice today."

"What?"

"Yes, ma'am. He said he'd sent tapes to an Atlanta station the same time he applied here, and he just heard back. Obviously, he's going to choose a major market

over us. That's probably what he wanted to tell you."
Ruthie decorously stirred her drink.

"So, like every other twentysomething, he blew
into town just long enough to pad his resume and now
it's off to the big city." It was one of Boo-Boo's
favorite rants. How Avalon's other young media
hotshots were career opportunists while he, Boo-Boo
Bailey, was content remaining a big fish in a small
market. As her thoughts skittered uneasily to Ira
Everhart, the most notorious radio reporter still standing
in Central Louisiana, Joy sensed Ruthie was waiting for
her to say something else.

"I guess that means adios Avalon and hola
Hotlanta then." Feeling that was linguistically
insufficient for someone who talked for a living, she
added, "Arrivederci, bon voyage, and don't let the
screen door hit ya where the good Lord split ya."

Ruthie wrinkled her forehead, confused. "I thought
you liked Nick."

"For about a day," Joy exclaimed. "Let's put some
quarters in the jukebox and I'll tell you all about it."
Twenty-five cents later, she was slightly hoarse and
fully finished with Nick. "Georgia can have him. As
can Carolina or Virginia or whatever that tramp's name
was," she said quickly, as the needle dropped on the
next record.

Ruthie rattled the ice in her glass and leaned closer
so she could be heard over the deafening intro of Joy's
favorite Aerosmith song, which she played every time
she came to Ship O'Hoyt's.

"Speaking of moving," she yelled, "did you hear
about Ira and Dianne?"

Joy's entire body convulsed. Did Ruthie just use

the words "moving" and "Ira" in the same sentence?

Ira was *moving*? That explained everything. No harm in flirting if he was *moving*. As Steven Tyler howled, Ruthie mumbled something that sounded like, "Ayatollah sheep be black."

"*What did you say?*" Joy wailed, on the verge of tears.

"I said," Ruthie hollered, spacing out her words like an SOS, "I. Told. Ira. She'd. Be. Back."

Joy stared dumbly, certain she still hadn't heard her correctly. "*Huh?*"

Ruthie leaned closer and yelled louder. "Haven't you heard? Dianne's moving to New York City."

The hand clutching her Tom Collins suddenly felt like it could crush glass. Scooting her stool around till she was nearly on top of Ruthie, she bawled, "*What?*"

"What rock have you been under, Joy? You mean you haven't heard about Ira and Dianne, either?"

"No!"

"Well, Dianne got into some school up there. Seems she's always wanted to study painting."

"*Fainting?*"

"*Painting.* Drawing. Art. Stuff like that."

The hand holding her Tom Collins was now exhibiting signs of palsy. "When are they leaving?"

Ruthie laughed at Joy, who was nearly in her lap. "Ira's not going. He says he'd rather move to—forgive me, Lord—Bumfucked Egypt than New York City."

Dianne was leaving and Ira was staying? What did that mean? Where was this place? When would that infernal song end? Ship O'Hoyt's went totally black as a band closed around her ribs, pressing out all air. Joy hadn't free-fallen into such a bottomless stupor since eighth grade when, for kicks, she and her friends would hyperventilate and squeeze each other till they passed out. Then someone said you kill brain cells every time you do that. Joy wondered if she would have any brain cells left at all after Ruthie's revelation. Ira's thin wife was moving? And Ira was staying? By the time the music blessedly rumbled to an end, Joy had just one question she could barely manage to ask.

"Are they getting divorced?"

Ruthie crinkled up her crooked nose as though the thought hadn't occurred to her. "Not that I know of. From what Boo-Boo said, Dianne just decided it was time to explore her creative side. I guess they'll have one of those newfangled marriages where they live apart and visit once a month or something."

So this bombshell came by way of *Boo-Boo*? Her second-best friend in the world? Whom she just had supper with Saturday? Boo-Boo knew Ira's wife was moving away and planning to visit monthly and hadn't told her? A lot could happen in a month. A month is an eternity for some things. Houseflies. Mayflies. Wives that fly the coop. Surely even Boo-Boo knew that. After another round, during which Ruthie encouraged not a single biker and Joy lapsed into a pensive silence impervious to even Harley Davidson Happy Hour, they gathered their purses and headed for the door. Blinded once more, Joy lurched toward Sally in the setting sun, feeling as if she had spent a lifetime not seeing anything clearly.

After dropping Ruthie off back at her car, she headed home and called her grandparents in Kentucky. Maybe her mother was there. Maybe she'd like to know she was about to be the real star throughout the state she'd just left that morning. But her grandparents' phone rang and rang, so Joy hung up and went to stand in front of the bathroom mirror, looking for answers to the question she kept asking herself like an incantation. *What's going on here? What's going on?*

Joy Savoy did not have the kind of life where one good thing piled on top of another like they had that day. Mother gone. Show syndicated. Ira abandoned. She had a Dick and Sonny kind of life. She had a trollop for a best friend and another old buddy as a program director who had apparently decided to tell everyone except her about Ira's new marital arrangements. Feeling slightly bewildered and fully betrayed, she gazed into the mirror at a flawed reflection soon joined by a host of her favorite neuroses, the countless inadequacies that had always justified any slights or sorrows, particularly during the last two and a half years. Since Jessie.

As night mournfully thrummed and called across the bayou, Joy once again imagined Ira soon forsaken in a duplex across town. Holding on to the sink as the bathroom spun, she searched the mirror for signs of alien occupation—sudden widow's peak? Hollow cheeks? Glass teeth? But all she saw was the same old benzoyl peroxide addict in need of a good night's rest.

Chapter 9
"I Ain't Living Long Like This"

Deep asleep, Joy Savoy barely heard the phone ringing. Fumbling for the receiver, halfway remembering calling her grandparents, she mumbled "Hello?" and groggily waited for one of them to speak.

"I hope yore sittin' down," her mother blared into the phone, instantly opening Joy's eyes and blanketing her in panic.

"I'm *lying* down," she said, checking the bedside clock. "I do that at two thirty-seven in the morning."

"I know what time it is," Quida Raye snapped. "I just thought you might like to know Doyle's in jail and it's a miracle I'm not, too."

Joy sprang up in bed. Doyle was in jail? Had they run over someone? It was her worst fear, the thought of her mother hurtling through the night, a tawny, heat-seeking missile shot from charred, mangled metal. If there *had* been a wreck, Joy realized with some degree of relief, at least she was still alive.

"*What happened?*"

"They got him for grand theft," her mother said.

"*What?*" Joy heard a quick gulp of breath, nicotine nerves rushing to neurons near and far. Not even that steadied her mother's voice when she spoke again.

"Joy Faye, you know full well that truck we've been drivin' is stolen property."

She said this as if stating actual fact, as if stealing an eighteen-wheeler was a minor maternal detail that had simply slipped her daughter's mind. Joy Savoy knew what brand of beanie weenies her mother preferred. She was pretty sure, even jolted from a sound sleep, she would have recalled some mention of a snatched semi.

"I most certainly did *not* know any such thing," Joy proclaimed as the ceiling spun. Or maybe it was the bed. Or maybe her eyeballs had popped out of her head and were playing craps by themselves over in the corner. Seven, come on lucky seven. *"You stole that truck?"*

"*I* didn't steal nuthin'," her mother hollered. "Doyle did."

"Okay. So you've been riding all over kingdom come for years in a truck your boyfriend stole? Doesn't that make you an accessory or something?" Joy leaned against her headboard and considered a veritable dictionary of other crime jargon. Aiding. Abetting. Accomplice. Alibi.

"Not accordin' to the state trooper that hauled Doyle off," her mother said. "Or at least not yet."

"Not yet?" Joy asked.

"That's what I said," her mother grumbled.

"How about you say more because I am completely discombobulated here," Joy said. "This is either the end of a bad dream or the beginning of a true nightmare. I vote for dream but, if not, would you mind filling me in, please? Maybe start with what just happened and work backwards?"

****

Three states away, Quida Raye Perkins mashed out

one cigarette and reached for another. "What just happened was Doyle didn't listen to a word I said, as usual. Instead of stoppin' in Tompkinsville like I *told* him to, he was bound and determined to make Luavul tonight. We were a few miles outside a E-town when he said, 'Hang onto Sugar Pie!' and hit the shoulder. I thought we'd had a blowout. Till I saw the blue lights. In no time flat, a trooper had him yanked out and sprawled across the side of the truck, handcuffed. Sugar Pie was barking her head off."

"Poor Sugar Pie," Joy said. "What did the trooper do to you?"

"Let me sit in the truck till backup arrived and roared off with Doyle. I kept Sugar Pie quiet with some chocolate-covered caramels and waited for one of 'em to come jerk me out, too. But all they did was hand me back my license and say I might have charges pressed against me 'at a future date.' But that, for the time bein', I was free to go."

"Free to go where?" Joy asked. Elizabethtown was two hours from Tompkinsville. A world away.

Quida Raye took another long drag off her cigarette. "To the county jail in the back of a blame squad car. That's where I sat and waited for Mama and Daddy to get there."

"Poor Grandma and Granddaddy!" Joy yelped. "No wonder they didn't answer when I called."

Quida Raye felt the first stirrings of shame. Yes, her broken-down old parents had been forced to drive two hours after dark in an ancient hardtop to retrieve their youngest daughter from a jailhouse. Remembering them shuffling in together in their stiff church shoes and dusty funeral best, she saw her daddy squinting behind thick glasses, one blue eye turned white and blind decades earlier by part of a walnut shell. Saw her Parkinson's-riddled mama, quaking hands clutching a pocketbook stuffed with every rainy-day dollar they had squirreled away inside canning jars and old coat pockets for decades. Nobody said boo all the way home.

"They went to bed a while ago, but I cain't sleep," she murmured. "My stomach's all tore up, and I've got a sick headache. If the po-lice don't come back for me tonight, I'm gonna go get my car and clean out the apartment tomorra. So, if you call, wait till later."

"I still don't understand," Joy said. "How in heaven's name does anyone steal something as huge as a big rig?"

Quida Raye Perkins sat in the dark of the old house her daddy had built and decided she had never felt so tired. Tired of life, and definitely tired of talking. As it did during most conversations, her focus soon floated off to a place where she could have a little peace and quiet.

Teetering on a stool at her mama's sticky breakfast bar, knees up to her chin, chewing what was left of a thumbnail, Quida Raye held the phone to her ear and peered into her most familiar darkness. A night wind moved through the window screens of the old place, never air conditioned but generally bearable, stirring a half-century stew of lives that had been lived, for better and for worse, inside those sturdy walls.

Twirling the cord of the wall phone, which had hung in the same spot for decades, she let herself drift on a breeze borne of yesterday's fried baloney sandwiches and cornbread sticks, old songs and sharp cars, good dogs and dear friends long gone. In the wee hours of a morning, she would dare anyone to tell her the old place wasn't haunted. All around her small creaks and groans never failed to conjure happier times and fresh faces she could clearly see again just by closing her eyes. Her two wisecracking brothers with their crewcuts and old jalopies were always first on the scene, tinkering on clunkers out back or gobbling up Mama's fried chicken before running off to the dirt track outside of town with girls they would turn into mothers, wives, and women, in about that order. Then there was her bossy big sister, raven-haired and too beautiful for her own good, now dead for years.

Hearing her daughter clear her throat six hundred miles away, Quida Raye thought of the kids the four of them had produced, some shiftless, a couple thoroughly worthless. Till that night, in fact, several of her no-'count nephews, long since given up on by everyone else, had been the only hoodlums her mama and daddy had been forced to pick up from a jailhouse. Those boys had brought intolerable disgrace to a good name, a name hauled to the tobacco patches and cornfields of western Kentucky in the days of Daniel Boone, then handed down by good country people ever since. Till those delinquents came along.

Nearly toppling off the bar stool, Quida Raye suddenly realized *she* was now in the same league as those hooligans. If the thought didn't make her so furious, she might have broken down and cried. Instead, she forced herself to carry on with her story, get it over with.

"For yore information, it ain't that hard to steal a damn truck," she crabbed. "Or so I found out three years ago, when we was drivin' around Lake Barkley and Doyle told me to pull into Woodie's Truck Stop. Then he got out of the car, walked over to a semi that was sittin' there idling, got in, and drove away, big as you please. You could've knocked me over with a dern feather. I've never been more surprised in my life. Other than the day Jessie was born." She heard a sound and knew Joy Faye was flinching, like she did anytime someone mentioned Jessie's name. Which Quida Raye Perkins almost never did.

"By the way, she was with us that day, too," she quietly added. "We was goin' to the stables at the lake so she could ride a real Neigh-Neigh for the first time in her life." It was the only confession of the night that had made her breastbone feel like it might crack in half. "Doyle said they'd probably bring her in for questionin', too, if we ever got caught." She listened to Joy Faye cluck her tongue three states away and maybe even drop the phone.

But Quida Raye frankly couldn't care less what her daughter thought just then. Saying Jessie's name had opened the floodgates of other memories. Her only grandchild at five and a half. And four. And three. And, well, every sparkling second from the first moment they laid eyes on each other. As stupefied as she'd been that Joy Faye wasn't just seventeen and fat but also seventeen and pregnant—*pregnant!*—none of that mattered when she peered into the bassinet and that surprise newborn swiveled her bitty red face around and reached out a teensy hand—as if they'd known each other all of eternity.

Winning a million dollars wouldn't have dumbfounded Quida Raye Perkins more, and she immediately set about filling the days with endless ways to keep that feeling coming. Which it did, as long as that munchkin mug was trained on her own deeply tanned, hopelessly devoted one. All she had to do was squeeze her eyes shut, which happened any time Jessie's name came up, and the reel-to-reel of those five and a half years started flickering once again across the paper-thin screen of her tired, withered lids, complete with sights and sounds she would never—no, never— forget.

And always in the background was the tinkling of bells. Little bells. Tiny bells attached to the first toy she herself had bought Jessie, that little red rolling horse with gold trim and real leather reins on four tinkly wheels that Joy Faye took one look at and squawked, "She's *three days old*, Mother!"

Jessie's first, best—and last—Neigh-Neigh.

The thought momentarily caused Quida Raye Perkins to lose her balance on the stool at her mama's old breakfast bar. Opening her eyes to a pitch darkness she knew would shroud the rest of her days, she switched the receiver to her other ear, as ready as she'd ever been to get on the far side of the past two and a half years.

Clinging to sweet memories slipping back into the night, she offered the first lame excuse that came to mind. "Jessie might've only been five, Joy Faye, but Doyle swore they'd make her testify if I ever told anyone what he'd done, and I believed him. Don't forget the po-lice are *still* grillin' them kids about those little green men in Kelly. And that was back in fifty-five."

"First a dang stolen truck and now some old

Kentucky UFO hullabaloo?" Joy howled, agitated to the point of near hysteria. "I think you've lost your mind!"

"Maybe I have," her mother hissed. "Or maybe I'm just sick of talkin'. Talkin's probably what landed Doyle in jail in the first place. He couldn't get within two feet of a bottle of Jim Beam without runnin' that damned big mouth a his. I'm surprised it took the law *this* long to catch up to us." Thinking about Doyle's indiscretions moved her that much farther from the sad slide show her traitor brain always tortured her with. Changed her tone from shaken to swaggering, from little-girl-lost to pure Belle Starr braggadocio.

"So what are you going to do now?" Joy asked.

Her mother clicked her cigarette pouch shut. "Only thang I *can* do, which is stay 'round here a while. One of the troopers said if I don't turn state's evidence, I could be sent up, too."

"Sent up?" Joy said. "As in jailed? Or imprisoned? Or whatever you call it?" It was three in the morning, her mother's thieving boyfriend was behind bars, and she was using judicial jargon while inquiring into her mother's plans for avoiding prison. Prison! Her mother! "So are you?"

"Am I what?" Quida Raye grumped.

"Going to 'turn state's evidence.' "

Quida Raye Perkins fell into another pensive silence before speaking again. "I don't know *what* I'm gonna do except go fall into bed. I guess I'll either call after the apartment's emptied out. Or if I'm headed to the Kentucky State Pen."

****

Several hours later, after Joy had eaten an entire box of strawberry toaster pastries, it occurred to her that she had completely forgotten to tell her mother how notorious she was about to be in Louisiana, too.

Chapter 10
"Beware of the Tall, Dark Stranger"

"I heard from Mother a few hours ago," Joy Savoy told a good chunk of Louisiana that morning. Since KLME was running a network test before Monday's rollout, the snippet introduced a vast, new audience to her maternal shtick. "Lock up the family jewels, folks, 'cause she's picked up the torch Ma Barker dropped in a hail of gunfire a few years back. Grandma bailed her out, and I'm laying down the law, so that ought to teach that little felon a thing or two about runnin' with the wrong sorts. If not, I suppose I'll find out everything I never wanted to know about body-cavity searches. Ooo-la-la!"

"Wait. Are you saying your mother got *arrested*?" Boo-Boo said when Joy carefully pulled off the headphones so as not to mess up her hair. She'd been behaving strangely since stomping in without a word to anyone except WildDog. All Boo-Boo had gotten from her so far was barely a nod when he explained the network test. If her mother had had a run-in with the law, that could explain the chill.

Though he was sitting just four feet away, Joy turned and stared searchingly at a spot to the right of his head. "Is someone speaking, WildDog?" she asked. "All I hear is an annoying squeak."

Despite his admittedly limited experience with

members of the opposite sex, Robert Bailey had picked up a few pointers regarding the female propensity for utter insanity during his eleven-year friendship with the owner of the cold, hard face currently aimed at the wall. Evidently, *he* was somehow the problem, though hell if he knew what he'd done this time. Baffled as thoroughly as he'd been anytime he had incurred Joy's wrath, Boo-Boo just sighed at the prospect of a morning spent measuring statewide radio signals with a DJ who had suddenly decided to completely ignore him.

Ever the problem solver, he turned to the baseball-capped intermediary beside him. "WildDog, could you please ask Joy if her mother was arrested?"

"Joy, did your mother get arrested?" WildDog asked, kicked back in a rolling chair and enjoying his new position at the top of this tense little triangle.

"Why, no, W.D. Thank you for asking. Half the patrolmen in Kentucky hauled her boyfriend off and impounded the big rig they'd apparently stolen in broad daylight three years ago. But *she* wasn't arrested. Yet. She might be at a future date, but as of this morning, her wardrobe is still void of black-and-white stripes."

Turning to Boo-Boo three feet away, WildDog said, "No, Joy's mother did not get arrested."

Pantomiming a goofy form of sign language, Boo-Boo slapped and smacked his hands together while saying, "Please tell Joy, 'Thank you for that explanation.' "

"Thank you for that explanation," WildDog repeated, minus the hand gesticulations.

"Not a problem, WildDog," Joy sweetly replied.

And so it went for the first ten or fifteen minutes of the first full day of Joy Savoy's becoming a statewide phenomenon. It was a still unimaginable announcement she might have been able to more fully appreciate had the previous twelve hours not been mined with a pair of additional bombshells—her mother had been riding shotgun in a pilfered eighteen-wheeler since before Reagan was elected, and Ira's wife was moving away.

While the former was a shock to everyone, she knew the latter was a revelation her dear friend Boo-Boo Bailey had been privy to and had shared with Ruthie and probably everyone else at the station. Except her. As retribution, Joy had decided never to speak to him again.

After several more entreaties went frostily ignored, Boo-Boo handed WildDog a wire to plug in. "Since it appears Joy has mysteriously fallen deaf to my voice only, would you mind hanging around and serving as a go-between? You know, in case this test we're running requires actual communication with the brand-new show's brand-new star."

"Sure," WildDog said. "I don't have anything to do till ten or so, at which point you two ding-a-lings will have to excuse me. I've got a date with the visiting NLC cheerleaders."

"*All* of them?" Boo-Boo asked, astonished.

"Why, certainly," WildDog replied. "I wouldn't want to hurt any feelings by excluding some." Boo-Boo shook his head as Joy clomped around the cluttered studio, snatching up songs to play in a silent huff broken only by her stints on air, which she kept short and sweet. For expediency's sake, she even revisited a few of her earlier zingers, as any that involved trucks were once again unfortunately fitting.

WildDog hadn't enjoyed himself more in days.

When it came to detecting tension between the sexes, he prided himself on being as sensitive as a forked stick in the hands of a talented water witch. It was an analogy that brought to mind the one dowser he'd had the pleasure of passing a long weekend with, a freckle-faced, hefty gal named Darla, who knew her way around rods of every sort. Witch-hazel twigs, willow branches, peach sprigs, etc. Especially et cetera. Momentarily awash in vigorous recollections, WildDog jumped when Joy slammed a clipboard down.

"If you want, Bobby, old buddy, I can give you a few pointers on navigating the oft-troubled waters atop which members of the fairer sex blithely bob," WildDog dreamily said. "It looks like you could use some help."

"God knows that's true, Archibald."

Archibald. Joy stifled a smile. If ever there was a question about DJs inventing on-air monikers, Archibald settled it. Turning away until she could compose herself enough to scowl again, Joy was staring through the big plate glass window into the darkened newsroom just as Ira Everhart opened the door, flipped on a light, and strode in.

Quickly turning away, she caught Boo-Boo's eye, then wheeled around to look him square in the face. Tipping her head and fixing him with a cocked-jaw stare, her steely glare gave the impression of being tethered somehow to the activity unfolding through the plate glass window behind her. Glancing from Joy's indignant scowl to Ira and then back to his old friend, Boo-Boo sensed he was being provided clues of some sort. After some mental charades—involves Ira, sounds like trouble—he had it. Joy must have heard the latest office scuttlebutt, and not from her usual source.

While it was true Ira had mentioned his wife was going back to school, it was also true that Boo-Boo had decided against repeating the exchange—barely more than a couple of sentences—to Joy. When it came to her infatuations, he knew how carried away she could get for no reason whatsoever. After all, he'd been playing sideman to her endless fantasies since she'd been a whimsical girl with a weakness for dark-haired bad boys and anything purple back during the Vietnam War. He had in fact been her accomplice in *amour* the day it all vanished in a purple haze.

"WildDog, have I ever told you how Joy and I first became friends?"

"Can't say that you have," WildDog said. Sitting up, he resituated his cap and clasped his hands in his lap like a boy at bedtime, ready for his story.

"Well, I was a junior at Pitts High School, and she was a freshman, which means I could drive to school and she couldn't. So I took pity on her and ferried her around."

"It's not like I had a choice, other than taking the *bus*," Joy told WildDog, plopping back down at the turntables and deigning to engage in a three-way conversation as long as she didn't have to speak directly to her former second-best friend in the world.

"Ah, yes. The big yellow taxi. A fate worse than death," WildDog agreed.

"So I picked her up and took her home," Boo-Boo continued. "And one afternoon—I guess I was a senior and she was a sophomore by then—we had company."

Joy well knew the day he was referring to and, with over four minutes left on "Pancho and Lefty," allowed herself to drift back to that pine-scented, white-bright spring afternoon. It was a day she probably would have remembered forever anyway since Paul Cruz, one of the best-looking boys at PHS, was behind them. Suggesting they meet after school was the most attention Paul had paid her, and she could only imagine the gains they would make once they got to the trailer and Boo-Boo left. Her mother would still be at work for another hour or two. And, since she and Dick had recently separated after yet another battle royale, Joy didn't have *him* to worry about anymore.

"Some guy Joy had a crush on was following us," Boo-Boo told WildDog. "She lived in the back of the biggest trailer park in Morrow Parish, so any new beau required a guide."

Joy recalled grinning at her own reflection in Boo-Boo's car window that day as they passed the jumbled loop-the-loop of long, silver trailers and tall, jade pines, their two-car caravan weaving its way toward a wooded dead end. Her mother not only preferred living in fancy new mobile homes since houses were so "old-timey," she also insisted on a corner spot as far as possible from the Spec. Fours and local riffraff typically drawn to a life of lot rent and butane gas. Though she'd had stiff competition for Lot of the Month in such a large park, Quida Raye Perkins had, as usual, risen to the challenge, paintbrush in hand.

Joy couldn't wait till Paul saw their place, a wonderland in yellow, beige, and brown, clunky with color-coordinated yard bric-a-brac and aswarm with pets—several dogs, assorted ducks. Joy even had a horse, though he was pastured five miles away. In other words, Paul was about to behold what every cent and all the credit an occasionally contrite if genetically combative E-Seven could scrape together.

"But when we pulled up to Joy's place…" Boo-Boo began.

"Something was missing," she said.

"There was the fence, the dogs, the ostriches, and so forth," Boo-Boo said.

"They were *ducks*," Joy told WildDog. Boo-Boo hunched his shoulders and shook his head, as if ducks made any more sense than ostriches.

"Anyway," she continued, "in addition to the *ducks*, there was the cinderblock storage shed, freshly painted yellow and brown to match the brown fence posts and yellow bird bath."

"I think there were even some yellow plastic flamingos still standing in the yard," Boo-Boo recalled.

"Yellow?" WildDog wrinkled his forehead.

"My mother thought pink clashed with her yellow-and-brown color scheme," Joy explained, as if that made sense.

"Everything was just the way it used to be," Boo-Boo said.

"Except for one thing," Joy noted, memory flitting once more across the unsettling what's-different-about-this-picture sensation that gripped her as Boo-Boo pulled up to the driveway, Paul idling behind them. After studying the scene a few seconds and adjusting her depth perception by several degrees, it finally hit her. That wasn't her trailer she was looking at. It was the one parked *behind* her trailer.

"Her trailer was gone," Boo-Boo said.

"Gone?" WildDog exclaimed.

"Poof," Joy replied. "If you can imagine anything

fourteen feet wide and seventy-two feet long disappearing into thin air." Joy felt again the dawning dread of those first few thunderstruck moments, her instant inventory of everything else that had disappeared—her purple carpet, purple walls, purple towels, sheets, bedspread, candles, stuffed animals. Sixteen years' worth of cherished possessions. Most of it purple. All of it gone.

"And soon, the guy who'd followed us there was wisely gone, too. I'll never forget what she yelled," Boo-Boo said, chuckling.

"That Dick!" Joy yelled again.

"To which I said, 'What'd you expect him to do? Make out with you where your bedroom *used* to be?' Then it occurred to me that she was talking about her father."

"Probable *step*father," Joy told WildDog. "His name was Dick and he *was* a dick!"

"So your father, step or otherwise, came and took your trailer while you were at school?" WildDog asked, attempting to wrap his mind around a domestic tableau featuring yellow plastic flamingos and snatched mobile homes.

"Yep. He always did like going out with a bang no matter where the battlefield was," Joy explained. "And that wasn't all he took, either."

"First Sergeant Dick Perkins had clearly given some thought to his little blitzkrieg," Boo-Boo continued. "Next up was Joy's mother's brand-new vehicle."

"Brown with a beige vinyl top, to match the yard," Joy told him.

"Gone," Boo-Boo said. "Dick went to the PX

where Joy's mother worked and drove off with it, leaving in its beige-on-brown place his old rattletrap junker with an ooga horn."

"So if it had wheels, Dick took it that day," WildDog observed, wagging his head.

"Or hooves," Joy added. While she flipped on a commercial and WildDog helped Boo-Boo mute the feed so other stations could slot their own spots, Joy recalled the rest of that black afternoon. Her mother rattling up in the old clunker, tan hemorrhaging into a burgundy rage. Boo-Boo's speedy exit. The two of them sitting on their wooden stairway to nowhere for a few long minutes before heading out to the pasture where Joy called and called but no bay Quarterhorse stallion cantered up, eager for his molasses and corn.

"At least that's one less mouth to feed," her mother had snarled, glaring across the empty pasture into the pine-fringed distance toward Fort Dewey as if she wouldn't mind seeing a well-placed mushroom cloud forming. Following her mother's murderous gaze, Joy studied the far horizon, her stolen future.

"But it all worked out," she insisted with a reassuring smile. "Both of us stayed with friends for a few days till Mother got a second job and rented us a place. Life went on." Albeit in a small secondhand trailer on a different street in the same park. Next door to the Spec. Fours and local riffraff Quida Raye had spent a lifetime avoiding.

"Did you ever find out what happened to your trailer?"

Boo-Boo harrumphed. "Don't forget who we're talking about here."

"Oh, yeah. It didn't take her long to track down

Dick and our *very* mobile home. He'd had it pulled to a vacant lot on the other side of Fort Dewey."

"That's good," WildDog said hopefully.

"Sort of," Joy said. "Remember his whole goal that day had been to hijack a huge trailer before we got home and, as a final, oh-so-funny farewell, put the yard back exactly the way it was. That means he didn't waste time packing or securing anything. Imagine everything—from food to furniture—flying around a mobile home going sixty miles an hour down a highway." WildDog and Boo-Boo frowned.

"Yep, it was hurricane-level destruction in there. Cabinets and shelves were emptied, couch and chairs knocked over, the refrigerator had nearly gone through the floor. Curdled milk and mayonnaise and flour and sugar and raw hamburger meat were all mixed up with busted ash trays and undrained toilets and trashcans slung everywhere in a trailer that, to top it off, had been stewing under the blazing Louisiana sun without electricity for days." Ten years later, she still gagged at the memory.

"If you were inside, where was Dick?" WildDog asked. "Don't tell me he and your mom had patched things up."

"Lord, no," Joy exclaimed, shuddering at the notion. "Though it's true he *did* try to grovel back into her good graces. But she never let him. Not entirely. At least not till she was sure she'd have the last word. No, *that* day he was outside with the MPs while we were boxing up whatever hadn't been destroyed."

"And the MPs weren't there to protect her mother, either," Boo-Boo noted.

Joy laughed. "That's for sure. I did a little

genealogical research later and realized Dick was lucky she didn't whip out some Confederate sharpshooter recessed-gene action on his ass. Maybe she would have, but thanks to the MPs, Dick survived and we were able to get our photos and records and clothes and, you know, carry on."

"Which is not to say her mother didn't reenact her own little Battle of Bull Run later," Boo-Boo said. "Remind me to tell you *that* story some time. Suffice it to say the next time the MPs arrived, it was the end of the Army line for old Dick Perkins."

"Okay, but how did the stolen trailer saga end? With everyone living happily ever after?" asked WildDog, ever the optimist.

"Well…" Boo-Boo began, standing up to flip through a rack of forty-fives.

"Sort of," Joy said. "While it's true I never had another purple bedroom or bay Quarterhorse stallion, we also never got messed up with another shell-shocked, vindictive, mean drunk, either. Which is to say the future was not without its high points."

"Which is *not* to say it was without its low points, too," Boo-Boo added. "For example, Paul Cruz wasn't the last black-haired bad boy to come and go in a flash." Joy knew they were moving on to the dreadful subject of Sonny Savoy, a segue she didn't care to make that morning. Besides, Boo-Boo was already off at college by the time Sonny showed up at the door of that old rented trailer, no guide required. Sonny had definitely known his way around her new, rundown world.

Feeling her spirits sink on the first day she was being broadcast across the boot-shaped state, Joy realized she and her mother hadn't come that far after all. Quida Raye Perkins had hooked up with yet another man who'd managed to yank another set of wheels out from under her. And Joy had fallen for yet another black-haired aloof sort who, somewhere during her Pitts recollections, had slipped out of the newsroom and was also gone.

"All of which is to say the moral of this story can, as usual, be found in a country song." With the nimble timing of a program director, Boo-Boo flipped on the forty-five he had just cued up—"(Beware of the) Tall, Dark Stranger." Ira walked back into the newsroom just as Joy hurled an empty donut box at her old friend, who only laughed and brushed the sugar flakes and candy bits out of his long, black hair.

"WildDog, help me?" he said. "Forty-fives? Albums?" As the two of them rolled their chairs to the racks of records behind them, crunching across a carpet of rainbow sprinkles, Joy glanced through the glass at Ira, something she did no less than fifty times a day. This time, however, to her absolute shock, he was staring back at her. The sensation was not unlike straddling a set of railroad tracks and looking up to see a locomotive twenty feet away. Then he smiled and held up a scratch pad. Heart thumping, Joy read: "A star is born."

Looking over her shoulder to see if some real celebrity had materialized behind her, she saw only the back of Boo-Boo's head and WildDog's baseball cap. A red flush began crawling up her neck. But it was a good red. Like Valentine's Day.

Numbly, she smiled back as Ira began his first newscast of the day, wrapping it up with a promo for her show. "Be sure to tune in next Monday morning as Lady Bug, Mouth of the South, kicks off something special you're not gonna want to miss."

"WildDog, would you mind giving Joy this," Boo-Boo said. WildDog obediently took the record and handed it to her. The 1960 hit "I'm Sorry."

"Actually, *I'm* sorry, WildDog," Joy said, "but I already know what our next oldie's going to be." Soon, the mournful opening chords of "Help Me Make It Through the Night" filled the studio. Though the song was smolderingly suggestive, it could also be construed as nothing more than an innocent—if somewhat obscure—songwriter-turned-movie-star reference to Ira's scribbled note. Glancing in his direction once again, she saw he was grinning. Bingo! By all means let the devil take tomorrow.

Years later, when Joy Savoy cast her memory back to that day, she knew the format for her syndicated country show crystalized at that moment, the first time Ira signaled receipt of a message she had sent him over the airwaves.

Giddy at the thought of pouring out her soul to him in song, the formula that paved the way for her small-time fame was simple—more banter about her mother, and every love song she could think of for Ira. Or, as an ad campaign targeting working folks would later call it, "Quips to earn by, clips to yearn by." Combined with the hits Boo-Boo made her play, those pumping, thumping, steam-the-joint-up country lust songs seemed just the right equalizer for her mother jokes.

By 9:30, she had played "Slow Hand," "Easy Loving," and "Daydreams About Night Things," thrilled to see Ira's head bobbing along to each.

"WildDog, would you mind asking Joy if she thinks we might possibly, pretty please, play 'Common Man' on our *Hot Country* station," Boo-Boo said, holding up her next selection, 1972's "Rated X," alongside an expression of utter exasperation.

Ever the good sport, WildDog said, "Hey, Joy, whatcha say we play the number-one country song in the land. As opposed to some oldie moldie from Nixon's first term?"

She was opening her mouth to respond when Vernon appeared in the doorway to let them know the test was going well. "Ferriday had a few signal problems, but they got it ironed out." Shooting an A-OK through the glass at Ira, who was standing up, car keys in hand, poised to take every ounce of Joy's euphoria out the door, Vernon turned back to them. "Ray and Jimmy called to say you're coming through loud and clear in Bogalusa. They've already had a ton of calls, most of them after your"—cough, cough—"reprise of that Mother Trucker bit."

"Wasn't that a hoot?" Boo-Boo asked, laughing. "I'll bet mothers all over Louisiana loved that."

"If you say so," Vernon nervously allowed. "I have, however, liked the music you've been playing. It's off format, with all those sixties and seventies cuts, but it seems to be flying. If you want, maybe you can tweak her format some, Bobby. But make sure the other jocks stick to the old one."

"Of course," Boo-Boo said.

"Uncle Vernon?" they heard Ruthie call behind him. " Brother Stanley's on line one. You want to take it in there?"

"No!" Vernon shouted. Glancing sheepishly back

at them, he added, "I'll get it in my office, Ruthie." Then, to Joy, quickly, "Just back off the double entendres for the rest of the day. No more mother truckers or mother trucking. Or trucking anything. Just punchy little bits about mama, okay?"

"Okay," Joy said. As he darted out the door and toward the phone call from his preacher, Joy finally looked at her old friend again. His straight face was ruby-red from the effort.

"Truck it," Boo-Boo snickered.

"Truck *him*," Joy said, giggling.

"Truck me runnin'," WildDog said.

"Truck him if he can't take a joke," Joy said.

"Truck him and the horse he rode in on," Boo-Boo said, and the three of them laughed and laughed. They laughed so much that Joy forgot she was supposed to be permanently mad at one of her oldest friends in the world. By the time Boo-Boo said, "Oh, me," and wiped happy tears from his eyes, their earlier unhappiness was ancient history. "Well, Mable, your latest come-on song is about crooned out, so what's next? Maybe some prehistoric singing cowboy?"

She smirked. "Very funny. You'll be glad to know that very little of what I want to play predates the Nashville sound."

"Whew. So no fossilized yodelers or petrified fiddlers?"

"Nope. Just the kind of classic country people our age might have actually heard. Along with the hits we've got to play, of course. I never thought I'd say this, but some of my mother's old records seem to have grown on me. Like grits and greens."

"I'm right there with you," Boo-Boo said. "While I

was running the needle through 'Four-Way Street' in my bedroom, my mom was blaring 'Tennessee Birdwalk' in the living room. I still know all the words to that stupid song."

"We had that. And 'When You're Hot, You're Hot'," WildDog said. "I just ran across 'Amos Moses' the other day. Want me to get it?"

"Well," Joy said, twirling her headphones, "I wasn't exactly talking about *that* kind of old country song. What I have in mind is more along the lines of 'Sweet Dreams' or 'Pure Love.' " Then, feeling the beginnings of another blush, she added, "Or 'The Year That Clayton Delaney Died.' "

"Uh-huh." Boo-Boo grinned. " 'Heaven's Just a Sin Away' is more like it."

"So? People like love songs," she yelped, popping the headphones on.

"Whatever you say. Anyway, I think I get what you're doing here." She gingerly slipped the headphones off. "Old lovesick songs mixed with whatever's running up the charts. 'Stand by Your Man' alongside 'Swingin'.' " Joy nodded, though she hadn't given it that much thought yet.

"I guess that's fine." Then a smile snaked across his fuzzy face. "How about 'Long Black Veil' next? An upbeat little ditty about adulterers, a trial, and a hanging. You know, fun stuff that happens when married folks stray."

"Boo-Boo!" she squealed, punching him.

"Ouch," he said, not even flinching. "Speaking of judges and alibis, why don't you tell me all about Quida Raye's latest crisis."

Joy was preparing to embark on the tale of the

eighteen-wheeler bandits when she noticed a call coming in and clicked on the line first.

"KLME, Call Me Country."

"Hey, you crazy little mother trucker," Tanya hooted on the other end.

"Well, if it isn't the long-lost Tanya," Joy said for her co-workers' benefit. "Where in heaven's name have you been?"

"Heaven didn't have a whole hell of a lot to do with it," Tanya replied, her laugh deep and bawdy. "But my question first. What are you doing on the Anacoco station? Gary had it on in the bus, and I thought, Kick my country ass, Joy's been fired and hired again. Then, when we lost Anacoco and they tuned into KLME, there you were again! What's going on? Houdini radio? Merlin the musician?"

"If you hadn't been Lord only knows where for days, you'd be up on a few minor details. Like my show is going to be broadcast across the entire state starting Monday. Or at least the tiny outposts that Poi-Son Communications owns. And they're running a test today. Now, where have you been?"

"Let's see. Beaumont first, then San Antonio and Austin and now, voila, Pitts. The boys are on their way to Nashville, but they took a little detour to drop me back off at Gran D.'s."

"So how was it? Or should I ask how *many* was it?"

WildDog motioned to the clock and wiggled his hips, a reminder of his date with the NLC cheerleaders. Boo-Boo held up five fingers and followed him out. Evidently, neither cared to hear a one-sided conversation concerning all the musicians Tanya had slept with since Friday.

"Everyone except Gary," she announced. "Challenge accepted. Thanks for a great night at the Wagon Wheel, by the way."

Joy just shook her head. "Speaking of, have you heard anything about Lonnie? You know, if he's alive or a paraplegic or anything?"

"Lonnie Luneau can kiss my ass. I've got *far bigger* fish to fry, if you know what I mean, jelly bean." Then she began wickedly snickering. "*Waaay* bigger fish. *Lots* bigger."

"I get it," Joy grumbled, hearing something like wax paper crinkling on the other end. "What are you eating?"

"Everything in sight," Tanya replied. "Since I had to eat like a stinkin' bird in front of the boys for *days*."

"Which is the real reason you're back in Pitts, isn't it? So Ethelene can feed you."

"Exactly," Tanya happily admitted before outlining life so far as a groupie. With her piles of snacks as inspiration, most of her wanton recollections leaned heavily on culinary references like "stuffin' the muffin," "riding the baloney pony," and "playing hide the cannoli."

Other than Joy's quick story about her mother's near arrest, which she pointed out she managed to tell without resorting to a single dietary euphemism, she barely uttered another word before Warren Piece shuffled in to do his show prep. Nodding at the silver-haired co-worker Boo-Boo liked to say was old enough to have beaten Marconi to the invention of radio, unable to contain herself any longer, she swiveled her chair around and whispered, "Guess what? Ira's wife is moving away. She's going back to school. In *New York City!*"

"Fascinating," Tanya groused, loudly crunching her food wrappers. "Assuming she falls off the face of the earth—and, last I checked, furthering one's education doesn't quite qualify—have you heard of something called a rebound relationship? Be a good daughter for once instead of a sad stalker. Run up to Kentucky and check on your mom before your show kicks into gear."

"Thanks for that swell advice," Joy grumbled. There was no way she was leaving Avalon now that Ira was writing her notes through the glass. "Anyway, gotta run." Then she clicked off the call and spun back around to Warren Piece, owner of KLME's best voice, a silky smooth baritone that Boo-Boo said emanated from the shrunken head of Methuselah. Realizing her mother might be in the market soon for a new beau, hopefully one with some maturity, Joy didn't realize she was staring until Warren smiled and gently shooed her from the chair. "Time to fly away, Miss Lady Bug."

Recalling Ira's note, fly away she did, straight to cloud nine.

Chapter 11
"Lead Me On"

Halfway through her first week of syndication, Vernon walked into the studio with two of the best-looking men Joy had ever seen in such a small space. Boo-Boo and WildDog sprang to their feet, a first-ever in-tandem respectful gesture that instantly tipped her off.

"Here she is," Vernon announced. "Lady Bug, Mouth of the South."

"Ray Poisso," one of the heartthrobs said, reaching out to shake her hand.

"James Sonnier," said the second, taking her other hand. "But everyone calls me Jimmy."

"Ray and Jimmy just wanted to drop by and say hi," Vernon stiffly announced, all business.

"Hi," Joy chirped, seeing she should also stand. Since she had yet to let go of either man, their lingering handshakes transitioned into somewhat awkward heave-hos as Ray and Jimmy jokingly pretended to haul her to her feet.

"Upsy-daisy!" She laughed, relieved to be wearing one of her more slimming new dresses, and watched them turn to greet Boo-Boo and WildDog, exchanging long-time-no-see sentiments. How had Ruthie failed to mention Ray and Jimmy were absolute Cajun hunks? Maybe Ruthie was gay. Maybe Joy should have been taking her to gay bars.

"We had some business up this way," Jimmy began, turning back to her.

"So we thought we'd swing by and say what a good job you've all been doing so far," Ray added.

Several minutes then passed as the five men stood around the cramped studio, discussing the mechanics of just how Joy's good job was getting done. Joy meanwhile sat back down and took extreme care in cueing up the next record, the most routine part of radio.

"In fact, you're doing such a good job," Jimmy said, nodding at her, "that we just might have to give you a raise one of these days."

"Be my guest," she gaily replied. *Since both of these goobers I work with probably get raises on a regular basis.*

"Till then, how does having your own music director sound?" Ray asked. "We're doubling up old Bobby's duties here. In addition to program director, we're making him your music director, too."

Joy turned to the one person, besides her mother and Tanya, who gave her roots. Overpriced roots, no doubt. But deep ones all the same. "That sounds wonderful," she gushed.

"We got you the best," Jimmy said.

"Actually, they got *me* the best," Boo-Boo demurred. "Can you imagine working with a guy whose specialty is sounding like a jackass?" Though Joy knew she was a second-rate DJ with a flavor-of-the-month schtick, she appreciated her old friend's charity.

"We never were sure how barnyard noises would play in less rural parts of the state anyway," Ray conceded. "Which is another way of saying, dear Ms. Savoy, we couldn't be happier that Bobby will be helping you give our listeners one 'Mother' of a good time."

"*Laissez les bons temps rouler*," Jimmy declared.

Joy was thinking life couldn't get any better when another thought nearly sent the needle through "Dixieland Delight." Anxiously scanning the long mental list of future steamy tunes she had lined up for Ira, she said, "I'll still get to pick some of my own songs, won't I?"

A chorus of affirmations rang out.

"You'll definitely get to add input," Ray insisted. "The only thing Bob's gonna do is the dirty work. You know, humdrum radio stuff so we can all keep earning paychecks. We're gonna be getting our money's worth out of this old boy, that's for sure."

Everyone laughed as Jimmy banged a humorously overwrought-looking Boo-Boo on the back. "All you have to do is kick back and knock our socks off. *With* some songs of your own choosing."

Joy made the one forceful comment that came to mind. "Yabba dabba doo!" At least Boo-Boo chuckled.

It was only after all five men wandered out that she turned to see if Ira was in the newsroom. He was. And he was holding up a scratchpad. "If Hollywood Don't Need You (Honey I Still Do)." She smiled and cued up that new cut.

****

Day after day, Ira continued scribbling comments on the other side of the glass for her eyes only, often naughtily reinterpreting lyrics of the song currently playing. "Blood Red and Going Down" triggered a

138

flurry of teasing "going down" references. For years, she couldn't hear "First Taste of Texas" without flushing, recalling Ira's "menu" detailing the main course's blue eyes, golden hair, and other select ingredients. Then, heaven help her, there was "Love in the Hot Afternoon." If only.

Similarly memorable were his helpful attempts to expand her playlist with questions like, "Who said he was looking for a gal who could suck the chrome off a trailer hitch?" Relieved that she actually knew the answer, Joy cued up "Mamas Don't Let Your Babies Grow Up to Be Cowboys," from the soundtrack of the movie featuring that classic line. Another note asked, "What were the two things in life that Waylon said make it worth living?" Also easy. As "Luckenbach, Texas" filled the airwaves, Ira wrote, "That's right. Firm-feelin' women. Make that one thing."

Despite the racy repartee that had sprung up between them on either side of the plate glass window, Joy was nothing but blundering when she found herself alone with Ira for the first time since their stroll down Vernon's long hall. It was the end of her second week of syndication, and she was headed home alone to an empty weekend. Ira was walking toward the staff car, notebook in hand, as she headed toward Sally.

"Callin' it a day?" he asked.

"Uh-huh, you?"

"Not a chance. I've got a city council meeting to cover, which means I'll be stuck in this fucking place a while longer."

Hearing Ira say the word "fucking" had the unsettling effect of emptying her brain of any cogent thought, though she did manage to say, "Too bad. Hope it's not a late night."

"Wouldn't be the end of the world if it was. It's just me and the cat, and he's an asshole. Dianne's off in the Big Apple, picking out her apartment."

"Oh, right. I heard," Joy said. "That's going to be exciting."

"I suppose. Someone will have to ask the lovely Dianne one of these days. Let me know what she says."

Joy felt her eyebrows rising.

"You haven't heard?" Ira asked, staring off across the parking lot. "When she leaves the middle of July, that'll be the end of the line for sweet Dianne and me. And the middle of July can't get here soon enough."

"No, I, uh…hadn't heard…*that*." The scorching pavement beneath her sandals seemed to be liquifying.

"Well, we're not shouting it from the rooftops. In fact, the longer Vernon stays in the dark about all this, the better. The last thing I need is him whipping out his Bible and trying to save my damn marriage."

Noticing Joy's eyebrows were now arched into a widow's peak, he shrugged and said, "Shit happens. I had seven years to get it right. Which reminds me of another song suggestion for you. Make that two. 'Seven-Year Ache' and 'D-I-V-O-R-C-E?' " Turning to go, he said, "I'll try to come up with more ideas by Monday."

"Monday," Joy repeated, floating toward her car, then home, without one memory of the drive. Parking, frantic to run in and squawk to someone about Ira's D-I-V-O-R-C-E, she remembered Tanya was on the road again with the band. Boo-Boo was at some promotional event. Ruthie wouldn't have a clue. And the last thing her mother would want to hear was news about any man. So she sat in her car, spirits sinking, feeling as isolated as the old sharecropper shack in front of her.

She stared at the rundown porch of the rundown place. The peeling swing blistered by the ruthless sun, the yard grown up as high as an abandoned field. Then, feeling the last traces of Ira euphoria wane in the face of her lonely reality, she headed inside to a houseful of additional reasons to feel lousy. The furniture that hadn't been dusted or rearranged lately. The orange throw rug Sugar Pie snored on while her mother sat cross-legged on the couch after a long day of tanning, slamming a spoon like a post-hole digger through a tall glass of buttermilk and cornbread. The runners and tablecloths she had embroidered. The countless peace offerings she had made—feed-sack pillows, wooden-crate tables, ham-can lanterns, paper-bag placemats, ice-cream carton lamps. Everywhere Joy looked, she saw some trinket or doodad her mother had made or bought so that old place, rented well after the heart had left them both, could at least impersonate a home. Turning to the altar area clustered with frames adorned by spray-painted, glittery macaroni surrounding Jessie's photos, Joy knew that, after two and a half years, no place would ever truly feel like home again.

Peering through the dusty picture window, past the sagging front porch, across the stock-still bayou and live oaks, into a white sky too hot even for birds, she caught a whiff of someone somewhere mowing, perfuming the clammy air around her shack with the one scent, besides cigarette smoke, she would forever associate with her mother. Kicking off her shoes, she lingered by Jessie's kindergarten photo, then wandered into the bedroom. Changing into shorts, she continued on to the back porch and that nagging olfactory reminder, the picnicking, gingham-checked tang of fresh-cut green.

A couple of hours later, she used the garden hose to squirt the dirt off her legs. She hadn't accomplished much before the lightning bugs came out, barely cutting more than the front and back yards. But at least her mother would have less to mow when she came back. *If* she came back. Then she went inside and, still feeling adrift, wondering if Ira had made it back to that fucking place yet, stepped out of her cutoffs and into the shower. As slivers of grass and every fleck of hesitancy eddied around her heels before slipping down the drain, she envisioned her outfit—the tightest jeans she owned and a pink, crepey, vaguely translucent top.

Later, she paused in front of the mirror. Perfect, save one detail. Reaching under her blouse, she unhooked her bra and let it fall to the floor. Then she found her keys and headed out.

****

Nick's replacement, John "Nine Ball" Linebaugh, was giving a paid, upbeat description of the new AA facility downtown when she jiggled into the studio.

"I think I forgot something," she said after the red light went off. On the other side of the glass, Ira launched into the last news report of his long day. She leaned against the wall and watched, making small movements that kept her somewhat see-through blouse in deliberate motion.

"Have you been drinking?" Nine Ball warily asked.

"Not yet," she answered, staring a hole through the glass at Ira, who wrapped up the news, then yanked his head toward the door.

"But the night's still young," she said, slipping out.

As the doors to the newsroom and studio simultaneously closed, Ira turned to her in the hall and said, "I'll follow you home."

"Good," she managed.

And if they said anything else the rest of that long, hot night, she couldn't recall what it was. There would be time enough for talking. Time enough for everything except, as her compatriots in the country field might say, the pressing business at hand. That, and making sure her front door was shut and double-bolted after she and Ira tumbled inside.

Later, when she finally heard from Tanya and attempted to detail every magnificent moment since Ira had followed her home, she was at a loss. She knew Tanya didn't want specifics, and she couldn't abide generalities.

"Don't you dare say the P or V words," Tanya screamed. Joy held the phone away from her ear and decided that was just as well. Precious few details she had so far memorized, rhapsodized, and apotheosized regarding Ira began with those letters anyway.

"When I think about what Ira and I did all weekend, Tanya, my thoughts turn more to verbs than nouns anyway," she said, happy to settle for goading her.

"I don't want to hear those words, either. Ew! Yuck! Can we talk about something other than Ira Body Parts please?"

Thanks to WildDog, Joy likewise didn't have to spell everything out for Boo-Boo, either. After Ira pulled her into a broom closet first thing Monday morning and didn't let her go for two glorious songs, she staggered back into the studio, unwinding her hair from around her neck and tugging the hem of her slip out from beneath the waistband.

"What in the world happened to you?" Boo-Boo exclaimed.

WildDog looked at her, then back at Boo-Boo. "I know you haven't dated much, Bobby boy, but do you really need someone to tell you about the birds and the bees, little buddy?"

Then they all looked through the glass at Ira. He was once again at his desk, leaned back reading the paper. Only his thick hair, recently elevated on either side into an ardent Einstein updo by Joy's greedy fingers, belied his time in the broom closet.

"Before you have *the talk* with him, WildDog, why don't you see who can find 'Happiest Girl in the Whole USA' first." Joy decided to take the easy way out and let songs tell her co-workers everything she couldn't. Not with Ira close enough to trigger a nuclear reaction.

Telling her mother she had a new beau, however, proved more of a challenge. In call after call, Joy meant to bring the subject up, or at least drop some hints. Instead, weeks flew by as she did little more than listen to her mother bellyache about the Kentucky judicial system, about her parents treating her like a child instead of a forty-four-year-old grown-ass woman, about the fear that Doyle would flip and rat her out if she didn't keep him in cigarettes and spending money. Then they would hang up, Ira would come over for a few inconceivable hours of fantasies sprung to incomprehensible life, and Joy and her mother would pick up where they left off the next day.

The truth was, Joy couldn't figure out a way to talk

about Ira without starting at the beginning—that horrendous night two and a half years earlier. How could she possibly explain wanting a man she first saw the night her daughter died and then initiating their affair on one of the rare days she had spent missing her mother? Joy felt she could sooner converse in Zulu with Quida Raye, but she kept trying. Given Doyle's host of legal woes, she thought she had plenty of time.

As it turned out, she was wrong. The wheels of justice that had been grinding so slowly up in Tompkinsville exponentially sped up as soon as Doyle, hoping to avoid a trial, pled guilty to a lesser offense and was promptly delivered to the Kentucky State Penitentiary in Eddyville.

Quida Raye Perkins appeared back at her daughter's door without warning the very next day, before Joy had mentioned a single word about her savage new romance. Which turned out to be just as well.

Because, by then, Ira Everhart was already gone.

Chapter 12
"The Night They Drove Old Dixie Down"

"Who out there has been to Natchez, Mississippi?" Joy asked her fans the first of July. "I went this weekend, and boy, is it a heartbreaker of a place." Truer words had not been spoken since her syndicated show began, but she soldiered on that Monday morning.

"In addition to being achingly beautiful, Natchez reminds me of a quirk of Mother's I don't believe I've mentioned. She can see ghosts."

"Really?" WildDog said into another mic, serving in his unofficial capacity as on-air sidekick. Ray and Jimmy had floated the idea during their visit and now WildDog hung around after his own shift to follow whatever Joy got a wild hair to say. Which, that day, evidently involved channeling dead folks.

"Yep. And this weekend in Natchez, I realized I might have inherited a touch of her sixth sense. So I thought it would be fun to dedicate today's show to ghost stories. If any of you have spooky tales to tell, call me here at one-eight-hundred-lady-bug."

Flipping on "Louisiana Woman, Mississippi Man," she prayed the phone would light up so she could fill her shift with other people's words. Since Saturday, the thought of speaking—or eating or sleeping or laughing ever again—exhausted her to the point of tears.

Boo-Boo's own spirits sank just watching her stare

off into the darkened newsroom, brown eyes brimming. If ever he needed to act like a music director and direct something, the sight of his morning jock's heartsick gaze suggested this could be a good time to start. No matter what Ira had done over the weekend, and Boo-Boo had a pretty good idea what that might have been, he needed to pry some air time out of Joy before Vernon was in the studio, hopping up and down.

"Ghost stories," he said to the back of her head. "That's different." Nodding at WildDog to play along, he said, "We'll wrap some call-in accounts around your Natchez adventures. Shoot for a whole dark-and-stormy-night vibe. Dawg?"

"Works for me. It can be a dry run for Halloween, which is only, what, three or four months away?" WildDog said lamely.

Joy shrugged, which was all the encouragement her co-workers needed. As they bustled around piecing together what early fans would consider one of her more offbeat shows, Joy drifted back to Saturday morning and Ira's suggestion of a road trip.

"It feels like we've been under house arrest for a month," he grumbled. As glorious a month as it had been, Joy agreed they hadn't exactly been painting the town red. Ira, come to find out, had some old-fashioned notions about the sanctity of marriage. As long as his soon-to-be estranged wife was still in Avalon, he refused to be seen out and about with another woman.

Faced then with the prospect of two more weeks of stolen hours passed under cover in Joy's stuffy old shack, Ira had said, "Let's ride."

And ride they did, into ripples of heat radiating off an asphalt ribbon winding north toward the flat, fried edge of Louisiana. Joy popped in the latest eight-track tape she had made, a mixed bag of boogie she had assembled for specific biological reasons—country for Ira's heart, rock for his body, then soul for exactly that and nothing less, all laid on top of a steady, thrusting beat.

Monday, after a caller shared the first of several tales involving pennies from heaven, Joy slipped the headphones on and exhaled deeply. No matter what might come out of her mouth that morning, she knew some of it had to reference her mother, Vernon's lone requirement for every shift. Looking over at Boo-Boo and attempting a smile, she leaned toward the mic and said, "You know what I think's interesting about Natchez? How the land goes from flat as a flitter cake, as Mother might say, to something almost alpine in comparison, over the bridge. For any of you who might be sneaking around out there and are looking for a town where you can pretend to be footloose and fancy free, Natchez, Mississippi, is your place. City built on a bluff."

"Har har," WildDog said.

"Dripping with wisteria, draped in lore, and dotted with about a thousand historic places on the National Register," she continued, "Natchez is a deliciously romantic, subtly spooky place where, if you're not careful—and sober—you might just think you've seen a ghost or two." Joy nodded, and Boo-Boo went to another caller.

Several commercials and another song bought Joy five more minutes to drift back to their first stop Saturday, Natchez Under-The-Hill, one of the most captivating districts in the entire Deep South. Ira had arched a brow and said, "You know, these saloons have been down here on the bank of the Mississippi since at least the early eighteen hundreds, when whores and pirates stumbled off steamboats to raise five kinds of hell. Let's drink to them, shall we?"

"Cheers," she said, raising the day's first mimosa. Soaking in the old pub's nineteenth-century ambiance, the chunky bar swayed by decades of resignation, the peeling walls hung with Civil War dioramas, she found the bar's gilded mirrors galore particularly eye-catching.

Stealing glimpses of the two of them in those hazy old mirrors, Joy kept drinking and thinking how good they looked together, how handsome Ira was, tipped back in his ladderback chair, tapping a toe to the player piano, like a rakish gambler from days of yore. Since her fantasies always ran wild where he was concerned, she found herself imagining haunted old mirrors with the power to merge modern-day reflections atop misty impressions from long ago, finally uniting lost lovers from another time and place.

"First, full disclosure here," Joy told her listeners. "I *might* have had a mimosa…"

"Or two…" WildDog said.

"Or three," she added, laughing. "But I can't be the only person who looks in old mirrors and thinks she's experiencing déjà vu or some sort of historical hallucinations. From the corner of my eye, I swear I saw smoky, empty-eyed forms drifting past. Forlorn, war-weary faces sporting forage caps and wool kepis in varying shades of nearly sheer Confederate gray."

"Did you see any ghosts you recognize?" WildDog asked, playing along.

"Who can say for sure? But my thoughts did turn to Mother's own Rebel blood, an eagle-eyed Kentucky farmer named Deacon Starnes. I did a little research a while back. Called myself an 'armchair genealogist,' though Mother cackled and said 'a *La-Z-Boy* genealogist' was more like it." Pausing to give WildDog time to snicker, she said, "Nevertheless, I determined my great-great-great-grandfather was on the front lines for some of the worst of it. Fort Donelson, Champion Hill, Vicksburg, and a number of other hell holes."

"Avalon?" WildDog asked.

"Except Avalon. Banks had his own plans for Avalon," Joy replied. "At any rate, when Lee surrendered, Deacon was among only eight survivors from his regiment of ninety-three men, described by one historian as the best young men of Sprigg County. Four years later, skeletal, near death, and mostly barefoot, those eight survivors dragged themselves nearly three hundred miles home from eastern Mississippi to western Kentucky. And if Deacon ever left again, it's lost to history. What we do know, however, is he divorced his first wife, married her sister, and changed the spelling of his last name so his second life—and second wife—wouldn't be confused with the first." Everhart, she thought. Ever*heart*.

"Here's an interesting aside that speaks to the crazy power of heredity," she rattled on. "Thanks to an ancient family Bible my grandmother had in the attic, I discovered Deacon was an old family name beloved by each of the many earlier generations whose names, birth dates, and death dates had been noted on the inside of that falling-apart Good Book. But even though this particular Deacon lived another twenty-nine years after his amazing Civil War exploits, not a single child was ever named in his honor. Zero."

"Ouch," WildDog said.

"Exactly. War hero or no, however he behaved—or *mis*behaved, as the case may be—sealed the deal. The famous Confederate sharpshooter would be the last in a long line of Deacons. Which is not to say his legacy isn't alive and well and skirmishing still in the form of a rowdy great-great-granddaughter who no man, Yankee or not, has ever been wise to cross. Isn't that right, Mother?"

"Remind me never to tick her off," WildDog said. "Or, if I do, to keep an eye out for any suntanned snipers."

"You wouldn't stand a chance," Joy replied. "No man ever has against Deacon Starnes' banty little body double."

"I guess all's fair in love and war," WildDog said. "Speaking of which, Ginny from Coushatta's on the line. She's going to talk about her grandparents, who passed away within an hour of each other. Now, when the moon is full, they can still be seen arm-in-arm out in the rose garden of the old home place. Idn't that right, Ginny."

With WildDog and Boo-Boo once again running the show and her Mother well covered, Joy turned back to the empty newsroom, recalling Saturday afternoon's near heat stroke-inducing hike to the bars on top of the bluff in Natchez proper. She attempted recovery by transitioning to Tom Collinses. Ira moved on to boilermakers.

It was there, somewhere along the sweltering,

boozy line, that they began striking up fast friendships with genial, like-minded tipplers who seemed drawn to them in every bar. Happy to be socializing alongside Ira at last, Joy lost herself in the rowdy crowd, sipping and listening to restless peals of tinny laughter mingling with Natchez's ever-present player pianos, as if hilarity had also been laced into perforated paper rolls pounding out "Red River Valley" and "Yellow Rose of Texas." Only later did she notice their jovial new acquaintances' odd attire. They were all clad in Civil War garb. Frock coats and suspenders for the men, hoop skirts and shawls for the women.

"Where's the reenactment?" Ira asked. "Aren't y'all dying in those outfits?" Their new friends only howled in merriment and continued leading the charge to bar after bar, staggering past grand lawns and sprawling oaks in a hearty, hammered cavalcade.

After another penny-from-heaven story, Boo-Boo kicked on "The Ride," about a hitchhiker's eerie trip to Nashville in an antique Caddy driven by a ghost-white stranger named Hank. Listening, Joy got goosebumps remembering how, as quickly as they had appeared, their Natchez friends were gone in a whoosh of ruffles and sashes. Then again, other parts of that gin-soaked day had similarly vanished from memory. Except the way it ended.

Announcing he was hungry enough to eat hardtack, Ira had spun around till he thought he was facing the river again. Then, grabbing Joy by the arm, they staggered back toward restaurants Under-The-Hill, drunkenly waltzing toward a ridge of green splashed against a lavender Mississippi sky slipping into purple, stopping for Ira to read every historical marker they passed.

"Here's a piece of advice," Joy told her listeners. "If you're ever tying one on in Natchez, beware of the historical markers. They're everywhere and, in an altered state, it's easy to get knocked over the head by history. Literally."

On cue, WildDog cleared his throat and read from a tri-fold brochure Ruthie had brought in, "Most of the old buildings came through the Civil War unscathed because no major battles were fought near Natchez. Union gunboats did, however, fire on the city in retaliation for actions of sharpshooters on nearby bluffs."

Saturday, when Ira recited words to that effect, Joy could have sworn she saw those sharpshooters still, ragged bands of brothers and neighbors, fathers and sons, peering round tree and rock, their gray long since gone to heather, fixing her with sad, smudged cellophane stares. Then again, she always had read so much more into Ira's every word.

As Boo-Boo cued up the mournful "An American Trilogy," she let her mind's eye drift once more across that land of cotton, knowing some things there would never be forgotten. That Saturday, as Ira read marker after marker, Joy stood under arbors humming with bees and heavy with blooms, filling her lungs with the sticky-sweet scent of decay and defeat that hangs even now in the shadows of Dixieland. That melancholy, soul-tickling smell seemed to grow wild in Natchez, running up trellises and winding toward bewitching woods, catching in the throat of anyone too addled by alcohol to know when to speak and when to keep her big mouth shut.

As a phone somewhere in Natchez rang and rang, Joy heard herself say, "So."

"So?" Ira said.

"Soooo, have you thought about what you're going to do after Dianne leaves?"

"Like?" Ira said.

"Like, if you'll, you know, ever get married again?"

Ira kept marching on, the far-off phone kept ringing, and something like a distant flute song began sounding in Joy's head.

Finally, stopping at the day's hundredth marker, he sighed and said, "I guess there's something I should tell you." Her heart cleaved open, dumping endless possibilities into her roiling stomach. He and Dianne were getting back together. They'd never broken up. He'd met someone else.

Ira studied the bronze plaque as if preparing to recite the words written there. But what he said was, "I called Vernon this morning and gave him my two-week notice. I'm going back to New Orleans. For a job."

Looking over her shoulder to make sure the call-in line was blinking, Joy motioned to Boo-Boo to keep the stories coming. Then she turned back to the darkened newsroom and remembered night falling with a thud in Natchez. Or maybe it was her heart. Or maybe her gut was just recoiling from the final, savage strike against a rope-tension drum, an instrument she was sure she'd seen slung around the neck of a scruffy young lad she had caught bleary, gossamer glimpses of all afternoon. He had fluttered like a wisp of gauze through the verdant shadows as he trailed the two of them, providing a backbeat for a fine summer day with his friend the fifer. Finally, Joy recognized their catchy little tune. "When Johnny Comes Marching Home Again." *Hurrah, hurrah*, her poor heart sobbed. And the drum fell silent.

Central Louisiana's last hard-nosed reporter was leaving. It was the dire inevitability she had dreaded for over two and a half years, the foreordained event that had haunted her from the moment she first heard the name Ira Everhart.

"Which reminds me," Ira said. "I need to call and have the utilities disconnected. I already gave my landlord notice, so at least that's done. Funny how everything worked out. Dianne and I will be leaving the same day."

Later, after supper and a pot of coffee, they headed back to the middle of Louisiana. Feeling more like she was coming out of anesthesia than Mississippi, Joy concentrated on keeping her voice steady. "Why do you have to go?"

"Because it's one of the biggest stations in the state. More money. Back in civilization. My hometown. Need I go on?" Reaching over to run a hand down her thigh, he said, "Don't worry. We'll see each other every weekend or so."

But they hadn't even seen each other Saturday. Now here it was Monday, near the end of her shift, and Ira was only now entering the newsroom, distracted by a multi-car pileup on the Pitts Highway.

WildDog got up to leave, shaking hands with Boo-Boo, as Warren Piece shuffled in. Complimenting everyone on a fun, quirky show, Warren said, "The Civil War's one of my favorite subjects."

"Oh, that's right," Boo-Boo said, chortling. "We

should have called you for some first-person commentary. How was Chickamauga anyway?"

Warren grinned at their running joke, old blue eyes twinkling. "We won," he said, holding up a V for victory.

"Yay," Boo-Boo mouthed with muffled little claps as Joy opened the mic.

"If we didn't get to your ghost stories today, no worries," she said. "Next time, we'll talk about an even more haunted place—New Orleans." With that, Ira finally glanced her way.

"Thanks again for visiting Natchez with us," she said, "where the past plus the present doesn't always add up to the future." Then she cut to "The Night They Drove Old Dixie Down," swiveling her chair away from the plate glass window.

Chapter 13
"Why Lady Why"

The next time Quida Raye Perkins showed up unannounced at her daughter's door, the sun was high and the mood was low.

"They've got this great invention called the telephone," Joy said, holding the door open as her mother and Sugar Pie floated in on a perfumed cloud redolent of recent coiffure. While her mother's hair was higher and harder than usual in honor of the previous day's courtroom appearance, the exact opposite was true of Sugar Pie. When under stress, Quida Raye plucked, teased, waxed, exfoliated, colored, tinted, and bleached various of her own parts. Then she unleashed any remaining pent-up frustrations on her poor dog. Sugar Pie looked up at Joy with a pair of woeful eyeballs bulging from a shaved pink head. And the rest of the formerly black-and-white Pekingese was the same fleshy rose. The only sprigs of hair Sugar Pie had left erupted like sprays of scraggly baby's breath from the middle of her skull and the tip of her tail.

"Poor wittle sing," Joy cooed. "What happened to woo?"

"It made me hot just lookin' at her," Quida Raye grumped, marching in and hurling paper bags toward the couch. The crumpled sacks, Joy noticed, held clothes. The fresh ones brimmed with groceries. "And since when do I have to call and make a reservation with my own damn daughter?"

With Ira gone for two weeks and one more day of a pointless weekend to fill, Joy had not an ounce of energy for a fight with her clearly agitated mother.

"Heavens to Betsy," she breezily said, shuffling over to pick through the sacks. "I'm not asking for reservations. Just a little heads-up." Her mother responded by collapsing on the couch and fuming out the window, gnawing a fingernail. Sugar Pie hopped up beside her, pinkly sniffing the grocery sacks. "After all, you never know when I might have company." Joy had no idea why she said that. Having nearly broken his neck getting out of town, Ira hadn't shown the first sign of returning anytime soon.

"If someone decides to up and come over here, you just say the word and I'll clear out," her mother snapped, sounding like Baby Face Nelson, holing up till the heat arrived.

"Don't be ridiculous," Joy exclaimed, though she indeed hoped there would come a day—and soon!—when having her mother disappear might be convenient. "Where would you go anyway?"

Quida Raye gnawed her nail some more before spitting out an answer. "I could always go to Harvey's. Or the side of the road. For all *you* care. But right now I'm goin' to the bathroom, assumin' it ain't been condemned yet." Joy watched her stand up, scrawny, two-tone legs swimming in size-six shorts, and figured she must have lost five more pounds since May. She had obviously found time to tan, just not to eat.

Glancing into one of the grocery bags, Joy spied hamburger meat, a green pepper, and something more peaceful to discuss. "Want me to go ahead and start the spaghetti sauce?"

"I thought I'd fix minute steaks tonight. I brought back some of Daddy's tomaters and purple hull peas," her mother replied, turning to sourly scrutinize the kitchen. "But I have no doubt that filthy-tail kitchen a yores needs a good scrubbin' first."

"You'd be surprised. I cleaned up a couple of weeks ago."

Her mother's head bobbed backward in silent skepticism. "Since when have you cleaned a single thang? You've always been so lazy dead lice wouldn't fall off you."

"Since two weeks ago," Joy insisted, rubbing one of Sugar Pie's pink ears. "I was fixing a special supper for a...*friend*...so I tidied up."

"Let's hope that boy survived," she snarked. "Or not."

Joy smiled, pleased to have kept so much a secret. "If you mean Nick, he's ancient history. But my guest did live." In fact, the stuffed shrimp she'd labored over put an extra spring in Ira's step as he hopped on his motorcycle after supper and nearly burned the rubber off both tires tearing away to New Orleans.

Quida Raye dubiously crimped her mouth and kept walking into the bedroom, only to leap two feet in the air and screech like a demon.

"Get the broom! There's a big black cat in here!"

Sugar Pie tore off the couch and flew past Joy, barking with every shrill *"Scat!" "Scat!"*

Joy whipped past her mother and the bald, baying dog, amazed at how their appearance at her screen door could eliminate most functioning brain cells.

Scooping up the hissing hump of bone and muscle arched in the middle of her bed, she said, "This is Cole. My new cat. Get it? Black as coal? Only I spell it C-o-l-e."

In a rare display of utter stupefaction, Quida Raye Perkins' mouth fell wide open.

"Joy Faye," she sputtered, "the only thang black cats spell is t-r-o-u-b-l-e."

Joy responded by rubbing Cole's flattened ears.

"You might as well bust a mirror to smithereens as to have a dern black cat in the house."

It was true that, after twenty-five years of hearing her mother recite endless superstitions as if quoting Biblical verse, Joy's heart had seized at the sight of a black cat at her door. But, with Ira gone, she had let him in, if for no other reason than to have something with black hair and warm blood around once more. Feeling her eyes fill yet again, she glanced down, as if admiring Cole's ebony pelt.

"*This* black cat is perfectly fine," she said over Sugar Pie's head-splitting yaps. "He's been here nearly two weeks and hasn't been a bit of a problem. Someone probably drove him out here and dumped him. I can't imagine why."

"Well *I* know why," her mother declared, hands on bony hips. "Whoever had him realized they'd be better off walkin' under a dang ladder than havin' *this* thang loose in the house while they slept. Hush, Sugar Pie! Go lay down! Why in the world would you want a blame black cat when everyone knows they're nuthin' but bad luck?"

"You've got Sugar Pie," Joy said, watching the little pink dog cower behind her mother's rock-hard, knobby calves, glaring menacingly at Cole. "I wanted a pet, too."

"You need a pet like I need a wart on my ass," her mother roared, stomping off to the bathroom. "'Specially a dern black cat. That's all I need right now. More bad luck."

****

And more bad luck is precisely what she got, though the jury's still out on whether all of it was Cole's fault. Who can say how everything might have unfolded had Quida Raye not tossed him into the yard before she even started supper that day.

"Get out and stay out!" she hollered, hooking the screen door to keep Sugar Pie from lunging through it. Cole was still outside and her mother's one-piece bathing suit was on the bed, near her mowing shoes, Monday when Joy left for work.

As she told Boo-Boo and WildDog, Quida Raye had a few more acres to bushhog before she could lay out in peace. "Since the thought of field mice going about their business while she tans herself rocks her with a shudder that could register on the Richter scale."

"Sounds like fresh material," Boo-Boo observed. "Let's ask listeners a new question—'What's Your Mother Afraid Of?' " The idea immediately triggered a torrent of calls involving spiders, snakes, bugs, bats, heights, drowning, flying, bridges, and even touching dryer lint.

"Dryer lint," Joy said, grinning into the mic. "That's a new one, but I get it. Heck, I grew up watching hamster tanks in dime-store pet departments elicit shows energetic enough to put Tippi Hedren's performance in *The Birds* to shame.

"Time after time, I've seen my mother shriek and flail around and appear electrocuted at the mere sight of endless items not even remotely ratty. Kittens. Various breeds of newborn puppies. Dark socks balled up and left on the floor. That kind of behavior will scar a kid for life. Though I suppose I don't have to tell any of you that."

"No, ma'am, you don't," WildDog said into the other mic, having just admitted his own mother had an irrational fear of poultry. Or, as he put it, "She's chicken about chickens."

****

Back at Joy's house, Quida Raye and Cole would not come face to face again until the clear-cutting was complete and she was once again motionless and well-oiled on her chaise lawn chair. Sensing movement, she cracked open an eye and saw Cole sitting near her pop bottle. Her first thought was maybe he had licked it with his filthy little sandpaper tongue. Her second was, "Mmmooouuussseee!"

As Joy later reconstructed for her fans, using information she had been provided in a raging gush, her mother had flown straight into the air before landing, feet first, on the lawn chair's straps, sorely compromised by a full summer of sweat, baby oil, and iodine. And there she tottered, shrieking and swinging her swirly glass bottle like a billy club at the bewildered Cole, who soon picked up his furry gray peace offering and strode away.

Her mother's last word on the horrifying experience was a declaration that Cole wasn't coming back in the house as long as she was there.

And that proved to be the case—for most of the

week. While Joy sanitized certain details in order to keep Vernon out of the studio, the plain truth was her mother had been sitting on the commode in her usual fashion—squatting with a bare, brown foot slapped on either side of the toilet seat, a position she had struck since a mouse had scurried across her toes mid-pee as a child. And that's when the door to the cabinet beneath the bathroom sink began banging. She was still squatting there, brandishing a plunger, when, first, a black paw, and, soon, an entire black cat leg hooked around the cabinet door, holding it open long enough for the rest of Cole to emerge.

"You know, Joy Faye, if a big ol' thang like *that* can get in the house, just imagine what else is runnin' in *by the droves*," she yapped five minutes later, hanging on to the door frame between the living room and bedroom lest she faint straightaway.

Once recovered enough to kick Cole outside again, she set about plugging the hole beneath the bathroom sink with scouring pads and duct tape. Then her eyes fell on what she considered a blood-curdling array of mouse entrances all over the house.

"Like every structure at Happenstance Plantation," Joy said on air the next morning, "my place is antebellum, which, in Avalon, we know means pre-General Banks. It's been twelve decades since that dastardly Yankee set fire to everything in and around town except Sweet Magnolia Blossom Plantation, which folks said was saved purely by happenstance. The name stuck, and that's about all that does, anymore. Over a hundred and twenty years of gravity have pulled windows away from sills, floors away from doors, baseboards away from walls. And everywhere

Mother can see the outside, she knows in her heart there's a mouse ogling the inside."

Sure enough, Quida Raye's worst suspicions were confirmed that very night. Rousing herself for a midnight snack, she shuffled into the kitchen, flipped on a light, and started rummaging. From Joy's hot, cramped bed on the couch, she lifted a knowing brow when the rustling came to an abrupt halt. By the time she made it into the kitchen with a shoe in one hand and an old copy of *Valley of the Dolls* in the other, her mother, courtroom coiffure bent by several nights in Joy's comfy bed, was still frozen in front of the worst objects she could have found in any cupboard. They were black, about the size of birdseed, and sprinkled around the sleeve of nibbled-through crackers she *had* been reaching for.

"Those mouse turds may as well have been bits of nuclear waste pooped out around my tubes of saltines for the near-fatal effect they were having on their disheveled discoverer," Joy told her fans the next day. "I said, 'Just step away from the cabinet, and I'll buy some mousetraps tomorrow.' Then I dropped the shoe I was holding and nearly sent her through the roof."

Mousetraps, however, were not what Quida Raye Perkins had in mind. "Yesterday, she went out and spent a good chunk of her monthly check on tin foil and steel wool," Joy reported on air. "Since I've witnessed similar shopping binges involving the likes of cling peaches and potted meat, I'm not alarmed. In fact, I find the thought of a decade's worth of shiny household products soothing, in a dry goods kind of way. Plus, I never have liked the idea of mousetraps anyway. If she can rig some sort of aluminum sling-type device to catch them with, all the better."

Joy came home late that day, having stopped at Ship O'Hoyt's with Boo-Boo, Ruthie, and WildDog, where she'd spent hours playing the first country song Hoyt had allowed on his jukebox—the rocking "Mountain Music." When Hoyt threatened to snatch the record right off if Joy played it one more time, the merry foursome called it a night, and Joy headed home, blaring her eight-track with "Mountain Music" full blast.

Easing up beside her mother's old brown jalopy, her headlights fell on Cole, stoically perched at the end of the porch, and Sugar Pie's flat little pink face aimed at him from behind the screen door. But those were the only signs of life at her shack. Though the sun had long since set, there wasn't a single light on inside.

As a niggling sense of dread gathered in the pit of her stomach, Joy pulled out her tape, turned the car off, opened the door, and was immediately hit with a gust from half a carton of cigarettes. Combined with the house's dispirited darkness, the gloomy smoke cloud suggested a scenario that, till then, she had not considered—maybe her mother was sitting in the dark, ashtray pulled close, despondent again, à la Dick. It all made immediate sense. Clearly, Doyle's trial had left her more emotionally fragile than Joy had bothered to notice, fixated as she'd been on Ira's absence and having fun on-air at her mother's mouse-fearing expense. Tiptoeing across the porch and easing the screen door open, Joy was trying to imagine where steel wool and tin foil fit into the dreary new picture as she reached for the light switch.

"When I could see again, I noticed Mother was not

only grinning, but was also shimmering like fool's gold," Joy told her fans the next morning. "Tin foil and steel wool were crammed everywhere—around the baseboards, in cracks between the paneling, above doors, in keyholes. My old house twinkled like a disco skating rink. Adding sparkle to the spectacle, Mother had shoved all the furniture to the middle of the room, away from her glittering masterpieces. And there she sat, hunkered down on the ottoman, knees tucked under her, ashtray beside her, ears perked up for nibbling sounds anywhere around her.

" 'I'm gonna keep an eye on that tin foil to see if somethin' gnaws through it,' she informed me. 'I imagine if anythang can gnaw through THAT, *we're* gonna gnaw ourselves into a new house.' "

A day or two later, Joy came home and her mother's .38 was on the coffee table.

And a day or two after that, she came home and she didn't live there anymore.

Chapter 14
"I Don't Wanna Play House"

Joy unlocked her front door and it swung open in that loosey-goosey way doors do in vacant houses. She had been away eleven hours and forty-two minutes. And all her worldly possessions were gone.

Staggering through the rooms, she saw the floors had been mopped, the windows cleaned, the tin foil removed. The only slightly smudgy spot was a four-foot circle around the corpse of a gray mouse. A dime-sized hole in the floor suggested there had been a forty-degree angle on the murder weapon. As if the perp had been sitting on the couch embroidering when the urge to shoot had suddenly struck.

Joy didn't have to sit in her car long, there in the driveway of the house where she used to live. Soon, her mother's beige-on-brown bomb came rattling down the bayou lane. She pulled up beside Joy, aimed her smug, satisfied mug out the window, and said, "Why ain'tcha inside watchin' TV? Somethin' missin'? Like the TV?" Then she erupted into volcanic fits of hilarity that rocked her barge of a car.

"Very funny," Joy growled. "*Where is everything I own?*"

Gasping for breath, still convulsed in hysterics, Quida Raye nodded toward the vacant house and choked out an answer. "After seein'…what was…runnin' around…all over that place…I figured…it was…high time…we got the hell out!"

Joy stared bullets at her until she wiped her eyes and could produce full sentences again. "So I moved you into somethin' big enough for the both of us. And guess what? Monthly pest control is included."

Sitting in the driveway of a house where she had lived a mere half day earlier, watching her mother having a good, long laugh at *her* expense for once, Joy felt something pop in her brain. Possibly an aneurysm or a blood clot.

"Did it ever occur to you that I might not *want* a place big enough for the two of us?" she croaked, rubbing her temple. "Or monthly pest control?"

"And I might not want a golden goose," her mother replied, flapping a dismissive hand. "You got yore own syndicated radio show now, Joy Faye. It's time you had somethin' to show for it. Follow me." And, with that, she spun her car around and roared off toward Avalon, fast enough for Joy to risk getting a ticket trying to keep up with her. Tearing through downtown and up to the banks of the Little River, she ground to a bad-brake halt in front of a flimsy narrow bridge, and Joy's spirits bottomed out. Not only were they about to cross the most perilous span still in service, they were also heading for the town with the worst reputation in all of Louisiana. Ferndale.

In addition to a state charity hospital and numerous shelters for the down and out, the town was home to so many facilities with shadowy mental-health functions that its name had come to symbolize insanity throughout Louisiana.

If you were crazy, you belonged in Ferndale.

Joy drummed her fingers on the steering wheel as they waited at the foot of the old Little River Bridge for oncoming traffic—a motorcycle—to pass. Then she followed her mother over raging torrents on a slightly swaying one-and-a-half-lane bridge that Avalon's mayor had been trying to get condemned for years.

Joy held her breath all the way to the other side, where her mother flew off again. In a few short blocks, they sped past the John F. Kennedy Memorial Charity Hospital, the Louisiana Training Facility for Underaged Offenders, and Northside Behavioral Services. Then, just past the gun shack and electrified gate of the area's star facility—the sprawling Central Louisiana Institute for the Criminally Insane—her mother turned left and swung into a driveway.

Joy eased up beside her, noting they had entered a circa 1940s development that catered to families of the institutionalized by painting houses in colors crazy people might consider pretty. It was a highlighter-bright neighborhood, and Quida Raye had chosen for them the sunburst yellow model. Springing out of the car and darting up onto the porch, she flung the door open and bopped up and down, anxiously motioning for Joy to get out and follow her.

Once she grudgingly determined the pain in her brain wasn't going to kill her, Joy heaved herself, fuming and snarling, up the stairs to see her mother's handiwork in all its backbreaking glory. Sure enough, there was every large item she owned—from couch and chair to console stereo and bed—all of which must have presented relocation challenges for a woman without a truck. Then there were the incidentals, like Cole, that could be crammed into a trunk. And it was all situated, albeit with considerably more wall space, in roughly the same locations as in her previous house. Before, as her mother hastily outlined, she had paid a neighbor twenty dollars to help her rope every stick of furniture onto the roof of her jalopy so they could rumble through downtown with the whole hillbilly mess.

Joy's stomach churned at the realization that her mother must have made at least fifteen trips back and forth past the radio station. What if someone had seen her Okie-from-Muskogee self with box springs see-sawing over the Barge-mobile's windshield? She was still shuffling around, numbly gazing at her furnishings and craft-book curios as if they were pieces in some stupefying museum, when she came upon the kitchen table. Supper, she could see, was ready. *Supper!* On *moving day!* Crumpling into a chair, she numbly reached for the French bread, more out of habit than hunger. In the living room, the devil was going down to Georgia.

Taking a bite and not tasting a thing, Joy Savoy began attempting to make sense of her mother's most outrageous exploit yet. Oh, yes, she knew she'd milk the day's events for months to come. The only challenge would be trying to explain it to listeners with normal mothers. Mothers who didn't surprise daughters with brand-new addresses at day's end. With spaghetti! Twirling her fork round and round, Joy couldn't decide if she should feel honored...or homicidal.

"At least now you won't have to be ashamed to invite anyone over to supper or anythang," her mother announced with a note of happy finality. She started in on her own spaghetti—which, in Quida Raye's case, meant sauce atop mashed potatoes—and finished half before putting the rest down for Sugar Pie. Then she got up and hummed around, color-coordinating hand towels and dishrags. Every few minutes, she erupted in fits of twitters at the memory of Joy Faye's bullfrog face aimed toward that empty rat hole in the country.

Realizing her mother had the unmitigated gall to still be laughing at her, Joy slurped up the last of her noodles, then stormed off to her new bedroom. Slamming the door and hurling herself onto the bed, she glared at the phone, wondering what her stupid new number was and what message Ira might get if he dialed the old one.

Later, when she heard through the paper-thin walls the familiar sound of her mother losing her supper, Joy's central nervous system only issued a few writhing corkscrews of fretful distress. Quida Raye knew she wasn't well enough to be working as hard as she had that day. Why, oh, why did she persist in pulling such outlandish stunts then? Joy flopped on her side and scowled out the window, not an answer in sight.

By falling asleep with her clothes on and resisting the urge for a midnight snack, she avoided her mother the rest of that night. They in fact didn't exchange another word until after her shift the next day, during which she made the most of the move with a new installment in the daily call-in question Boo-Boo had named "Can You Beat This Mother (Please!)?"

****

"Thanks for tuning us in this morning," she said, adjusting the headphones. "That was 'She Got the Goldmine (I Got the Shaft),' a song Mother's boyfriend probably can't get off his mind these days.

"Anyway, it's time for our daily call-in contest.

You know the drill. Ring me up if you've got a story you think can beat the one I have about *my* mother. On the off chance someone has a wilder woman they call mama, they win two free meals at any of the Chop House's many fine locations. Today's question is— What's the most unbelievable thing your mother has ever done to you? Go ahead and call if you want—one-eight-hundred-lady-bug—but the only way I'm losing today is if Joan Crawford's daughter is listening, and even then it'd be a toss-up."

As WildDog tended to the callers, Boo-Boo leaned back in his chair and wagged his shaggy head. "I can't believe you walked in the house and absolutely everything was gone."

"With the wind!"

"To Ferndale, of all places." He shook his head and laughed again.

"And just think, if you hadn't come up with our daily call-in contests, you and I wouldn't be going to the Chop House for lunch again."

"What'll it be," he said, "three weeks in a row?"

"I guess we should start letting someone else win, huh?"

"As if it's in our control," he cried. "If anyone comes even *close* to what your mother did yesterday, I'll send them a week of Chop House vouchers and take you to the finest steak place in town."

"Deal," Joy said, though she was already visualizing the Chop House's buffet line and what she would pile on her plate. Correction—plates. That day, after yet another slam dunk, she had three. Then she and Boo-Boo headed back to the station to spend the afternoon in production, which is when Ira called.

"So that's what the problem was," he said after a terse summary. "I tried to call last night but got a recording saying your number had been disconnected." So her mother's caper had cost her one of Ira's rare phone calls. She stopped twirling a pencil she'd been jotting commercial ideas down with. Then she snapped it in half.

"Yep, then reconnected in a pineapple yellow house in the middle of fruity Ferndale," she said. Encouraged by Ira's "humph," she considered more snippets from her morning show. Boo-Boo, who'd heard it all before, tapped his watch, held up five fingers, and slipped out. "You might say the hue and cry of my new house approximates, in a semigloss sort of way, what happened when everyone within walking distance went bananas."

"Sounds like you could use a weekend away," Ira said, and Joy's heart soared. "It's short notice, but why don't you come down after work tomorrow? Just till Sunday," he quickly amended. "Monday's Labor Day, but I'm low man on the totem pole, so I'll be working."

"Friday through Sunday sounds great," Joy said in as even a tone as euphoria allowed. "I have to work Monday too." Though she would have quit on the spot had Ira suggested a longer visit. Which he didn't. He also didn't stay on the phone much longer. Joy was staring at the wall, broken pencil in her lap and delirious grin on her face, when Boo-Boo walked back in behind a half-grown, fully wild hound.

"What's this?" she whooped as a gray-brown tornado whipped into the production room.

"Security. You might need it in Ferndale," he said, trying to keep the dog's wagging tail out of the

173

oscillating fan. As a stack of forty-fives flew across the room, he said, "You might also need to put her in the restroom till you leave."

Joy stared at Boo-Boo, dear sweet Boo-Boo, and jumped up to smooch his prickly cheek. It must have looked like fun, since the dog hopped half a foot in the air, frantically lapping at his bristly chin.

"The pound said she's half St. Bernard and probably some Great Dane and Shepherd, too," he said, prying paws the size of catcher's mitts off his shoulders.

Bending down and getting slathered with more ecstatic dog kisses, Joy tried to piece together a timeline. "When did you do this? You were here all morning before we went to lunch."

"I made the call, and Ruthie went and got her," he said with a shrug. "She even came up with a name. What about Annie? As in Little Orphan."

"Little Orphan Annie," Joy crooned as a one-hundred-seventy-five-pound canine shoved her to the floor and filled her lap. "I think she likes it. I also think she just snapped my hamstring."

****

That night, Tanya called from Memphis, where she was on a two-night stand with Gary and the Giddyups.

"What happened?" she asked. "Miss Syndicated couldn't pay the phone bill?"

"Whatever do you mean?" Joy twirled the cord around her finger, enjoying the way this story was playing out among her non-listening public.

"I called and got a message that your number had been disconnected. So I had the operator check your line, and she gave me your new number."

"What is it?" Joy asked.

"What's what?"

"My new phone number. Mother hasn't bothered giving it to me yet. Of course, I haven't asked for it. Mainly because that would involve speaking to her and, since she up and moved me to Ferndale without my knowledge or consent while I was at work yesterday, that's something I'm currently not doing." A wall away, Joy heard her mother yelling *"Sit!"* at Annie.

There was a brief, staticky moment of long-distance bafflement. "Your mother moved you to *Ferndale*?"

"Yep."

"Without even telling you?"

"Uh-huh. My old house had *mice*," Joy said, sarcasm dripping off each syllable, hoping to finally win some sympathy from her hard-hearted best friend.

Fat chance. By the time Tanya spoke again, she had come to some crazed, only-in-Tanya's-mind resolution absolving Quida Raye of anything more than well-intentioned maternal concern.

"Well, I'm sure she at least got you a *better* place. Which wouldn't have taken much. Your old house was a real dump."

Before Joy could splutter a response, Tanya continued yammering. "Speaking of better places, you should see this Peabody Hotel. I told the guys I wanted to stay behind and see the ducks. Which of course is code for running up the phone bill and ordering everything on the room-service menu."

Tanya hawed as Joy sat in her new, hated bedroom, realizing her best friend had hopped over this major life crisis of hers to focus on the more pressing subject of the amenities at the Peabody Hotel. Staring incredulously through the window at her new, hated neighborhood, she decided Tanya might be her mother's only competition for maniac of the month. Surely they have that here in Ferndale, she thought, winding the cord tighter and watching her fingertip turn blue as it registered that Tanya had had the operator check her line. Ira, conversely, had simply hung up and called work the next day. Late.

"Well, eat a bonbon for me," Joy grumped.

"I will," Tanya chirped. "Talk to you when I get back to Gran D.'s this weekend. Till then, be nice to your mother. All she ever does is try to improve your life."

Joy dropped the phone in its cradle. She hadn't bothered to say goodbye or even mention Ira's invitation. But she also hadn't told Tanya to go to hell, either. That was something.

Then, through the wall, came Ms. Big Ear's loud voice. "The number's eight-eight-six, one-nine-two-six!"

Chapter 15
"I'd Love to Lay You Down"

A month and a half after Ira moved, Joy was finally
on her way to New Orleans. Listening to Warren Piece
till static started popping, around LeCompte, she
slipped in a tape and kept driving. Past signs for towns
like Mansura and Bunkie, Lebeau and Morganza.
Through prairies, woodlands, marshes, and deltas. Over
farm trails crisscrossing 71 and then 190. By roadside
shanties and faded businesses advertising everything
from bait and boudin to gas and gator.

Making her way through the bottom half of her
new listening audience, Joy Savoy began appreciating
the wonders of syndication. For starters, it gave her a
new driving game—challenging herself to name callers
from some of the outposts she flew through. Mixed
results were had till Krotz Springs. Harold from Krotz
Springs had called just that morning. She remembered
Boo-Boo and WildDog warning her to slow the hell
down in Krotz Springs. She also recalled why Harold
was calling. He was burying his mother that weekend.

Joy played "I'll Fly Away" for Harold. She had
started playing "I'll Fly Away" any time listeners called
in to memorialize their moms on air, which was
happening more and more often. Sometimes the passing
had occurred years earlier. Other times the loss was
fresh. Always, Joy paid homage via that oft-recorded

hymn while checking any wisecracks for a song or two.

As Boo-Boo observed after Harold called, if going live with gripes about her own cantankerous mom had accomplished nothing else, it gave fans a forum to send their own mamas' names over the airwaves, across the flat, baked Louisiana land as far as Joy could see that Friday.

"Why, up past the pearly gates, for all any of us can tell," Boo-Boo had said, brown eyes misting.

"Well, don't get all busted up about it, Mama's boy," WildDog yawped at the sight of their steadfast program director getting teary.

"Jackass," Boo-Boo countered, throwing the clipboard he was holding at WildDog, who caught it and threw it back.

"Titty baby," he grinned and said.

"Prick," Boo-Boo grumped. And back and forth they continued to go, hurling the clipboard and an escalating torrent of insults until Vernon stuck his head into the studio.

"What's all the commotion?"

"Just Batman and Robin acting like fools again," Joy quickly said, worried the kerfuffle might delay her departure to New Orleans. "Send Ruthie in to do their dumb jobs and you won't hear another peep."

Vernon just shook his head at the very idea and eased back out the door. Boo-Boo and WildDog meanwhile leaned toward each other in renewed gender solidarity, fixing her with matching glares of utter betrayal.

"Ruthie wouldn't know country pop from soda pop," Boo-Boo proclaimed.

"Or dobros from bongos," WildDog added.

"You couldn't make it without us," Boo-Boo said.

"Oh, yeah?"

"Yeah." Without looking, he reached toward her pile of pending tunes and held up the first forty-five he touched. "Tell me about this record."

"It's round," Joy said. "And black."

Turning to his blue-jeaned new best friend, he confidently lifted his face and dryly said, "Dawg?"

WildDog resituated his baseball cap and struck a professorial pose in the rolling chair. "Well, Bobby, what you've got there is '(If Loving You is Wrong) I Don't Want To Be Right,' nominated for CMA Single of the Year in 1979. Want to know more? Maybe about its first go-round as an R&B hit in 1972? Or the 1974 version that garnered two Grammy nominations? Or…"

"No," Boo-Boo smugly said. "I think it's obvious Joy couldn't make it without us."

"No one cares about all that minutia," she said with a flip of her wrist, praying she was right. "You two are just lucky my focus on the *music* leaves a pair of dweeb-shaped holes to fill."

"Right," Boo-Boo said, curling the corners of his mouth. "*We're* the lucky ones."

Later, on the road to New Orleans, Joy knew she'd be lucky if she didn't get pulled over. Sally hadn't been pushed that hard since her mother had run that state trooper off the road. Slowing down, she thought again about Harold from Krotz Springs and wondered if any of the many roadside cemeteries she was passing would be his mother's final resting place.

It was a depressing thought that dampened her drive and turned her morose attention to graveyards and their increasingly tall tombs all the way into below-sea-level New Orleans. Sufficiently dispirited, she managed to pull off I-10 without getting run over, stopped to freshen up at a gas station without getting mugged, then found Ira's duplex to the right of an exit ramp that appeared to be hosting a panhandlers' convention.

As she sat in Ira's driveway, looking at twin doors leading to two separate living quarters, another miserable realization occurred to her. Of all the housing options available in this big, terrifying place— apartment, condo, camel-back shotgun, Creole cottage—Ira had selected a duplex. The same type of domicile he and Dianne had shared in Avalon.

As she stared at the duplex, Joy felt her big-city jitters vibrating dangerously close to a full-blown panic attack that could easily send her straight back to I-10 and her safe, if dull, life four hours up the road. Then she thought of her mother rattling around that big yellow house four hours up the road. And, soon, she was reaching for her purse, her bag, and the pot of still-chilled stew on the passenger-side floorboard.

Hands full, she knocked on the far door with her knee. Ira instantly appeared, a tight, host-like smile slitting his face.

"Need a hand?" he said.

"Sure, you can take the stew."

"*Stew?*" he repeated, much as he might have said, "*Entrails?*"

A small voice that sounded as distant as deep graves said, "I thought we might work up an appetite." There she stood, freshly powdered and spritzed, all dressed up in her best jeans and a blouse her mother had insisted on starching, quivering with a cloying desire every bit as tangible as the Dutch oven dripping condensation across Ira's new front porch. All she needed to complete her country-come-to-city ensemble was a blacked-out tooth and a corncob pipe.

Registering her chagrin, instantly hoisting his expression into something more closely approximating graciousness, Ira said, "Actually, stew might not be a bad idea. Especially since I didn't have time to shop." Then he took the pot and proceeded to lead her on her first tour of his world. At least the parts Dianne hadn't packed in their only car and driven to New York City.

He was tidy, a collector—tea cups—and had a stereo sitting on cinder blocks in a dejected, single-man way. There was a couch, chair, and coffee table in the small living room. Blinds on the windows. A few photos on the mantel—one, unframed, of Dianne. Joy could see the sparsely outfitted kitchen beyond the living room, and, behind that, the bedroom. To keep from staring at his unmade, queen-sized bed, she focused instead on the album playing.

" 'Quarter Moon in a Ten Cent Town'?" she asked, grinning.

"In honor of you, madame," he replied, setting the stew down and reaching an arm around her. As he started to sway, he slipped the purse strap off her shoulder, peeled the bag strap out of her hand, and began unbuttoning her stiff blouse. Soon, he had undressed them both in a tangled trip and slide through the kitchen and into the bedroom, where Joy quickly discovered he hadn't gotten around to bolting the headboard to his bed yet. Any little movement made the woven rattan panel thump the wall separating the duplex's bedrooms. Big movements, she soon realized, nearly sent it slamming through the sheetrock. For half the night, his new neighbor had no peace whatsoever.

Around midnight, they staggered into the kitchen looking for the pot of stew, only to find it sitting in a puddle in the living room. Giggling, they put it on the stove, kicked the clothes out of the way, and rifled through Ira's echoing cupboards for bowls, glasses, spoons, and some bread-related product to sop up the gravy, settling for a couple of bagels. Then, exhausted by carbs and a clamorous headboard, they slept through their first full night together.

Saturday morning, Ira made the strongest coffee Joy had ever had, in a white French drip pot. Bringing her a cup in bed, along with the *Times-Picayune*, he informed her he didn't have anything for breakfast. "We ate the bagels last night."

Then he took the sports section and, thirty minutes later, they had made their way through the slim Saturday edition and an entire pot of coffee. Strung out on high-test caffeine undiluted by food, sticky from a soggy late-summer, deep Delta morning seeping through the duplex's damp, white walls, Joy felt the unexpected stirrings of something like regret stealing upon her. Propped against a pillow, staring at the relentless slant of the sun on the ceiling, she knew their first full night together was now being cast in the least flattering light, reduced to smeared mascara, greasy hair, and countless imperfections previously concealed by flesh-tone cover stick. Then there was the neighbor's muffled movements next door.

"We've got to get out of this place," said Ira, ever the mind reader.

Soon, he was driving her past his radio station, then through the Garden District, then to the French Quarter, where they parked and walked and drank and ate and juked to a different tune blasting out of every bar they passed. After stuffing themselves on all the requisite touristy fare—hurricanes at Pat O'Brien's, shrimp tempura from Takee Outee, coffee and beignets at Cafe du Monde, more hurricanes at Pat O's—Ira said he hoped she'd had her fill of the Vieux Carré because they wouldn't be getting near the place the next time she visited. Eyes aglitter at those two words—"next time"—Joy traipsed down Bourbon Street beside him in yet another starched blouse, elated to careen back to his duplex later and keep the neighbor up most of that night, too.

Sunday morning, after more invigorating chicory coffee, Ira pulled on his tennis shoes and went for a run. With nothing better to do than study Dianne's photo on the mantel, Joy called Tanya collect. Ethelene accepted the charges and yelled, "Tanya Lynn, pick up! That strangy-haired girl's on da line."

"Thank God you called. I've never been so bored in my life," Tanya groaned. "The only thing I've accomplished so far is figuring out when the drop date is for all my dumb classes."

"You're not dropping any classes. Gran D. would have your head. Besides, think of all the frat boys and college jocks you'd leave crying in their corn flakes."

"Good point," Tanya happily agreed. "Speaking of male distractions, where's Elvira?"

"He went for a run," Joy answered, stretching out on Ira's scratchy sofa.

"A *run*?" Tanya scoffed. "*Why*?"

"Either to get away from the murderers and muggers outside his door, or to stay in shape. Why does anyone run?"

"Beats the hell out of me," Tanya proclaimed. "Though I must say the first thing that springs to mind is a newly single man who takes such pains with his appearance must be trying to look good for the ladies. The ones he sees day in and day out." Irritated, as usual, by her hateful best friend, Joy's gaze drifted over to Dianne's photo.

"So when are you heading back?" Tanya asked.

"Later," Joy snapped. "Why?"

"Because Ethelene's got a pot of gumbo on the stove and a hummingbird cake on the counter. Leave Carl Lewis in the dust and come have a late lunch with us."

"I'll think about it," Joy said, hating herself for already fixating on that cake. "Let me see what Ira has planned."

"Please do," Tanya exclaimed. "I certainly wouldn't want to take priority over some still-married radio hack who left you high and dry for all the new women he's staying in shape for."

"You're such an ass. Why would I want to go out of my way to see you?"

"Because you've always loved Ethelene's gumbo and cakes. And because it wouldn't be but an hour or so out of your way. And because, last I checked, you don't have anything to race back for. Unless you want to see where your mother moved you to this weekend. I'll have Ethelene set you a place."

"Don't wait for me. If I do leave early enough, I'll just drop by for some cake." Hearing Ira's running shoes hit the porch, she lowered her voice and said, "He's back. I'll talk to you later." Hanging up and resituating herself on the opposite end of the scratchy sofa, she watched through the blinds as Ira gasped for breath and stretched and did whatever else it was that people do to survive after running an hour in the hot soup of New Orleans in early September.

While she kept watching to make sure he didn't pass out, Ira's neighbor emerged from his side of the duplex, rattling car keys. After a comment or two that Joy didn't quite catch, she adjusted her head so she could read Ira's lips through the slits in the blinds. And what she clearly saw him say was "No," and "Just a friend."

When he came in a few minutes later, dripping wet and still breathing hard, Joy was flipping through a copy of *Esquire* that the pot of stew had sweated a wrinkly circle into Friday.

"Good run?" she asked, getting a breathless nod. "Hey, I forgot, but I've got a thing I need to do up in Avalon. Hope you don't mind if I hit the road."

Ira looked relieved, which hurt Joy's heart nearly as much as his "just a friend" comment. But she was all smiles as she hurriedly packed the Dutch oven and her wilted clothes into the car, consulted a state map, and made her way back to I-10.

Past Baton Rouge and Lafayette, on into Lake Charles, she turned and headed north through another string of towns sprinkled with fans whose names mostly came back with every city limits sign. Jeanne in Moss Bluff. Angela in DeRidder. David in Rosepine. Then of course there was Tanya, queen of crazy, in The Pitts.

Even after four hours on the road, Joy still wasn't up to dealing with Tanya. So she turned left at the largest Pentecostal church in Morrow Parish and drove fifteen more minutes, toward Morrow Lake and some of the most beautiful country in all of south central Louisiana. Boo-Boo's parents had had a fishing camp out there before his father died. Now the only reason Joy came down that road anymore was located off to the right, behind one of the parish's smaller Baptist churches. Easing into the circular drive, she pulled up beside the beige-on-brown two-door, turned her engine off, rolled down the windows, and waited.

Few places are more peaceful on sunny Sunday afternoons than little country-church cemeteries. Joy guessed that might be why so many folks in the South frequented them. In her own family, visiting graveyards had been a prime recreational activity during the summers her mother worked and she stayed with her grandparents in Kentucky. Some of her happiest childhood memories, in fact, were wrapped around trips to old family plots. All-day affairs, her grandmother filled those excursions with cousins, fried chicken, wasp spray, and subtle lessons that lasted. As a result, Joy knew where five generations of her family were buried on a pair of tranquil hills a mile apart in the Land Between the Lakes. She also knew some of the more interesting ways many of them had met their maker. On her grandmother's side alone, causes of death stretched from stillborn to syphilis, with endless old-fashioned killers in between: consumption, dropsy, grippe, lockjaw, palsy, kicked by horses, drowned in wells, shot by Yankees.

It had been over two and a half years, however, since Joy Savoy had experienced any emotion approaching peace at a graveyard, particularly this one. As her gaze skimmed the fenced-in acreage, avoiding the small grave in the far right corner and the two shapes moving around it, she knew if she waited long enough, her mother and Sugar Pie would eventually emerge.

Soon, the gate clicked open and four shaved paws and a pair of dirty work tennies filled her field of vision.

"Are you all right?" her mother asked.

Settling into a more casual pose against Sally's fender, Joy smiled and said, "Absolutely. It was hot in the car, so I was just bent over getting some air."

"It's not exactly the North Pole out here," her mother said, slipping off her work gloves. "I just hope I left that new hound a yores with enough water. Whew. I'm so hot my hair's flat as a flitter cake." Joy glanced at the brown globe she was patting with the back of her wrist. It was half a foot high.

Walking on to her car, Quida Raye popped the trunk. In went her trowel, rake, sack of old flowers, and camera. She had a photo album devoted to pictures of Jessie's grave done up for every holiday—a red heart stand for Valentine's, bunnies in a circle for Easter, flags instead of flowers on July Fourth. Joining those photos, Joy knew from her one glimpse into the far right corner, would be a shot of her Labor Day labor of love—a ribbony red-white-and-blue festive affair. She also knew her mother would come back the next weekend, disassemble it, save what could be recycled, and replace the rest with silk flowers in colors appropriate to the season.

"I'm plum pooped," she said as she came and leaned against the fender beside Joy. Fishing a wet washrag from a baggie, she snapped it open and wiped her face. For the briefest instant, it seemed that she had not only rubbed off all the red Morrow Parish dust, but every last, lingering hint of youth, as well. Instead of reviving her, working in the dirt, in *that* dirt, seemed to have the exact opposite effect.

"Have you eaten yet?" Joy heard herself ask, silently bidding farewell to Ethelene's gumbo and hummingbird cake. "I've been thinking about catfish."

"Humph," Quida Raye chirped. "Catfish dudn't sound half bad." As Joy hoped it would, mentioning one of her mother's favorite foods scrunched her face into an impish, almost girlish grin. Just thinking about something other than Jessie's grave softened some of the grooves, smoothed a few of the creases. Her hair even seemed to grow two, maybe three inches. Folding the washrag and stuffing it back in the bag, she said, "My palm's been itching off. Since it's my right one, that means I'm gonna be comin' into some money. I'll buy if you wanna go to that catfish shack on the Avalon Highway."

"Sounds good to me."

"Give me a minute to get everythang situated," she said, heading back to arrange the trunk to her liking. Then, scratching her palm again, she whistled Sugar Pie into the car and took off.

Before Joy followed, she looked back at the little grave in the far right corner. For over two and a half years, she had thought of that patch of land as the final resting place for several stories that would never be told again. But that September day, she saw she had been wrong.

Just as surely as she had come to know so many details that weren't written in stone in several Kentucky graveyards, she realized an entire cemetery full of survivors in Louisiana had undoubtedly learned a few concerning her, as well. And, for however long future generations think there is no place more peaceful than that country cemetery on a sunny afternoon, she knew how the story would go, too.

"See that little heart-shaped stone way back in the corner? Well…"

Chapter 16
"The Man That Turned My Mama On"

Every few weeks, Joy headed to New Orleans. And
every few weeks, against her better judgment, she
called Tanya during Ira's runs. Soon, their chats were
little more than recaps of various Dianne ghost
sightings Joy had experienced in all of Ira's favorite
haunts, the bars and restaurants where he trained empty
black eyes on familiar old walls, mumbling, "Who do
you have to fuck to get waited on here?"

"Don't tell me you're surprised the guy who
moved back to the place where he met, married, and
lived with his estranged wife is taking you everywhere
they used to go," Tanya said. "Go somewhere new.
Take some road trips."

Surprised that something Tanya said made sense
for once, Joy cued up "Islands in the Stream" and
presented Boo-Boo and WildDog with another
opportunity to collaborate.

"Name some fun things to do or good places to eat
within a few hours of New Orleans," she said. Then, as
Kenny and Dolly sailed away to another world, she sat
back, notebook in hand, jotting down their salvo of
suggestions. Two songs later, she was still scribbling
restaurant recommendations from the gastronomes she
evidently worked with.

And shortly thereafter, she and Ira began leaving

Dianne and The Big Uneasy far behind.

****

As autumn settled across Louisiana, summer's hot pink begonia blushes faded into poofs of Halloween-colored mums and fall's flashy pansies. Heading down back roads aflutter with fallen leaves and high hopes, Ira at the wheel, Joy prattled away as the gaudy blur flew past, yard after country yard of Mardi Gras parades in petaled beads. Purple, yellow, and green, the same shades her mother had recently strewn around that flaxen house up in Ferndale, too.

New season, new scenery, new start. Determined to finally win Ira's undivided attention and, with any luck, his heart, Joy devised a plan. She would spend their drives telling him everything he hadn't bothered to ask about her life. While Tanya considered the strategy debatable, there was one clear benefit to Joy's weekend diatribes—they jostled loose fresh ideas for her radio show, which pleased Boo-Boo.

In early October, Boo-Boo rolled the latest Nielsen ratings into a jolly baton, conducting a bit of "Somewhere Between Right and Wrong" before declaring the trio of Quida Raye, Joy Faye, and country music were like a braid. "Twist the three of you up together, and you've got a stranglehold on anyone forced to listen to you for any amount of time. Which I suppose is as true of poor old Ira as it is your fans these days." Laughing as Joy swatted at him, he tapped her on the nose with his paper Nielsen wand. "Take that," he said, dodging left and right. "And that."

Joy unplaited that braid every chatty weekend she could. She told Ira about her first husband, Sonny, her No. 1 father, Frank, and her No. 2 father, Dick. But, mostly, she told him about her mother.

"That's original," Tanya drawled after the first play-by-play.

"It makes sense, if you think about it," Joy said defensively. "Driving reminds me of her. Which reminds me of dying in a terrible accident."

"Which reminds you of Sonny," Tanya continued.

"Which *mainly* reminds me of all the country stars who died far too early," Joy said, ignoring Tanya's efforts to personalize the trauma, which was already personal enough.

As Joy told Ira, on the way to Paw-Paw's in Lake Charles, she would never forget the night in 1963 that Patsy Cline's plane went down.

"Ironically," she began, "that event triggered a road trip, too." To get her mother back in the kitchen again, anywhere other than curled in a ball on the couch, Dick eventually piled them into his new convertible and drove the ninety miles from Fort Lipton, Kentucky, to Camden, Tennessee, just so Quida Raye could sit and smoke and shed some tears near where Patsy had drawn her last breath. Patsy, who bore a striking resemblance to Quida Raye's headstrong older sister. Patsy, whose haunting, achy voice was more familiar to Joy at age five than that of her own frequently mute mother. Months later, not even Kennedy's assassination would make as lasting an impression on a first-grader.

"Probably because JFK didn't leave behind a stack of forty-fives my mother would play for the next twenty years," she said into the mic several days later, opening the line for melancholy memories of Mom.

Another weekend, heading to Soileau's Dinner Club in Opelousas, Joy had two hours each way to talk,

talk, talk. First, she told Ira about her mother's stomach-cancer diagnosis in '77, when she was given three months to live. "Despite steadily losing weight, and not being able to work, and refusing to darken a doctor's door again, she seems okay. Aside from some occasional, um, digestive issues. I mean, it's been *five years* and she's still alive *and* kicking."

"Interesting," Ira said, sounding not very interested at all, which Joy thought she could remedy with another medical report—her own incredible story of impossible survival.

"Then again, she hasn't believed a thing any doctor has said since the end of 1957, when she was about seven or eight months pregnant with me," she began, chills running down her arms. "That's when the family GP moved his stethoscope all around her stomach, stepped back, hung his head, and said, 'I'm sorry, little lady, but I can't find a heartbeat. I'm afraid your baby has died.' "

Until Ira came along, spending part of her time in utero as a dead fetus had pretty much been the high point of Joy Savoy's life. She got a rollercoaster rush every time she imagined the doctor telling her mother she had two choices. She could either end the pregnancy, or wait until nature took its course.

"Grandma said Dr. Bishop just shook his head that day, watching Mother waddle off, choosing what she considered the least troublesome way out. Which made sense, I guess, considering how rocky the pregnancy had already been."

"How so?" Ira asked.

"Well, by the time anyone found out she was expecting, she was already too fed up with both of the likely suspects—Frank and Dick—to tell Grandma which blond, blue-eyed buck private was responsible. So Grandma basically flipped a coin and dropped in on Frank's company commander out at Fort Lipton. In 1957, company commanders still made sure their recruits did right by the local girls. Meaning Mother and Frank had been married about four months when it looked like it could have been all for naught."

"Shotgun wedding?" Ira inquired.

"More like an M1 rifle wedding. And I was no sooner declared dead than Grandma sent Frank packing back to his barracks on post."

Two miles outside of Opelousas, Joy rushed to wrap up her origin story. "As a result, Grandma was the only one at the hospital when, right before Mother was wheeled into delivery, Dr. Bishop found a heartbeat and drew a big, red circle on her belly over the spot. Then I arrived, kicking and screaming for what they tell me dragged on for three solid months.

"In other words, I was dead. Then I was alive. A *joy*ful miracle!"

But as Ira slowed down to look for the restaurant, she mulled over the story's true end. How she and her mother became Quida Raye and Joy Faye, so alike you couldn't tell one from the other in early school photos. So alike no man had seemed involved. So alike, Joy knew, glancing back at Ira, no man had ever been all *that* involved.

Pulling up to Soileau's, he said, "So which one's your real father then?"

"Who knows. Frank hung around about a year, then Dick swooped back in and spent the next fifteen making us pay for that early uncertainty. As I like to say, I have two fathers, but you could put them both together and they still wouldn't add up to one whole dad. And Mother, of course, still isn't talking."

"Of course." Ira sighed and said, "Let's go eat."

On the way back to New Orleans, Ira, as usual, didn't ask another question. And Joy, as quite usual, didn't force the subject. By Port Allen, the rain began, sending temperatures tumbling and silence settling around them like snow blown from a coming storm. Determined to salvage that afternoon, at least, Joy resorted to the only activity that had ever earned her Ira's undivided attention, which also served to nicely heat things back up for the moment.

"I'm trying to drive here," he laughed and said, peeling her hand—briefly—off his ropy thigh. Watching him try to keep all four wheels on the highway during what he dubbed a "Joy Ride" or "Radar Luv," however, wasn't the only danger related to hitting the road with Ira.

As she told listeners that next unseasonably cool week, "Since I'm spending some of my weekends out of town, Mother's whiling away the hours— unsupervised—in Ferndale. For a woman with more energy than the TVA, being stuck in sedate, or, shall I say, *sedated* Ferndale is not safe for anyone. Especially when you throw in her old friends nicotine and caffeine, in both carbonated and analgesic form, which crank her up tighter than a choke chain on the Iditarod's lead dog."

It was the best explanation she could come up with for what happened to the big white couch.

****

"Want to go to Ship O' Hoyt's tonight?" Joy asked

WildDog and Boo-Boo the week before Thanksgiving. The former was enjoying a late breakfast. The latter was shelving a stack of albums. "Ruthie's coming, and I thought we could have a little early birthday party for her."

"Her birthday's Tuesday, right?" Boo-Boo asked, reaching for "The Closer You Get."

"Yep," Joy said. "She's turning thirty, and, with any luck, she'll finally meet someone tonight. Just between us, I think the jig is about up on all this virginity nonsense. With a nose like she's got, you'd think she'd be more proactive about striking while the iron's still a little hot."

"First of all," Boo-Boo announced in a brisk, clipped voice, "I don't see one thing wrong with her nose. So it seems to lean the slightest bit if you look really closely. I happen to think it's cute. Second of all, since when is a woman's virginity some kind of national tragedy, Joy?" Though he had his broad back to her, she could imagine what his face looked like. He had only used that tone with her one other time in eleven years, and that was when she told him she was marrying Sonny Savoy a few months shy of her seventeenth birthday.

"Excuse the hell out of me," she huffed. "Someone's certainly in a pissy mood today." Boo-Boo's only response was to yank up another album and nearly crack it in half.

WildDog reached in his donut bag, pulled out a white napkin, and waved it as he scampered out of the studio, leaving Joy wondering just when Ruthie and Boo-Boo had become such good friends.

"I'm not saying her status as the oldest virgin in the

western hemisphere *is* a national tragedy, Boo-Boo. I just think she'd be happier if she had a boyfriend or something."

"Why? Because *you're* so damn happy?" Wheeling around, he glared at her and banged a finger atop the next record in line, the mournful "I Don't See Me in Your Eyes Anymore."

"You know what I mean."

"No, I'm afraid I don't. You've been a wreck since Ira Everhart gave you the time of day. Why in God's name would you wish that on a perfectly sweet woman who, up till now, has so far been spared the utter misery of finding out just how fucking heartbreaking being in love can frequently be?"

Joy sat there blinking at him, stunned. "Good grief, Boo-Boo," she finally sputtered. "What would *you* know about being in love?"

Wordlessly, he spun back around and attempted to remodel the studio by slamming albums through the wall.

"What?" Joy said. "What?" But he didn't speak to her again until they were at Ship O' Hoyt's later. WildDog spent most of the evening counseling Hoyt on possible new jukebox additions. Ruthie was her usual delightful self, not the least bit tortured by her chaste status or wayward nose. And Boo-Boo was back in fine fettle, too. In fact, the more he and Ruthie leaned their heads together and chattered, the happier he seemed to get.

As for Joy, something seemed to be drifting peculiarly off course, out of kilter for reasons she couldn't grasp. And the sensation only swelled and slithered around her gut the more Boo-Boo's long, black hair brushed ever so casually alongside Ruthie's adoring, freckled face.

"You need a haircut," Joy announced between songs. "If I've got to wear dresses to work, I don't think it's fair that you get to traipse around looking like Alice Cooper."

"Oh, Joy," Ruthie twittered. "His hair's nowhere near as long as some girl's."

Not even that drew Boo-Boo back into the chummy accord he and Joy had always privately shared. In fact, he all but ignored her. So she ordered another drink and started griping about everything that came to mind—brown jalopies, glow-in-the-dark subdivisions, groupie best friends, dilapidated death-trap bridges. By about drink number three, she had made her grousing way to the crocus-colored cavern her mother had moved her to. Specifically, its vast expanses of wall space.

"I make enough to afford a bigger place," she said, slamming down Mr. Collins. "I just don't make enough to furnish it."

Ruthie, in dear Ruthie fashion, tore herself away from Boo-Boo long enough to offer a solution. "My mom and dad have a couch they're not using. It's white and, with as many grandkids as they've got running around, a white couch is the last thing they need. I'm sure they wouldn't mind if you used it a while. But I'm warning you, it's really big."

Joy sat back and studied her glass. "There's an idea. But how would we get it to my house?"

"We can use my truck," Boo-Boo offered as Ruthie beamed up at him.

"Of course we could," Joy groused.

Two days later, after Boo-Boo, WildDog, Joy, and Ruthie finally got a monstrosity nearly as long and white as Daytona Beach shoved up against most of one wall, Quida Raye stood back and scrutinized the colossal couch. It was the same look she reserved, scissors in hand, for shaggy Sugar Pie every summer. But Joy didn't give it another thought as she and her moving crew staggered off to Ship O' Hoyt's for some alcohol to apply to their aching muscles.

The next weekend, she and Ira lingered over crab and shrimp au gratin in eggplant pirogues in Washington, then strolled along Bayou Cortableau. Passing a pop-up stand that took photos to apply to various knickknacks, Ira relented and let Joy get a mug with his mug on it.

Sunday, she returned home and walked in to a living room that seemed different somehow. Looking around, she couldn't decide what was off, aside from two instant snapshots she picked up from the coffee table as she set her new mug down. One was of the white couch, so long the far arm was a blur. The other featured a vaguely familiar, short, bright blue loveseat of a thing, all four feet of which were in perfect focus.

Then the area behind the photos swam into focus as Joy realized she was holding the pictures directly in front of the actual new loveseat itself. It was on the same wall the white couch had previously engulfed. Smiling at how blind she could occasionally be, she inspected her newest, boldest piece of furniture. Unless she was mistaken, the arms bore the same scrollwork as the white couch. Thinking she might compare the two, she turned around to see where her mother had shoved Ruthie's parents' hulking piece of furniture. But it was nowhere to be found. Not in the living room. Not in the dining room. Not in her room or her mother's.

Back in the living room, hands trembling now, the photos slipped from her grasp and fluttered back onto the coffee table, alongside something else she hadn't noticed earlier.

Her mother's compact one-handed reciprocating saw.

She ran a finger down its bi-metal demolition blade, bile rising in her throat. The white cottony tufts clinging to the smirking silver teeth were, she fully understood, *stuffing*.

Once again Joy turned toward the tiny object along the wall. And she knew the huge white couch was before her still. Only it wasn't white. And it wasn't a couch anymore. It was basically the size of a recliner built for two and newly covered in loud material she had last seen illuminating the linen closet.

She stood there absorbing the enormity of her mother's latest enterprise. Quida Raye had taken a massive couch that belonged to the parents of Joy's co-worker—her *boss's* sister and brother-in-law, no less—sawed off two-thirds, resprung the remaining wad, nailed an end back to it, recovered it with a jazzy sheet, and stained the woodwork. All in one weekend. With enough time left over to smear the extra stain on the kitchen cabinets, table, and chairs.

"*Mother!*" Joy yelled.

"Out here," came a distant reply. Assuming combat stance, Joy marched through the house and into the backyard, startling Cole, Annie, and Sugar Pie, who had been watching her mother hammer something into one of the trees.

"What's that?" Joy screamed. "The *rest* of Ruthie's parents' couch?"

"Just a few of the bigger boards," her mother said with the same daffy smirk she'd worn on moving day in the driveway at Happenstance. "Why?"

"Oh, no reason," Joy shrieked. "Except that couch did not *belong* to us!" This was clearly a piece of information her mother had not considered.

"It didn't?"

"*No!* Ruthie's parents only *loaned* it to me."

She thought a bit. "Well, by the time they want it back, maybe they won't remember what it uset to look like."

"They'll remember we needed a *truck* to get it here. Not a *little red wagon*! They'll remember it was *white* and not *azure*."

"Whose-yer?" Quida Raye snorted before shifting her attention north. "What daya thank of this doomaflidgy I'm buildin'? Since Cole spends mosta his time out here, I thought if he had a nice place to sit, maybe he wouldn't go off lookin' for..." She shuddered. "...*thangs*."

Joy just stood there, agog. She had a best friend who'd entertained more troops than Bob Hope and couldn't say "vagina" and a mother who built tree houses for cats and couldn't say "mice." Through the pines, to the left of Quida Raye's spherical do, she could see the twin smokestacks of the Institute for the Criminally Insane. She wondered what their phone number was, and if they had a SWAT team.

Incapable of speech, she wheeled around and stepped right on the flat head of a field hoe her mother had leaned against a tree. The solid wooden handle recoiled, slamming her square in the face and sending her to her knees, where Annie tried to lick the blood away while her mother got a wet washrag. For two full days, she looked like Ruthie's twin sister, beak-to-crooked-beak.

While such shenanigans didn't hurt her ratings, they did give Joy pause when considering out-of-town trips. The next time Ira called, ostensibly to make plans, she hemmed and hawed till he switched gears and started doing what he'd probably called to do anyway. Complain.

"Guess what I did after work today," he snarled.

"What?"

"Nothing. Same as yesterday. Same as tomorrow. Same as every fucking day you don't decide to drive down here and save me from my own fucking self. This living alone shit is not for me."

Joy sat on her bed and stared out the window. Dusk had come to her neon neighborhood, but night was falling fast. If Ira didn't like living alone, what—or *who*—were his options?

"You could always move back up here and rent a room from the Demolition Derby Queen," she shakily joked, attempting to delay what she suspected might be the inevitable. "She'll either keep you company or kill you, one. You should see my nose."

"I wish I could. Right this minute." Alone in her bedroom, Joy blushed. "I actually had something else in mind," he said, freezing her heart. "There's an opening here at the station." Then heaven parted and the angels sang as Ira Everhart said, "You could always apply for it and move down here. That wouldn't be so bad."

Chapter 17
"Blue Eyes Crying in the Rain"

"Mother just informed me that I'm not applying for any job till she goes shopping," Joy told Tanya, cradling the receiver, still reeling from Ira's invitation to get herself hired at his station.

"Quida Raye to the rescue again," Tanya proclaimed. "You could certainly use some spiffing up. And, since she never leaves the house unless everything from her key chain to her license plate matches, you couldn't be in better hands. Remind me what she says you drape yourself in?"

"Garb," Joy replied.

"That's right." Tanya hawed. "*Garb*. And it really is a four-letter word the way she uses it."

"I thank that's some kinda *garb* you've got on," Joy said, acing her mother's twang. "She used that exact phrase five minutes ago when I went and sat on that weird little loveseat and asked how long a lease she'd signed on this place. She immediately weaseled the entire story out of me and made plans to leave for Harvey's first thing in the morning."

"There goes her next disability check," Tanya said gaily. "Or will she have to hock her rings again?"

"Who knows," Joy mumbled, feeling the excitement of a new dress fizzle. Thinking about how her mother financed most of her heart's desires always dropped her down in the dumps. "I told her I could wear one of the new dresses she bought me in May."

"To which—let me guess—she reminded you that showing up to a job interview in *December* wearing a *summer* frock might lend a certain down-in-the-boondocks air that may not go over well at a major-market station?"

Joy glanced at the clock, anxious to get off the phone before Tanya got really wound up. "Something like that. Till then, there's a small-market station I need to be at in not too many hours. Where, by the way, I'm not breathing a word of this to anyone. Not even Boo-Boo."

"I won't call and spill the beans then," Tanya promised. "As long as you swear to act grateful for whatever your mother and Harvey pick out for you."

****

"See if these shoes fit," her mother said two days later, pulling a box out of a bag and bopping Annie's sniffing nose with it. "You ain't eatin' these, dawg."

Dumping the contents of Joy's old purse into a new one, she added, "I guess I could get uset to livin' in New Orleans. If I *had* to." While Joy tried on three new dresses, oohing and aahing and spinning around in what she was sure even Tanya would deem a suitable display of appreciation, she couldn't help but smile. Buying a few new dresses for her daughter had naturally struck Quida Raye Perkins as a sound investment in her own future.

Friday, a record three hours and twenty-five minutes after she told Boo-Boo she had a doctor's appointment and ran out of the station, Joy Savoy picked Ira up at his duplex and careened to the three-story offices of his employer, nearly wrecking twice.

"Calm down," he cried, grabbing the dash. "You're a syndicated disc jockey, remember?"

"Yeah, at a sprinkling of small stations in a few tiny towns," she wailed. She knew she was a pitiful excuse for a DJ. She also knew the only reason anyone listened was because griping about her own crazy mother gave everyone else an excuse to call in and gripe about theirs.

"You don't have to be Ralph Emery to work the graveyard shift," he pointed out. "And this isn't WSM. Relax." The opposite of relaxed, she parked and followed him on wiggly spaghetti legs through the lobby and up to the station manager's office, where Ira made quick introductions before dashing back to the elevator.

Watching him go, the smiling station manager and genial program director began showing their panicky job applicant around an office suite chock full of autographed eight-by-tens even more impressive than the ones lining Vernon's long hall. Only then, surrounded by countless country singers so familiar they practically felt like family, did Joy Savoy finally stop twitching convulsively.

Strolling past photos of the industry's biggest stars, the pleasant station manager mentioned tapes Ira had shared, the friendly program director asked about stations where she had worked, and they all compared notes about executives they each knew. Then, settled in comfy leather chairs around a big oak desk, they chatted more about the pros of a young woman like Joy working her way up in a major market. After asking if she had visited New Orleans much, they then began rattling off favorite restaurants and dive bars, detailing which dishes and drinks were best and whether jazz brunch, Friday lunch, or happy hour was the time to go.

It occurred to Joy that she had never had a job interview go so splendidly. It was only a matter of minutes, she knew, before an offer would be made, a salary proposed, medical and dental detailed. This is a breeze, she realized, mind sliding across the satin promise of every glorious certainty that would then come to pass. She would either move in with Ira or they could get a bigger place farther from I-10. The Quarter would be interesting. Loud but interesting. Surely they'd get married, once his divorce was final. Invite her mother to visit every now and then. Boo-Boo and Tanya, too. Joy Savoy couldn't believe life was about to get so good, but all evidence was pointing to nothing short of paradise here on earth.

Then, sensing she was being spoken to, she stopped picking out colors for bridesmaid dresses long enough to wrap her mind around what the station manager had said and was now repeating.

"As I was saying, if we offer you a job, you don't have a husband back in Avalon who's going to throw a wrench in the whole deal, do you?"

"Husband!" Joy declared, face rumpling in amused incredulity. "Nope, no husband here. At least not anymore. I always say the best thing I ever did was leave that man, may he rest in peace since I certainly can now."

"Oh, I'm sorry," the station manager said, simultaneously startled and confused by this blasé attitude regarding what sounded like—could it be?—her husband's untimely death? "Was there an accident?"

"Maybe, though that's debatable," Joy allowed, smiling and waving the gloomy ordeal into history, more than ready for her rosy future to get rolling here. "Trust me, it wasn't anything he didn't have coming."

"Goodness. Well then," said the man entrusted with hiring and firing for one of the largest radio stations in the South, Ira's station, "I take it there weren't any children?"

The room tilted sideways.

Children?

"Children?" Joy whispered, her voice dangerously slipping a notch or two higher. Children. It was just one word. Two syllables. But if ever a word carried the overwrought weight of a solemn vow, a sacred oath, this was it. Children. The one subject she had not discussed with a single soul in over two and a half years.

Oh, boy, Joy thought, chest tightening. This is not good. Not good at all. Her throat swelled. Eyes stung. Nose burned. Quick, she told herself, tip your head back and study the ceiling and maybe these sudden hot pools will evaporate. Something, however, was whirling terribly out of control. Blood drummed in her ears. Ditches joined her brows. And instead of disappearing, those fat lakes began flooding down both sides of her face. Rivers and rivers of tears. All the tears that had been dammed up for over two and a half years.

"Ah, yes," she managed, swallowing hard and pinching her nose. "Children."

The stunned program director sprang up and began rummaging around for a box of tissues. The alarmed station manager tipped back in his chair, stricken, like any man might be after triggering such a commotion.

"There was," Joy continued, head still craned back, nostrils flaring, deluge unabated, "*one* child…but…well, there *was* an accident…and she… well, she…she…"

Joy Savoy had never seen anyone have a complete breakdown before and, judging from their faces, neither had the station manager or program director. At least not during a job interview that had been going swimmingly until one word obliterated it.

Children.

But, even as the room spun and every one of Joy's most cherished desires flew out a third-floor window, she was pretty sure that was what was happening here. A complete and total breakdown. Still, on she fumbled.

"…She…well, she didn't make it…she…" Both the station manager and the program director waved their hands and shook their heads and tried to let her know in every way possible that she didn't have to keep talking. First a dead husband and now this? Yes, they had heard quite enough. Really. Please.

"No, no," Joy kept saying. "I'm okay." But she was not okay. Hadn't been okay for over two and a half years. Probably would never be okay again. Finally, the station manager cleared his throat and murmured something about the two of them stepping outside for a few minutes.

"Oh, God," Joy whispered, reaching for a tissue. *This is bad. Bad, bad. Bad, bad Leroy Brown.* She was still humming when they came back in. And while she was once again dry-eyed and upbeat, she knew she was as far away from moving to New Orleans and living happily ever after as she would ever be.

****

That night, after the dishes were done and the stereo was on, a storm blew down from Baton Rouge. Eyes nearly swollen shut from the most disastrous job interview in the history of radio, Joy leaned against Ira's open door and smelled the rain coming, a gravel-scented headwind of splatters smacking warm asphalt. Sucking in the too-sweet breeze, she memorized the wet air, the tangerine rings the mist cast against the circles of street lights, the throb of the city itself. She was never moving to New Orleans. As a result, she was going to lose Ira Everhart. She knew it as well as she knew every beat of the song jarring the duplex, Phil Collins' baleful "In the Air Tonight."

"Want to talk about it?" he asked, pulling her away from the door and down on the floor. As the rain began falling in earnest, he snapped off the light and turned down the stereo.

"I wouldn't know where to start."

"The beginning's always nice."

"Well, there are *two* beginnings," she said. "Sonny. And Jessie."

"Screw Sonny," Ira said.

Good. It would have taken a road trip to the moon to explain *that* teen-aged madness. How a crater left by a trailer with purple carpet was soon filled by Sonny Savoy. Brash, black-haired Sonny who did everything in record time. From running the bases to falling into—and out of—young love. It was no surprise then when he responded to Joy's mouthy slide back toward sanity by swiftly returning plenty of purple to her world. Months of mauve, she thought, as if on air. Vast quantities of violet. Even the car Sonny died in—*her* car—was bruise purple.

"Okay then," she told Ira. "Jessie it is." But as she listened to the storm building and stared into pitch dark lacerated by so much more than lightning, she knew what she had known long before that day's cataclysmic job interview. She was as incapable of calmly talking about her daughter as she might be—for all the opposite reasons—Sonny, prince of purple. Archduke of amethyst, she nonsensically thought, again as if on air.

As if on air.

As if she were talking about *her mother* on air.

And for the first time in over two and a half years, Joy Savoy saw in a stormy black night the spark of an idea that might help her speak the unspeakable. As long as she kept her mother in sight, like a bulbous lighthouse in the distance, she might finally make her way through this wretched darkness. All the memories her soul could never part with—the touch of Jessie's still baby-soft skin, the smell of her hair, the funny words she said, her darling face tipped up for goodnight kisses, and a million other glimmering moments shot through with the cherished essence of a precious child—could stay tucked inside, privately persecuting Joy Savoy the rest of her days. By focusing on her mother, however, she might find a way to share the easy bits. The facts. Just the facts.

"When Jessie was born," she began, inhaling deeply, "my mother was thirty-six. And, for the first time in her life, she experienced love at first sight. Having steeled herself against exactly that by a diagnosis of dead baby before *I* arrived." Encouraged to hear Ira huff at the memory, she soldiered on. "With Jessie, she basically woke up one day and became the most crazy-in-love grandmother on earth."

It helped, Joy knew, that her mother actually did wake up one day and discover she was about to be a grandmother. That day!

In her own defense, Joy had proof she was raving mad to insist on marrying wild, truculent Sonny at sixteen because what she did next was truly certifiable. When she came up pregnant and didn't bother to inform anyone outside the chaos of her ridiculous marriage. Including her mother. Talk about ridiculous! What kind of daughter doesn't tell her mother she's pregnant? What kind of mother wouldn't know? What kind of mother, indeed.

"When Jessie and I were released from the hospital—Ferndale's JFK Memorial, incidentally—Mother picked us up and brought us straight back to her trailer, no questions asked." About what, Joy didn't elaborate. Knowing Ira probably wouldn't overly care, she decided to at least spare herself a bruised ego all those years later.

"Virtually overnight, she had filled the place with everything an infant could possibly need or want, from crib to toys." Stumbling across the recollection of one plaything in particular, that little red riding horse no one in her right mind would have bought a newborn, Joy rubbed her forehead, tempted to stop speaking completely. With a rapt audience of one, however, she groaned and forged on.

"And there we stayed, me barely leaving my room while Mother, Harvey, and the others buzzed around filling bottles, burping Jessie, and batting around ideas for giving Sonny what he deserved."

Ira snorted.

"I'd be lying if I said the words 'alligator bait' and 'deep bayou' didn't float up to that front bedroom," she said, chuckling. "While they could have just been singing their favorite songs, I stayed in bed, figuring it was safer there." Weeks, in fact, passed as Joy stared at the shifting shadows on the walls, the mottles in the mirror fading back to beige. Then, once she could fit into something other than Sonny's big, ambiguous shirts, once no stiff-haired woman was sitting around with a binky in her hand and revenge in her heart, she ventured out.

"I hiked through the woods to Pitts' little radio station where Boo-Boo was working his usual summer job. Soon, some DJ ditched a shift that I was offered out of pure desperation. And, boy, if you think I'm bad now, you should have heard me then." Ira amiably humphed.

"When I was handed my first paycheck, I knew Jessie and I were going to be okay. I also knew walking to work was getting old. It was time to go get my car and everything else from Sonny's." Voice trailing, Joy sat up and reached through the dark for her glass of wine.

"But, of course, that didn't happen. Not after Sonny got that hospital bill. Did you know charity hospitals send out bills?" It was a rhetorical question meant only to buy time for more wine. "Well, they do. At least JFK Memorial did. And Sonny jumped in my car the day it arrived to come and, um, *give* it to me."

In small towns, tall tales grow like weeds around bad news. And Joy had heard them all. That the rattletrap VW was a piece of junk anyway and it was just Sonny's sorry luck that his own jalopy was up on

blocks that day. That someone had it in for him—
maybe Joy herself?—and boobytrapped it. Why else
hadn't she already claimed her own car? Then there
was the theory that Sonny had loosened the lug nuts
himself. Had known Joy would eventually drive off in
the purple Bug bought with $200 in wedding checks
from her uncles in Florida. Joy herself could easily
imagine how a few lug nuts turned counterclockwise
weeks earlier might be totally forgotten in the face of an
astronomical hospital bill with Sonny Savoy's name all
over it.

"And I've told you the rest. How they said it was a
miracle he didn't spin into any other cars when the
wheel flew off." And how his hand was still wrapped
around that hospital bill when they pulled him out.

"Served the bastard right," Ira said curtly. "Again,
screw Sonny. Go on."

"Is there more wine in that bottle?" Ira obviously
didn't want to hear it, but Joy always thought time
might have smiled upon Sonny one day. Without her
fevered teen-aged manipulations, who knows what the
future could have held. As it was, handsome, sulky
Sonny Savoy was dead at twenty-two, before Jessie
ever met him, so she never missed him. Quida Raye
Perkins made sure of that.

"Mother had tried for years to get pregnant after
me, probably to give Dick a baby he'd believe was
actually his," Joy continued, hearing Ira grunt at
another familiar story. "But, in a rare stroke of medical
acuity, Dr. Bishop had said her ovaries were the size of
an infant's and she'd been lucky to have had one child.
To be perfectly honest, one was more than she usually
acted like she wanted anyway. Until Jessie came

along."

Smiling at happier times flooding back, Joy told Ira about it all, from cabinets stacked with jars of Jessie's favorite Blueberry Buckle to the puppies and tea parties and bulging dress-up bins filled with miniature versions of Quida Raye's favorite honky-tonk outfits. They even had identical teased balls of country-western hair— Jessie's baby fine and dirty blonde, her Grammy's thick as a snarl of brown barbed wire. They were like some newfangled family act zooming around the trailer, Jessie's western fringe flying as her Grammy raced her up and down halls atop that little red riding horse with wheels. Neigh-Neigh.

Wine. Much more wine.

"Thanks," Joy said, reaching for the new bottle Ira brought back. "Anyway, Jessie could get Mother to do anything. That was true the first two years in Louisiana as well as the next three in Kentucky, when we moved to be closer to Grandma and Granddaddy and farther away from the specter of everything with Sonny.

"Then I started working two jobs, and Mother met Doyle, and…well, I suppose Jessie got lost in the shuffle. By the time Mother got sick, Jessie had begun shrieking uncontrollably any time visiting hours were over. Grandma said it was being left at babysitters round the clock. But I was afraid it was something worse. I got it in my head that, like conjoined offspring do, Jessie sensed what I didn't tell her—that the doctors only gave her Grammy months to live. What would one do without the other?" An impossible notion. Joy eventually settled on an equally implausible solution.

"The summer of 1980, when Boo-Boo called to say he knew plenty of stations back in Louisiana paying enough so I'd only have to work one job, I convinced myself that separation was the best thing for Mother and Jessie, the unlikeliest of Siamese twins."

Sitting up, she scooted back to lean against the couch, glass in hand, steadily sipping as she considered—for the first time in two and a half-plus years—this point in her story. The moment when one or two different decisions would have changed absolutely everything.

"Mother told me to go. She said she and Doyle could get loads in and out of Louisiana all the time. I think, as always, she was trying to prove me, the doctors, and everyone else wrong. I'm sure she figured that having Jessie ten hours away would be just what she needed to build herself back up. To show us all.

"So Jessie and I went."

Joy paused, as if standing once again at the threshold of the old house she would rent. The cheapest listing in the want ads of that Louisiana town's small newspaper, it didn't have appliances. It also, to her everlasting regret, did not have air conditioning. Boo-Boo was with her as she walked through the four shabby rooms and flipped on the big attic fan, which shook every board as it rattled to life. What she told Boo-Boo that day she repeated to Ira over two and a half years later, still trying to convince herself.

"An attic fan didn't seem so bad. My grandparents have one just like it, and it's kept things bearable for fifty years."

What Boo-Boo said that day and she repeated to Ira years later was, " 'That's Kentucky, and this is Louisiana. Kryptonite melts here.' He wanted me to find a better place to rent. Like I could afford that."

Calculating the true costs of that decision once again struck Joy as easy as pi. Endless.

"How I wish I would've listened to him," she said softly. "Though, again, my grandparents have an attic fan just like it."

In reality, that monstrosity had terrified Joy throughout her childhood. An abominable sight, the device was comprised of massive blades bolted into place beside the attic steps. Beneath it, a louvered covering slid open when the fan was on and vibrating her grandparents' entire house. But above it, in the attic, those solid steel shanks were protected by nothing at all.

Joy drained her glass, wishing her story was similarly spent. Because, before the worst, came the best. Six months of working just one job, seeing her mother rally and—best of all—finally getting to know her adorable five-year-old after years of nonstop babysitters. The utter happiness of those six months was every bit as torturous as any other detail Ira expected her to recall.

"Fast forward to Christmas week," she said at last, feeling him nod in the dark. "Mother had been at our house again, looking almost good as new. She said Doyle had some long-distance runs she was going on, but I could give Jessie whatever I'd bought her and we'd 'have Santy' when she got back, probably after New Year's. Then she was gone in a puff of smoke and a cloud of truck fumes.

"So Jessie unwrapped her first round of gifts. Then, Sunday night, we did what we did every year after Christmas—we went through all her old toys, the raggedy dolls and sad stuffed animals, making a pile to donate so we'd have room for the mounds more I knew Mother had for her.

"And off in the corner, missing most of its mane and all its gold trim, was that little red riding horse. Jessie's Neigh-Neigh."

Saying the name of her daughter's first and favorite toy all but stopped her cold. Years later, still trying to make sense of what she did that night, Joy told herself that, like stacking rings and building blocks, Neigh-Neigh was a toddler toy, one that was never touched anymore unless Joy herself tripped over it. Too small for Jessie to ride and too large for Joy to save, she made a split-second decision that shaped the rest of eternity.

A few long moments passed before Ira said, "And?" After more wine, she racked her brain for a better answer. But there was only the reprehensible truth.

"And so I told Jessie it was probably time we donated Neigh-Neigh, too."

Again, she fell silent. As the rain poured outside, she once again saw the waterfall of emotions that had cascaded across Jessie's upturned, incredulous face. From an infant's silent cry to a preschooler's imminent tantrum to, finally, "Okay, Mama." A big girl's bravado.

Big girl. Five-and-a-half isn't big at all. It's small. So small it can easily fit inside the average human heart for more years than Joy Savoy could ever have a chance to count. How had she not realized that then? How had she not known so much more, like where she *should* have stashed those old toys till she could haul them away? Anywhere other than the place she chose.

"Since our house was so cramped, the attic seemed

217

the best place. Out of sight, out of mind, right?" Joy continued, barely above a whisper. "So I pulled the ladder out of the ceiling, tapped the wall plate in the hall, and told Jessie what my grandmother had told me a thousand times—'Left switch light, right switch fan. Left light. Right fan.' "

She didn't think it was too difficult a lesson for a bright kindergartner to grasp. Left light. Left light. *Left light!*

"Jessie and I carried the old toys upstairs. And the last sight I saw before going back down was that little red riding horse. It was next to the box nearest the…" Joy swallowed, unable to continue.

"Attic fan," Ira offered, propping himself up on an elbow, recognizing another familiar point in her story.

"That's right," Joy mumbled. " Anyway, I tucked her in, then collapsed on the couch. The local rock station was airing a memorial to John Lennon, dead for twenty days. And I must have dozed off, because the next thing I vaguely recall is hearing a palpitating bass hum that only lulled me deeper asleep. I might have heard some creaks, too, but they were small noises. Tiny sounds I probably wouldn't have paid attention to even if I'd been awake."

Years later, however, no matter how tightly she squeezed her eyes shut, trying to blind herself to the unspeakable sights stenciled across the rest of her tomorrows, she had no trouble whatsoever matching the squeaking of a set of spring-loaded steps to a little girl going up, up, up.

Then there was another sound, one so wholly unearthly as to bring with it Joy's first vision of God. He told her to run.

"In an instant, I was in the hallway, under the ladder I had...*forgotten!*...to spring back into the ceiling. My God! *My God!*"

Ira refilled her wine glass and, five or ten minutes later, she spoke again.

"It was days before the Florida State Police tracked Mother and Doyle down at a truck stop outside of Delray Beach. I'd already been talked into burying Jessie beside a little country church out near Boo-Boo's parents' camp, and I knew with one look at my mother's haggard gray face that I had ripped the heart out of her as surely as I'd left that ladder down."

Casting about for some way to wrap up a story she hoped never to tell again, Joy's desperate mind eventually seized on a musical metaphor. "So you might say I killed my daughter. And now I'm killing my mother." She paused, because she had to. "Softly, with my song."

If Ira caught the tuneful reference, it didn't register. She didn't feel like spelling it out for him, either. Other than obsessing over the man now prone beside her, she hadn't felt like doing much of anything for over two and a half years.

"I'm hardly the only person who's lost a child, you know," she continued, wrapping up loose ends. Like a braid.

After ticking off a long list of country stars who had tragically lost children, from infants to adults, she named the dearly departed one by one, like an incantation. Then she heaved a ragged sigh and said, "It helps, some, to remember them. And, heaven knows, countless others forever memorialized in the hearts of everyone left behind." Jessie Jaye Savoy, she thought.

Age five and a half. Dirty blonde hair and big blue eyes. Good with papier mâché and coloring books. Beloved grandchild of Quida Raye Perkins.

"And that's about it," she said, setting her wine glass down on the coffee table. "You were there. You could probably tell me more than I've told you."

"I didn't realize you noticed," Ira said softly.

"Better you than anything else," she replied, deciding to leave out the rest.

After her Psych 101 class, it was Tanya who suggested Joy must have somehow substituted Ira Everhart for the five stages of grief. That she had staved off immortal despair by opting for obsession over a less appealing mishmash of denial, anger, bargaining, depression, and acceptance.

All Joy knew was Ira's two black eyes were forever attached to the period at the end of her darkest night's death sentence. Dot-dot-dot. Life would...go on. Ira, her dear ellipsis.

Thunder rolled and lightning flashed, and Joy looked into those sloe eyes again. She saw what she saw every time she looked in a mirror. Disappointment. She didn't blame him. She was disappointed in herself, too. Would be till the end of time.

With nothing left to say, they soon wandered off to bed, the storm still raging, the headboard as silent as a wicker headstone behind them.

Chapter 18
"Why Not Me"

Quida Raye Perkins heard her daughter pull into
the driveway Saturday, not Sunday, then watched as she
stayed bent over, petting the animals, far too long. And
she knew success had not been had in New Orleans.

"I just fixed some sammin patties," she said when
Joy stood up and sniffed. "Want a couple? Got some
field peas, mashed taters, vinegar cucumbers, and
biscuits, too."

"Maybe later," Joy muttered, shuffling toward the
bedroom, oblivious to the line dance of living creatures
following her. Hurling two paper bags on the bed,
thinking they may as well be filled with price tags and
empty dreams for all the good any of it did, Joy opened
the closet and kicked her new shoes against the wall.

Locating the twin black scuffs the shoes made so
she could deal with them later, Quida Raye reached for
several wire hangers to clamp between her teeth.
Shaking out, hanging up and admiring each new dress,
she said, "You'll get some good use outta these this
winter. It won't hurt to look sharp for all them singers
droppin' by the studio."

Joy tossed new underthings in a drawer, slammed it
shut, then threw her new purse near the door, making
the dogs run. She couldn't name one country star she'd
met who'd care if she loomed up in flour sacks, let

alone a Gunne Sax. As long as her mic was handy.

"That's all right," Quida Raye said, bobbing her head matter-of-factly. "I didn't lose nuthin' in New Orleans anyway."

Oh, but I just might have, Joy thought, bending down again and pretending to reach for a balled-up pair of socks that had rolled under the bed. As if her disastrous job interview hadn't been bad enough, Ira topped it off by sharing some news of his own after Joy woke up that morning, eyes glued shut, head pounding. He was going to have a white Christmas. In New York. With Dianne. He had, in fact, booked his flight just after she had been kindly, but firmly, shown the radio station's door after her oh-so-cinematic collapse.

"I'm leaving the twenty-third and coming back the twenty-sixth," he said. "I couldn't get any more time off." Joy lay beside him in the crumpled new dress she had fallen asleep in, wondering what she was supposed to say. Too bad? An extra day or two and you could take in Ellis Island and the Empire State Building while falling in love with your estranged wife again?

Ira rolled over and reached for his running shoes, saying he'd fix coffee when he got back. It was a straight shot from the bed to the door, through which she watched him do a little jig. Then she got up, slipped out of her job-interview dress and into jeans and an old high school T-shirt Ira had worn the night before. Shivering, she pulled one of Boo-Boo's worn-out XXL flannel shirts from a bag, then looked around to make sure she wasn't forgetting anything. But all she saw was the short shadow she cast across the ruined bed.

Among the many revelations awaiting Joy Savoy was a perspective on Ira's mental state while she was returning to Avalon on a Saturday for once. As she drove, she did the math—subtracting trailers with purple carpet from wives in New York City—and decided Ira was at the same point her mother had been years earlier, when she'd let her sixteen-year-old daughter get married. Separated was a good word for it. Split. Cleft. Severed. Adrift.

Drifting toward the kitchen, Joy shivered again. "It's freezing in here."

"You'd better get uset to it," Quida Raye warned, reaching for the plate of salmon patties and biscuits she'd left on the stove. "The weatherman says this is gonna be the worst winter we've had in years."

Sure enough, a cold front blew in that night, serving as a portent for the misery yet to come. During the winter of 1983-84, one of the coldest on record in over fifty years, pipes froze, engine blocks froze, people froze. Even worse, all roads heading out of town stayed so impassable in patches that trips to the Crescent City were soon a distant memory.

****

"We've discovered a slight problem with the house Mother rented," Joy announced, adjusting her headphones. "It only has one heater, which is small and in the dining room. The other five rooms are without heat of any kind, not counting the gas oven and four gas burners. So, if I don't show up one morning, let me say it's been *a gas*."

Boo-Boo's eyes were the size of forty-fives when the "on air" light went off, causing Joy to snort and jiggle through the next record. "Don't worry," she told him. "I'm not going to gas myself. Not anytime soon, at least. Besides, I've found two places where I can do something other than shake uncontrollably—in a bathtub filled with blistering hot water, and at work. Since work doesn't wrinkle me up quite as badly, that's my preference."

"Good," Boo-Boo exclaimed, comically exhaling.

"We'll *try* to keep you out of hot water here," WildDog said.

"Thanks. The only problem is getting here. Sally impersonates a puck when so much as the air conditioner is up too high."

"I can always come get you," Boo-Boo offered.

"At his usual oh-dark-thirty," WildDog noted, grinning.

"Thanks anyway. I'd rather sleep in and hitch a ride. I believe I know someone with transport experience and wheels from hell." So this is what it's come to, she realized, kicking the trash can and pretending it was an accident—Ira will soon be flying back into Dianne's arms while I'm at the mercy of a badass bomb imitating a Bradley armored vehicle.

****

As temperatures and Joy's spirits plunged that December, her mother's mood was naturally on the upswing. Quida Raye was always at her best when called upon to conquer anything as daunting as the elements. Morning after frigid morning, her alarm would go off an hour early so she could run out and crank up her car and its brutally effective heater. In addition to nearly melting her vinyl seats, the heater also recycled Quida Raye's cigarette smoke with a vengeance.

"I couldn't help but notice you floated in on a ciggie cloud again today," WildDog observed one morning, adjusting his headphones as Boo-Boo coughed and wheezed on cue.

"That I did," Joy said into her mic. "Because, while I've never smoked, I've *been* smoked. Every morning on the way to work with Mother."

On the iciest days, a skeleton crew, fetched by Vernon and his Bronco, filtered in. Soon, Boo-Boo declared he was also done with dodging amateurs on slick highways. Unfurling a sleeping bag in the dark hall heading to Vernon's office, he slept there during the worst of it, surrounded by duffle bags stuffed with various essentials—including a droopy pair of swim shorts.

"What's *that*?" Joy asked, frowning at the faded brown trunks flopped atop one of the bags. "Dead raccoon?"

"*Au contraire*. That's my trusty swimwear for a Polar Bear Plunge," Boo-Boo exclaimed, eyes asparkle. "If the Little River's ever going to freeze, this is the year. And I'm going to be ready to hop in." Joy studied the tic undulating one side of the previously most steadfast, fuzzy face she had ever seen, and decided it was going to be a long, hard winter for them all.

****

"Here's an idea," Tanya said on the phone that night, back in Pitts for winter break. "Why don't you let Boo-Boo come stay at your place? Your mother could take you both to work. And he could keep you from freezing to death." Sniggering, she added, "You know he's never wanted anything more than to slip between the sheets with you anyway."

"You are a lunatic," Joy announced. "And guess who else is going insane—Boo-Boo! He's planning to jump in the river if any of it freezes."

"That does sound crazy," Tanya agreed, laughing. "Which certainly qualifies him to slip between the sheets with *you*."

****

"I've got an idea," Boo-Boo said the next day as Joy sat and stared at him, trying to determine if he really was nuts enough to swim in the dead of winter, or if he was just carrying out one of his colossal pranks. "Let's throw some weather-related songs into your oldies mix. Like 'If We Make It Through December' or 'Snowbird.' "

Joy scrutinized his satirical grin. "Thanks for those depressing suggestions. One song about daddy getting laid off before Christmas and another about a love who's untrue. Really?" Instead, she found one of her favorite albums, "Urban Cowboy," then rolled back to the board.

He just grinned more. "And your point is?"

"My point is, can we change the subject? What are you doing for Christmas?" Not that she cared. Beyond knowing Ira would be celebrating in the Big Apple, she had no interest in anyone's yuletide festivities. Since 1980, as Boo-Boo well knew, Christmas had been a subject she dealt with only at work. "Grandma Got Run Over by a Reindeer" and that sort of thing.

"Actually," he replied, "I'm going to Ruthie's."

"Huh?" Joy didn't know what she had expected to hear. Maybe something about wallowing in swim trunks on a snowbank somewhere. Anything she might have poked fun at. But going to Ruthie's? For *Christmas*? This sounded serious. This sounded like something she should have seen coming, something that shouldn't be sending a thorny curlicue of…what?—Incredulity? Covetousness? Proprietorship?—spiraling through the churning center of her.

"You're going to *Ruthie's*? For *Christmas*?"

"Yeah." He shrugged. "She's making a big ham, which she knows I love, so she invited me over."

"How does she know you love ham?" Joy demanded, flipping "Urban Cowboy" end over end. What else did Ruthie know? Did she know he loved the Fab Four and *The Big Chill* and floats made with Dr Pepper and chocolate ice cream? Did she know he had a little duckling named Quack-Quack he won at the fair in third grade and slept with till he rolled over on him? Did she know no other girl at Pitts High School would go to the prom with big old Boo-Boo Bailey? No one except Joy. Did she know he hadn't always had this long, black hair and scruffy beard and faded jeans and wrinkled flannel shirt draped across six feet four inches of utter bewilderment currently sprawled in a rolling chair, staring at Joy as if she'd lost her mind.

"She knows I love ham because she's made it for me before," he slowly said.

"*When* did she make ham for you?" Joy bellowed.

"I'm outta here," WildDog announced, holding up his hands in surrender and goose-stepping through the door.

"A couple of times," Boo-Boo answered, leaning back, as if away from a sudden flame. "What's the big deal? It's just Christmas dinner."

"Which *we* could be having together."

"Which *you* never mentioned." Maybe she hadn't. Maybe she would have. If not that year then maybe some other.

"I've had a lot on my mind lately, Boo-Boo, in case you haven't noticed," Joy petulantly reminded him.

"That's where you're wrong. I *have* noticed. And that's why I'm going to Ruthie's for Christmas dinner."

"Go then," she spat, toeing her chair around till her back was to him and "Urban Cowboy" was all but snapped in half in her lap. "See if I care."

"I plan on it," he said. "And, Joy?"

"What?" she yelped, twirling back around just as a smile snaked across his furry face.

"Thanks for caring."

Before she could stop herself, she threw the album straight at his head.

"He ducked but the corner caught him above his left eye," Joy told Tanya that night.

"Trying to make sure he's still blinded by love, huh?" Tanya howled.

"Whatever *that* means."

"You know what it means," Tanya said, still laughing.

"No, I'm afraid I don't," Joy snapped, deciding that brutal winter was driving everyone out of their ever-loving minds.

"Well I'm not going to spell it out for you," Tanya said. "Speaking of *luv,* have you heard from Allah lately?"

"He called to remind me he's going to New York tomorrow." Flat on her back in bed, sudden tears slid toward Joy's scalp, detouring around the receiver clamped to her ear. So what if Boo-Boo was spending Christmas with Ruthie. He could move his ice-swimming self in with her and eat ham three times a day for all Joy cared. Ditto for Ira. Maybe Dianne was also fixing a juicy ham. Maybe that was the big attraction. Maybe they could all just take their hams and go gnaw on them in hell for all she cared.

"Don't you wish he'd get iced in or, I don't know, be involved in some kind of minor motorcycle accident? Anything that would keep his ass in New Orleans?"

"A lot of good wishing's going to do. As Mother always says…" Joy began, smiling and waiting for Tanya to join her in a favorite Quida Raye colloquialism.

"Wish in one hand," they drawled in unison, "and shit in the other, and see which one fills up fastest."

****

"Why don't you go to Pitts with me today?" Quida Raye asked the next morning. "The weatherman says another storm's comin', but we could scoot down to the Wagon Wheel's big Christmas party and get back 'fore it hits. Who knows, you might even meet someone."

"No, thank you," Joy said, reaching for another cinnamon roll. Meet someone. It was official. Everyone around her *was* going off the deep end.

That afternoon, she discovered her mother's Noel activities had not been nipped in the buds of the little Norfolk pine she had lovingly decorated to place beside Jessie's headstone. For there on the table next to it, comfortably close to the heater, sat their own three-foot-tall spruce. And all around it was a small mountain of gaily wrapped packages. An entire disability check in snowflakes and sleighs. Joy glared at her mother, huddled like Bob Cratchit by the heater. Then she shot off to her bedroom, slammed the door, and toppled onto

the bed, snorting icy musket balls into thin, gray air.
Cartoon balloons packed with penciled-in blasphemies.
Her best male friend in the world had gone and gotten a
girlfriend. The man of her dreams would soon have his
estranged wife on his lap, asking her what she wants
from Santa. And her mother was Mrs. Damn Claus.
Merry frigging Christmas.

Thirty minutes later, Quida Raye stuck her head in
to say she was leaving. Joy nodded so she'd go, which
she did, shimmying out the door with the Norfolk pine
ajingle with tinkling miniature ornaments. Joy
continued lying on the bed till she was nearly frozen.
Then she filled the bathtub with scalding hot water and
lay in there. Still. Very still. So still she could see her
heartbeat rippling through the steam. Throb. Throb.
Maybe it'll just. Stop. One of these days. Then, when
the water cooled to gray, she wrapped herself in a
terrycloth robe and stretched out beside the heater in the
dining room until she knew Ira was on his plane.
Scooting closer to the glowing ceramic plates, gazing
up at the branches of the little Christmas tree on the
table, she wondered how her mother could possibly
manage to be so damned jolly.

****

The next morning, she awoke stiff and cold, still on
the floor. Initially, she was only aware of how much her
backbone hurt, as if each vertebra had come unlinked.
Then sweet silence washed over her. There was no one
slamming around in the kitchen or running a chain saw
or belt sander. Nothing shattering the stillness of a
frosty Christmas Eve morn. She carefully rolled onto
her back, feeling bones click together, and almost as
painful, her last memories from the previous evening

similarly slip into place. Whatever time it was, Ira was almost certainly still in bed next to his wife who, being a student, surely couldn't have afforded a two-bedroom anything in New York City. Rolling on her side and curling up again, Joy concentrated on trying to guess what time it was, any subject other than Ira first thing in the morning.

Cole, illegally located on the table beside her mother's Christmas tree, yawned and stretched, suggesting Joy hadn't slept in too long. The dogs weren't even up yet, and their nails were always scritching across the hardwoods long before she cared to hear them. Just then, however, a loud knock sent the cat flying and the dogs ripping through the house, baying, "Murderer! Robber! Escaped psychopath! Thief!"

Clutching her robe around her, Joy crept to a window, peeked through the curtain, and gasped. Flinging the door open and getting hit with an Arctic blast, she said, "What are you doing here? Brrr!"

"Just dropping by to wish you a Merry Christmas," Boo-Boo said, hugging his leather jacket closer. "I wanted to catch you in case you're heading out of town."

"I'm not going anywhere. Come in before we both freeze to death." Quickly closing the door behind him, she said, "Give me your coat and come sit by the heater. I'll make us some coffee."

"Okay," he said, grinning and slinking oddly sideways out of his jacket, which he gently folded over and handed to her in a somewhat complicated pile.

"Be careful," he said, stifling a snicker.

"Why?" Joy asked as the coat started wiggling and

she all but sent it soaring.

"Don't drop it!" He laughed and said, cradling his arms underneath.

"What is it?" she yelped as a tiny black-and-white head popped out from a sleeve.

"A Shih Tzu," he announced, gleefully digging the entire puppy out of its black-leather package. "A Chinese breed. Happy and hardy. Full of character. Pleasant disposition. Merry Christmas!"

"Boo-Boo, Mother's going to skin you alive!"

"I know, but I couldn't resist her," he said, putting what looked like a Holstein tennis ball with legs down for Sugar Pie, Cole, and Annie to sniff and nudge. "Besides, Sugar Pie's getting on up there. You never know when you're gonna need another little black-and-white dog running around."

"Yeah, and till then we'll have the Bronx Zoo." Bronx, Joy groaned, wishing any other non-Ira-specific menagerie had blathered out. San Diego Zoo. Old McDonald's Farm.

Boo-Boo just grinned. "I'm sure it'll all work out."

****

Quida Raye walked in later and nearly climbed the wall. *"What's that?"* she shrilled in her best it's-a-mouse screak.

"It's a puppy," Joy said, bringing her back to her senses.

"Whose?"

"Joy's," Boo-Boo sheepishly said, getting up from Ruthie's parents' former couch. "And/or yours. Merry Christmas."

"Merry Christmas yore own dern self, Robert! That's just what we need. Another dang dawg to feed.

232

That last hound you gave Joy Faye's about to eat us outta house and home."

"I know. I'm sorry. What can I do to make it up to you?"

Quida Raye just stood there, hands on her skinny hips, scrutinizing the ball of fluff gnawing the toe of her tennis shoe. "I s'pose you could go get some newspapers and help me make it a bed. What's that over yore eye?"

Reaching up to touch the inch-long gash, he winked at Joy and said, "Cut myself shaving. Where are the papers?"

****

Sunday, Joy carved a turkey she didn't know they had and opened gifts she didn't know she'd want—a coat, scarves, mittens, stocking cap. Her mother, with a silver garland draped around her neck and a red glass ball perched like a cardinal in her high, brown hair, danced around the kitchen, mashing up some of Sugar Pie's canned food in a saucer of milk and scooting it close to the heater for the puppy.

Later, Joy was making a turkey, cranberry sauce, and cream cheese sandwich, humming "Jingle Bell Rock," when the phone rang.

"Doodness," her mother told the startled puppy in her lap. "Who could dat be?"

"Hello?" Joy said, hopeful.

"Merry Kiss My Ass," Tanya said.

"And a Happy New Steer to you," Joy replied, trying not to sound disappointed. "Speaking of mammals, I got a new puppy."

"Who from? Surely not Mr. Huddled Masses Yearning to Breathe Free."

"Correct," Joy said, watching her mother play with the frolicsome lump in her lap.

"Which leaves Boo-Boo, because I *know* it wasn't Quida Raye."

"Right again," Joy said. "Any ideas for a name? She's the cutest little thing. Black and white. The size of a roller-skate pom-pom."

"I don't know. How about 'Ode to Joy.' " Then a bawdy laugh began building. "Or, knowing what Boo-Boo surely hopes all these dang dogs are gonna get him some day, 'Joy Juice.' "

Joy groaned, as much to discourage further tangents along those lines as from the sudden reminder of Ira's own off-colored puns—Joy Ride. Radar Luv.

****

Monday, Joy reached for a cassette and turned to Boo-Boo.

"You wouldn't happen to have a Chinese-English dictionary underneath those droopy old swim drawers, would you?"

"Hmm," Boo-Boo murmured before wandering off to dig around his duffel bags.

"You've got to be shittin' me," WildDog declared when he walked back in brandishing a slim paperback. "Nerd."

"At your service," Boo-Boo said to Joy, bowing so his posterior was in WildDog's face, to whom he addressed an over-the-shoulder comment. "And *you* can kiss my hairy ass."

"I'll *kick* your hairy ass," WildDog hawed and said, rolling his chair back and doing exactly that.

Pretending to fall into Joy's lap, Boo-Boo grabbed each side of her own rolling chair and shoved her halfway across the studio, laughing and spinning her round and round.

"Whee!" she said, feeling hot breath in her ear, black hair against her face, thick arms on each side of her. "Whee!"

"Excuse me, ma'am, but is this guy bothering you?" WildDog officiously asked, standing up and shuffling lawman-like up to them. "'Cause, if he is, I'll kick his ass some more."

Boo-Boo jerked up and wheeled around, causing WildDog to drop his hand from his imaginary holster, squeal like a girl, and take off running through the small studio, Boo-Boo hot on his heels. Giggling and dodging them, Joy watched as a combined total of twelve-and-a-half feet of loping maleness nearly sent the needle through "Love Is On A Roll." Watching Boo-Boo's flannel fly, seeing it flip up to reveal a hint of fuzzy midriff, noticing his faded jeans tug against burly thighs before Vernon appeared and both men hilariously stopped mid-lurch, as if playing freeze tag, she was shocked as a silent answer to WildDog's question burbled up past the buffoonery in Studio A.

Why, yes, I *do* believe this guy might be bothering me.

****

That afternoon, still unaccountably chipper, Joy skipped out of the office, skidded across the parking lot, and slid into the Barge-mobile, where her mother was waiting for action like a smoldering, bubble-helmeted Red Baron.

"I've got a name for the puppy," she announced. "Leida Ai. I think it's Chinese for Radar Love." Quida Raye just stared at her daughter.

"Shih Tzus are Chinese dogs," Joy explained.

"A *shit zoo*! Is that what that thang is?" Quida Raye began to vibrate. Soon, she was wobbling all over the front seat, convulsed. Yanking it into "D," she whiplashed them across the Little River Bridge and into Ferndale, whooping all the while. Then she parked, marched into the house, and, still cackling, glared at the whimpering puppy in the clothes basket pulled up close to the heater.

"Shut up and lay down, Radar," she yapped. Then she tossed a couple of Christmas chocolates to the puppy, who Joy was surprised to see had a sweet tooth to rival her mother's.

Chapter 19
"Your Cheatin' Heart"

Trooper First Class Donis Wayne Broussard was on his way back to Troop Q headquarters after another productive Friday running radar. That afternoon, he had been parked south of Avalon on U.S. 71, stopping plenty of partiers breaking their necks to get to New Orleans. Mardi Gras parades always promised a steady stream of speeders. And Broussard, a South Louisiana native, knew this was the weekend for, among other unbridled debauchery, the Krewes of Choctaw and Pontchartrain. His ticket book was all but smoking.

****

"Hope you don't mind that I'm sneaking out early," Joy told Boo-Boo. "I thought I'd take advantage of the halfway decent weather and slip out of town."

"No problem," he said, waving her on. "If Vernon says anything, I'll remind him of all the remotes we've been doing. Not to mention the Possum's concert. Go. You've earned it."

"What about me, boss?" WildDog mewled pitifully. "Have I earned some time off, too?"

"All you've earned is my size fourteen boot up your..." Joy slid out of the studio as they started wrestling again, just the kind of ruckus that always got Vernon's attention.

She had finally decided to get to the bottom of

what Ira had done over Christmas in New York, not to mention whatever it was that had been claiming so much of his attention since. Regarding Dianne, all Joy had received so far was a curt report that they had discussed terms of their separation. But, as the ground thawed and winter relaxed its hold on Louisiana, she sensed something had similarly begun breaking loose inside Ira, too. Their phone calls had become more sporadic. And, when he *did* call, he spent most of the time complaining about work or living alone. Yes, a trip to the Crescent City was long past due, and she had been preparing for days.

The pot of chili was in the fridge at home. New tops had been purchased and faded jeans washed. And, most importantly, hours spent haunting the perfume counters of Avalon's upscale department stores had finally paid off.

"I'm looking for the smell of 'don't go,' " she had told a saleslady, who took one look at her and called in reinforcements. Eventually, Joy settled on a dove-shaped bottle that cost more than she used to make in a week.

"What's this?" her mother asked when Joy careened into the driveway and tore through the house, snatching up everything as quickly as possible so she could beat the Mardi Gras traffic.

"It's two weeks' worth of groceries."

"Humph," she said. Plucking the little glass dove off the bed, she popped the beaked top off, sniffed it, and appreciatively rearranged her face. An Eau de Door-to-Door woman from way back, Quida Raye had stuck to her favorite floral scent through Dick and up to Doyle. Joy had also dealt in L'Direct Sales. Sonny had been pinch-penny perfume. Ira was two weeks' worth of groceries.

"That's a purdy shirt," her mother said.

"Thanks," Joy said, doing some deep-knee bends to stretch out her jeans. "Stop fixing anything other than lean meats and fresh veggies 'cause I'm going on a diet Monday."

"Ha!" her mother yawped. Plugging the head back on the perfume bottle, she watched Joy run the chili out to the car, then hustle in again to get her bags and scratch the dogs' heads before bounding back down the stairs. It was the fastest she'd seen her move since she hit a patch of ice and skidded off the porch that winter. Seconds later, her little black car was out of sight.

****

After zipping in to a nearby Park 'n' Rob to fill up and grab a snack for the road, Joy was tearing past the turnoff for Happenstance Plantation, reaching for the bag of chips, when, through a mist just beginning to fall, a familiar brown hulk materialized alongside the road. Slamming on her brakes and swerving in front of the Barge-mobile, she wondered what could have possibly made Quida Raye ride like the wind till she knew Joy couldn't be in front of her.

Through the light rain, her mother came running. Wordlessly, she held out her hand. In it was a sort of baton being passed from one who knew far too much to one who hadn't learned quite enough just yet. Joy reached out and took the little glass dove.

"You left it on the bed," her mother said, backing up and motioning for her to go on.

How tiny she is, Joy thought, adjusting the rearview mirror and pulling away. How much weight she's lost. I won't leave you anymore, Mama. I won't.

But even as Joy Savoy opened the chips and resumed her race to the boot tip of Louisiana, she knew she was only kidding herself about deciding when to stay. And when to go, go, go.

****

After being delayed by a report of unusual activity near an abandoned warehouse, Trooper First Class Broussard was once again heading north on 71. Glancing at his watch, wondering if he had time to pick up a king cake, he turned his eyes back to the road just as a black streak shot past like a cannonball.

Joy Savoy had never been stopped—while driving—in her entire life. As the blood drained from her brain at the sight of blue lights in the rearview mirror, she jerkily pulled off the road and fumbled for her wallet, spilling the contents of her purse and the bag of chips around the pot of chili. Finally, license in hand, she weakly rolled down her window, outside of which a long, lean lawman was already standing, staring at her agog.

"It's about time you pulled over, Miz Savoy. I've been behind you for nearly two miles," Broussard exclaimed, grinning at the shock the sound of her name produced. "You don't recognize me, do you?"

Joy's rattled mind seized only on the melee in the Wagon Wheel's parking lot that May, when Tanya had ensured neither of them left in good standing with any members of the Louisiana State Police.

"Trooper First Class Broussard?" he said. "Your mother ran me off the road last summer on the Pitts Highway? I believe an attempted bribe was involved?"

"Oh, that's right," Joy said, emitting a squeak of a

laugh. "Sorry again."

"That's okay. Kept me on my toes. And guess what?" Broussard asked, smile splitting his tanned, chiseled face.

Joy smiled back, not quite believing her first traffic stop had snared this long, tall, genial trooper. "What?"

"I've become one of your biggest fans."

"Really?" Joy wondered if she should be worried or flattered.

"Your mother's quite a character."

"That she is," Joy agreed as a truck slapped past on the wet highway. "Am I far enough off the road? You seem awfully close to traffic, and I'm not sure how long this will all take." She waved at his ticket book.

"You're good," Broussard said. "Tell you what, if you dedicate a song to *my* mother, we'll just call this your lucky day."

Joy blinked. "You mean you're not giving me a ticket?"

"Do you realize how fast you were going?" he asked, censoriously dipping his cleft chin. "Truth is, I might have to take you into custody if I wrote you up. And I'm rolling off shift if I can ever make it back to town."

"Goodness! I didn't realize this old thing could go that fast."

"Oh, it can," Broussard said, nodding and recalling the scores he had stopped. Most, just like this one, with some lovely young thing behind the wheel. "What are you in such a hurry for?"

"Nothing really," she said, suspecting truer words had never been spoken.

"Slow down and arrive alive then. And bring me

back some beads." Winking, he tipped his Smokey the Bear hat and stepped away from her window.

"Will do." Joy watched a few drops of rain drip off his brim, trickling past a pair of the clearest glade-green eyes she had ever seen. Seeing his grin widen, his neatly trimmed head playfully cock to one side, she decided she was nowhere near ready for this state trooper to keep on walking.

"Wait," she said. "What song do you want me to play for your mom?"

"Hmm," he murmured, tapping a fingertip against his full, broody lips. "Why don't I call the station Monday morning, and we'll toss around some ideas. Make a few plans. Maybe see each other again, under less official circumstances?"

"Sounds wonderful," Joy proclaimed, giddy at the very prospect. She in fact thought of little else the rest of that aromatic weekend. That and her new goal of collecting unattractive qualities about Ira to wrap like a tourniquet around her heart. The cigar film that fuzzed his tongue. His bushy eyebrows, hairy toes, dirty mouth. The way he carried around a bag of Mardi Gras gewgaws during their one trip downtown, asking every well-endowed reveler they passed to show him her boobs for some beads.

She checked to make sure Dianne's photo was still enshrined on his mantel, which it was. She decided to stop pretending his pointed comments about her wardrobe—"Where have you been? A taping of 'Hee Haw?' "—didn't sting, because they did. And she was guaranteed to never forget the fact that his headboard still had not been bolted to his bed. When she sat down and heard it *thump* the wall and only *tap* it when he joined her, she said, "Why did it do that? *Thump* with me and *tap* with you?"

"Because you're fat and I'm not," Ira replied. While he laughed and apologetically reached for her, she yanked away and huffed off to the scratchy sofa, only mildly disappointed when he didn't come and try to change her mind.

****

"Kick his ass to the trash," Tanya yodeled when Joy called Sunday. "Mr. Hot-to-Trot Trooper evidently didn't think he'd stopped Big Mama Thornton. If you ever go back to New Orleans, Joy, I swear to God I'm driving down there and dragging you back by your hair." Then she chortled and added, "Maybe I'll speed, too, so *I* can arrange a little trade with a hunky trooper."

The next day at work, Joy rehashed her weekend adventures for Boo-Boo and WildDog, barely finishing before the phone line lit up. As soon as she heard her caller's deep Cajun drawl, she anxiously motioned to them to keep running the show, then spent forty-five minutes in the corner, whispering and giggling and making plans to meet Trooper First Class Donis Wayne Broussard—"Call me Donis"—behind an old abandoned warehouse after work.

"My roommate will be back at my place," he explained. "And your mother will be at yours, so…"

Later, when she played his request, "Mama He's Crazy," she tingled for a full three minutes and fourteen seconds.

"Do either of you believe in destiny?" she gushed.

"I most certainly do," Boo-Boo declared. "For instance, I believe it's mine to be driven absolutely insane by details of your incessant love life for the rest of gotdamned eternity."

Stunned, Joy's head rocked backward. "What does *that* mean?"

"That means," WildDog replied, "he's jealous."

Boo-Boo got up, walked over to WildDog and punched him in the shoulder so hard his chair spun completely around and his baseball cap nearly flew off.

"*What the hell?*" WildDog yelled, grabbing his arm with one hand and his cap with the other. "I was only kidding, asshole."

"Me too," Boo-Boo said, turning around and stomping out of the studio.

"What's crawled up *his* ass," WildDog crabbed, rubbing his shoulder.

Joy shrugged. "Who knows. How about you, Dawg? Do you believe in destiny? It just feels like getting pulled over by Donis was, I don't know, meant to be."

"The state trooper's name is Donis?" WildDog asked, gingerly rolling his shoulder, making sure nothing was broken. "Donis Broussard?"

"Uh-huh. You know him?" The longer WildDog took to respond, the more something that felt like alarm took a slew-footed walk down Joy's spine.

"I might know *of* him," he finally began. "I went out with a girl once who used to date a state trooper named Donis Broussard. Maybe it's not the same guy, but *that* Donis Broussard always suggested they meet way out in the country, behind fire towers and empty old shacks and such. He claimed he had a roommate back at his place."

Joy's heart sank.

"Then she found out why they needed to sneak

around," he said, preemptively rolling his chair across the room. "What he really had was a wife and four little kids—Don't hit me!"

To apologize for wrecking her new crush, WildDog virtually finished Joy's shift that day. She in fact reached for the mic only once more, making some halfhearted comment about her mother grocery shopping to buy her a set of encyclopedias.

"One volume with every five-dollar purchase," she said anemically. "And she only has one to go. Any of you need groceries? If so, call me. One-eight-hundred-lady-bug. WildDog delivers."

"He also fetches. Watch," Boo-Boo said, walking back in the studio and pretending to snatch at WildDog's cap, a playful amends.

Yanking his head away and rolling off in his chair again so he could remain securely behatted, WildDog cackled. "Asshole. If you don't want Joy dating a state trooper, just tell her."

"I don't think Joy should date anyone," Boo-Boo said, flopping into his own chair and spinning around to stare matter-of-factly at her confounded face. "Give it a rest already."

"Spoken like a true eunuch," WildDog said, screaming like a goat when Boo-Boo stood up again.

****

When the phone rang near bedtime, Joy had long since finished her supper of cornbread and white beans topped with diced green onions. It was the sharp fog of those green onions ricocheting off the receiver, in fact, that forever attached the evening's menu to other, far more consequential, memories from that unforgettable call.

Ira Everhart, former meanest reporter in Central Louisiana, wanted her to know he'd been informed his job in New Orleans was on the line. Could this day possibly suck any more, Joy wondered, pulling the phone into her room and collapsing on the bed.

"What did they say?"

"They said I'm not 'performing' as well as they had expected. They want to know if something about my personal life is distracting me. Fuck. I don't even *have* a personal life. Did I put it down and forget it somewhere? Did it get in a car and drive to fucking New York?

"I know," he continued, mocking now. "It's still in Avalon. Maybe I should come back up there. Move you off Crayon Road and into a place on the right side of the river. Settle down. Have a few kids. Play daddy. Would you like that? Would you?"

His dark, singsong tone lifted the hair on Joy's arms. He was finally saying all the right words. So why did they sound so wrong?

"I *would* like that," she weakly said.

"You would?" he asked, goading now. "Here's what I'll do, then. I'll tell Herb to take this job and shove it. Then I'll crawl back to Vernon and beg for my old job back. You and I can get a cabin in the woods. Raise some chickens and kids. Do like your people in Kentucky and make a little moonshine. That doesn't sound so bad, does it?" Joy shook her head.

"So what the hell," he snarled. "Why don't we just get married?"

Though she heard the taunt in his voice, all that lodged in her soul were the six words he had just spoken.

Why don't we just get married?

In total shock, Joy Savoy did something she rarely ever did. She said nothing at all. Ira didn't say anything, either. In the sudden silence, sprawled across her bed in his old high-school T-shirt, she wondered if her particular brand of neurosis had progressed to the point where she was now hearing voices, and they were saying all the sweet words she had always wanted them to say.

Why don't we just get married?

Just in case wild exhilaration wasn't the appropriate response, Joy opened her mouth and, to hours-old green onion reek, feebly requested clarification. "Wait. Do you really mean it?"

Then, in a voice as cold as distant graves, Ira said, "What the hell do *you* think, Joy? I'm not even divorced. I can't fucking marry anyone. Not you. Not anyone."

Not me.

Not *anyone*?

Who else was there?

Two hundred miles and Ma Bell away, Joy Savoy began suspecting she had already been telegraphed some sort of answer. Feeling like she might be ill, she sat up in bed, swallowed, and swallowed again. But the question burned like green onions in her throat.

"What do you mean 'not anyone'?" she finally asked. "Who else is there?"

Then Ira Everhart, the man whose two black eyes punctuated her darkest night…were her only hope, said, "I guess there's something else I should have mentioned this weekend."

Bits and pieces began streaking through the sudden

Kathy Des Jardins

darkness like falling stars. "Advertising department… young… blonde…. What the fuck's wrong with me? No wonder my job's on the line."

And, in a yellow house on the wrong side of the river, on a night when untold happiness had seemed not so terribly far away, Joy Savoy's heart broke, as they say hearts do.

"Anyway," Ira finally said, ready to get off the phone. "You left some barrettes and bobby pins and things here you need to come by and get sometime."

****

Once she could speak on air without a hitch in her voice and a box of tissues by her side, once her mother, Sugar Pie, and Radar had been driven to Kentucky, fueled by a full tank of her intolerable despair, once the phone stopped ringing and Boo-Boo ran through the million new ideas he suddenly had for her show, she decided she might never go and get her barrettes and bobby pins and things. At least not until Ira's little fling had run its course.

****

In May, a letter arrived from New Orleans. A single line written on a full sheet of paper. "What's happened to you?"

Well, Joy thought, folding the paper back up, I've moved on.

"Literally," she said out loud, reaching for the keys to the one-bedroom house she had just rented. It was back on the right side of the river. Conveniently located near several twenty-four-hour businesses and some outgoing neighbors. And, best of all, it was barely big enough for one person, let alone anyone else who'd never really been there in the first place.

248

Chapter 20
"Broken Lady"

"Did you honestly just move across the street from a *whorehouse*?" Tanya blared.

"Technically, the Sleepy Time Motor Lodge is a block away," Joy said, holding the phone away from her ear. "My across-the-street neighbors are Up Yours Bess and Fuck You Bubba."

"Yeah," Tanya said, not amused. "Lovely couple. I just got off the phone with Boo-Boo, and he mentioned them, too. Don't cluck your tongue at me. He also told me about the Stop 'n' Rob on one corner and the twenty-four-hour fried-chicken-slash-drug-dealer joint on the other. The Monopoly board of your new neighborhood sounds dandy, Joy. Let's just hope you've got a stack of get-out-of-jail cards."

"You stole that from Boo-Boo," Joy said, recognizing the observation from many rude comments made by her surly three-person moving crew earlier. "A whorehouse *and* heroin dealers," Boo-Boo had chirped. "I see you made good use of the Avalon Chamber of Commerce's relocation guide."

"Anyway, at least one of Mother's wild hairs worked out for once," she told Tanya, flat on her aching back in the bed Boo-Boo had insisted on assembling and making before he, WildDog, and Ruthie left. "There isn't one spot in my new place big enough for that original colossal couch. Or much else. I sent a truckload of furniture to Ruthie's parents as a belated apology."

"Boo-Boo mentioned how microscopic the place is," Tanya said. "He said outhouses are bigger. What we both want to know is where's your mother going to sleep when she comes back."

"I've got just the bright blue, four-foot-long spot. Talk about making your bed and sleeping in it." Joy grinned. "Assuming she doesn't get the hint and find her own place."

"Assuming you're still alive."

"So I rented a small house near a thriving business district," Joy groaned and said. "Big deal. I also happen to be moving from a place within shouting distance of the Institute for the Criminally Insane. Between the two, I'll take fried chicken and sharp-dressed neighbors any day."

"Up Yours Bess and Fuck You Bubba don't sound too sharp-dressed," Tanya observed. "Boo-Boo said they look like Big Bertha and Rasputin, back from the dead."

"Ah, yes. Them." Joy rolled on her side, wincing as much from back spasms as memories of the pitched battle that had raged all moving day long inside the trailer across the dirt drive from her new cottage.

"Jeez, the Titanic going down couldn't have made more noise," Boo-Boo remarked when they finished and Joy walked them outside. Nodding toward the trailer, all but rocking on its cinderblock stacks, he threw the last few boxes in the back of his truck and said, "Why don't you hop in, too, and ride away with us?"

Just then, an ice chest crashed through the trailer's front window, sending glass and beer cans flying across the yard and Ruthie very nearly under the truck.

"Yeah, Joy. Come on," she begged. "Now!"

Having spent the day valiantly suppressing countless Sonny-shaped flashbacks, Joy forced herself to smile and say, "I'll be *fine*."

WildDog calmly reached into the truck and pulled out a slim paper bag, soon shucked. "Some liquid courage might help," he said, screwing the top off a bottle of strawberry wine. "Sorry, your convenience store doesn't carry champagne."

The four of them passed around the bottle, mumbling "Cheers" and listening to more glass break and doors slam inside the trailer until the bedlam suddenly, eerily, ceased.

"Ever been in the eye of a tornado?" Boo-Boo asked, wiping his mouth on his shirtsleeve. Then they all slowly turned to behold the trailer, from which three words soon shattered the silence—"Fuck. You. Bubba!"—followed by a dark, hairy body flying out the back door, landing in the yard in a motionless, fuzzy lump.

"Is he *dead*?" Ruthie gasped, triggering hushed but intense debate over who should go and check for a pulse. Boo-Boo was halfway across the dirt drive when a big blonde hove out the same door and up to the woolly mound, which lifted his head.

"Up. Yours. Bess," he squeaked, earning himself a kick in the liver before the blonde teetered around and galumphed back inside without noticing the foursome draining a bottle across the way.

"WildDog said they probably only act like that the

first of every month, when the checks arrive," Joy told Tanya. "If his own family and friends are any indication, he said they'll be quiet as church mice the rest of the month."

Tanya was having none of it. "What are you trying to do? Get yourself attacked so Ira Everbarf will drop his hot little honey and come to your rescue?"

"I'm hanging up now."

"Oh, I know. You're waiting for that hunky state trooper to leave his wife and dozen kids and save you."

"Goodbye," Joy said.

"Don't you hang up."

But she did, only to have to hear it all again the next morning.

"You haven't returned the keys to your old place yet, have you?" Boo-Boo asked, drumming his fingers on the arm of his rolling chair. "You could always stay in Ferndale and take your chances with the John Wayne Gacy wannabes. At least they keep 'em medicated over there. Whatever Up Yours Bess and Fuck You Bubba are on, I doubt if it's legal."

"Don't you know every couple bickers?" Joy smirked. "Or are you and Ruthie the exception?" Since the Christmas ham incident, Joy had taken special delight in ribbing him about Ruthie, if for no other reason than to make him finally admit they were an item. But all he ever said was, "Now, Joy."

"Now, Joy. I don't think what Up Yours Bess and Fuck You Bubba did *all day yesterday* sounded much like 'bickering.' Unless you call what the North and South Vietnamese did 'squabbling,' during which we happened to lose fifty-eight thousand men."

"Can we work here?" she asked. "Make yourself

useful for a change and find 'You Never Miss a Real Good Thing (Till He Says Goodbye).' "

"Are you sure? We've been playing 'Don't It Make My Brown Eyes Blue' pretty heavily," Boo-Boo said.

"And 'I'll Get Over You,' " WildDog added.

"And all her thousand other he-done-me-wrong songs," Boo-Boo noted.

"So I'm on a Crystal kick. Humor me, please."

Indeed, after work, she put "Crystal" on the stereo and looked around at what probably was the smallest habitable house ever. Aside from the admittedly sketchy neighborhood, it was exactly what she needed. A wee bit of a spot she could curl up in, play her records, and think her new, blue thoughts without a lot of square footage—or her mother—getting in the way.

****

"I didn't realize BellSouth hadn't run lines to Kentucky yet," Joy said weeks later, holding the door open for her mother and her two-dog entourage.

"I didn't wanna call and wake you up," Quida Raye said, putting her bags and the directions to Joy's house on the kitchen table. "Though Lord knows how you sleep through all this commotion." Through the trees, Joy noticed a familiar red-and-blue glow.

"There are several twenty-four-hour businesses on the main drag," she said, flapping her hand. "I've gotten used to the noise. Besides, it's nice having the police never more than a block away." Rubbing the sleep from her eyes, she sized up her mother—bigger hair, smaller body. Everything about her was going in the wrong direction, as usual, including the self-guided tour on which she immediately embarked.

"Not bad," she said thirty seconds later. "Three

little rooms plus a bathroom. Not much to clean, at least."

"My thoughts exactly."

"I oughta be done by lunch. So if you wanna invite Robert or anyone to come grab a bite, I'm sure I could throw sumpin' together." Joy watched her mother casually picking through sacks and tried to remember the last time she had offered to cook for her and a man. The answer—1974, Sonny—suggested the invitation wasn't exactly off-the-cuff.

"I think you need some sleep. You're sounding delirious," Joy said, bending down to pet Sugar Pie and Radar. "I hate to burst your bubble, but Boo-Boo's got a girlfriend. Besides, we're working through lunch a lot lately. You're not going to believe what we've done with the show. I hardly have a free second anymore."

As had been her intent, that seemed to satisfy her mother. As long as Joy was back slaving away, she wasn't barricaded in a dark room, balled up in the fetal position.

"So what's going on with Doyle?" she asked, straightening up. "I thought you'd be in Kentucky a while."

"Doyle ain't goin' anywhere no time soon," she said, carrying her bags into the mini living room and shoving them under the coffee table. "And, since it kills Mama and Daddy's souls to see anyone so much as paint a dern, dreary wall, I thought I'd come back down here and find sumpin' to do." For starters, she kicked all the animals out of the house.

"This place ain't big enough for the both of us, dawg," she told Annie, who tucked her tail between her gangly legs and followed Sugar Pie and Radar through the carport and out to the fenced-in backyard. "And yore outta here, too, cat," she informed Cole, toeing him toward the door.

As it turned out, even with the animals evicted, Joy's new house still wasn't big enough for Quida Raye Perkins.

Joy came home that afternoon, waved at her mother sunning herself in the freshly mown backyard, and went in to change. Happily noting the pot of butter beans simmering on the glistening apartment-sized stove, she was hooking her purse on a chair when something on the table caught her eye.

She picked up the scrap of paper and blinked a few times to make sure she was seeing clearly.

"Mother!" she yelled, storming out the door, through the carport and past the gate, hand shaking as she shoved the paper in front of a deep brown, freshly oiled face. *"What's this?"*

"What's it look like?" Quida Raye asked, taking a swig of soda. Though the dogs had jumped up and run when Joy slammed the gate hard enough to rock all four corners of the chain-link fence, her mother hadn't moved a muscle.

"It looks like a receipt for two weeks at the Sleepy Time Motor Lodge," Joy shouted. Quida Raye Perkins just looked up at her daughter, as if pleased she could read. "Do you happen to know *what* the Sleepy Time Motor Lodge *is*?"

"A place where I can sleep," her mother replied. "Unless you was thankin' I'd sleep in the yard."

"No, I didn't think you'd sleep in the yard," Joy hollered. "I expected you to find somewhere halfway decent to live."

"Somewhere halfway decent costs an arm and a leg," her mother hollered back.

"Well, unless you're planning on bartering with *other* body parts, I think I'd spend the money and move somewhere other than a dang *cathouse.*"

"Where?" her mother yelled. "A *dog* house like you moved to?"

"It's good enough for me," Joy screamed, sending a flock of cedar waxwings flapping out of a nearby tree. "And you could find a nice place, too, if you tried."

"Not for no fifty dollars a week I cain't," her mother squalled. "Lots of perfectly normal folks rent rooms over there, for your information." And with that she plopped her big hair back against the lawn chair, squeezed her eyes shut, and resumed tanning. "Now go inside and leave me alone. I've got a sick headache."

Sensing movement, Joy turned and saw Bess and Bubba slipping toward their old jalopy. She hadn't seen them since their last sanctioned World Wrestling event, when humility had filled their downcast faces. Now they held their heads up high, beaming twin glares of solidarity straight at her.

"Congratulations. You fit right in with Up Yours Bess and Fuck You Bubba," Tanya observed later. "Carrying on like a lunatic outside in broad daylight."

"What do you expect?" Joy said, squeezing the phone. "My mother's back."

Because she *was* back. She might have spent every night watching TV and gobbling cookies and candy at the whore motel. But, after she fixed up her room with Priscillas on the window, pretty pillows on the concave bed, and a new tank and lid set in the bathroom, she spent all day every day at Joy's tiny house, cleaning, cooking, mowing, and suntanning. To get to Joy's faster, she even worked a couple of boards loose in the kudzu-covered fence separating the den of iniquity from Bess and Bubba's yard. She worked four more loose when Tanya visited the next weekend.

"Guess where I found the two of them when I got home," Joy asked Boo-Boo that Monday.

"Where?"

"At Sluts R Us. Sprawled across the hood of a low-rider, gangsta-whitewalled luxury automobile. They were flipping through some of Mother's mail-order catalogs with a couple of working girls who weren't otherwise engaged."

Boo-Boo grinned and leaned back in his chair. Was it Joy's imagination or had he lost weight? Maybe he was getting himself in shape for Ruthie. Maybe Ruthie had gone and lost her stupid virginity just when it looked like Joy would never have a man again.

"What was Tanya doing? Getting some pointers?" he asked, reaching for the latest Top-100 list.

"Probably giving them, knowing her," Joy replied, stealthily studying her oldest male friend in the world. Had he started lifting weights? Recalling an arcane fact she'd read somewhere, how females of every species—from houseflies to humans—are drawn to males who have recently mated, she was sure her suspicions were correct.

"Is Tanya still in town?" WildDog asked.

"No, thank God. She has finals. Then she'll probably be touring with Gary most of the summer."

"A girl after my own heart," he said, nodding approvingly.

"No doubt. Speaking of, how's this for today's oh-so-appropriate theme?" Joy waved the soundtrack to "The Best Little Whorehouse in Texas."

"Works for me," Boo-Boo said. "Gotta love country's approach to outlandish subjects."

"Like 'Fancy,' " WildDog noted. "Regarding that classic country theme of getting pimped out by one's own mom."

Boo-Boo laughed. "How about 'Would You Lay with Me (In a Field of Stone)' recorded by a fifteen-year-old."

Later, Joy reached for "The Best Little Whorehouse in Texas" again. Cuing up the last track, "I Will Always Love You," the most tremulous paean to heartbreak recorded in any genre, she sat back and listened to the only song she had wanted to hear all morning anyway.

"That's right," Boo-Boo said, fixing her with a knowing stare, the oscillating fan ruffling his long, black hair. "It was the *whorehouse* imagery we were going for today. What was I thinking?"

"You need a haircut," she said.

That night, she curled up on her little couch in her little house, nursing a little wine. Maybe it wasn't so bad to have her mother off organizing pinochle games at Sluts R Us and Bess and Bubba and the nearby businesses providing plenty of light and sound shows compliments of the Avalon City Police. Maybe she hadn't made a terrible mistake in signing that one-year lease. Maybe she couldn't have picked a better place to try and keep her mind off New Orleans after all.

****

As sleepless as Joy's hopeless nights were, they were at least short. Since none of her mother's naughty new neighbors stirred till noon, Quida Raye began slipping off to Joy's before dawn every day, still in her gown and hedgerow hair. Unlocking the back door, she'd slip into the kitchen and put on a pot of coffee. Then, filling a cup half full of sugar before stirring in coffee and milk, she'd take the goo to the concrete steps to sit and slurp and smoke, a study in polyester.

One morning shortly after Tanya's visit, Joy maneuvered around her and got into her car. Since the steps faced Bess and Bubba's trailer instead of the street, and since she was two cups of coffee away from caring anyway, Quida Raye had no compunction whatsoever about being outside at dawn with her dandelion do and dishrag gown. Flagging the somewhat frightening image for later, Joy turned the key at the exact moment she remembered she should have waited until her mother had carried her frumpy self back to the bordello. Too late, a shrill death whine lifted up and took wing from the general vicinity of Joy's windshield wipers. Instantly, Quida Raye mashed out her cigarette, set her coffee cup down, dislodged the nightie from all the usual crevices, and crept over to Joy's car like it was Seattle Slew, raring to go.

Joy rolled down the window. "Yes?"

"Why don't you take that bike a yore's to work? You need to work some of that butt off you anyway. And this car sounds like it needs a..." Joy waited. "...Oil change." By longstanding prior arrangement, her mother was allowed only to change her oil.

"An oil change, huh?" Joy warily asked.

"Uh-huh," her mother insisted. "An oil change."

****

Joy pedaled home that afternoon, and there, on the

259

floor of her carport, lay half her engine. Sauntering out from under the hood like she was part of a dirt track's pit crew, Quida Raye wiped her brow with a greasy rag and announced, "Starter's shot." Even Joy knew a starter wasn't involved in an oil change.

"While I had 'er opened up, I thought I'd check a few thangs." She in fact had so much fun fiddling with Joy's starter and heaven only knows what else that she'd picked up a starter for her car, too.

****

Days later, during a fresh installment of "Can You Beat this Mother (Please)," Joy simplified what had actually been a drawn out, mechanically complicated total nightmare.

"Long story short…" she began.

"For once," WildDog drawled into the other mic.

"…whatever she did to my car *and* hers has me on my bike and in the poorhouse. The actual mechanic both vehicles were eventually towed to said her car's starter wires had been incorrectly attached. But the *really* bad news is I made the mistake of driving my car after she did no-telling-what to it. And now *it* needs a new *engine*."

"Ouch," WildDog said, adjusting the headphones atop his baseball cap. "Cha-ching!"

"Exactly. So if any of you are feeling generous, the telethon is open. Call in and pledge now—one-eight-hundred-lady-bug."

****

Quida Raye wasn't fazed—until her check to the mechanic bounced. In quick succession, checks to the In-'n'-Out, Jewel's Golden Brown Breasts & Legs, four grocery stores, and—alas—the Sleepy Time Motor

Lodge also bounced. A few phone calls soon revealed the problem. Her only source of income—the Social Security disability check she had received since being diagnosed with terminal stomach cancer seven years earlier—had not been automatically deposited into her account. From the day she had changed both cars' starters till she discovered the funds to cover those and all other subsequent expenditures were missing, four hundred seven dollars and nineteen cents in bad checks had hit her account. Not counting twenty dollars a pop the merchants and bank were charging on each end.

First, she called every place of business to say they could run the checks back through as soon as her daughter, "the famous Lady Bug," got paid. Then, fury building, she dabbed a fresh coat of armor on her white tennies, sprayed her bulletproof do again, and headed out, loaded for bear.

The clerk at the Social Security office took her eyes off the brickbat in starched jeans cocked in front of her desk long enough to check some files. Then she shrugged and said the only explanation she could offer was the federal government must have decided she had gotten better. At five-foot-four and ninety-seven pounds, self-medicating with about twenty-five headache tablets knocked back by a case of sodas a day, Quida Raye Perkins assured the clerk "in no uncertain terms" that she had not been informed of any such miracle, as she later told Joy.

"What'd she say?" Joy whimpered, hopes collapsing.

"She said I could file a 'reconsideration notice' and wait *months* for it to be reviewed and *maybe* my disability check'll be reinstated. *Eventually.* I was so mad I coulda bit a tenpenny nail in two by the time I left that office. That woman teetotally pissed me off!"

Guessing her mother had made the SS official well aware of how she felt, picturing the clerk sending her paperwork straight to File Thirteen, Joy said, "I hope you didn't make *her* mad."

"Well she can just scratch her ass and get glad if I did."

****

The next day, with her bad debts now exceeding six hundred dollars, no money in her purse, and no prospect of any coming in, since her mechanical meddling had tapped Joy out till payday, Quida Raye Perkins heated up a can of chicken noodle soup on the hotplate in her room, crushed half a tube of crackers into it, ate it all, threw it up, then put her teeth back in and her tennis shoes back on. After driving to Abe's Pawn Shop and hocking her rings, she headed to every convenience store and nursing home in Avalon.

"She filled out job applications all over town despite having both a stomach and a work record with seven-year holes in them," Joy told Tanya that night.

"How is she going to work if she can't keep food down?" Tanya asked.

"Doesn't matter. It's been hard enough for her to survive on about four hundred and fifteen dollars a month. Zero dollars is going to be a stretch."

****

The last day of June, Quida Raye Perkins moved out of her room at the Sleepy Time Motor Lodge, leaving the fancy Priscillas behind for management. The girls—who, under her tutelage, had discovered crafts custom-made for a bunch of hookers—gave her a lovely crocheted toilet roll cover as a going-away gift.

"Looks like you've got yourself a permanent roomie," Boo-Boo said the next morning, trying not to laugh. "I can't imagine how you're going to squeeze her into that dollhouse of yours. Unless you're considering tiny little bunk beds."

"I'm going to make a call," Joy said. "Just keep playing records. And don't bother turning the sound down. I'll need all the help I can get."

"Whatever you say, boss," he replied, cranking it up.

After the district manager of Avalon's Social Security office got over being called by Lady Bug herself, he attempted to solve the problem. Working his way through information on several reforms, he finally hit on one that sounded plausible—a declaration ordering the cessation of direct-deposit checks if letters sent to beneficiaries on a certain date were returned due to insufficient addresses.

"Has your mother moved, perchance?"

Had her mother moved? Since being approved for SSI disability and receiving, at the time, about three hundred seventy dollars a month, Quida Raye hadn't figured out how to pay rent and utilities while keeping gas in the Barge-mobile and herself in nicotine and caffeine. So, what time she wasn't living in the cab of a stolen eighteen-wheeler or with Joy or with her parents or her brothers, she was living a month or two at this address, then a month or two at the next. Eight in all, Joy calculated, not counting the truck and the relatives and the Sleepy Time Motor Lodge.

"My mother's moved more than the nomadic bushmen of Africa," she gaily exclaimed, the gray cloud of insolvency parting for the rich, warm sun. "I think we've finally gotten to the bottom of the problem."

"Good," the district manager said, relieved. "I'll set up an appointment for her and you can tell her all she'll need to bring in are her doctor's records for the previous year or two."

"Doctor's records?" Joy asked, struggling to keep her tone peppy.

"Correct," said the SS official. "Doctor's records. Then we can fix this."

"Right. Doctor's records. I'll pass that little detail on to her." After promising to drop by with some autographed eight-by-tens, Joy hung up and stared through the glass at the darkened newsroom. Boo-Boo quietly kicked on "Skip A Rope."

Quida Raye Perkins of course had no recent doctor's records. Nothing even from that decade. Not since Jessie had died, at least. As Joy studied the empty newsroom, she clearly saw her mother would be sleeping on the loveseat in her miniscule house for a good long while.

Soon, Joy barely noticed Bess and Bubba's World Boxing brawls next door. The brisk business that Sluts R Us and the local crooks were doing similarly escaped her. She was in such a funk—Tanya's scholarly term for it was a "major depression"—that it didn't register until later that well over a year had passed between bumping into Ira in a bar parking lot and getting stuck in Lilliput with her mother, late of the red-light district.

What a difference a year makes, Joy thought, barricaded once again in a dark room, balled up in the fetal position.

Chapter 21
"I Fall To Pieces"

Quida Raye's initial reaction to suddenly losing her lone source of income was to plant a garden. Day after day, Joy spun "A Country Boy Can Survive" then detailed each new sprout and seed packet. Fan favorites, those "victory garden" segments ended with a few choice words concerning whatever entity had irked her lately, governmental or otherwise. Any off-color bits were drowned out by Boo-Boo blowing a kazoo into WildDog's mic.

And there was much that irked Joy Savoy the summer of 1984, as evidenced by one hell-hot July day. Fresh back from a trip to the grocery with one of Joy's blank checks, Quida Raye smirked and propped her hands on her bony hips. "Guess what a checker just said to me."

"That one person couldn't possibly eat so many Vienna sausages and stay so skinny?"

"Nope. She said, 'I don't know where that girl a yore's gets that viperous tongue in her head. Yore such a sweet thang she couldn't have got it from you.' " Quida Raye's grin slid into a full-blown simper. Joy snorted.

" 'A purdy lil' sweet thang' was her exact words," she announced, cackling. Her hair had grown out that summer and, while she still kept the top round as a hubcap, she had taken to drawing the bottom twigs into a shrimpy, sweat-drenched ponytail when she gardened. Cooing "Purdy lil' sweet thang" to herself, she trotted back outside to continue hoeing to China.

Joy pulled the curtain back and watched her swigging sodas and puffing cigarettes, cutoffs belling out around legs as spindly as a pair of tanned shish-kebab skewers. She did not particularly look like a pretty little sweet thing at the moment. She looked like a hot, thin cross between Abe Lincoln and a lollipop pried off a Siberian husky. Hot, Joy could take. She could even get used to that wacky, fluffy, ponytailed do. Thin, however—especially as thin as her mother was getting—was becoming increasingly difficult to tolerate.

"It sounds like you're taking this personally," Tanya observed. Joy could hear pages turning. "Like you think losing weight is some passive-aggressive move on her part or something."

"My mother's about as passive-aggressive as a ball-peen hammer," Joy exclaimed. "All I'm saying is I'm just tired of the two of us losing so much. She's losing weight and I'm losing my temper. That's all we do anymore. Lose."

Looking out the window again at the neat rows of red dirt Quida Raye was stabbing, Joy fumed with a bit more clarity. "Then again, since she technically still has Doyle, chain gang and all, I guess that makes *me* the biggest loser."

Tanya honked like a car horn into the phone. "Finally, a declaration of yours I couldn't agree with more."

****

266

Sometime during the protracted season of her mother's never-ending harvest, WildDog adjusted his ballcap and said, "Did you hear? Ira's living with that woman he's been seeing from his station."

"Is that so?" Joy said, turning toward the oscillating fan that suddenly needed adjusting in the worst possible way. From the corner of her eye, she saw Boo-Boo shake his head and WildDog hold up his hands.

"Can one of you find our copy of 'I Fall to Pieces'? It feels like forever since I've heard that song," Joy said, business as usual. Except she sounded like she'd taken several hits off a helium balloon. Boo-Boo found the record, slapped it on, and he and WildDog glowered at each other as she pulled on the headphones and opened the mic.

"I'm wondering if there's a single one of you who's never heard 'I Fall To Pieces,' " she began in that odd, wobbly register. "Don't call if you haven't. Just crawl out from under that rock and crank up what's about to come on. I promise it'll sum up better than any song ever has what it's like to hear your true love's name again. Out of the blue. Out of the deep, dark blue."

Kicking on KLME's disc, burned into seconds of solid static by decades of DJs cuing it up, she stared into the empty newsroom and rode a wave of pure heartache to the brink of utter despair.

Behind her, Boo-Boo hissed, "Asshole."

"I think you're shootin' the messenger, buddy," WildDog quietly replied.

"I think that sounds like an excellent idea," Boo-Boo growled as Joy focused on falling to pieces.

****

Quida Raye's second reaction to suddenly losing her lone source of income was to take the first job she was offered.

"At the convenience store around the corner from my house," Joy told her co-workers the next day. "She kept walking over there and putting in applications till they cried 'Uncle!' and hired her."

Celebrating at lunch, replete with two rounds of drinks—"On me," WildDog insisted—there was more cause to party two weeks later when Quida Raye used her first paycheck to move into her own cozy Section 8 apartment a few miles away.

Then, several paychecks after that, yet another triumphal moment occurred—Kentucky freed her man.

"Come get me, Grump," Doyle called to say that very day.

After replenishing her wardrobe with a speedy trip to the mall and trading her overtime for comp time, she rolled a window down for Radar and Sugar Pie and did just that, stopping at Joy's house first.

"Look at me," she hooted, hopping up and down. "I'm jumping for Joy!" Estimating her new end-of-gardening-season weight at about ninety-two pounds, Joy grinned at her scrappy little mother bouncing around the kitchen like a kid on a pogo stick.

****

At KLME, they had a heyday playing trucker songs and mama songs and prison songs, suitably complemented by a loop WildDog taped of the end of "You Never Even Called Me by My Name," the perfect country song part featuring all the classic tropes. Then, because Boo-Boo said they should, they segued back into the kind of love songs Joy used to play for Ira.

"And guess what?" she informed Tanya. "I've hardly thought of him at all."

"Alert the authorities," Tanya drawled.

"I've been too busy. We've had the most amazing shows since Mother's been gone. Which is good considering Ray and Jimmy just sold us to a few little stations in Mississippi."

"Too bad Quida Raye isn't getting royalties," Tanya noted.

"Too bad none of us are," Joy countered. "But at least we're having a good time. I just hope she's having as much fun as we are."

****

Joy was driving past her mother's new apartment a few days later when she glanced over and was shocked to see the Barge-mobile parked in front of the picture window, drapes drawn tight. Turning around, she parked and, keys rattling, let herself in, only to find her mother stock-still in smoke-filled gloom, knees up to her chin.

"I didn't know you were back already," she cheerily said. "Days early!" But Quida Raye, curved like a sliver of a thumbnail on her secondhand couch, just turned away. Her stone-cold silence said everything she never would. Doyle was gone. And she was alone, pretty much like she'd always been.

Joy knew there wasn't much worse for a daughter to see than her mother stripped of any hope for a shared tomorrow. Unless it was seeing it twice. But Quida Raye Perkins had been thirty-five and at her peak the last time a man had left, taking along a trailer with purple carpet. Now forty-five and going down fast, her

269

mother, once the picture of ponytailed, '50s drive-in dazzle, had little more than the shattered mess still standing by the door, rattling car keys.

Fighting back a wave of panic, Joy looked around her mother's fussy, thrift-store-filled apartment, desperate for any distraction. Spying the junk-filled kitchen table, she walked over and started picking through the piles, thrilled to see that whatever that low-down thieving dog had stolen from her mother, she'd taken plenty from him, as well. In addition to Doyle's driver's license and various notes and cards from his worthless kids, also heaped on the table and all four chairs were towering stacks of men's shirts, jeans, belts, hats, boxers, socks, tank tops and cowboy boots on which Quida Raye had squandered a good chunk of every disability check since 1977 and kept stored in the Barge-mobile's trunk throughout most of a fifteen-month incarceration.

"What should I tell Doyle if he calls, nude, from a phone booth somewhere?" Joy asked, trying to tease a grin out of her.

"Tell him he can kiss my ass and go straight to hell," Quida Raye spat, lighting another cigarette.

****

"All I managed to get from her is Doyle bummed a buddy's big rig and the two of them took one last ride for old time's sake," Joy told Boo-Boo the next morning. "Then he told her his estranged wife had been visiting him in prison and maybe they both needed a 'fresh start.' He said she ought to come back down here and get on with her life."

Joy wondered if Doyle hadn't simply been surprised by the new leaner, meaner Kentucky Cajun

Queen. Then again, as Ira had well demonstrated, sometimes no surplus of any stripe matters much in the end.

As he always had with her show, Boo-Boo provided just the input she needed to move from desperation to revelation.

"If she's that down in the dumps, you should buy her something she'd never in a million years expect," he said, ever the benevolent soul.

"I'm sure not getting her another dang dog, if that's what you mean," Joy blared. "And don't *you* dare show up with another one, either."

"Not a dog," Boo-Boo said, laughing. "Think big. Really big. Maybe a cruise or something."

Joy knew her mother would no sooner take a cruise than she'd take the prescription drugs that might actually improve her mood. No, a cruise wasn't the answer. But driving past the convenience store that afternoon and spying the poop-brown Barge-mobile parked there, Joy seized on a big-ticket item her mother might honestly appreciate.

"She hasn't had a new car since Dick took the trailer and her beige-on-brown custom coupe," Joy excitedly told Boo-Boo the next day. "To celebrate-slash-retaliate, she bought herself that 'gently used' Barge-mobile in the same color scheme the day her divorce was final."

"That's been a while," Boo-Boo observed.

"Yes, it has."

Joy couldn't look at the rattletrap jalopy, now old and battered beyond its years, without seeing every trip she wished she could forget since she was seventeen years old. It had taken her home from the charity hospital in Ferndale where Jessie was born. It had taken her mother to the hospital in Tompkinsville where her cancer was diagnosed. Had taken them both to the house where Jessie had died. Now it had brought her mother back from the last man who would ever care. Before it took either of them on a journey there might not be any returning from, it was time for that damned car to go.

****

Joy sat at her kitchen table that Saturday, doing the math, until she heard her mother coming from a mile away. Clanging up to Joy's carport, she turned the Barge-mobile off and waited for it to chug and cough and gulp and huff and eventually shudder to a standstill. Then she hauled in six loads of Joy's laundry she had washed and precision folded at the laundromat in her apartment complex.

Joy looked up from her calculations and grinned. "What would you say if I told you I'm buying you a car for Christmas?"

Quida Raye set the clothes basket down, adjusted her armload of dresses, and stood completely still in the narrow doorway.

"Would you rather have a big used car or a new small car?" Joy continued. "Neither of which you can smoke in."

Still nothing. Whatever reaction Joy had expected, had carefully tabulated there on paper to produce, was decidedly not forthcoming. Instead of jumping for joy again, all her mother did was look away and tear up. The rare times her mother cried, Joy thought of Jessie and, when she couldn't think of Jessie anymore, she thought of Dick and a trailer with purple carpet.

"Never mind," Joy muttered, stumbling outside to the dull thuds of Bess and Bubba hurling large objects around their trailer. Even that was an improvement over the deafening silence inside her own place.

The next day, her mother appeared again. "Yore refrigerator's growin' cobwebs," she announced, setting a plate of meatloaf, mashed potatoes, corn, and crowder peas on the stove. "Here's some biscuits, too. And, if you still wanna know, a small car's gonna get better gas mileage than a big car any day."

****

One Saturday in November, during their vehicular tour of Japan, Joy was focused on the front row, genuflecting in front of sticker prices under $10,000. She didn't realize her mother had wandered off until she heard a squeal, whipped around, and spied her back in the high-dollar section, parked beside a bad little number with racing stripes and fancy wheels.

"What's *this*?" she oohed.

"One look at the wedge-shaped body, sunroof, and five-on-the-floor—the only conveyance she's looked at twice in all this time—and I all but reversed my opinion on Hiroshima," Joy told Boo-Boo that Monday. "Somehow I found the strength to check the sticker and guess what. It's doable. Granted, it's in the high end of my low-budget Christmas calculations, but I think I can swing it."

Odell the New Car Salesman helped them work out the most ticklish details—red, black, blue, no, white, "To match the license plate," Quida Raye proclaimed— and the deal was done. The special-order Wedgie would arrive in time for Christmas.

It was the first new car Joy Savoy had ever bought.

And it was her mother's first new car since that 1974 coupe which, a few months after he'd stolen it, Dick had totaled coming back from a *cochon de lait.* As Tanya memorably said, the pig wasn't the only thing lit that day.

With the Barge-mobile's bad old days numbered, having Doyle as far out of the picture as Ira would ever be didn't seem so bad. In fact, Joy was on a high till Odell called weeks later to tell her the Wedgie was ready. Squealing and slamming down the phone, she sprang up and grabbed her purse.

Boo-Boo, who was with her in the production room, shelving carts, said, "I'll meet you at the dealership. I've got a little something to give your mother myself."

"Okay," she said, scampering toward the door. Then, spinning around and pausing for a moment to bask in his big, warm smile, she ran back and hopped up on tiptoe for a quick, celebratory hug. Instantly, as if the lights had dimmed and they had begun slow dancing, Boo-Boo leaned down, wrapped his arms around her and began swaying.

"Mmm," he said, nuzzling her ear, his long, black hair brushing her face. Slipping her arms around his neck, she moved closer, breathed in his minty gum, the cherry cola he'd had at lunch, his freshly washed shirt, the thick, male mist under it all. It felt so good to hear a deep voice so close, to be gathered up tight by a pair of firm arms and pressed against a body so large and hard in all the right places that, for a moment, Joy felt she might faint.

"Then again you always have confused physical contact with deep affection," Tanya pointed out that night, guffawing.

"True," Joy agreed, changing ears, mind drifting back to those breathtaking moments in the production room. She didn't come to her senses for a full minute or two, after it dawned on her that she and her oldest male friend in the world were locked in a swaying embrace, moving ever so deliciously slowly to "Amanda" pouring through the speakers from Studio A.

"So what happened?" Tanya asked. "I'm on pins and needles here."

"Nothing. I got hold of myself and said, 'What if Ruthie would've walked in here!' and he said, 'Now, Joy,' and I ran out the door to the dealership, and he came and gave Mother some nice floor mats, and that was that."

Trumpeting like an African elephant, Tanya yelled, "You irritate me more than any human being alive. Why didn't you just pucker up and lay a big wet one on him? Who knows what that might have led to?"

"Are you kidding?" Joy squawked. "It would have been like smooching *you*."

"*Yuck!*" they both shrieked.

That night, however, when the lights were off and a dazzling new Wedgie was parked beside the convenience store around the corner from her infinitesimal house, Joy lay in bed, eyes wide open, still tingling from head to toe.

Chapter 22
"Here You Come Again"

A month later, Quida Raye Perkins still had not taken full custody of her $11,476 Christmas gift, which had been parked under Joy's carport at least half the time since being driven off the lot. Her mother simply could not part with that four-bald-tired brown bomb. Till she did, she insisted on driving both cars equally.

"As if alleviating sibling rivalry between Cinderella and one of the stump-ugly stepsisters," Joy told her listeners.

Not that she was still bending everyone's ear about the Barge-mobile. After a quick Christmas trip to Kentucky, during which she and her grandparents were buried beneath mountains of aggressively beribboned gifts Quida Raye had barely managed to cram into the Wedgie's trunk, Joy had moved on to griping about other brown subjects. Notably the year's final crop—pecans. Pecans are big business in Central Louisiana, and the most productive pecan tree in town was in Joy's back yard.

"I am, of course, not telling my neighbors anything they don't already know," she said, adjusting her headphones. After months of hearing only the riotous Bess and Bubba, Joy awoke one morning to murmured commands and hushed hallelujahs. Peeking into her back yard, she saw her neighbors to the left.

Homeowners. Homeowners with a hankering for her pecans.

Soon, she was dedicating parts of every broadcast to them. Like, "What you don't know is I really don't mind you stealing my pecans. Be my guest. I've even got some grocery sacks you can have. It's the lean woman with a hungry look who answers to the name 'Mother' you need to watch out for."

Quida Raye had been rooting around in Joy's yard since the first green pecan parachuted down in September. She was determined to collect every single nut and shell it, bag it, and either freeze it or sell it on the side at the convenience store.

Until one Saturday in January when Joy ran out of pecans. Overnight.

Tickled to find themselves the occasional new targets of her broadcast, Joy's pecan-thieving neighbors had come up with a foolproof plan to also steal the show.

"They've been shop-vac-ing that tree," her mother wailed before dawn one morning, rattling a caved-in grocery bag in Joy's sleepy face. Three nuts cowered in the bottom. "They sucked up the pecans and even left the dern shop vac out by their back door."

Boo-Boo, at his producerly best, helped guide Joy through the next week's saga. Discovery. Complicity. Then, Friday, resolution involving an about-face and wishy-washy retraction.

It was all quite involved for a thin storyline featuring a few brown nuts. But, as Joy often reminded herself, this was radio. Nothing else besides maybe newspapers was as carnivorous, requiring a never-ending diet of fresh dollops of flesh. Ounces of confessions, pounds of slapstick, metric tons of just plain dumb, she spewed it all out as if the mic were a stiff liposuction device. In other words, Joy Savoy's fans knew better than to expect anything like Roosevelt's Fireside Chats.

"If you want the last pecans of the season, Mother, you'd better get to the house," she blared across radios first thing that Friday. "A few more came down last night, and there are neighbors everywhere!" Boo-Boo even chimed in with rare, on-air repartee later, after Joy talked him into playing devil's advocate.

"Bake them a pecan pie and be neighborly for a change," he suggested, headphones on. "Better yet, bake me one instead."

"Okay," she agreed, smiling at her old buddy, surprised she had forgotten how sexy he always sounded on air. "But only if my neighbors bring me some recipes. Just leave them in my mailbox, folks. And if you don't remember ever *seeing* my mailbox, simply walk out of my back yard, go around the house, and take a left. You can't miss it."

"You can't, huh?" said another good radio voice behind them.

"I'll be damned," Boo-Boo exclaimed, wheeling around and sliding off the headphones. "Look what the cat coughed up." Both he and WildDog jovially rose to shake hands with their grinning visitor, cheerfully pounding him on the back. Joy meanwhile was incapable of any movement whatsoever.

"When did you leave the good-paying world of producing for life as a lowly jock again?" Ira asked, pumping Boo-Boo's arm.

"Hell, that wasn't my idea. You know how

persuasive Joy can be." Somewhere in the dim recesses of her bleary mind, Joy registered a pair of black heads swinging like wrecking balls in her direction.

"I think I recall something along those lines," Ira said, nodding at her. "Hey. Been a while."

"Hey," she genially said. "Yes, it has."

"What's shakin' in the big city, man?" WildDog asked. Ira leaned against a rack and answered by regaling them with some of his more sensational newscasts. Boo-Boo and WildDog then filled him in on his substandard replacement as well as the revolving door of DJs who had been vying for WildDog's old shift since he became full-time sidekick to the syndicated host suddenly absorbed in the minutiae of her job.

"What about you?" Ira asked. "What's new with you?"

"Not much," Joy said, glancing up from the ad log and smiling congenially, like she did at every meet-and-greet.

"Not much more than the full-time girl they've got handling her fan mail, appearances, bookings, what have you," Boo-Boo said, winking at her.

"Wow," Ira said.

"Yep, there went my raise."

After a couple of beats of total silence, never a good thing in radio, WildDog said, "So what brings you back to Hooterville?"

"I finally had a couple of days off, so I decided to climb on my bike and take a ride. I haven't been back up this way since before last year's blizzard."

"You don't say," Boo-Boo exclaimed. Joy cringed, wondering if Ira heard what she had—Boo-Boo all but admitting that every other song he'd been subjected to for so many months had ticked off the minutes without the tall guy in faded jeans currently sucking all the air out of Studio A.

"Yeah, what a fucking winter," Ira said. "At least it looks like we're gonna have a mild one this year."

To keep from having to speak again, Joy idly spun around to review her upcoming tunes. Once the men had moved on to other subjects, notably how much the Saints sucked, she slipped "Some Broken Hearts Never Mend" off the top.

"I guess I'll go and let Vernon know I'm here before he calls security," Ira eventually said.

"I'll go with you," Boo-Boo offered. Following Ira out, he turned and screwed his face up at Joy. She screwed her face up back at him. It beat bursting into tears. Later, after Warren Piece had taken over and she had gone to the production room to be by herself, Boo-Boo came in and closed the door.

"Ira and Vernon went to lunch. You okay? You don't look like you feel good." She hunched her shoulders. "Come here and let me see if you have a fever." She rolled her chair over and submitted her forehead for inspection. Feeling him brush her bangs aside, she closed her eyes and leaned into his gentle touch. "No fever," he said, easing his big hand down the side of her face and cupping her chin, a tender turn that very nearly opened the floodgates. "You want anything? Water? Pop? Some aspirin?" She shook her head, locomoting her chair back to the board. "Why don't you go on home then. We can finish the promo tomorrow."

****

Long past dark, collapsed over her stereo and every song that summoned every time she had lost in love, Joy Savoy heard a sound that unhinged her as much as Bess and Bubba's bass-tone demolitions next door. It was the *rip-rip-ripping* of Ira's motorcycle sputtering up to her kitchen door.

With everything inside her a-flitter, leaning against the wall for support, she opened the door and casually said, "Oh. Hey."

"Hey. Boo-Boo told me where you were living now. Took a walk on the wild side this time, didn't you?" Ira slipped off his helmet and ran a hand through his wavy black hair.

"It's not as bad as it looks. Everyone pretty much keeps to themselves. And, when they don't, I've got the Avalon City Police on speed dial."

Ira nodded. "New car?"

She glanced at the Wedgie under her carport, yellow sticker beginning to peel. "Sort of. But it's not mine." Not much was anymore.

"I hope you don't mind that I dropped by."

"Not at all," she insisted, smiling. As Annie barked from the yard at this stranger and a curtain was surreptitiously pulled back in the trailer across the way, Joy wondered how a man who had been so central to her world could be unknown to everything and everyone currently in it. Then again, she supposed that was the nature of obsession. Nothing is more achingly private.

"Can I come in?"

"Certainly," she said, moving away from the door she had been blocking like a landslide.

"Cozy," he observed, strolling past her. "Not a lot

to clean up."

"My thoughts exactly." Following Ira through her bit of a house, downwind from the road soaked into his leather jacket, the salty, slightly sour man smell of him, the warm sheen she knew was matting the fur beneath his flannel, she once again remembered her first glimpse of him. Night without end. Amen and amen.

"Conway?" he said dourly, reaching the living room.

"What'd you expect? AC/DC?"

"Now that you mention it, yeah, I did."

Craning her head to the side, as if recalling something other than sad country songs for a change, something with a hot jungle beat, she turned the turntable off and the local rock station on. Ira slipped out of his jacket, sat down, and reached for his motorcycle boots—"Do you mind?" How many times had she imagined this scene, and now here he was, on her small blue loveseat.

"Not at all. Make yourself at home," she said, heading for the kitchen. "What can I get you? Coffee? Tea?" *Me?* she didn't say, throat tightening around the notion.

"Tea would be good. Or a beer."

"Sorry. No beer." Continuing on to the fridge, bending her mind away from a thousand questions she actually wanted answers to, she sloshed some tea in a glass and carried it back, asking about work instead.

"I haven't been fired yet, so that's something," he said, taking the glass. "But big-city news is the same fucking grind. Crime in New Orleans is a bitch. Traffic's a bitch. Tourism's a bitch. Life's a bitch, and then you die, right? And on that happy note," he added, smiling wryly, "how's everything here in big Avalon?"

Joy chuckled and, seeing what little space was left on the blue loveseat, sat down across from him on the coffee table instead. "Not much new to report here either, except they keep letting me have my show, for no good reason that I can tell."

"Boo-Boo said your ratings are off the chart," he noted, taking a sip.

"Yeah, with the thirteen people who can actually hear me," Joy glibly replied. "And Lord knows why, but that seems fine with Vernon and Ray and Jimmy. For now."

"Well no job in radio is forever, that's for damn sure," Ira said, setting the glass down beside her on the coffee table. "Speaking of…"

Just then, a tap on the kitchen door made them both jump.

"Who could that be?" Joy exclaimed, leaping up and darting off. One glance through the thin curtain on the window and the big, round shadow behind it, and she knew.

"Yes?" she hissed, cracking the door enough to glower at her mother.

"I was just pickin' up the Wedgie when I noticed you had comp'ny," she said, grinning ear to ear. "Need anythang? I could run back to the store for some cheese and crackers."

Joy couldn't help but imagine what cheese the In-'n'-Out might sell. Probably something with a shelf life of an eon or two. "No, thanks," she said, closing the door. "See you tomorrow."

"Your mother?" Ira asked as she flopped back down on the coffee table.

"None other. For a solid month she's come and gone without a word, dropping off one car and picking up the other as if playing some elaborate game of keep away. But tonight of all nights she decides to be Miss Hostess with the Mostest. Anyway, you were saying?"

"I was saying I think the writing's on the wall," he began again. "I doubt if I'll be at the station this time next year. And I'm not getting any younger. So I'm wondering if it's time for a change."

As Joy listened to Ira talk about trying his hand at TV news writing, she silently complimented herself on her composure. They could have been any old friends catching up. But of course they were so much more, and so much less. All they weren't was whatever it was they used to be. And she knew how she would describe it later to Tanya, too. Recalling her mother's offer to run back to the In-'n'-Out for snacks, she decided she and Ira were like sliced cheese after the advent of plastic wrappers. The ingredients might have been the same, but the taste sure wasn't. Funny how nothing more than being separated can completely change a thing, but it can. Oh, yes, it can. Blinking to keep Ira from swimming around on the little loveseat, she sniffled a bit and mumbled something about coming down with a bug.

"It's that time of year," he said, continuing on. "Anyway, as I was saying, I figured, what the hell. Maybe I'll give some of my old stories more of a TV newsmagazine treatment and send them off, see what happens."

"Sounds good."

"Thanks," he said, reaching for his jacket. "I actually brought some with me. I was hoping you'd read a few and let me know what you think." Pulling out a thick packet, he folded his jacket back up and handed her the envelope.

"After all, such a big star should know quality work if she sees it, right?"

Joy heard the taunt in his voice and grinned. "Poor you, if I'm the biggest star you know."

"Poor me is right," he said as she reached for the envelope and accidently brushed against his hand. Instead of pulling away, he turned his fingertips toward hers, sliding down to her palm, then her wrist, where they lingered atop a long, blue, pulsing vein, the only thing moving at the moment in her entire diminutive house. Down her arm his fingers slowly slid, then back up again, till sparks were all but shooting off every short, erect hair. Dropping his voice to a raspy whisper, he said, "But that's not all I came back for. I think I also need to explain a few things."

Repositioning himself on the loveseat so his legs were on either side of her knees, he leaned forward and reached for her just as she decided she would be more comfortable sitting beside him rather than basically in the middle of him. Flying into the far corner of the loveseat, which rocked and groaned and reminded her that she might very well get a backside full of nails if she didn't stop jumping around on the jerry-rigged thing, she grew completely still, staring at the envelope she'd dropped on the floor. Then, glancing up at Ira, watching him consider their new cramped quarters with a bemused smile, she felt...not much.

Where was it? The heat, the want, the burning need? She knew it hadn't vanished. It still ached too much to be gone. But, then again, didn't amputees feel phantom pain? Maybe Ira was like an arm she'd lost back in the war. The war between the mates. Maybe they just needed to kiss and make up. What could that hurt? Ira had his girlfriend, after all. And Joy, well, Joy had a few more pecans, if she was lucky. Who would have to know if she let herself hang on for dear life one last time?

When he reached for her again, she reached back, sliding her hands up his arms, reacquainting her heart with every rock-hard hill and valley beneath his flannel, arching toward him as he scooped her closer. Running his lips down her neck, he quietly said, "Relax. You're not seeing someone, are you?"

She was opening her mouth to say—*what? Yes? No? Maybe? It depends on if you're still living with someone?*—when from the kitchen door there came a deafening salvo of blows that lifted her straight off the loveseat.

"What the fuck!" Ira exclaimed. "It's like Grand Central Station around here. Ignore it."

But she was already hurtling toward the kitchen, preemptively gritting her teeth. How dare her mother come back again when she knew Ira was finally there. How *dare* she!

Blam, blam, blam!

"I'm coming," Joy shouted, snatching the door open.

"That's actually what I was afraid of."

"Boo-Boo," she squawked. Barefoot, blue work shirt unbuttoned, long black hair wild as if someone had spent half the night raking her hands through it, he looked like he'd just rolled out of bed to take a midnight drive. "What on earth are you doing?"

"Several things," he calmly replied. "One of which is checking to see how you're feeling."

Remembering his big hand on her forehead, across her cheek, she blushed and said, "Better."

"Good. I also wanted to make sure Ira was able to find your house." As if on cue, Ira slipped up behind her.

"Yeah, no problem," he said.

"Great. I'll just be going then." Moving as if to walk back to his idling truck, he stopped and turned around. "You know, man, if you don't have anywhere else to crash tonight, you're welcome to come back to my place." Boo-Boo might have been talking to Ira, but he was staring straight at Joy. And she supposed she was staring back. As she told Tanya later, how could she not, the way the black tangle scribbling his chest disappeared into a wide, shocking snarl just above his unbelted jeans? In all the years she had known Boo-Boo Bailey, she had never once seen him shirtless, a situation that suddenly seemed practically criminal. "I've got a bed in the guest room with your name all over it."

"Thanks, but I thought I'd see if Joy had anywhere to stick me here."

Joy remembered all the places she had stuck him in the past. And, when she looked back at Boo-Boo, she guessed he was consulting a similar checklist.

While Ira's charged presence two inches behind her still had enough energy to ignite a power grid, and while part of her yearned to lean back against every solid memory she had missed for so long and say, "That's all right, we'll figure something out," she was surprised to find she was having technical difficulties processing a response. It was as if Boo-Boo in his wide-open shirt and low-slung jeans was scrambling the signal somehow. She looked at her old friend-turned-producer and sensed him directing her still, guiding her toward a brighter future she couldn't quite see for the residual steam still rising off Ira. But Boo-Boo had never steered her wrong before. And if he didn't think Ira should stay with her that night, then she didn't, either. Not really. At least not entirely.

"You know what?" she said, turning to Ira, "Boo-Boo's got a point. You probably *would* be more comfortable at his place. As you can see, I really don't have anywhere to stick you here." Not now. Maybe not ever. Certainly not as long as Boo-Boo was ten feet away, looking like he'd been making love for hours.

"Fine," was all Ira said.

"Why don't you follow me," Boo-Boo suggested, heading for his truck and winking at Joy. "It can be a little tricky at night."

It can be a little tricky indeed, she thought, winking back and watching the man she had considered the love of her life for more years than she cared to count collect his jacket, slip on his boots, give her a Scout salute and, just as he had come, be gone, *rip-rip-ripping* into the night.

Three weeks later, tucked between some pecan recipes, Joy found a familiar postmark in her mailbox. "I guess you've dropped out of sight again? You sounded so happy to get to read my news stories, so I left them with you, expecting a call at least. No call. No more stories for you. Try calling some time. Try writing. Try keeping in touch. No charge. No obligation."

Oh but Joy *had* called. Filled with regret about the way Friday had ended, wishing she had slammed the door and dragged Ira straight to bed, hoping in fact to drive to New Orleans and do exactly that, she had dialed his number Saturday afternoon and got the answering machine.

Ira's girlfriend: "This is Robin."

Ira: "And this is Ira."

Both: "We can't come to the phone right now."

They giggled.

Ira: "So leave a message at the beep."

Robin: "Ciao!"

And Joy hung up.

****

Living across from Bess and Bubba was more educational than she could have imagined. Building on their favorite exhortations, she trained herself to automatically repeat one calming mantra any time Ira entered her mind—"Up yours, Ira Everhart. Up straight the fuck to fucking yours."

Bess and Bubba did her that favor. They did her mother one, too. Shortly after Ira's visit, the couple who were on a first-name basis with every Avalon City beat cop bought the Barge-mobile.

"*What?*" Joy screamed, slamming Sally's door, eyes bugging out at the brown heap parked across the dirt drive, next to the trailer. "You sold *them* that damn car? Jack the Ripper and his blonde accomplice?"

"I wish you could see yoreself," her mother snorted from her perch on Joy's concrete steps, fishing a fistful of tablets from her cigarette pouch and knocking them back with a slug of soda. "You've been pesterin' the daylights out of me to sell it and drive that thang over there." She yanked her head toward the Wedgie, still boasting factory plastic over its sweet red seats. "They had the money. Now they've got the car."

"They also have a matching pair of semi-automatic pistols and no remorse," Joy yelled. "What's going to happen when that damn car dies again, probably sometime later today, and they come banging on *my* door wanting their money back?"

"Squall, why doncha," her mother hissed, darting her eyes toward the trailer. Then, standing up, she goose-steeped to the gate, opened it, whistled Radar and Sugar Pie into the Wedgie, and peeled out.

"Maybe you could move," Tanya said, once Joy had calmed down enough to call. "Into an actual, full-grown house. They have those, you know."

"Maybe I could come stay with you till all this blows over," Boo-Boo suggested the next morning, a smile flirting around the corners of his mouth. "I'm not too much bigger than Ira. I'm sure I'd fit wherever you were going to stick him."

"I'm sure you would," Joy said, shoving his shoulder as she walked to the coffeepot.

"I'm sure it'd be fun trying," he said, grinning and handing her a song to play—"If I Said You Have a Beautiful Body Would You Hold It Against Me."

"Whoa, Nelly," WildDog whooped. "Should I give you two some privacy?"

"Why?" Joy asked. "So I can beat him with this record? You don't have to leave for that." To illustrate, she smacked Boo-Boo on top of the head with the forty-five. "Bad boy," she said. "What would Ruthie say?"

"Now, Joy."

She bapped him again.

Chapter 23
"If It Weren't For Him"

Any time her mother wasn't at work the next few months, she was parked at Joy's kitchen table, peering out the window at the Barge-mobile. Bess and Bubba, for whom stakeouts were nothing new, beefed up their phony public act.

Little did they know that Quida Raye Perkins didn't care if they whipped each other like lard icing. She simply wanted them to do it inside their trailer, not in or even near that beige-on-brown bomb. At the first sign of trouble brewing near her former car, she was prepared to march over, make a citizen's arrest, and impound the vehicle as evidence.

Despite all the thought Joy had given to exterminating the junker, she spent the first half of 1985 kicking herself for failing to consider what parting with it might mean to her mother. Far too late, Joy realized that, in addition to entire tobacco fields of cigarette smoke permanently soaked into every fiber, that bucket of bolts was also filled with ten years of life, including every precious second of Jessie's. Now someone else was driving the highs and lows of Quida Raye's previous decade. And they were doing it in nothing short of a daily Firecracker 400.

"They're too burly to land any really good punches inside the car," Joy said one warm May afternoon. Not that her mother was listening. She was doing what she had done for months—sitting by Joy's kitchen window, faraway eyes trained on the corner, waiting for the Barge-mobile to turn and head back home to her.

Joy sighed and stirred the soup her mother had started—vegetable, not many calories, but food was food at that point—while contemplating her upcoming schedule.

"Did I tell you I'm judging a talent contest at the Wagon Wheel next weekend?" The announcement was really a warning. Joy would once again be invading Quida Raye's raucous weekend retreat. Therefore, no dancing barefoot on tabletops.

"Idn't Gary Ferris gonna be there again?" her mother asked, drawing back the curtain and narrowing her Rebel eyes. Movement had been spotted across the way.

"Yep, and they're pulling out all the stops. In addition to the talent contest, they're having a crawfish boil and raffling off a new car. Everyone from KLME will be there, not to mention TV and newspapers."

"Well, Gary's a big star now." Her mother exhaled and let the curtain fall. False alarm. It was just one of Bess's juvie boys, briefly in from reform school and probably off to expose himself to some of her bored floozy friends past the big red fence.

Joy stirred the soup and hummed Gary's new smash hit, the patriotic ballad, "Cut Me and I Bleed Red, White, and Blue." Until recently, she had spent her entire career spinning pretty much the same smallish collection of singers, most of whom were around her mother's age. By mid 1985, however, a younger generation was steaming up country as much as Joy's soup-simmering kitchen. That very subject, in fact, had been a hot topic at work just the day before, after Ruthie firmed up Joy's itineraries for the next weekend at the Wagon Wheel as well as Nashville in June for Fan Fair.

"Wonder how many of the new crew's gonna be at Fan Fair," Wild Dog said, inspiring Boo-Boo to rattle off fifteen or twenty names, many of which Joy was hearing for the first time.

"Who?" she asked, prompting WildDog and Boo-Boo to snicker derisively. Her superficial grasp of the entire subject of country music remained a running joke between her pompous-ass co-workers.

"One of 'em's next up right now," Boo-Boo said in his kindergarten-teacher voice.

She flapped a dismissive hand. "Whatever. I don't pay attention to most of those flash-in-the-pans you make me play anyway."

"We know," WildDog said, cutting his eyes at Boo-Boo and sniggling again.

"Well, pay attention to this one," Boo-Boo said. "Every word."

"Is that what's been playing the last few mornings?" WildDog asked. Boo-Boo nodded, a little sadly, Joy thought. She knew the two of them arrived well before she did, and she also knew Boo-Boo treated the production room like his own living room, playing records that would never get airtime on her show. His musical tastes had always been more cutting-edge than KLME's programming allowed, which Joy considered humorous since one of his jobs was dictating what got played and what didn't. And it looked like some new song by some new guy was about to be introduced to small-town audiences near and far.

Boo-Boo sat back and examined the floor as the studio swelled with swoon-worthy, heartrending lyrics about a secret, would-be love thwarted by some other man. Once the tune trailed off and stations went to national news, all Joy could manage was, "Goodness!"

"Yeah, and check this out," WildDog said, standing up and grabbing the album cover, which he held next to Boo-Boo's head. "Just shave that infernal five o'clock shadow off this sucker, and trim a few inches off his shaggy-ass head, and ta-da!"

"Goodness," Joy said again, looking from the picture of her newest heartthrob to the face of her oldest male friend in the world.

"And add about twenty pounds," Boo-Boo noted, shoving WildDog away. "While subtracting a couple of on-air personalities if the two of you don't get back to work."

Joy smiled again while stirring her soup, listening to the song playing in the living room.

"Who's that?" her mother asked.

As if she had been in the know for years, Joy ticked off all the details she had first heard the day before. If Joy Savoy had learned anything during her time as a country DJ, it was how to dress up total ignorance as deep knowledge with nothing more than a few snippets of well-placed trivia. In truth, all she had ever really known was what sounded good. And she could listen to heartbreakers like this one nonstop—as long as she could keep the old classics in rotation a while longer. At least until the name Ira Everhart no longer came to mind.

"Humph! I like him," said Quida Raye, who adored

anyone new out of Nashville, and plenty were on the cusp the middle of 1985. Glancing at her mother, face glued to the window while she twitched a toe, Joy clanked the spoon against the pot and scuttled into the living room to start "If It Weren't for Him" again, pulling out Gary Ferris's latest album to play next. It wouldn't hurt to get ready for the weekend, when Tanya had her heart set on introducing Joy to all her paramours in Gary's band.

"Doesn't a big star like Gary Ferris have fresh *wee* groupies he can choose from?" Boo-Boo had asked the day before, earning himself a thunk on the arm.

"Maybe," Joy had coolly said, rubbing her knuckles. "But, for your information, Tanya's got something those other girls don't. She's got a drawer full of lucky panties. And she can't wait to grab a fistful and introduce me to the entire Giddyup gang next Saturday."

Joy picked up her spoon and tittered again at the memory of Boo-Boo's face, a slack-jawed mix of professional horror and personal alarm.

"Danger, Will Robinson," WildDog had cried, robotting his arms.

"Don't worry," she had said, and chortled. "I'm a little pigeon-toed and plain for a country groupie. But Tanya swears there's hope for me yet."

"Here come them fat asses now," her mother said, ducking behind the curtain as the Barge-mobile rattled up. And, for a confused second, soup spoon in hand, Joy thought she was talking about her and Tanya.

****

The next Saturday dawned like so many May mornings in Louisiana, buggy and muggy, blue with hope and humidity. Joy waited till the afternoon to get ready so she wouldn't sweat off all her perfume. Then she picked up her mother, dropped her off an hour later at Harvey's, and headed to Tanya's grandmother's house, wondering if that bantam rooster of a bouncer was still at the Wagon Wheel and, if so, would he realize the chain-ripping, riot-inciting duo once banned for life had returned with backstage passes?

"Where you been keepin' yoself?" Ethelene asked, swinging open the door.

"Up the road, where I belong. I get into too much trouble when I come back home."

"It's the comp'ny you keep," Ethelene cackled. "Yes, lawd."

Then Gran D. swooped in with a big, blinding hug. "Joy Faye! Have you lost weight?"

"I doubt it," she said, sucking in her stomach. "Certainly nothing more than a pound or two, and that's only because I still have to ride my stupid bike any time my mother looks at my car sideways."

"Let's go shopping tomorrow, then, and get Tanya a bike," Gran D. exclaimed.

"Okay, I've got a ten-speed, which she might like." Just then, a sound like a locomotive toppling down the stairs erupted behind them.

"If I come home and there's a bicycle anywhere around here," Tanya declared, landing in the foyer, fright mask gleaming and six-inch heels nearly chipping the marble, "it better be one built for three, because you stooges will be the only ones riding it."

Grabbing Joy's arm, Tanya thundered past her grandmother and the housekeeper who had raised her, through the door, and across the porch. "I hope you're hungry," she bellowed. "Because I'm ready to eat myself into a diabetic coma."

"Tanya Lynn, don't forget you only have two vegetable exchanges left," Gran D. called, scurrying out to the porch. "That's one cup of green beans, young lady."

"They on the stove now," Ethelene hollered.

But Tanya only whanged Sally's door very nearly off its hinges. "I gotcher green beans, Granny," she said. "Shit fuck! How fast can this thing go?"

Joy turned the key and eased around the circular driveway, waving at the women scowling on the wraparound porch. As Tanya bounced around beside her, Joy made her way to Pitts' main drag, registering how much the town had changed. With all the money Reagan was pumping into Fort Dewey, investors hadn't been able to slap up fast-food joints and new-car lots swiftly enough. As a result, the Wagon Wheel, situated in the middle of what was quickly becoming a serviceman-oriented industrial park, was a mob scene even when one of the biggest names in country wasn't making a special appearance for old time's sake.

As they approached the newest hotel in town, Tanya cried, "There are the buses in back." Twisting around to check out the parking lot, she motioned for Joy to pull in. "Let's see if any of the guys are around. This'll be a great time for you to get acquainted with some of them, if you know what I mean."

Lewd hilarity filled the car as Joy pictured Tanya accosting multiple fellows in cowboy boots while she stood primly back—Miss Jane Hathaway to her Elly May.

"I thought you were hungry," she said, speeding

up. "The sooner we get to the Wagon Wheel, the sooner we can hit the crawfish boil. Think of the pile of crawdads we'll have. The potatoes. The corn. Mmm."

"Hell's bells," Tanya howled as the hotel faded behind them. Flopping back around and goggling at Joy, she yelled, "I thought I left my grandmother at home! What am I saying? You've been without a man so long you may as well *be* my grandmother."

Joy felt a guilty twinge, remembering how often Tanya had listened to her moan about Ira or groan about her mother. Of course, Tanya had usually been as aggravating as both of them put together. Still. Making up her mind to be as frisky and fun as possible the rest of the evening, Joy playfully jabbed Tanya in her sequined side. She felt like an iguana.

"Stop it," she crabbed. Joy poked her again. "Cut it out." She nudged her again. "The only way I'm forgiving you is if you give me your potato *and* your corn. And, for that matter, your dessert, too. Oh, speaking of *sweet thangs*, guess what I heard… Lonnie Luneau's getting married!"

"Really?" Joy said, careful to keep her eyes on the road. "To who?"

"The girl whose father has the new Weenie Queen franchise in town. Bitch."

Unhappily registering various similarities to the melee of two Mays earlier, Joy weakly asked, "You don't think they'll be at the Wagon Wheel, do you?"

"They'd better not be," Tanya roared, laughing till tears glistened in her crazy eyes. "Lonnie was the love of my life, at least for a split second. If he shows up to rub my face in his dumb, soon-to-be-newlywedded bliss, I'm afraid the National Guard might have to get involved."

Tanya was still cackling when Joy shakily pulled into the Wagon Wheel's parking lot, where a feast soon recalibrated their attention. Collecting plates heaped with mudbugs, they joined Boo-Boo, Ruthie, WildDog, and the others by the KLME van. Hits were blaring and little black eyeballs were everywhere.

"Why anyone would eat food with the face still on it is beyond me," Joy said, rolling the potato and corn onto Tanya's plate, then handing hers to Boo-Boo, looking away while he picked the tails. Noticing the swell of excitement their arrival had sparked, she glanced around to see what everyone was looking at.

"A whole crowd's watching Boo-Boo peel your crawfish for you," Tanya pouted.

"Don't worry, darlin'," WildDog crooned, sliding over beside her. "Those two are dull as dirt. The real stars will be shining soon enough." Tanya turned to behold long, tall WildDog. Painted-on jeans, black western shirt open to his navel, white cowboy hat atop shoulder-length, feathered brown hair. Then she made a noise that sounded like a cross between a gurgle and a coo. Recognizing admiration when he heard it, not to mention a good dancing tune, WildDog took Tanya's plate of crawfish and set it down, slipped an arm around her waist and returned the compliment by two-stepping her around the parking lot to "Baby's Got Her Blue Jeans On."

"Fire, meet gas," Boo-Boo said as WildDog and Tanya whipped past. WildDog had been right; all eyes were now on the two of them. Cool Hand Luke and big Jane Russell, dazzling in a blinding red swirl.

"She sure can dance, can't she?" Joy proclaimed.

"Yep, even in six-inch heels. Though, if she trips, they'll probably have to call a vet to come put her down." He was amusing himself, if no one else, and Joy popped him on the arm.

"Stop it," she said. "Her grandmother's buying her a bike tomorrow."

"Does that mean she's giving her lucky panties a rest tonight, then?" he asked, cocking an eyebrow.

"It doesn't look like it," Joy said, sighing as the song ended and WildDog and Tanya whirled back to the KLME van, bowing and waving to their cheering fans.

"Whoo! That was fun!" Tanya gasped. Snatching up one of the station's promotional giveaways, a hand-held fan emblazoned with "Lady Bug, Mouth of the South," she flapped at her kabuki face that was beginning to melt. Then she snuggled up to WildDog and waved it at his chiseled, handsome countenance, grinning as he closed his eyes and moaned in mock ecstasy.

Neither of them seemed to be cooling off much, Joy observed, as Warren Piece opened the mic and announced the good folks from Palmer Ford would be drawing for that new Escort in five minutes.

Tanya jumped as if stabbed. "I haven't bought my raffle tickets yet. Quick, WildDog, can you break a twenty?"

"Darlin'," WildDog drawled for all to hear, "I could break your heart."

As a gaggle of females swooned in agreement, Tanya gave a thumbs up, grabbed the fives out of his hand, and tottered off to buy raffle tickets, tossing the promotional fan over her shoulder. But as Joy reached to catch it, her supper slid off her paper plate and her right foot slipped through the mess, causing her to nearly do the splits across the pavement.

"You okay, Grace?" Boo-Boo cracked, hoisting her up. "Don't worry, everyone was watching Tanya strut her stuff, so they missed your smooth Nadia Comăneci moves." Suddenly mindful of the Lady Bug bobbleheads also up for grabs, not to mention her now-empty plate, Joy gingerly minced toward a trash can, thinking about a newspaper clipping Boo-Boo had handed her that week, a story detailing the job high-school students considered the "coolest"—radio disc jockey.

Examining some of the other stellar examples of humanity collecting KLME paychecks, she heard WildDog belching a few chords of "When You're Hot You're Hot" while Warren Piece pretended to wave away a fart and Boo-Boo laughed so hard a fizzy stream of beer shot out his nose.

Yep, we're a bunch to be admired, all right. Sucking crawfish juice off her fingers, she slid up behind Boo-Boo and kneed him in the back of the legs, giggling as he pretended to lose his balance and fell back against her. Wrapping her arms around him, resting her head against his broad back for the briefest moment, she filled her lungs with the sweet, damp scent of him, a sweaty gust of peppermint and well-worn denim that smelled like home. Then she opened her eyes and saw Ruthie by the KLME van.

"Ugh. Get off me," she said, shoving him upright and ambling over to lean against the van. And that's when she felt it. The music. The thing that really jars admiration out of the masses. Flattening her back against the quarter panel so she wouldn't miss a beat, Joy Savoy closed her eyes and fanned her face. Coolest of the cool. *Right.*

****

At twilight, Boo-Boo and Joy were getting off Gary's bus when Harvey's sedan eased into the parking lot with its big-haired payload. Boo-Boo let fly the two-note coyote howl from *The Good, The Bad and The Ugly.*

Joy watched her mother and the others climb out looking as grimly determined as a pack of freshly starched, heavily teased bounty hunters. Especially the slim one in pink, the one who looked like Huck Finn under a Moonlit Brown wide-brimmed hat.

"Let the games begin," Boo-Boo announced.

****

Later, when the music was but a dull thud in Joy's brain, she walked her co-workers back to the KLME van.

"Keep it classy," Boo-Boo sternly said, nodding across the parking lot at the busses Tanya was skittering around, tapping windows. Behind him, WildDog stuck out his tongue and waggled his fingers on either side of his white cowboy hat.

"Don't worry," Joy said, wishing she had ridden with the goobers in the KLME van. Instead, she was left standing in a bar parking lot, watching them leave, while Tanya bounded up bus steps.

"Wait till you see what I've got for you," she bawled. Catching a flash of red and the lacy edge of a lucky pair of panties, Joy knew her chauffeur services were no longer required. Mood drooping, she got in her car and headed back to a small house an hour down a winding road, making her way by the dark side of a melancholy moon.

She would be on the phone with the top-selling country artist in the land in a couple of days, on assignment with the King of Country soon thereafter, then chatting with the Grand Ole Opry star whose chart-topping "Rose Colored Glasses" was one of the rare songs from the late '70s Boo-Boo never minded hearing. Folks kept telling her what a great life she had, but Joy Savoy just couldn't see it. Hitting her brights, she felt as in the dark as ever.

Chapter 24
"She's Got You"

Besides being able to belch entire songs, WildDog had another talent that came to light the summer of 1985. Come to find out, he was also quite the amateur photographer. A closet shutterbug who for years had been smuggling his 35mm backstage at concerts, he also prided himself on always getting the best images of whatever wedding he was attending, empty-handed save his autofocus camera and roll of 36-exposure film.

In late June of 1985, WildDog took his roll to a one-hour processor, then showed off his shots before slipping them in the mail to New Orleans.

The bride wore powder blue. The groom, who had stopped shaving, wore a navy suit. "Don't you think Ira looks better with a beard?" WildDog asked, pondering the images over Joy's shoulder.

"I think he looks like shit," Boo-Boo snarled, grabbing for the photos Joy was studying like a handful of cards upon which the ranch had just been bet.

"Wait," she said, twirling her chair around. Maybe it wasn't exactly powder blue. Maybe it was more like that sugary blue generally only seen on bakery cakes. Sweet, creamy blue. Baby blue.

"Why didn't either of you tell me?" she managed, staring wounded and raw at her second-oldest friend in the world. "Did *you* go, too?"

"Hell, no. And I *was* going to tell you," Boo-Boo said, lunging for the photos again. "I just didn't realize a gotdamned wedding photographer was going to beat me to it."

Joy spun away once more, giving WildDog fits. "You better not bend those. They're my wedding gift, dammit!"

With that, Boo-Boo stood up, seized the arm of Joy's chair, snatched the photos out of her hands, and flung them against the door. "There's your fucking wedding gift."

Joy watched the pictures flutter briefly through the breezy air, thirty-six oscillating bits of baby blue. Picking them up and peevishly wiping each one on his jeans, WildDog slowly straightened himself, pausing a few tense moments toe-to-toe with Boo-Boo.

"I'm going to the post office," he quietly said. "And you, Robert, can go fuck yourself." Snatching the door open, WildDog stormed out, Boo-Boo hot on his heels.

Then Joy also stood up and walked toward the door. But, instead of following the men, she reached down and flipped the deadbolt left over from the days when Studio A had been some long-ago engineer's private apartment. Then she turned and wandered toward the rack of forty-fives. Flipping through the Cs, she found the record she was looking for, sat down and, without a single lucid thought, cued up a song that would serve as the centerpiece of a stunt far more in keeping with her shock-jock counterparts.

For the rest of her show that day, not to mention all of Warren Piece's shift as well as those of several other DJs, Joy Savoy played just one record. She skipped lunch and supper and was even considering forgoing breakfast the next day just to play it more. All told, Lady Bug, Mouth of the South, spun one lone tune for slightly over eighteen hours and fifty-seven minutes, the amount of time it took to hear every heartbreaking word three hundred sixty-three times in a row. No commercial breaks. No news. No words. No regrets. Just one song, three hundred sixty-three times.

During the first nine or ten hours, the entire office was on the other side of the glass in the newsroom, hopping up and down and mutely flailing around. Vernon scribbled stern notes on a yellow legal pad— "You're not too big to fire!!!" and "Ray and Jimmy are servicing the plane right now!!!" and "I could have this glass popped out or that door knocked down in no time!!!!!!!"

But on the record played, over and over, until only Boo-Boo remained. Turning off the lights in the newsroom, he dragged a chair up to the glass, propped a boot on the ledge, rested an elbow on a knee and touched a hand to the glass. Soon, the count on each side was ten fingertips, between which vibrated the absolute best Nashville had ever offered on the subject of being shattered beyond repair.

About having his picture while "She's Got You." And having their records while "She's Got You." And having so many other little things while "She's Got You." For one long day and most of a night in late June 1985, Joy Savoy held the airwaves hostage, pouring nothing but Patsy's "She's Got You" across little towns throughout Louisiana and beyond. It wouldn't be long before even the smallest stations would have technology to prevent half-crazed DJs from pulling such shenanigans. The day Joy learned Ira was lost, however, all that existed at KLME was a single-minded determination to purge the name Ira Everhart from the farthest reaches of her unsettled soul.

Well after midnight, finally on the far side of caring, she flipped the deadbolt. Just as she had met Ira in that hallway two years earlier, Boo-Boo was standing there now. Nodding to the graveyard-shift guy, who had also been waiting in case she ended her siege on his dime, Boo-Boo turned to her and said, "Ready?"

"I guess."

"I'll drive." And he didn't say another word till long after he'd swept her into his house and onto his couch, encasing her in a warm, swaddling crook of bended knee and folded arm. "There, there," he said, gently kissing her forehead as if, Joy found herself thinking, that could put Humpty Dumpty back together again.

Somewhere, a clock struck two. She needed to be at work in less than four hours. Assuming she still had a job, which she guessed she probably didn't. Burrowing deeper into the soft crush of couch cushions behind her and the firm sanctuary of her most steadfast friend in front, she reached once more for the man she had leaned on through so many years of losing, starting with a trailer with purple carpet and ending with what just might be the best job in the world. The anguish in between drew her deeper still. Sonny. Jessie. Ira. Gone. All gone.

As Boo-Boo started rocking her, Joy swayed in his arms, mind adrift, free floating to random, thrumming thoughts of beached whales and wave-battered sailors of yore, many of whom never learned to swim so as to hasten the inevitable should they be lost at sea. Yearning for the same deep, dark peace, she was distracted only by whispers stirring the surface, murmured promises floating up, foamy but firm.

"It'll be okay," Boo-Boo was saying. "It'll all be okay."

Turning fully toward him, reaching a hand up to his long, black hair, pulling him closer so she could anchor herself to his craggy roughness, feel the fire of his five o'clock shadow burn across face, lips, neck, she became increasingly aware of a tightening in him, the possibility that, as long as he kept holding her this fiercely, there was no chance she would ever hit bottom again. Feeling parts of him begin fitting into places they had probably always belonged, her heart began softly singing again at last. *Boo-Boo, oh, Boo-Boo! How could I have been so blind?*

As their lips brushed against each other, then circled back deeper, harder, hungrier, over and over and over again, twelve years of friendship flew away like shingles in a hurricane. Tasting a summer-warm sweetness she had never known, Joy rocked to a rhythm that perfectly matched her own, synced to a private soundtrack only they seemed to hear. Stirring to greedy caresses, devouring eager kisses, she covered his big hands with hers, exploring long, thick fingers on a quest all their own. Turning her own touch to the heat beneath his shirt, thrilling to the warm tangle her fingers twisted through, she heard him catch his breath as she slipped toward denim.

Then, at the very moment she knew she would never want anything more than this man with her, beside her, throughout her always, he groaned and pulled away.

"Wait," is all he said.

Shuddering in agony, wracked by despair, she gazed into the dark eyes that owned her now, that had truly punctuated her every unspeakable night...every one. Convulsed by that realization, clinging to the man now smiling sadly down upon her, she knew there would be no getting over *this*.

"Is it Ruthie?"

Silencing her with a kiss, he heaved a sigh and said, "Now, Joy."

Chapter 25
"A Thing Called Love"

By the time Ruthie walked down the aisle and took her place beside her long, tall, gorgeous groom, it had been over two months since Joy's blue "She's Got You" day. Although it was touch-and-go for a while, Ray and Jimmy soon discovered her stunt was just what they needed to sew up the market. She was suddenly the outlaw DJ. That crazy, unpredictable Lady Bug. Joy Savoy had never been so much in demand. It also didn't hurt that the movie featuring that track, *Sweet Dreams*, was soon all the rage, applying—at least for her fans—an irresistible psychic sheen to Joy's temporary insanity.

"Just no more three hundred sixty-three times of the same dang song," Vernon had said. "Deal?"

"Deal," Joy agreed. And her raise of twenty-five dollars a week went into effect. She bought Ruthie and WildDog a place setting of their everyday dishes to celebrate.

"Boo-Boo wanted to get them some of their silver," Joy told Tanya at the reception. "But each spoon costs more than my raise, and I don't want him paying for it all. I'm doing everything by the book *this* time."

"I still can't believe you spent all that time thinking he and Ruthie were dating." Tanya hawed, ladling herself some punch—into which WildDog had just dumped a magnum of champagne, much to the horror of Ruthie's Pentecostal contingent primly lined up against the wedding hall's far wall.

"We've discussed this a thousand times," Joy said tiredly. "How was I supposed to know he was only a foil for her Holy Roller family?" Nibbling a finger sandwich, Joy grinned again at the thought of their silly charade, born after some legitimate, if uninspiring, dates and a drop-in visit from WildDog one night at suppertime. Boo-Boo went to get a bucket of chicken, and by the time he got back, Ruthie had all but lost her virginity to KLME's biggest womanizing scoundrel right there on his living room floor.

As he explained the night of her raving "She's Got You" delirium, months of agony followed as Ruthie begged him not to breathe a word to anyone—*especially* Joy, who she was afraid might blurt it out on air, like she did every personal detail involving her own mother.

So Boo-Boo Bailey, the most suitable of suitors, kept picking Ruthie up and dropping her off at WildDog's rocking pad, returning hours later to deliver her back to her parents' house. Their secret was safe—until WildDog fell to his knees during KLME's remote at the King of Country's concert and, in front of thousands of adoring fans, swept his cowboy hat off his half-hairless head. Exposing a gleaming dome only dear Ruthie had adored, clutching his hat to his heart, he asked her to become Mrs. Archibald Dale Dolittle.

When her startled father had given his grudging blessing, he had one question for the long, tall rascal whose hairy legs were poking out all over his skintight falling-apart jeans. "Son, all I want to know is if my precious Ruthie is still pure."

"Sir," WildDog answered, "I swear I still don't know if Ruthie's a girl or a boy. But I aim to marry her and find out. With your blessing, of course."

Boo-Boo said he didn't mind being Ruthie's "beard," especially since it seemed to bug Joy so much. Even now, all he had to do to make her knees wobbly was grin and slowly rub his bristly chin, something he was doing at that moment, standing across the room with Vernon, Ray, and Jimmy.

"But that's not even the half of it. Remind me how long it took the two of you to finally do the dirty deed. You know," Tanya said, elbowing her. "Makin' bacon. Sinkin' the sausage. Hidin' the salami."

"If what you're referring to with your deli-counter allusions is intercourse involving body parts I could name for you," Joy said, laughing as Tanya set her cup down and stuck fingers into both ears. "You know what Boo-Boo said that night."

Tanya unplugged her ears and picked up her cup. "Yep, that he had a twelve-year head start and you had a lot of catching up to do. While I'm aware that neither of you have ever been the quickest rabbits to the proverbial hole, as *you* might so crudely put it," she said, bugging out her eyes, "I still can't believe it took you *days.*"

"Yes, but they were *divine* days. *And* nights," Joy said, snickering as Tanya squirmed.

From the first morning after her "She's Got You" jag, when WildDog walked into the studio to find her in Boo-Boo's lap and declared, "It's about damn time!" until that day at the wedding, every second had in fact been divine, with the possible exception of the tense negotiations related to Joy attempting to retain her job.

"Whatever. I still think the funniest part is how he let you twist in the wind. After doing it himself since, what, eleventh grade? In making him bide his time for twelve full years, you singlehandedly turned Boo-Boo Bailey into the most patient man on earth," Tanya observed, maniacally cackling.

"You know, every time you laugh like that I expect 'Wipe Out' to start," Joy observed, lifting her cup to the tallest man in the room, the one she now casually referred to as the *real* love of her life.

Taking note of her salute, Tanya checked out the company Boo-Boo was keeping and said, "Why don't you see if he can get you a better raise than twenty-five measly dollars?"

"I'm lucky to still have a job, Tanya, let alone more money. Besides, it'll come in handy on my trip."

"You're going to be stuck in the sticks with five Pentecostal women," Tanya reminded her. "Where are you going to spend twenty-five measly dollars?"

She knew it had been a mistake to tell Tanya about her latest plan, how she was going to a "wilderness retreat" with Vernon's wife and her prayer group. While part of the original motivation had been to suck up to Vernon and keep her job after three hundred sixty-three times of "She's Got You," Joy had actually started looking forward to the trip, scheduled for the next long weekend after Ruthie and WildDog's nuptials. "A short vacation will be nice. Other than being without Boo-Boo for three whole days."

"You'll also be without running water or indoor plumbing or heat," Tanya pointed out, scooping up another ladle. "You'll be peeing in the frosty woods with a pack of lady snake handlers. Yippee. Can I come, too?"

****

Her mother dropped her off at Vernon's church before dawn the next Friday. Parking beside a van the women would take to their rustic retreat near Greenwood, Mississippi, Quida Raye nodded when Joy said she'd see her Sunday night.

"We'll be back around six. Remember, Boo-Boo's got a ribbon-cutting, so he can't come get me."

"I'll be here," her mother said.

Then Joy gathered her bags and climbed on the van. Looking back at Quida Raye's slight silhouette under the parking lot's vapor lights as they pulled away, she saw her thin arm, little more than a bone with suntanned skin dangling off, stuck out of the Wedgie's window, pinching a contraband cigarette beneath a cone-shaped mist of creamy yellow.

****

Tanya only had it half right. Yes, there was no running water, indoor plumbing, or heat at Camp Pisgah. But there also were no walls on the tent cabins, no dry wood for fires, and no road. Meaning they had to hike two miles through a damp chill, lugging all their luggage, and Joy brought the most. Train case, pilot case, and square duffel. The other five women, veterans all, had little more than fanny packs.

Despite the autumn briskness, Joy sweated more hiking those two miles than she had since the summer she biked to work after her mother's automotive meddlings. If mascara melting into her eyes didn't blind her, hair spray-tinged sweat dripping off her bangs very nearly did. She practically needed a damn Braille Bible by the time she dragged up to the church campsite, swollen-eyed, soaking wet, and gasping for nippy air. The other women—each with at least ten years and fifty pounds on her—hopped around like barely winded Christian Olympians. Weightlifters maybe.

Most Pentecostals don't wear mascara, Joy fumed to herself. They also probably don't sit around playing records all the livelong day. She clearly needed to start riding her dumb bike again. The notion ticked her off so much she flopped down outside her tent cabin and stayed put till night. Sensing the truth of the matter— that Joy had been in the same spot for hours because she couldn't move—the other women gathered around her and began singing and praying. Praying and singing. That's pretty much all they did for three straight days. Sing and pray. Pray and sing. That and pee in the frosty woods, those five lady snake handlers and Joy.

While she originally suspected she might spend three days in the wilds of Mississippi wondering why in hell's name she had played the same damn song three hundred sixty-three times and got herself into such a pickle, that didn't quite turn out to be the case.

What she did was something else entirely. She learned to sing. And she learned to pray. The lady snake handlers weren't settling for less. Converting Joy Savoy had, in fact, been something of a secret mission for them all, and they were way too big to tick off. Come to find out, she wasn't such a hard nut to crack. She liked having people tell her God loved her and they did, too. With the exception of Boo-Boo's recent, fervent declarations, no one had told Joy they loved her in years. In fact, the closest Quida Raye had ever come was in stacks of notes signed, "Love, Mother."

By trip's end, Joy was consequently very nearly a lady snake handler herself, having lost her mascara in one of her suitcases, yanked her knotty hair into a Pentecostal ponytail, and gotten way on down with the amens and the praise Jesuses, hallelujah!

Till those spirit-filled days in Mississippi, it would be safe to say Joy had spent much of her twenties worshipping a different god. An aloof, moody—and now remarried—deity. While a change of religion in a barren survivalist's camp in Mississippi felt as right as every precious moment with Boo-Boo, another sensation eventually joined her newfound tranquility. And it wasn't anywhere near as peaceful. Instead, it was jumpy and anxious, as if Joy was missing something important. Quida Raye called it "being afraid someone was gonna fart and you wouldn't smell it."

Remembering her thinner-than-ever mother aglow in the church parking lot, Joy soon convinced herself that ticklish sense of missing was connected to her. Maybe she had gotten sick again. Maybe more. Joy couldn't call and have her worst fears confirmed, however, until the retreat ended, they hiked two miles back to the van, and drove another twenty miles to civilization. When her trembling fingers finally got her mother's number right, the phone rang once, twice, three times.

"M'hello," Quida Raye finally said.

"Can you tell me why you always let the phone ring three times before you answer it?" Joy barked, weak with relief.

Her mother didn't say a word. Joy pictured her on

her secondhand couch, hair stuck straight up, collecting her crabby thoughts. "I happen to have been nappin', if that's all right with you," she finally grumped.

"Good thing I called, then," Joy gaily said. "You have to pick me up in five hours."

"I'm well aware a that." Joy heard a lighter clicking. "Now I'd like to go use the bathroom, if you don't mind."

"Sure. Fine. Whatever. See you soon."

Joy hung up and stood there watching the phone cord swing. As the lady snake handlers pumped quarters into nearby candy machines, she wondered—if it wasn't her mother, what was it?

She would not have an answer until Monday morning. Under a stack of "While You Were Out" notes were the two words that had wound their way through the Mississippi woods.

"Ira called."

Chapter 26
"Old Flame"

The phone rang and rang, almost long enough for Joy to lose her nerve.

"Hello," Ira finally said.

Once she succeeded in squeezing a response past the adrenalin speedball shooting through her veins, he said, "Well, well. I was hoping you'd call back."

"You were? Why?" she asked, trying not to twitch the feathery pile of forty-five sleeves she was nervously fingering onto "Old Flame."

"Why not?"

While a sane individual might have mentioned certain recent developments—namely his new marriage and her new love—what she said was, "Why not indeed." And thus began a chummy exchange of low-key commentary between Joy and the man whose every word once shimmered like diamonds.

Once.

"The song's almost over, so I'd better go," she finally said. "But, first, what *did* you call for?" So much was riding on his response, so much more than he could have guessed. And, at last, Ira Everhart didn't let her down.

"I was thinking about taking a trip back up to Avalon." Mistaking her silence for an invitation to continue speaking, he said, "And I was hoping we

318

could see each other again."

"Okay," Joy slowly began. "But didn't you just say 'I do' a few months ago?"

"I did."

"Well…have you gotten a divorce? Or run *her* off somewhere?" What if he had? What if Ira Ever*hart* had had a change of *heart*? Would Joy be *joy*ful? Smiling at the answer, she knew what she—and he—would both finally be, in their own individual ways.

Joy*less*.

"No," he said, laughing. "Nothing like that. I just thought you and I could get together again. You know, for old times' sake."

"For old times' sake," she repeated, feeling oddly embarrassed for him. "Wonder what your new bride would think of such a rendezvous. Even one for no loftier reason than 'old times' sake.' "

"I doubt much," Ira said. "Especially in view of the fact that I wasn't planning on telling her about it."

Confident at last that Ira Everhart deserved nothing less, Joy eased around and smiled at Boo-Boo, languorously tipped back in his chair, boots crossed, casually keeping time to the song that had been his own suggestion.

"Funny, but something tells me the new Mrs. Everhart might find out anyway."

Reaching toward the elaborate new board Ray and Jimmy had recently installed to prevent any more runaway trains the likes of which Ira's nuptials had triggered in the first place, Boo-Boo made sure the tape from which Joy would play knee-slapping snippets for years to come was still recording. Then he nodded at WildDog, who rolled full bore into one of his most popular impersonations—that of shrieking, wronged-woman, psychopathic shrew.

With Boo-Boo hard at work on the bleep button, WildDog let fly a verbal eruption in a volcanic soprano that would become one of his most requested on-air performances.

"You mother*****ing, c***-sucking, son-of-a-dog-humping-b***!" the "new" Mrs. Everhart shrieked across the airwaves. "I'm gonna shove this wedding ring so far up your godd***ed cornholed a** that you'll be spittin' white gold and sh***n' black mold for years, you lying, cheating, sister-screwing, farm-animal-f***ing inbred mutant ******head b*****d!"

Vernon, in full cardiopulmonary distress, was in the studio and on the verge of either apoplexy or destroying thousands of dollars of new electronic equipment before Boo-Boo, doubled over in hysterics, succeeded in cutting to a commercial. But the tape kept rolling until, on the other end, a final click was recorded.

From that day forward, Joy Savoy rarely cued up an old somebody-done-somebody-wrong song without prefacing it with a few, choice, bleep-riddled, clanging ululations to Ira from his shockingly bawdy "bride." It was her way of performing a fairly regular, thoroughly public exorcism of Ira Everhart from the darkest corners of her erstwhile existence. And the original expulsion proved particularly popular with Joy's biggest fan.

"That woman called him everythang but a white man," Quida Raye dashed over to giddily exclaim after work that day.

"Yes, she did," Joy said. "But you do realize that

'woman' was WildDog, right?"

"Uh-huh," she peeped. "I also know who he/she was talkin' to, and that's all that matters. Idn't that right, Robert?"

Boo-Boo pulled Joy closer on the little loveseat and smiled. "Yes, ma'am," was all he said.

Chapter 27
"If We Make It Through December"

Joy Savoy walked down an aisle herself the first Sunday in December. She was one of three people joining the First United Methodist Church of Avalon, which Boo-Boo attended. As it happened, she was too attached to her mascara to turn Pentecostal. Ruthie and WildDog came. Her mother wanted to be there, too, but she didn't have a dress that fit anymore.

After church, Joy's usual moving crew helped pack up Quida Raye's old, big clothes—the twos and fours left behind when she'd moved to her apartment. Then they hauled everything to Joy's new full-grown house. With two bedrooms, a den, central air and heat, and a fenced-in back yard ringed by rioting camellias, her latest rental also had an unbeatable location. It was two doors down from Boo-Boo.

"Why didn't you just move in with the man?" Tanya bellowed after everyone left.

"I thought I'd focus on being a Methodist a few minutes before I start cohabitating with my boyfriend," Joy said, cradling the receiver.

Tanya snorted. "Last I checked, Methodists don't take vows of celibacy. Several have even been known to engage in premarital, um, trysts."

"True. And, last *I* checked, two people don't need to live under the same roof to spend every second together. Think of it as a gas-saving move on my part while affording me plenty of storage space for bright blue loveseats and the like."

"Speaking of premarital *you know what*," Tanya continued, chortling, "how's stuffin' the old taco going? Still fun?"

Joy opened her new back door, admiring the fencerow festooned with red and white blooms. Considering her true love two doors down and her unnatural disaster of a friend on the phone, the camellias' color scheme seemed a fitting mix of Valentine's and the Red Cross.

"I've decided I'm not telling you every little thing Boo-Boo and I do anymore. It's too precious."

"Aww," Tanya baby-talked. "It's too *pweshush*."

Joy hung up then and smiled as the phone rang and rang while she unpacked her dishes. Later, she wandered up her safe new street to doze off beside the true love of her life.

Across town, Quida Raye was catching a few winks, too. Catnapping before heading off to the In-'n'-Out, she woke with a start from a terrible dream.

****

"Look at this," Boo-Boo said Monday morning, rustling the newspaper. Joy pecked him on the head while examining the Police Log section he was tapping with a finger. "The In-'n'-Out was held up again last night. Good thing you moved. Now if we can just get your mother to stop working there. The paper didn't name the clerk on duty. It wasn't her, was it?" He glanced up just as Joy staggered backward, reaching for the phone.

One, two, three rings later, her mother finally

answered. "M'hello."

"Is there something you'd like to tell me?" Joy yelled. Hearing nothing more than a cigarette pouch snap open and a lighter click, she gripped the phone till her knuckles turned white. "Boo-Boo's got the newspaper right here. Why didn't you call and tell me?"

"Tell you what?" her mother finally said, exhaling. "That the po-lice came and filed a report and everythang went back to normal?"

"Tell me that my own mother was the victim of an armed robbery! Or do you think everyone should glean such facts from their daily newspaper?" Vaguely aware of WildDog politely slipping out of the studio while Boo-Boo focused on lining up the next hour of programming, Joy fumed while listening to her mother smoke some more.

"I didn't see no reason to call and wake you up," she said. "Besides, knowin' somethin' never changed nuthin'." Then she casually mentioned the heads-up she had received during her catnap. "I dreamed every single thang that was gonna happen, just like I've done a thousand times before."

She said the dream woke her out of a sound sleep, so she got up, fixed a plate of butter mashed up with syrup, sopped it up with a can of biscuits, then lost most of it in the bathroom. "Must've been nerves," she claimed, as if this was something new. Joy tactfully kept quiet for once, listening to the rest of the dream-come-true.

Knowingly heading off to work, she said, she rang up each pack of gum, every tank of gas, scrutinizing face after face. But it wasn't till after dark that the man she'd been expecting arrived.

"I was cleanin' up 'round the pickled pigs' feet when he ran up behind me. Grabbed my arm and twisted it. Waved a gun in my face. Shoved me over to the register and yelled, 'Open it up!' Took the money and run. Every single thang just the way it happened in my dream."

When the police arrived, Quida Raye Perkins, queen of cool, said she was shaking so badly she could barely unlock the door she'd bolted in terror. Later, she went back to running the register, sweeping, mopping, cooking hot dogs, and regulating gas sales. The racing stripes on her getaway car sparkled under neon near the pumps, but she knew she wasn't going anywhere. And that was okay, because her dream had told her so.

"Just as I knew full well what was gonna happen 'fore I went to work," she said matter-of-factly, "I also knew everythang was gonna be all right. For that night at least."

Joy was still fuming an hour later. "Can you believe it? She says she didn't bother calling because she 'knew' everything was going to be all right, 'for that night at least.' "

"Huh?" Boo-Boo said.

"'Huh' what?"

"The last part. The 'for that night at least.' What do you think she meant by that?"

"Hell if I know," Joy crabbed. "*She's* the psychic one."

****

The rest of that first week in December, fans jammed KLME's call-in line with gripping tales of their own paranormal experiences. The "Can Your Mother Tell the Future" call-in question of the week would prove one of Boo-Boo's most popular ideas.

The cue to call was "Highwayman," Joy's favorite number-one hit dealing with otherworldly subjects. As four of country's biggest male megastars took turns singing about one soul with four different incarnations, fans called nonstop to talk about past lives, out-of-body experiences, visits from the dead, and similarly spooky subjects Boo-Boo and WildDog paired with other eerie country tunes, of which there were plenty.

As her co-workers brainstormed supernatural song suggestions, Joy mulled over Quida Raye's off-handed comment, how she knew everything was going to be okay "for that night at least." The only thing worse than being a new Methodist with a mystic for a mom, she decided, was being a new Methodist with absolutely no ability to see the future herself.

****

Several days after the robbery, as Quida Raye was again emptying her stomach so she could go to work, something else came up besides olive loaf and mayonnaise on white bread. Something she was more accustomed to passing with both feet slapped like catfish on either side of the commode seat. Calling in sick for the first time ever, she flipped through the yellow pages till she found a doctor whose name sounded nice and who took the In-'n'-Out's surprisingly good health insurance. The doctor in turn sent her straight to one of Avalon's two private hospitals. Surgery was scheduled for the next week, after IVs had built her back up. As the doctor told Joy on the phone that day, "I'm not sure if you're aware of this, but your mother's severely malnourished and dehydrated."

"I wasn't even aware my mother had been admitted into the hospital," Joy said through gritted teeth. "She has a bad habit of not calling when she should."

Later, while Boo-Boo played an unprecedented ten in a row and went to tell Vernon he might be getting a "Best Of" show soon, Joy kept shaking her head and wondering if this was what her mother had meant—that everything was going to be all right...until now.

****

Days later, Quida Raye's doctor finally wavered like a wisp of blue smoke down a hall Joy had stared at so long she wondered if he might be a mirage.

He wasn't. "She's stable and resting," the doctor said. Glinting between the surgical mask tugged under his chin and the V in his scrubs, Joy saw a Saint Christopher medal. "Everything went exceptionally well." As a gurney rattled past and the twelve-alarm bell in Joy's central nervous system kept jangling, the doctor said something that sounded like, "We didn't find any cancer anywhere."

"I'm sorry," she said, reaching for Boo-Boo's hand. "I didn't hear what you just said."

"I said your mother doesn't have cancer. Not in her stomach, not in her liver. Not anywhere. She just had a gastrocolic fistula, which explains the most recent difficulty she's been experiencing."

Her mother didn't have cancer?

Not in her stomach? Not in her liver? Not for eight years?

As the world spun and a fantasy not even Joy Savoy had been brazen enough to entertain sprang to unfathomable life, the doctor went on to mention several areas of concern, notably signs of emphysema.

327

But he assured Joy that the prognosis was much better than he had expected going in.

No cancer? Joy wouldn't have been more stunned if her mother had died on the operating table. *No cancer?* No wonder some people come to think of their doctors as gods. Joy stood in that hospital, a newly minted Methodist, fully believing this Saint-Christopher-medal-wearing physician had pulled off a miracle of heavenly proportions. And all along she thought Quida Raye had been the crack magician, stretching a three-month death sentence into eight years.

****

A few days later, her mother was out of ICU and in a softly lit, nicely furnished private room that had done absolutely nothing to improve her attitude.

"How's Wonder Woman today?" Joy breezed in and asked, only to see her mother was still glowering at the cheery yellow walls.

Frowning, Joy dabbed at a puddle the water pitcher had wept across the nightstand. From the moment she'd come out of anesthesia and received the stunning diagnosis that she did not have cancer, Quida Raye had been incensed. Which tended to kindle a similar emotion in her daughter.

"Don't you think a woman who's just been told she's *not* going to die would be a little happier?" she fumed to Tanya.

"Eight years is a long time to think you know how the story's going to end, even if it's a sad ending," Tanya replied. "Especially since she's had a different ending in mind since Jessie."

"I realize that," Joy grumped, eyes filling, mind on

her mother's main objective since Christmas 1980—resting at last beside her dear girl. "All I'm saying is who would think being stripped of such a heartbreaking goal by a positive prognosis would tick her off more than getting held up at gunpoint."

"That's Quida Raye for ya," Tanya said before hanging up and running to class.

****

"My mother and grandmother are on an Atkins kick now," Tanya called to announce days later. "Either they're both about to need Quida Raye's new doctor, or I'm escaping to Avalon. I'm finished with all my finals, so why don't I come get her in a good mood again?"

Joy no sooner agreed than Tanya was there, freeing her to race off to the glorious refuge of work. Flying out of that hospital room, she glanced back as Tanya unpacked a needlework project and Quida Raye reached for her antique embroidery hoop, an old wooden oval burnished to a deep umber from decades spent adorning linens with flowers and teacups, kitten-filled slippers and birds, ribbons and puppies, bells and hearts, butterflies and monograms. All sewn with a loving pastel sweetness that, thanks to Dick, had existed nowhere else throughout Joy's entire childhood except inside the oval of that fragile old embroidery hoop.

"I can't imagine a nuttier scene," Boo-Boo said once Joy was contentedly ensconced back in front of a mic. "A woman who bunked in a brothel sitting around doing textile arts with a gal who's entertained more men than Gypsy Rose Lee." Nevertheless, they had nearly finished a quilt top for Joy by the time Quida Raye took a turn for the worse again.

****

Before curling up on a couch in the ICU waiting room, Joy called Boo-Boo in Nashville, where he was taking her place at some awards show, and read what she had jotted down from her mother's chart during one of her five-minute visits—hepatic coma and hepatic encephalopathy. Dilantin toxicity, malnutrition, and persistent hypoalbuminemia. No "terminal." No "cancer." Not even four words in a row that she understood or could even pronounce. So, again, she slept.

Mornings come to ICU waiting rooms, all windowless in Joy's experience, on squeaking crepe soles behind clanging carts. Medicine carts. Laundry carts. Equipment carts. Naturally, the food cart was her bugle call. "I'm so hungry even that smells good," someone said. Joy got up, stretched, and decided she may as well call Tanya, who had grudgingly gone back to Pitts several days earlier. Bending to check the time on her couch-mate's watch, she knew the hour would convey just the right note of alarm.

"She's having a relapse," Joy explained. "The doctor said everything would probably be fine if she could just keep food down." Fingering the coin-return slot and leaning against the wall, she said, "It's just frustrating. She's certainly not acting like a woman who doesn't have terminal stomach cancer."

"Well," Tanya said, yawning, "you know your mother when she makes up her mind."

A week later, Quida Raye and Tanya were embroidering again, up on the sixth floor. And a week after that, Joy's mother was finally paroled back to her apartment with strict orders to eat.

Joy thought she caught a glimmer of new hope,

too, when she dropped by with lunch and a fresh outlook on all things red and green.

"So," she said, depositing a sack on the coffee table. "What do you want for Christmas?"

"You really wanna know?" her mother replied, peeking in the bag.

"That's why I asked. It's barbecue, by the way."

Taking the slaw and beans out and setting them side by side, Quida Raye Perkins looked up at her daughter. Eyes aglow, she said, "I'll tell you what I want. I want you to come spend Christmas Eve with me. Then I want you to get up and spend Christmas Day with me, too. Just like when you were little."

****

Near midnight on Christmas Eve, Joy was nodding off on the couch when her mother called from the kitchen, "Come get these cookies and milk. Why don't you leave 'em by the door so you-know-who won't miss 'em." As Radar ran past with a red sugar cookie and Sugar Pie patiently waited for hers, she added, "Santy gets awfully hungry on Christmas Eve, you know." Joy hadn't heard this happy, singsong tone since she'd had a bedroom with purple carpet.

She was dozing off, hand around Boo-Boo's gift, a gold locket bearing Jessie's picture, when her mother asked, "Do you hear what I hear?" Playfully tipping her head sideways, she gasped and said, "Is that reindeer feet?" She lived in a first-floor apartment of a two-story building. They would have had to be some mighty big reindeer.

But what Joy said was, "Now that you mention it…"

It was 1972 all over again. Dick was back in

Vietnam. And it was just her and her mother, waiting for Santa, whom Joy would merrily believe in, like so much else, until the Christmas of 1980. Kicking off the dress shoes she had worn to the early service with Boo-Boo, she decided maybe it was time she started believing in Santa Claus again, too.

Her mother plucked up the shoes and whisked them into the bedroom. Ten minutes later, she flounced back in wearing her gown and every over-the-counter unguent that had ever promised to ward off wrinkles. Slathering herself up always put her in a rompy mood, and Joy watched the kooky dance begin.

"I feel human again," she squawked, flopping across the room to turn up the stereo. Joy considered her mother's grinning, shiny mug—the face she had spent decades frying day after day and sleeping on night after night so as not to muss her globular do. Next Christmas, she decided, you're getting a facelift.

"I think I'll hit the sack," Joy said, standing up and yawning again. "But do feel free to dance the night away." Her mother responded by twisting ahead of her into the apartment's lone bedroom, where she gestured to the already turned-down bed, then wheeled around and twisted back out the door.

Although the sheets and blankets were freshly washed, all Joy smelled when she went to bed Christmas Eve was thousands of cartons of cigarettes eternally seeped into every object in her mother's smoggy, festive apartment. Falling asleep to rustling sounds on the other side of the bedroom door, visions of smoldering sugarplums danced in her head.

****

The sun wasn't up the next morning before she was

dragged from the soporific depths by a playful whisper. "Josey Faye, Josey Faye." She opened an eye and saw her mother standing over her, cooing the nickname she hadn't used since Joy was in elementary school. It was a stroke of genius, however unintended, because Joy heard her childhood pet name and instantly leapt over all her most intolerable adult recollections. Instead of waking up a grizzled, wizened twenty-seven-year-old, she was a trouble-free kid again, if only for a moment. "Josey Faye, come see what Santy left you."

Historically, two types of Christmas gifts appeared under Quida Raye Perkins' tree—wrapped ones from her, and unwrapped ones from Santa. The Christmas of 1985, Joy walked out of her mother's bedroom and into a head-on collision of them both. No yuletide display had ever been merrier, or more jam-packed. On every surface sat heaps of boxes so heavily ribboned they looked like many litters of metallic sheepdogs. And all around them were enough artfully arranged kitchen, bath, and personal items to fill two houses. That had been her mother's intent, Joy later learned, since Quida Raye had bought matching sets of everything for herself. Pitts' Five and Dime was going out of business, and it was clear who had liquidated their stock.

"Shoot," she yelped as Joy stood speechless, gawking at the bounty. "I forgot to get film."

But that was okay. For the rest of her life, all Joy Savoy had to do was close her eyes and the Christmas of 1985 came back as clearly as if her mother were once again standing over her, calling, "Josey Faye, Josey Faye." Despite a childhood filled with holidays every bit as lavish, it was the Christmas Joy and her mother once again spent alone, two full-grown women without a shred of innocent whimsy between them, that would linger forever.

For one thing, it would have been difficult to forget a pile of a hundred or so bridal-shower-worthy gifts all bearing her name. "Just in case you ever come to yore senses and marry poor old Robert," her mother pointed out.

For another, who could forget a holiday cast against a backdrop as outlandish as Quida Raye's chockablock apartment, a veritable memorial to interior decorating on a shimmering shoestring. With countless flea market knickknacks cluttering old store displays spray-painted silver, white, and gold, adorned with gobs of glue and double rainbows of glitter, walls of mirrored glass and nightlights oozing from every socket, Quida Raye's apartment was luminously, if eccentrically, cozy all year. Christmas Day, however, it was utter havoc, a riot of red and green with the rest of the color wheel closing in for the kill.

At noon, after she had called her grandparents in Kentucky and her uncles in Florida, after she had stolen a few minutes to speak softly with Boo-Boo, who was at his own mother's in Pitts, then chat briefly with Tanya at her father's house in Missouri, Joy heard her mother announce dinner was ready.

Radar sprang like a wallaby through the squall of debris toward the Christmas candies in her dish. Sugar Pie, creaky, half-blind, and incontinent at seventeen, snowplowed her way through. Christmas music was playing. And the groaning board was richly set.

Joy surveyed the feast and grinned. Cornbread dressing, candied yams with bubbly brown marshmallows, mashed potatoes and gravy, corn, lima beans, green bean casserole, English peas, deviled eggs, pimento-cheese-stuffed celery sticks, cranberry sauce, pecan pie, pumpkin pie, coconut cake, ambrosia, and rolls. And the total number of guests invited to this repast was tabulated in glasses of iced tea, Joy's an unsweetened chestnut, her mother's a tall muddy fish tank with an inch of white sand at the bottom.

Taking a seat, she waited as her mother struggled to carve the turkey before hauling it to the table. Though still weak and bowed from surgery, Quida Raye wanted no help whatsoever and continued sawing away at the bird with the equivalent of a big butter knife.

"You could ride to town on this thang and it wouldn't cut you," she yelped, tossing the dull blade aside. As she rummaged around the silverware drawer for something sharper, Joy noticed that Abe's Pawn Shop once again had her mother's rings. But that was okay. At least this was a Christmas to remember.

Chapter 28
"Life Turned Her That Way"

January passed. February and most of March did, too, and still Quida Raye Perkins wasn't completely back on her feet, despite another two weeks at another Avalon hospital. The primary reason seemed to be she had all but stopped eating.

"She says everything goes straight through her," Joy told her mother's doctor. "What part of it she doesn't, um, *lose*." As usual, the doctor had returned Joy's call within the hour. One thing her mother certainly didn't suffer from was indifferent medical care. To spare the guys yet more graphic details, she rolled her chair into a corner and flipped the fan on high. "She says it doesn't even have time to…digest…so I was wondering if, maybe, there might be some problem with all that intestinal work she had done in December?"

She was also wondering what she had wondered for a while—was her mother's purging medically related to having only half a stomach, or was it psychological? The latter was a theory put forth by one of her uncle's wives, who ran a medical supply business in Florida and was therefore considered by her grandparents to be on par with a board-certified physician. Her aunt had used the A word: anorexia. Which Joy considered another A word: absurd. Her mother was about to turn forty-seven years old, for Pete's sake.

"Forty-seven-year-old women don't get anorexia, do they?" Joy asked the doctor.

"It's not unheard of," he replied. She sat there blinking into the fan, feeling her eyelashes bend backward. Why couldn't her mother have something other mothers had? Like varicose veins or excessive facial hair. Why was it always some life-threatening forecast with her? Rain, rain, and more rain, till not even Noah could help them. What was so damn bad about blue skies and sunny days?

"Instead of searching for terms that may or may not accurately describe her particular situation," the doctor continued, "what I think we should concentrate on at this point is helping her get her strength back. Which is why I'm recommending she go into a nursing home."

"A *nursing home*," Joy exclaimed. Behind her, Boo-Boo knocked over a stack of carts.

"Just for the short term," the doctor said. "Till she's built back up some. The only other option would be to have her move in with you for a while."

Both suggestions struck Joy as equally nightmarish.

"Hang on here," she began, scrambling for some sort of middle ground to this lunacy. "What if she stays at her house and I make sure she eats?"

"I'd advise against that," the good doctor diplomatically said. "However, if that's what you wish, it's my opinion you might want to consider hiring skilled nursing care."

****

Rattling a sack of Weenie Queen slaw dogs—

which were more in line with her budget than private-duty RNs—Joy let herself into her mother's apartment after work that afternoon. "Hello?" No answer. Looking out the window for Sally, she saw her car was indeed gone. Without the strength to manage the Wedgie's stick, Quida Raye had been reduced to an automatic transmission and Joy's old clunker, which she generally attempted to avoid driving. But not that day. Joy soon heard Sally rumble up and waited for her mother to come in. Which she eventually did. Slowly. Weakly. Having done some light housecleaning at Joy's as well as several loads of clothes.

"I'm plum tuckered out," she gasped, wilting into a kitchen chair.

"Are you sure you're well enough to be doing all that?" Joy asked, nudging the Weenie Queen bag.

"I just gave it a lick and a promise," she said, burying her face in her hands. "I'll be fine onct I rest a while." With her dogs beside her and her clothes falling off her, she looked like Mrs. Bojangles on her last leg.

The hair rose on the back of Joy's neck. "Why didn't you just stay in bed instead of running off to my place and working like a dang horse?"

Lifting her head and dropping her hands to the table, she pointed her bacon thin, weary, tanned face at her daughter and said, "*Somebody* had to do it. And it shore wudn't gonna be *you*."

That was the first indication that, in her mother's estimation at least, Joy was once again striving for the highest rank Dick had ever achieved, the uncivil service position of Major Disappointment. More clues would follow.

A few days later, Joy pulled up to her mother's

apartment to find neighbors swarming around a card table set up outside her door and stacked with linens. A lifetime of embroidered linens. All the most beautiful pastel parts of Joy's otherwise black-and-white childhood, flying off the card table as neighbors tossed bills in a cigar box and straggled off with priceless treasures.

"Stop!" she screamed. *"What are you doing?"*

"Makin' something to live on," her mother replied.

"Why didn't you just ask me for help?" Joy was still yelling, and neighbors were staring.

"Yore busy. I didn't wanna bother you."

"*This* bothers me. Tremendously!" Joy hollered, spinning around to announce the sale was over. Eyeballing the pitifully short stack of pillowcases and tablecloths that remained, attempting to form words, she croaked, "Why would you *do* this?"

"Why not?" her mother shrugged and said. "Who woulda thought you cared about a thang?"

****

Matters had not much improved by March 21st, when Quida Raye made a point of ignoring the celebratory catfish, coleslaw and hushpuppies Joy brought by. Even before she stepped into the smoky, overwarm apartment, Joy was filled with apprehension, thanks to a worrisome call earlier from her grandmother.

Sure enough, there were no lights on, no music playing, no sound at all except the paper Fishy Business sack she crinkled all the way to the bedroom, where her mother was perched on the bed like a centipede, all points and angles, dogs by her side. Joy put the food on the bedside table with a flourish.

"Happy birthday!"

Quida Raye turned away and glared at her drawn curtains, gumming the thumbnail pinching a smoldering, inch-long cigarette.

"Are you going to sit there and act like I didn't just bring you some of your favorite food to celebrate?" Joy crossed her arms and leaned against the doorframe. "Maybe because I've done some unspecified something wrong again?"

"You ain't done shit, as usual," she spat. While her deficiencies as a daughter were becoming an ongoing theme, Joy knew—for once—she wasn't solely to blame for this black mood. Joy knew her grandparents had also called to wish her a happy birthday. And she knew what her mother had asked for.

Quida Raye Perkins wanted to go back home to Kentucky. And Joy's grandma had said what Joy had been contending for weeks—they were too old and sick themselves to also take care of her.

"I just feel so bad," her grandma had called to say, shaky words dimpled by decades of Parkinson's. "We just cain't, Joy Faye. 'Course, her daddy threw a fit. But he knows we just cain't."

Anxious to appease at least one relative, Joy assured her grandmother she had made the right decision. "She and I have been fighting about this for days," Joy said reassuringly. "Even if you and Granddaddy had said yes, she's in absolutely no shape to drive ten hours. And *I* can't bring her since I'm out of time off."

Somewhat assuaged and, as always, worried about running up the phone bill, her grandmother said "Okay," and "bye now," then spent a full minute jiggling and joggling the handset in the general direction of her old wall phone.

Quida Raye, however, clearly did not think much was okay.

The fact that her daughter was too busy to do anything more than some drive-by feeding paled in comparison to her own mama and daddy's refusal to make up the bed in the back room. To fry her sausage in the morning and chicken at night. To fire up the floor furnace when she was cold and flip on the attic fan when she was hot. To tend to her every want and need as only a parent can. They had said what she herself had always tried not to—from Joy marrying a thug to moving her precious granddaughter into a house with another godforsaken attic fan—Quida Raye Perkins' own parents had said no when she herself had always said yes.

The crushing injustice of it all came through loud and clear after Joy said, "Grandma told me what you asked her today."

Looking up with red-rimmed eyes, shaping her gravelly voice into an oath, Quida Raye spaced her words apart so as to be perfectly understood. "I just want you and Mama and Daddy and everyone else to know one damn thang. I *am* goin' back home. Even if I've gotta take that thang you call a car."

"You aren't leaving Louisiana in either one of our vehicles," Joy announced, rearranging the hushpuppies and slaw with a yank and a snatch. "There's absolutely no way you can drive to Kentucky in your condition. Now eat this before it gets cold."

Joy stopped relocating containers long enough to glance in her mother's direction again. She looked like one of those kids with that horrible aging disease, sitting cross-legged on the bed, all crumpled up and caved in and about to cry, dogs whimpering by her side.

"Have you smoked up all the air in this room?" She choked, swaying slightly. "I can't even breathe in here anymore. It's a miracle Radar and Sugar Pie haven't keeled over." At the mention of their names, both dogs wagged their tails, stirring the pollution. Her mother responded by cinching up her mouth like a drawstring purse. Joy studied the puckered skin, the rumpled anger, and felt the walls closing in. Something had to be done before they were just a stew of snarls and spit.

"Where are your teeth?" she heard herself asking. "You didn't leave them at the hospital, did you?"

"If you must know," her mother replied, "they don't fit me no more. They just swallow me whole."

Joy had friends who had starved themselves till their rings no longer fit. She had even heard of women getting pregnant after dieting down a size or two in diaphragms. But she had never known anyone who had lost so much weight that her false teeth swallowed her whole.

She couldn't help herself. A little wheeze shot out her nose. "Your own teeth are swallowing you whole?" She snuffled again.

"Snort some more, Miss Piggy," her mother announced with a grudging grin. Soon, they were both grunting and spluttering while Radar and Sugar Pie hopped around the bed, goofy with relief.

"While we're on the subject of your mouth," Joy gayly continued, "do you plan to stop sticking cigarettes in it anytime soon, or am I gonna have to sic your doctor back on you?"

342

"I'll make a deal with you. I'll stop stickin' cigarettes in mine when you stop crammin' yores fulla food. How's Robert ever gonna haul yore big ole butt across a threshold, assumin' you ever come to yore senses and marry the poor man."

"Whatever," Joy muttered, picking up the hushpuppies.

"I don't *thank* so," her mother impishly said, snatching them away. "Go getcher own."

"I will. And, while I'm there, do you want me to pick you up some birthday pie, too?"

"I called myself eatin' a piece of pie from there onct," Quida Raye declared, reaching for the catfish. "Shoe leather couldn'ta tasted worse."

Ah, such whimsy, if only for a day.

Chapter 29
"Ready For The Times To Get Better"

Despite such rousing encounters, the spring of 1986 went downhill fast. More and more often, Quida Raye Perkins began acting like Carrie getting revenge at the prom, and her daughter responded accordingly.

Some days she accused Joy of stealing money—"Money!" Joy screaked at Tanya. "From a woman who hasn't drawn a paycheck in nearly five months."

Other days, irritated by Joy's snarky ministrations, Quida Raye snapped at her to leave her alone and "go hole up with Robert," directives Joy happily followed. Except, the more she stayed away, the angrier her mother became.

"Have you read *Catch-22*?" Tanya asked, chuckling.

"Who has time to read?" Joy shouted.

She in fact wouldn't have time for much—except feeling like Dick's *official* replacement as Major Disappointment—the next time she returned to the battleground of Quida Raye's airless apartment. After she got her mother off the floor and back into bed, once she was sure she was sleeping and not in a coma, when the chain of command had finally established Joy Savoy as the real drill sergeant from hell, she called her mother's doctor.

"Joy, I'm sorry to have to tell you this," the doctor

began, "but it's come to my attention that your mother no longer has medical insurance."

No medical insurance? Joy leaned against the wall, scalp beginning to sweat. No medical insurance? How could that be? What did that mean?

"What does that mean?"

"That means neither of the hospitals I practice at in Avalon will admit her. Your only option is to take her to JFK Memorial in Ferndale."

JFK Memorial? The charity hospital where Jessie was born?

Joy felt herself sliding down the wall. JFK Memorial? Just as surely as Jessie had come into the world at JFK, Joy knew her muleheaded mother would enjoy nothing more than taking her leave of it there. No, Quida Raye Perkins was *not* going to JFK Memorial, not if she had anything to say about it.

Crawling to the bedroom, checking to make sure her mother was still asleep, she pulled the door closed and slumped against the wall again, lap filling with two small dogs. "Is there anything I can do to get her policy reinstated?" she quietly begged. "Anything at all?"

"To be perfectly honest, I don't deal with insurance companies. My office does," the doctor kindly explained. "But my guess is you probably don't have much recourse at this point. I'm assuming that, since she's been out of work, her employer hasn't kept up with her premiums."

Her daughter hasn't either, Joy thought, wild-eyed. She had paid her mother's rent and utilities. Had even gotten her rings out of hock. How had she not thought to similarly keep her health insurance premiums current? What would that oversight mean? Hundreds of thousands of dollars in medical care? *Any* medical care at all?

As a cauldron of roiling emotions—regret, shame, fiery anguish—churned in her gut, Joy sat flat on the floor, stunned into abject silence. Finally, the doctor offered another, familiar solution.

"The only suggestion I have is one I've mentioned before. You could take her home with you and try to keep her well-nourished. That's basically all a hospital can do."

Long after Joy mumbled a few words of appreciation and hung up, she continued sitting with the dogs on the floor, listening to her mother's ragged breathing a wall away, speculations scattering a million desperate directions. Might there be loopholes with the health insurance problem? Could cashing in on her meager celebrity fix any of this? Exactly how much did Boo-Boo make anyway? No frenzied scenario, however, produced anything approaching promise in Joy's clenched mind. Frantic and feeling physically ill, she eased the bedroom door open, found her mother's purse near the bed, then continued quietly on, past a table filled with Jessie's photos, into the bathroom, pulling the phone behind her. Locking the door and turning on a faucet, she sat on the toilet lid, opened her mother's wallet, and began pulling out every item shoved in slits and pockets during all the years her mother had loaded her life into this quality leather clutch.

Front and center was the insurance card. Sure enough, the woman who answered the 800 number validated every grim assumption the doctor had made. Thinking there might be some back-up insurance, Joy kept looking. But all she found, besides many photos of Jessie, was every laminated document her mother had ever received that bore her own likeness. All her old driver's licenses and store IDs, years upon years of shiny, pliable proof that she hadn't always looked the way she did now. It was the ultimate in vanity, this billfold medley of comely mug shots, and, with nothing more pleasant to do, Joy studied each one, the sick feeling in her heart assuaged somewhat by slightly faded memories of long-ago Quida Rayes at twenty-eight, thirty-one, thirty-four. Then, on an ID card stuck in the last compartment by years of inertia, she saw her yet again, this time at thirty-five. Using her thumbnail to scrape something gummy off her face, Joy remembered this lovely woman well. In fact, she vaguely recalled the actual card, her military ID, the magic piece of plastic that had granted them entrance into every facility on Fort Dewey, from the commissary and swimming pools to the PX and post hospital the time Joy had mono.

The *hospital*, she thought with a gasp, nearly dropping her lapful of cards and photos. The *Army hospital*. Where everything was free. At least it had been for wives and children of active military. But what about ex-wives, she wondered? Ex-wives of retired military? Ex-wives who had given every bit as much in fifteen battered years as one drill sergeant surely had during a couple of tours in Vietnam?

"Joy Faye," her mother weakly called, causing her to jump there on that toilet lid and the edge of this outrageous notion. "You still here?"

"I'm in the bathroom," Joy calmly responded. "Be right out." Hurrying to put everything back like she'd found it, she suddenly didn't feel quite so queasy. Countless end-runs around possible roadblocks began forming in her conniving mind. Was there an expiration date on that card? How would the Army know they were divorced anyway? What was there to stop her from taking her mother to Fort Dewey and claiming she'd lost her latest ID card? By the time the truth was discovered, maybe she'd be good as new.

All that and more seemed plausible—for a person who hadn't been pummeled into Army-green submission for fifteen years. Sighing, suddenly miserable once more, Joy snapped her mother's billfold shut, well aware she would never have the nerve to commit any offense that, for all she knew, the punishment might be to stand at attention in front of an entire jury full of Dicks.

Dick, Joy thought, slipping the wallet back into her mother's purse. *Dick.*

One door away from her mother withering into oblivion, it occurred to Joy Savoy that there might be one possible way to eliminate every single complication, every possible federal violation.

Dick.

Then, shuddering at the very idea, she reached for the doorknob. Maybe a little home cooking would indeed be just what the doctor ordered.

****

That afternoon, Boo-Boo helped settle two small, matted dogs and a nearly catatonic woman into Joy's spare bedroom. The dogs weren't much trouble, aside from being in bad need of their usual spring shearing. The woman, however, was a different matter altogether. Accustomed to sitting all by her brooding self in a dark, smoky apartment, Quida Raye joined her daughter in a rare, shared assessment—neither of them wanted her in Joy's spare bedroom.

"But we're going to make the best of it," Joy informed her once Boo-Boo headed back to work. "As soon as you start eating again and gain some weight, I'm taking you straight back to your apartment, where you can stay."

"Good, 'cause wild horses couldn't drag me back to this pigsty," her mother yelled, slamming the bedroom door.

"Too bad they can't drag you away," Joy shouted back, already smelling a lit cigarette. Rapping on the door, she added, "Don't forget, no smoking in the house," jumping as a shoe or pop bottle slammed against the other side. Within the hour, Joy's new place reeked like the Wagon Wheel on a rocking weekend.

"Are you at least feeding her?" Tanya asked later.

"Everything she'll swallow. Which basically means chocolate bars, candy corn, and jelly beans."

"Yum. Set a place for me, too."

As April wore on, however, Joy grudgingly sensed a *Whatever Happened to Baby Jane* situation simmering two doors down from the man she hoped to marry one day. Luckily, before she resorted to cooking Radar and Sugar Pie and feeding them to her mother—intravenously if necessary—Quida Raye came up with a dish she promised to actually eat. Liver and onions.

Joy prepared the stinking stuff the very next day. And it was only when her mother took two bites—two!—that she finally lost it. So what if Quida Raye was angry because she was rarely ever around. Joy was absolutely furious with *her* for always being there. And not just that April, either.

"Why did you come back here anyway?" she demanded, waving her slotted spoon through the air. "Why didn't you just stay in Kentucky? I was doing fine till you showed up at my screen door three years ago."

"You thank you was doing fine?" her mother roared, shoving her plate aside. "Funny, but all *I* saw was a ghost where you useta be. You didn't even care who you laid up in bed with no more." Before she stopped speaking, face black with rage, Quida Raye had one last point to make. "Somebody had to take care a you till you learned how to feel again."

If all those years of Ira and her infuriating mother were what "feeling" felt like, Joy thought, slamming down her spoon, you could stick both it *and* this stinking liver and onions where the sun doesn't shine. Which would have been just about anywhere that April.

In a peculiar twist on the "when it rains, it pours" cliché, Joy found that, when it was stormy inside her house, it was invariably radiant everywhere else. So she extended her leave-taking. Work provided endless diversions, as did Boo-Boo. Joy even spent half a day with Ruthie at the beauty parlor of one of the lady snake handlers, leaving hours later with feathered bangs hot-ironed and standing in a cylindrical bush on top of her scalp while the rest of the mop flopped past her waist.

Quida Raye gaped at her when she finally came home. "I thought you was a Methodist."

"I'm trying," Joy said. *And failing*, she didn't say.

****

Toward the end of April, Joy slid off the

headphones, picked up her purse, and told Boo-Boo she'd see him later. "I'm going to the grocery after I check on Mommie Dearest."

"Behave yourself," he said, smacking her on the rear.

Smiling all the way home, she tiptoed into the bathroom to see if her mother had eaten that day—her only evidence was the bits that didn't flush—and was examining what appeared to be hot dog chunks when Quida Raye slipped up behind her.

"Find what yore lookin' for?"

Filing the fact that she no longer made noise when she walked, Joy said, "Actually, yes. The commode's where I left it this morning. That's a relief."

Frail as she was, Quida Raye had been up to her old tricks, moving Joy's furniture around willy-nilly. As Tanya observed, "She's like an ant, able to lift a hundred times her own body weight."

"The hardwood floor's in the same place, too, in case you hadn't noticed," Quida Raye deadpanned, signaling a pleasant enough mood. Then she said something that made April feel like December. "Unless yore headed off down to Robert's again, I was wonderin' if we could go sit on the porch and talk. I haven't moved the porch, neither."

Her mother wanted to talk? As in have a discussion? This couldn't be good. They hadn't said much to each other most of Joy's life. Surely they didn't need to start now. Joy couldn't tell who was more unsteady as they shuffled toward the front door, her malnourished mother or her own fussbudget self, easing down atop the concrete steps. On either side of them, ancient azaleas erupted in hot-pink heaps.

Flanked by fuchsia, Joy thought. Blooming crazy.

"What's up?"

"I've been thankin'," her mother began, "and there's a few thangs I want to make sure you know." Across the street, a pack of strays tramped past.

"Shoot," Joy said.

"For starters, there's a dress hangin' up in my closet. The pretty blue one I wore to the truckers' ball." Lighting a cigarette, she slowly emptied her lungs. "Remember?"

"Of course."

"Good. Cuz that's the one I want you to use. When the time comes."

Joy had a picture of her in that gown. Golden shoulders against sky-colored chiffon. The corsage was probably the last her mother had been given. She had never looked lovelier. Two months later, a small-town Kentucky doctor would hack away at what he would declare was terminal stomach cancer. And, for the next eight years, Quida Raye Perkins evidently saved that dress for one last special occasion, when she hoped she would once again be the prettiest belle at the ball.

Everything—road, strays, pines, porches, fences—slanted sideways in the soft April sun. It had taken considerable energy and boundless negligence to avoid the subject of her mother's mortality through eight years of thinking she was going to die and several months of it looking like she might at any minute. But Joy usually got what she wanted and—aside from Boo-Boo and several details regarding an attic fan—she hadn't wanted anything more than for her mother's strange, lingering ailments to simply disappear. She found she could make that happen, too—as long as they never talked about it.

"What are you saying?" Joy stammered. "It sounds like you think you're going to, I don't know, *die* or something."

"I certainly don't plan on livin' forever. D'you?"

"No, but I'm also not calling it quits any time soon. And you're not, either. Not if your doctor has anything to say about it. That's why they have hospitals, you know. To keep people from dying."

Her mother humphed. "Well, one thang's for sure. I ain't dyin' in no hospital." Joy must have made a noise because two of the strays glanced back before trotting on. "I called the store the other day, and they said my insurance has run out cuz I haven't had a paycheck in so long."

"So?"

"So I cain't die in no hospital. Not a regular one, at least."

It was at that moment, that week-long, cerulean second in April, that Joy should have turned to her mother on those front steps and asked the questions she had been meaning to get around to for years. Like, how many eggs do you put in your cornbread dressing? And what did you do with my baby shoes? And what should I tell Doyle or your ex-husbands if they call? And, you know, everything considered, on a scale of one to ten, would you say I've been a passable daughter? A three? Maybe a four?

But, of course, Joy Savoy said none of that. During no finer a moment for understanding, if not reconciliation, she opened her mouth and heard these words fall out—"If you aren't going to die in a hospital, just exactly where do you plan on doing it? No one's going to rent this place again if they find out someone croaked in it." Blinking, blinking, she waited.

"A person don't have to die in no bed. I could just drive off a bridge somewhere."

Drive off a bridge? Of all the organs that writhed at the idea of her mother driving off a bridge, only two— her eyes—betrayed her. Before Quida Raye could light up another cigarette, Joy had seized on the Wedgie and could not tear her gaze from it.

"Don't worry, I won't take *that*," she said, and rising from the inferno of her words was a trace of amusement. Then a chortle deep in her throat rattled like a sack of bones. That's it, Joy realized, nearly passing out. She's pulling my leg. She's just kidding. Silly kidder. Drive off a bridge. Yeah, like this is Chappaquiddick you're driving off a bridge.

"Don't think you'll go for a dip in Sally, either," Joy declared. "She's going to be a collector's item someday, and I don't want you getting mud all in her."

"Collector's item, my foot."

"Drive off a bridge in either one of those cars, and I'm sticking you in the ground in that ratty old housecoat of yours." Joy snickered again and, for a moment, all seemed as right in the world as it had ever been between them.

"May as well bury me nekkid as a jaybird."

"Drive off a bridge, and I will," Joy promised. "With an open casket."

"I thank that'd be a purdy sight," she said, snorting and gnawing what was left of a fingernail. Smoke swirled through lank hanks of two-tone hair that— unteased, uncut, and uncolored—brushed past her shoulders. Suddenly aware of her own vertically moussed bangs, it occurred to Joy that her mother was letting her hair down just as she was standing hers straight up. That Quida Raye was now the homebody while she was the gadabout. That, somewhere along the miserable line, they had reversed course and passed each other by, going in their usual opposite directions.

****

"It sounds like your mother needs to go back in the hospital," Tanya said.

"Yes, it does," Joy agreed, dragging the phone to her bedroom so she could look out the window and see when Boo-Boo pulled in his driveway.

"When are you taking her then?"

"When I can take her somewhere other than JFK Memorial."

"*JFK?*" Tanya exclaimed. "Where Jessie was born?"

"None other."

"Why in the world would you take her there? I mean, *come on!* You don't have to be a psychology major to see *those* red flags."

"I'm well aware of that," Joy said. "Which is why I have a proposition for you."

"What?"

Remembering that old military ID card in her mother's billfold, the absolute and utter last resort, Joy Savoy said, "What are you doing this weekend?"

"Why?" Tanya demanded suspiciously.

"I thought we might take a trip."

"Where?"

"To Missouri," Joy replied.

"*Missouri?*"

"Yep, Missouri. Land of the men who raised us."

Chapter 30
"Forgiving You Was Easy"

"Too bad your dad's in Hawaii," Joy said that Saturday.

"Convenient, huh?" Tanya observed, chortling.

"Well, it's not like we gave him much notice. And I'd say he more than apologized." They had just left Tanya's father's sprawling ranch, where his housekeeper had served them lunch, then pushed a bulky envelope across the table. Opening the belated birthday card, Tanya pulled out a set of keys to the five-year-old luxury car in the driveway. Joy patted the dashboard and settled back in her comfy leather seat, happy someone else was driving after ten hours on the road.

With three more to go, they headed across Missouri, singing along to every song on the radio. Harmonizing turned to talking, which segued into hours of free, third-party psychoanalysis for all the men Tanya and Joy had ever known. Which, given their course that sunny April day—due west on I-70—inevitably ended with Dick.

Joy wondered what over a decade had brought to bear on Dick's life. After years of witnessing how nimbly Tanya maneuvered around her own paternal disappointments, chief among them her dashing father leaving when she was seven, Joy wondered if she, too, might be capable of such emotional agility. If she could similarly overlook all the recriminations she'd held dear for so long in the hopes that, somewhere in the fantasy world where such a bout of unconsciousness could occur, she might resurrect something redeeming from her own past. Where Tanya's father gave her luxury sedans, Joy Savoy would settle for a little peace of mind from Dick. That and a small piece of plastic.

"Back when Mother was still humoring him," she reminisced, "we used to visit his family up here sometimes."

"I remember that," Tanya said. "She was always such a bear after those trips."

"Oh, she hated it up here. All of Dick's folks were seriously country people. I mean, they still used outhouses *and* corncobs for toilet paper. In the *1960s*. It's a miracle we came as often as we did."

"I'll tell you what's a miracle," Tanya said, laughing so hard the car shimmied down the interstate. "That you found a man who'd stay with your mother for a whole weekend while you left town."

"Boo-Boo's not a man, Tanya. He's a saint."

"He'd have to be, to put up with you," she howled, driving on.

****

Joy had not been a particularly attentive child, but, with the help of landmarks large enough to make lasting impressions on even small, dim minds—bridges, bluffs, rocky cliffs—they were soon knocking on the door of a house where one of Dick's brothers once lived. Amazingly, "Uncle" Larry still lived there. After he got over the sight of two strange women on his front porch, one of whom he eventually recognized, he gave

357

them directions to Dick's place in the boonies.

"He's been there since he left Loozeanna," Uncle Larry said. "You girls just go on out and surprise him." Lowering his voice, he pulled Joy aside and quietly added, "Don't worry, hon. He ain't took a drink for years now."

****

The big diesel did not make a bad all-terrain vehicle, which was good since Dick lived miles from the nearest pavement. Poking down dirt roads along which herds of cows studied their bobbing progress, they soon made their way to a property Uncle Larry had perfectly described.

"There's the outhouse with 'Shit Rolls Downhill' painted on the door," Tanya dryly noted. "Right next to five junked toilets turned into flower pots. Cute."

"At least he has a theme," Joy observed. "I don't, however, see his, uh, vehicle." What was that in her voice? Disappointment? Was she disappointed because she might not see the man who still made guest appearances in all her Army-green nightmares?

"Maybe the neighbors know where he is," Tanya suggested as three or four spilled out of the bare wooden house next to Dick's, hitched up their overalls, and nosed around a junk-filled yard, glaring at an automobile they knew full well had not been manufactured in Kansas City.

"Isn't the Jesse James museum up here somewhere, too?" Joy asked, fumbling for the lock.

"Can I help yew?" a booming voice roared. Jerking around, they beheld a hairy-eared, bushy-nosed, veiny-eyed face mashed against Tanya's tinted window.

"Floorboard it," Joy screeched.

Instead, Tanya placed a crimson-red fingertip atop the window control panel and pushed. "Why, yes, sir, you can," she burbled, batting her black-and-lavender-outlined eyes. By the time she finished, the whole clan was clustered around the car, wagging their shaggy heads and making comments like, "Why, ain't that the sweetest thang you ever heard?" and "Dick's baby's come back home." Demurely turning down invitations to come inside for some possum they'd just cleaned, Tanya and Joy continued sitting in the car until the only one still interested was the young, worldly one.

"This here's one of them German automo-biles, ain't it?" he asked, grinning.

"You're a Mr. Smarty," Tanya said, not a trace of anything but girlish awe in her voice. "Have you been to junior college?"

"Nope," he said proudly. "Almost gradiated high school, though." Embarking on a tale of vast travels throughout Missouri *and* Kansas, Nimrod was soon interrupted by the clangorous arrival of a hearse that had been converted into a camper. It seemed appropriate that all movement came to a halt in that hollow once the fenders ceased clattering. Joy, for one, had virtually stopped breathing.

Nimrod, apparently from heartier pioneer stock, shouted, "Recognize anyone in this here German automo-bile?"

The captain of the hearse/camper stepped out of his vehicle and turned their way, letting the padded, gilt-edged door bump him from behind. He was waiting for identification and clearly expecting the worst. Apprehension didn't much alter the open, furrowed face of every man who has ever stopped to help a stranger fix a flat. There was, however, a steely dare glinting off his aviator glasses. Dick Perkins had lived with Joy's mother long enough to know only bill collectors or lawyers drove deluxe ascot-gray coupes. And he had lived in places like rural Missouri and Southeast Asia long enough to be impressed by neither. Glancing in the general direction of the antennae, his gray-blonde buzz cut bristling beneath the mild Missouri sun, he said, "I'm not expecting company." Then he let the satin-padded door slam shut, turned around and headed toward his house.

"I'd look again 'fore I went off half-cocked," Nimrod hollered.

Wheeling around with the daunting, imperial poise of a drill sergeant informally addressed by a buck private, Dick slowly removed his sunglasses. After he finished daring Nimrod with a stare, his blue gaze slid to the diesel's windshield, raking first across an iridescent face, then to one that was much less colorful. In fact, it was probably pale enough to look like it belonged in that hearse/camper of his.

The last time Joy had seen the man who raised her from the time she was one till she was sixteen, he was yanking the distributor wires off the car her mother had just bought herself. After a solid year of trying to woo her back despite his disappearing-trailer trick, Dick Perkins had given up and stayed drunk, reduced to complicating her life any way he could. And disabling a damn beige-on-brown coupe seemed as good an idea as any. If nothing else, it would keep her out of the bars for one night. Joy, her mother, and Jessie watched from the door of the repo trailer Quida Raye was working three jobs to afford.

"Go on," her mother had yelled. "Show yore ass."

Then, like magic, one of her bar-hopping buddies drove up, got out of his pickup truck, walked over to Dick and knocked him to the ground with a single right to the jaw. Joy felt then like she would eleven years later in Tanya's new car. Like there wasn't anything she wanted more than for Dick to pick himself up out of the dirt, for him to be a better man.

"I'll. Be. Damned," Dick finally said, like a prayer. Then he took off running. Swept up in the moment, Joy jumped out and met him in front of the car's celestial hood ornament. "My baby, my baby!" he cried. Before he got hold of himself, he must have told her he loved her a hundred times.

"I love you, too," Joy reflexively blurted. In twenty-eight years, she had never said those words to her mother. But there she was, deep in the wilds of Missouri, blathering them to a hearse-driving, shell-shocked Vietnam vet who had treated her like the enemy for fifteen long years. Did she mean it? No! Had she lost her mind? Certainly! But she was also clearly a sucker for one sentiment she had not anticipated and, come to find out, could not resist—nostalgia.

When he finally stopped hugging her, Dick was as loud and cheerful as he'd ever been when he wasn't drinking. Something one of her aunts said once finally made sense—"Dick was always so much fun. We never could figure out why your mother ran him off."

While he made a fuss over Tanya, who had been a precocious fourth-grader the last time they'd seen each other, Joy studied the man she hadn't laid eyes on in over a decade, marveling at time's interminable tug on a life. His face was much the same, only saggier. His jawline was droopier, his neck goosier, his whole body shorter somehow, as if he had been compacted into a recycled, human-shaped container that bulged at the belly, withered at the rear, hung loose on the leg. It was as if she had blinked and Dick had gone from a mean, green, fighting machine to a wilted middle-aged man.

Joy looked at Dick, who had once seemed ten feet tall and bulletproof, and realized he only had a few inches on her. Why, I could take him, she realized, startled. And if I can't, Tanya surely can.

There would, however, be no fisticuffs that day. Only frivolity. And, if Joy was lucky, more than a little philanthropy on Dick's part. Leaving Nimrod lurking around outside, Dick ushered Tanya and Joy into his house, falling all over himself with jubilant hospitality. He offered them coffee or colas or fresh well water or anything they saw that would fit in Tanya's trunk, but Joy just shook her head, barely managing a "No, thank you."

Because, as if it weren't enough that the villain of her youth had gone and grown soft, she walked into Dick's house and realized that, for the first time since 1974, she had just stepped inside the trailer with purple carpet. Only it wasn't a trailer. And it didn't have purple carpet. But it *did* have every doodad and stick of furniture her mother had cherished and Dick had seen fit to run off with, plunging Quida Raye into near persistent poverty and Joy into an ill-fated teenaged romance with Sonny Savoy, the other side of the same coin now shimmering again like a not-so-shiny penny in front of her.

"Wow," she said, beating back an overwhelming sense of being smothered, concentrating instead on one glass-covered, carved-wood, Black Forest table, then the next. "I remember this."

"Of course you do," Dick declared, spreading his arms wide. "This is your home."

Trying to match his enthusiasm for her stolen past, she said, "I guess you could say that." The throw rugs were the same. Even the knickknacks were the same. Her mother had long since moved on to other collections, notably carnival glass and amber tchotchkes. Dick, however, was forever stuck in her cypress-stump lamp phase. Something told Joy her mother wouldn't think that was anywhere near as pitiful as she did.

Opening the creaky lid of their old console stereo, he snapped on the radio and, with it, lit up the pair of kaleidoscopic light boxes Quida Raye had rigged for rainbows so many years before.

"It's all yours, you know. Always was. Always will be," he said with a sad smile, blue eyes misting. "After all, you're the only child I ever had."

Of all the pronouncements he could have made, she was least prepared for this one. Her mother had been her only parent for so many years, and he had been such a mean drunk all the others, that Joy had long since fallen out of the habit of considering Dick any kind of dad, actual or otherwise. She had stopped thinking of him as anything except, well, a dick. As she stared at tears leaking from ice-blue ponds, however, her liability grew clear. Whatever their true ties might be—and her mother still wasn't talking—when he died, Joy could inherit everything she had lost so many years before. It was at that moment, a foot away from Dick's earnest, grizzled face, that she remembered she was her mother's beneficiary, as well. What was Quida Raye's would also ultimately be hers.

It would have taken computer technology to simulate what she felt then—floor falling away, walls flying off, ceiling whirling. As she stood in Dick's version of the trailer with purple carpet, mind scrambling for the "escape" key, the objects of her conflicted inheritance seemed to melt before her eyes. She might get some German coffee tables and, in her mother's case, God only knew what else. But without the driving force that had made any of it matter—Quida Raye's girlish desire for pretty things, the soft spot she'd always had for any gewgaw that could make her often crushing life more bearable—how much would any of it matter?

"So all this is mine, huh?" she wheezed, suddenly aware that Tanya and Dick hadn't flown off with the walls and ceiling. "Great. I've got just the spot for that china cabinet."

"Just hold your horses," Dick gaily boomed. "I ain't dead yet."

"Well, don't hurry on my account," Joy said, laughing her hearty, on-air laugh.

"You two are ghouls," Tanya announced with a shudder. Looping her arm through his, she said, "Why don't you show me everything else Joy can't wait to get her grubby mitts on." Joy hung back, ostensibly to marvel over plaster cats and stuffed alligators, old friends she hadn't seen since tenth grade, while Dick trotted Tanya through the rest of his house, regaling her with memories of Tanya herself as a nine-year-old in fishnet stockings as well as long stories about each room's unique architectural features. In the kitchen, that included a hardwood floor he'd nailed for some inexplicable reason to the ceiling.

Later, after he had shown them every picture he'd taken since the mid '70s, every musty pile of books and maps he'd pilfered from abandoned old houses, every medal and commendation he had received during twenty-one years in the Army, Joy finally saw her opening.

"Twenty-one years in the Army," she exclaimed. "That's quite an accomplishment."

"I suppose so," Dick said, closing the case to one of his Purple Hearts.

"Twenty-one years. Man, that probably gets you, what? Free medical care for life?"

Dick shrugged. "I imagine it might, as long as it's at a VA facility."

"The VA treats women, doesn't it?"

He shrugged again. "I guess so. Probably. After all, there are all sorts of women in the service, not to mention wives and whatnot." He stared at Joy, clearly wondering why she cared about the military's medical provisions when she hadn't asked the first question about any of the thousand other far more riveting topics he'd been holding forth on for hours.

"I wonder how a woman would go about doing that," Joy pointedly continued. "What she'd have to do to be seen by a VA or Army doctor?"

"I wouldn't know, honey. It'd probably depend on who the woman was and how many years of service she, or her husband, had."

"Say it was twenty-one years," Joy said, tingling with a terrible combination of desperation and tremulous need. "And say it was her *ex*-husband."

Suddenly, as if catching sight of a squad of VC at the end of a long, winding trail, a light began shining in Dick's old, blue eyes. "Are you saying what I think you're saying?"

****

Later, after inviting them to stay for supper, after offering them his spare room, after telling Joy she could move down the road to the place he'd just traded for a bored-out muscle car—he was sure he could have water piped in by the time she made it back with her stuff—Dick gave up and walked them out. Opening her door, he said, "I'll check on everything, honey. Like I said, I can't promise anything. But I'll check."

"That's all I'm asking," Joy said, scrambling to make sure she had covered all the bases. Every long, hard mile she had traveled to get here, every cherished recrimination she had cast aside for this, her mother's last chance at halfway decent medical care, maybe her last chance, *period*, hinged on this—persuading Dick to bend whatever rules he could to keep her mother out of the charity hospital where Jessie had been born.

"Remember," she repeated. "If they don't come out and ask if you're divorced, you don't have to tell them, right? Just get her another military ID if you can—even a temporary one. Here's my address. If you can do that really soon, that would be great." Then, afraid she sounded as desperate as she felt, and because she didn't want him knowing what her mother might actually do with a new ID card—Quida Raye had expressly forbidden her to breathe a word about the past few months on air, and telling *Dick* would be incomprehensible—she added a hazy disclaimer.

"You know what a shopaholic she's always been,

so don't you think being able to hit the PX again would be the perfect Mother's Day gift?"

Dick threw his head back and guffawed. "I s'pose. As long as I don't get court-martialed in the process." Then, reaching to hug her again, old blue eyes filling once more, he took the slip of paper and said, "You have no idea how much this has meant to me. I've had a lot of time to think about some of the things I did back then. Back when I was drinking." Tanya started the car. "And all I've ever wanted to say is…I'm sorry, honey."

"I know," Joy said, hugging him back, surprised again by how much he had shrunk. "I'm sorry, too, Father."

"Tell Mother I'm sorry, too."

"Will do," she said, climbing into the car.

"You know, I've never loved another woman like I loved that little wildcat."

"Well, she hasn't changed a bit," Joy said. *Give or take fifty pounds and everything a better man might have left behind,* she didn't say. She had seen Dick eat dirt once, and she had no desire to see it again. At least not until he made a few phone calls.

He pushed the door closed, and Joy lowered her window for a final farewell. Then Tanya blew a kiss to Nimrod, who tripped over a junked engine block, and pulled out. Dick was still standing in the road when a hill erased him from Joy's rearview mirror, like a wave over a dorsal fin.

"Despite your fiendish ulterior motives, you did a good thing today," Tanya said. "That wasn't so hard, was it?"

"I guess not."

"He wasn't such a bad guy. I mean, what's the

worst thing Dick Perkins ever did anyway, besides spank you a few times? Which I can certainly attest you probably deserved."

While Tanya hawed and playfully shoved her, Joy's mind skidded across a veritable top one hundred of Dick's greatest hits, none of which she knew would wring an ounce of sympathy from her obstinate best friend. For that, she would need to focus on Quida Raye.

"Here's something," she began. "Besides busting up two trailers full of her prized possessions before *stealing* the last one, he rolled in drunk another time, beat Mother to a bloody pulp, and broke her arm between his two bare hands. *Snap!*"

Tanya glanced over, eyes slit, not believing a word. "I don't remember your mother with a cast on her arm."

"Of course you don't. She never went to the hospital. How would she explain it to the Army doctors or her co-workers or anyone else? You know it's always been about appearances for her. If you don't believe me, look at her left arm when we get back. It's still sort of curved like a crescent moon, after dangling down by her side for months."

Suddenly, in an ascot-gray diesel in nowhere Missouri, Joy realized she was absolutely justified in asking retired Army First Sergeant Richard Perkins for help. He owed her mother quite a few trips to a hospital, if nothing else.

"It sounds like he's at least sorry," Tanya offered.

"Oh, he's sorry all right," Joy agreed. "Yes, ma'am, Dick Perkins is definitely sorry."

"And it also sounds like he might try to get her that new ID, too," Tanya continued archly. "Even though you and I both know *she's* the one who drove him out of his precious Army." Joy grinned. She always grinned when she thought about her mother's *pièce de résistance*, the final magnum opus of her entire marital existence.

"Remind me again how all that went down," Tanya said, rolling through a stop sign. "Didn't she hook up with his boss or whatever the Army calls them?"

"Yep," Joy answered. "Not long after Dick had stolen the trailer, she saw his command sergeant major nursing a cold one down at the Wagon Wheel. Come to find out, he was also recently divorced, so one thing led to another until she made a deal with him—she would go back to his place if he would drive out to the NCO club with her. And, if her bastard of an ex was inside, all he had to do was walk up and say something like, 'I hear you thank yore platoon is the best in the company. But I thank it's a piss-poor platoon full of piss-poor soldiers thanks to a piss-poor drill sergeant.' "

Tanya laughed at Joy's spot-on twang. "After the MPs arrived to arrest Dick Perkins for striking a superior, the last sight he saw from the back of that Army Jeep was his command sergeant major strolling across the NCO club's parking lot and getting in the passenger side of a beige-on-brown coupe. Just like Mother planned it."

Joy waited till Tanya stopped vibrating with laughter to finish the story. "An Army buddy of hers said Dick was still trying to make sense of it all when his battalion commander slapped him with an Article Fifteen. The way he put it was, instead of being busted, rather than having twenty-one years of exemplary service that stretched from the ass-end of the Korean

War to two godforsaken tours in Vietnam dishonored by the Army or any damned body else, before the memory of all the fine men he had led and fought alongside could be further profaned, Dick Perkins drove to headquarters and submitted his retirement paperwork that very day."

"That's right," Tanya said. "And your mother celebrated at the Wagon Wheel that night."

"Yes, she did. She drained a can of tomato juice into a mug of beer and declared, 'Let's see that son of a bitch steal another damned trailer. Cheers!' "

Eleven years later, Joy smiled and said, "Trust me, Tanya. Dick's got nobody to blame but himself."

For once, Tanya didn't argue. Joy was tired of talking, too, so she spun the dial, searching for a good country station as they drove on toward the mountains in the distance.

Chapter 31
"Hungry Eyes"

Joy got back to Avalon minutes after the ambulance left. Boo-Boo met her at the door and said her mother had been suffering from periods of vomiting and diarrhea. She was also incontinent, mute, and so weak she had been using a walker, but she fell again anyway. That's when he called her doctor, who said they had no choice except to send her to JFK, which was where the ambulance was headed.

"No!" Joy screamed.

"Go!" Boo-Boo yelled back. "There was no other option. I'll meet you as soon as I clean up here."

At the foot of the rickety Little River Bridge, waiting for oncoming traffic to pass, Joy stared at the lights of the dingy white hospital high on the far bank. The last time she had gone to JFK Memorial, her mother was in the driver's seat and Jessie was a breath away. Now Joy was behind the wheel and no new signs of life were anywhere in sight, certainly not on that bleak Ferndale hill.

****

"We'll put her on an IV and stabilize her," the ER doctor said. Joy nodded and looked down at her mother on the gurney. She had two inches of alabaster roots. All of it, Moonlit Brown and starlit white, stood straight out from her head. Like she had teased it for a night at

371

the Wagon Wheel and had simply forgotten to comb it out.

"Mother," Joy commanded. "Mother." A great struggle got underway beneath Quida Raye's eyelids. Even though the light eventually won and her head flopped toward the child calling "Mother," Joy saw not a speck of recognition in those faraway eyes, eyes the same brown as her beat-up old Barge-mobile. Standing in that charity hospital's emergency room, watching her wasting-away mother drift in and out of consciousness, Joy Savoy swore she'd buy that damn car back if she just didn't die. Just don't die, Mama.

An attendant appeared, and Joy stepped back, joining the rest of the writhing masses drawn to JFK Memorial that Sunday night. Name the victim— stabbing, beating, rape, shooting, influenza, life-in-general—and there they gathered, dripping blood, leaking resignation in the harshly lit, poorly maintained, archaically outfitted emergency room of Central Louisiana's only charity hospital.

While admissions chiseled her mother's information into stone tablets, Joy feigned a need to stand as far as possible from everyone else. "I've been sitting all day," she told the dirty green wall. Her ears grew hot. Body parts began falling asleep. She was about a minute away from running out of that place when a nurse announced they were finally taking her mother to ICU.

Following them up in the elevator, Joy watched as they rolled her mother in and began lifting her off the gurney.

"Got everything?" she hastily asked. Without waiting for an answer, she said, "Good. I'll be in the waiting room if you need me."

****

"So she's finally come full circle, huh?" Tanya said.

"What do you mean?" Pinching the pay phone between her ear and shoulder, Joy turned toward the wall and unsnapped her jeans. She had eaten way too much in Missouri, and this was going to be a long night.

"I mean she's back where it all began."

A half hour later, her mother's doctor's service patched Joy through. No, he didn't see patients at JFK. No, he didn't think her quality of care would necessarily be greatly compromised at a charity hospital. JFK did a fine job with a tough task, he said, often treating the sickest of the sick and always the poorest of the poor. No, he wasn't aware of special programs for indigent patients at Avalon's Baptist and Catholic hospitals, not with JFK across the river. Their business offices didn't operate like his, he said, at which point he informed Joy that he would not be charging her mother for her last relapse or two. Joy stood there beside the ICU waiting-room pay phone, head bowed, trying not to cry.

She knew this good doctor, this Saint Christopher-medal-wearing man, had lost his first wife and young son in a small plane crash six years earlier. He could tell Joy everything she wanted to know in a voice as soft as angel's wings. But how could she ask the questions? How could she say her mother might not have cancer or any other end-stage ailment with a definitive medical name. *But she's got something bad all the same. And it's taken her all the way back to the place her dear departed only grandchild was born.* Was there a cure for that? A cure for a grandma who seemed to want nothing more than to quit her lonely world and be back with the only person who had ever loved her unconditionally?

"Joy," the good doctor said, "it's in God's hands now."

For the fifth time in nearly six months, Joy spent the night in an ICU waiting room with another collection of rumpled families summoned by late-night calls. She, however, had an advantage. She knew her mother didn't have cancer. She also knew what she had known since she saw the first man do a double-take at Quida Raye Perkins—she had sprung from an untamed source. Thick lava from a live volcano. Though her mother was dormant for the moment in a bed in ICU, Joy told herself it was just that—for the moment. Her mother had a will no one—certainly no man or even her own mama and daddy—could bend. And, for the moment at least, it was apparently not her will to do anything more than two-step up to the pearly gates over and over on the teasing strains of the devil's own fiddling.

During one of Joy's five-minute visits, she checked her mother's chart and told Boo-Boo little written there made any sense. "Severe chronic malnutrition and hypoalbuminemia, acute non-anon B viral hepatitis, grand mal seizure disorder, and chronic obstructive lung disease." Satisfied that the word "terminal" wasn't anywhere on the page, she laid her head in his lap on the waiting-room couch and did something no one else seemed capable of. She slept.

****

Not even a week later, Quida Raye Perkins was on a regular ward getting no more strenuous treatment than food she largely ignored. *Don't they have adequate IVs in this place,* Joy wondered, stomping down a hall that didn't smell anywhere near clean enough.

She had skipped lunch to take her mother the candy bars she had requested. She didn't care what it was anymore. Antacids. Toenails. Vaporizing salves. If it could be swallowed and her mother wanted to eat it, Joy was game. She might have been late delivering this last jolt of pure sugar—she latched onto any excuse to avoid getting grilled by the guard outside, not to mention strafed by the memories inside—but she more than made up for her tardiness with generosity. Carrying a bag stuffed like Santa's sack with pounds of chocolate and sugar, Joy was hustling down the stuffy hall when she heard, "Psst, psst!" coming from a dark nook barricaded by a brace of loaded-up gurneys. She stopped and stared at the mound of blankets and pillows. And that's when she saw the smoke.

"Over here," her mother hissed.

"What are you doing?"

"What's it look like?" Quida Raye asked, cackling and peeking out from a foxhole of laundry that appeared to be on fire.

"It looks like you're trying to burn the place down," Joy replied. "Though Lord knows you might be doing everyone a favor."

Her mother humphed. "Did you bring everythang?"

"Yep, and then some. Now where are you going to hide it so, if nothing else, the roaches don't haul it away?"

"They give you a big zip-lock baggie to put yore

stuff in. It makes a racket when you open it, so at least I'll know if anyone's stickin' their nose where it don't belong."

****

A week later, Joy made an appointment for Radar's first official visit to a dog groomer and what was looking like Sugar Pie's last. Then she and Boo-Boo went to the new po'boy place near the mall for lunch. It was a day for firsts. Although her mother was again in ICU, Joy finally admitted on air for the first time that she had not been feeling up to snuff.

"Don't get your shorts in an uproar," she had said before signing off, "but mother's been feeling a little puny lately." Boo-Boo had suggested she deflect any pity on the part of her listeners by launching into a litany of ills that had befallen various female country superstars. Which she did, accomplishing little more than confusing everyone. After spending fifteen minutes explaining to callers—no, her mother hadn't been abducted and, no, she hadn't been in a hit-and-run and, no, she hadn't declared bankruptcy (yet), she was just back in the hospital—she and Boo-Boo finally left for a long lunch that included several much-needed glasses of wine.

When they finally returned, Ruthie looked up from her typewriter and said, "Hey, Joy. Someone came to see you, but he didn't leave a name."

"I'll be in the production room," Boo-Boo said, continuing on.

"What'd he look like?" Joy asked.

"Medium build. Older. Crew cut. Carried himself like retired military."

"Yeah? Well, with Fort Dewey an hour away,

we've narrowed the cast of potential candidates down to a mere few thousand."

"I'll show you what he looked like, Miss Smarty Pants." Flipping over a "While You Were Out" pad, Ruthie picked up her pencil, doodled a bit, ripped off the sheet, and handed it to her.

Joy glanced at the pink square, surprised once again by a secret of Ruthie's. "I didn't know you could draw."

"There's a lot no one knows about me," Ruthie sweetly said, twirling her wedding band.

Joy looked at the pink square again. The crew cut wasn't all that distinguishing. The fine graphite details, however, were indisputable. Around a pair of aviator glasses, Ruthie had drawn the open, furrowed face of every man who has ever stopped to help a stranger fix a flat. A flicker of something like panic mixed with savage hope tickled the base of Joy's skull.

"The only person I know who looks like this is my number-two father, Dick. And he lives in Missouri and hasn't been back to Louisiana since 1975."

"He's got a twin then." Ruthie shrugged.

Joy went to the production room and showed Boo-Boo the sketch. "Who does this look like?"

"Dick."

"That's what I thought."

"Why?"

"Ruthie claims someone masquerading as him came to see me while we were at lunch," Joy said, plopping into a chair.

"Um, you *did* ask him to find out something rather important for you."

"He'd be a day late and a dollar short if he showed

up with good news now," she huffed, though in truth she was already imagining a military ambulance life-flighting her mother out of godforsaken JFK. "Besides, they do have phones in Missouri. Who would drive eleven hours when they could just pick up a telephone?"

"Your mother," Boo-Boo said. Then, glancing at the door and standing up, he added, "And your father."

"It's about time you got back from lunch," boomed retired Army First Sergeant Richard Perkins. "What do you get anyway? Half a dang day?"

Going to church had given Joy an appreciation for the oftentimes surprising manifestations of a higher power in this world. She heard all the time about prayers being answered and lives that were consequently changed forever. Till the moment she spun around to see Dick in the doorway behind her, however, she had never felt personally involved in any particular fell swoop of salvation. But as she stood in KLME's musty production room, looking into the ecstatic, aging face of the man who had made her childhood a living hell, she couldn't help but wonder if this sudden appearance wasn't part of some divine intervention. Had she been so blind that God had sent Dick to whack her upside the head some more in the hopes he might finally knock some sense into her? The thought scared her half to death.

"Wipe that look off your face and come give Father a hug," he commanded. And she obeyed. If Dick had been a Jekyll/Hyde drunk, she had become a Jekyll/Hyde daughter. When he was nice, she was nice back. There would be time enough for recriminations. But now wasn't it.

"I can't believe you drove all the way down here," she exclaimed, stepping back. He had to have good news, right?

"I was on my way to Alabama to see an old sergeant major of mine—you remember him, honey, Sergeant Major Vinson? He was over in Veet-Nam with me? He has a reunion for some of us every year, and I thought, what the hell, I may as well go a little out of my way and come shoot the shit some more. Besides," he added, voice dropping, "I wanted to tell you what I found out. I'm afraid it's not good news, honey."

Smile fading, hopes cascading, she drew farther back and looked at him. "You can't get her a new ID card?"

"No, I'm afraid I can't."

Joy stared into his ice-blue eyes and wondered. *Can't? Or won't?* Behind her, Boo-Boo began shuffling papers.

"That's fine," she said, though, of course, it wasn't. There she was, a minor celebrity in small markets near and far, and she couldn't spare her own mother the fate of wasting away in a charity hospital. "Something else came up anyway."

"Good," Dick declared, relieved to be done with the whole subject. Craning his head around her, he stuck his hand out and said, "Dick Perkins. Haven't we met, son?"

"Yes, sir, we have," Boo-Boo said, shaking Dick's hand. "But I must've been a junior or senior in high school. You've got quite a memory."

"I never forget a face, do I, honey? I remembered little Tanya—well, I *say* little. She's sure not little anymore!—and she wadn't but nine or ten the last time

I saw her. You're looking good, too, son. Looks like you did all your growin' in the opposite direction. What the heck are you now? Seven feet tall?"

"Not quite," Boo-Boo said, smiling down at Dick.

"He's just a little bigger than the average bear," Joy said, beaming up at him, thankful that at least one person in her life never let her down.

"Well, you're either gonna have to sit back down or I'm gonna have to go get a dern stepladder," Dick joked. "No wonder you two took such a dang long lunch. How much does a man your size have to eat anyway?"

"Too much. Always." Boo-Boo laughed, waiting for Joy to chime in with some similarly amiable comment. When she didn't, he continued. "Speaking of, if you're still here at suppertime, we could all go grab a bite somewhere. My treat." Joy glared at him, tipping her head sideways and generating a speedy amendment. "Though we'd certainly understand if you need to get back on the road."

"Supper sounds great," Dick whooped, tilting Joy's head even farther over. "But first I thought I'd drop by and see Joy Faye's mother."

The sound came to her as if from another time. "My mother?"

"Yessiree Bob," Dick said, turning to face her. "Where is that hardheaded woman anyway?"

"Where?" she said bleakly.

"At home? Work?" Clearing his throat, Dick lowered his voice and said, "Remarried? You know, I didn't come all this way to start any trouble, honey."

"No, no, she never remarried." Joy searched Boo-Boo's dark eyes for clues about what she might say.

"That's good. I definitely don't want to do anything that would tick her off." Turning back to Boo-Boo, he said, "You know Joy Faye's mother, doncha, son?"

"Yes, sir. Of course."

"Then you know that fighting with that woman is like wrestling with a dang chain saw." Dick let go a booming laugh that shook the walls. Boo-Boo joined in, too. Not even that lasted long enough.

"So where is she, then?" Dick asked, taking the emotional temperature of the room. "She's not sick, is she, honey? I heard you say something along those lines on the radio, but I couldn't figure out who you were talkin' about. That's not what you wanted that card for, is it?"

"Actually," Joy began, "she is. And it was. But, as I said, something else came up."

"Let's go wherever that 'something else' is then." Joy could tell Dick's good humor was wearing thin.

Boo-Boo reached out a hand, and Joy took it, turning it over and absently running a finger down the long life line, heart line, marriage line. But nothing there revealed any lines that might work on Dick. Like, "Are you kidding? She'd skin me alive if I let you see her in her current condition. We are absolutely not going where she is. Not in a million years."

Five minutes later, Joy and Dick were going where Quida Raye Perkins was. Dick was clearly on a mission, and if the Viet Cong could never stop him, who was Joy to try? Why, oh why, had she ever gone to Missouri?

"It'll be okay," Boo-Boo said. "I'll see you when you get back."

****

Alone with Dick in the Wedgie—Joy was categorically *not* taking his hearse-turned-camper to JFK—she barely knew where to begin.

"I've been meaning to drop you a line and update you on a few things since I got back," she lied. "You see, Mother's been a little under the weather for a while. Nothing too serious. She's just run down. And, well, she's in ICU again."

"ICU? Again?" Dick's face drained of color. "What is it, honey? Cancer?"

"No. It's definitely not cancer. We know that for sure. I'm telling you, it's nothing anyone can pinpoint other than complications from one surgery or another. The bottom line is she just needs to eat more and get her strength up." That sounded simple enough, and the beige dripped back into Dick's face. At least it did until Joy pulled up to the Little River Bridge.

"We're not driving over *this*, are we?" he asked, grabbing for the Jesus strap above the door.

"Unfortunately, we are," Joy answered, trundling on. "Every time someone tries to get it condemned, Avalon's business owners back there on River Street have a fit."

Dick craned his head over his shoulder at the neon "Open" sign in the storefront directly across from the bridge, Abe's Pawn Shop.

"As you can see, it's a straight shot to Abe's front door. Downhill all the way. The bridge's closing would probably cut his business in half. Anyway, as I was saying…"

By the time Joy pulled into JFK's parking lot, she had put as good a spin as she could on her mother's harrowing medical events of the past half year. "Just don't expect her to look like she did the last time you saw her."

"Fair enough, since I'm pretty sure she was chewing me up one side and down the other. Anything else would be an improvement."

Maybe, Joy thought, opening the car door. And maybe not.

Chapter 32
"He Stopped Loving Her Today"

Dick stood by while Joy got her usual grilling from JFK's guard. As always, multitudes surged past while the guard demanded her name, what floor she was visiting, what room, who, then went to labor over his log and make a phone call or two. Why me? Joy wondered. Why always me? Why not any of these other shiftless sorts who genuinely looked like they could be smuggling concealed weapons to the disgruntled patients inside?

"You know what your problem is?" Dick said, once they were finally waved through. "You stop and everyone else keeps walking. You give him the only chance he gets all day long to play policeman."

Joy had to laugh. The man who'd spent fifteen years ordering her to stand at attention and bark "Yes, sir!" and "No, sir!" was complaining because she was too obedient? Not that she was going to point out the irony. He had also taught her to respect her elders, something Joy Savoy was trying extremely hard to continue doing.

"And here I just thought he was either no fan of country music or a parolee from the Institute for the Criminally Insane next door."

Dick humphed and followed her toward the big double doors, beyond which her mother was hooked up to every machine the state could spare, which wasn't many. "Did I mention this is her sixth trip to ICU since December?" Joy asked at the elevators.

"No, honey, you didn't," Dick tensely said, and Joy could tell he was beginning to lose the cool that had carried him and his hearse/camper all the way to Avalon. Whatever he had come hoping to find—absolution? a meal or two?—Joy knew he was about to come face-to-face with a sight that would send him back to either Missouri or the bottle, in fairly short order.

"Just so you know, she's on a respirator and a few other contraptions," she explained, pushing the third-floor button. "So don't be alarmed when you see her. It's not as bad as it looks." It was every bit as bad as it looked, and Joy thanked God fresh horses had finally arrived. As the elevator opened and she glanced over at Dick, however, she saw him for what he had always been. A wild stallion that had never carried anyone safely off into the sunset. God may as well have sent fresh dingoes.

Joy stood outside the swinging double doors to JFK's intensive care unit and wondered if there was a med cart left unattended somewhere, preferably one piled with opiates. Then she turned to the man who had once taken everything her mother had—except Joy, whom he'd never really wanted anyway—and said, "If you're sure you're ready, let's go."

Where ICUs across the river hummed and blinked like *Star Wars* sets, JFK's intensive care unit wasn't all that different from any other ward. There were a few more nurses, a few more medical students working rounds, and one or two different machines, but that was about it. Joy was glad Dick didn't have the comparisons to make as they pushed through the doors and toward cubicle number four. He seemed busy enough reconciling the woman of the mid 1970s with what he could clearly see from across the room that eleven rough years had wrought. Any other man might have broken down and wept. Most other men, however, didn't have a couple tours of duty in Vietnam rife with images Joy figured he was calling upon to help put this one into context, send a little steel down his backbone, hurtle him onward to her side.

The twenty or so pounds of fluid her mother was retaining belied her true weight, which had to have been only seventy-something by then. She had hoses running from her mouth and nose, was out of it, swollen, an odd shade of orange, and bruised from head to toe by needles and tape stuck in or on practically every inch. But, other than that, she didn't look much different than she had for longer than Joy's aching brain could recall. Grinning as if they were in the nursery, Joy leaned over the railings and said, "Mother! Mother!" When Quida Raye's head started moving slightly, Joy glanced at Dick on the other side of the bed, white as the state-issued sheet folded beneath her mother's slack, puffy jaw.

"Mother!" Joy repeated. "Mother!" As Quida Raye's head rocked and her eyes darted beneath bulging lids, Joy knew she was once again summoning the strength to answer that primal urge—finding the child calling "Mother!" Finally, her eyes cracked open and swam around until they focused. The whites had gone crimson. Hemorrhaging probably, one of the interns had said. As Quida Raye attempted a blood-speckled smile around the tube stuck down her throat, a calloused hand steadied itself on the far railing.

After the usual questions—"Are you feeling okay? Do you need anything? Are you comfortable?"—and receiving the usual barely perceptible nods and shakes in response, Joy stalled some more. Checked the IV bags. Observed the heart monitor's numbers. Glanced around to make sure there were plenty of nurses and interns nearby. Dick shifted his weight to his other foot and, afraid the movement might get her mother's attention, Joy swallowed once, twice, then let out a ragged sigh that sounded more like a sob, and, in a too-loud voice, somehow summoned the courage to say, "You're not going to *believe* who's come to see you today."

One or two nurses intuitively looked over, and Joy braced herself in case her mother had a heart attack and died on the spot. She nodded to the other side of the bed and slowly, slowly, her mother's head lolled to the right. At the sight of Dick Perkins smiling like the day she met him so many years and a million miles before, her flaming eyes sprang open. She gasped at her respirator tube. Recoiled into her pillows. Twitched and squirmed and flailed around. Wailed and grunted and jerked uncontrollably. The beeping monitors shrieked, the nurses ran over, a young doctor appeared. Still, Dick stood his ground, clutching his ex-wife's hand amid the chaos, a stellar example of battlefield bravado.

Terrified, Joy stumbled back, watching as her mother's mortification finally turned to humiliation, then, after the machines eventually ceased their piercing alarms, faded to indignation. It was a sliding scale of sentiments well suited to the vainest woman on earth, lying there distended and discolored in a bed in ICU, inches away from a man she had once loved with all her hard little heart. It was the most frightening scene Joy had ever witnessed, and it wasn't over. Her blood-filled eyes finally found Joy again, and she glared as beseechingly as a baby left to cry it out. Joy knew what she was thinking. She was thinking Joy had summoned Dick because she was dying. She thought Joy had given up on her and sent for Satan himself.

"I didn't call him," she exclaimed, approaching the bed again and shaking her head. "Honest. He just showed up. Like *you* always do."

Once the nurses and doctor cautiously went back to other business, and after another five long minutes of staring straight ahead, her mother deigned to look back into the older, sober face of her worn-out second husband. Then she huffed, as if to say, "So it's you."

"Hey, honey," Dick said, still holding her swollen hand. "How're you feeling? Look at me. I'm so happy to see you after all these years I'm bawling like a baby. You doing okay, sugar?" Quida Raye blinked and looked at the wall, back to her grumpy old self.

"Father here was on his way to Alabama to see an old something or other of his when he decided to drop in without a single word of warning. Weren't you, Father?" Joy's voice had that forced, intensive-care sproing to it.

"Sure was," he said. "You remember him, honey, Sergeant Major Vinson?" Mother tipped her head in vague recognition. And, for what was left of their visitation, Dick prattled on and on about his old platoon's annual get-together, every detail of his house in Missouri, driving to Avalon in a secondhand hearse he had converted into a camper for hunting trips, some of the more interesting discoveries he'd made in abandoned old houses, and, well, enough small talk to make even Joy's head swim, and she didn't have several extra pounds of fluid floating around in hers.

Degradation having long since bowed to boredom, her mother nodded off while Dick rambled on, oblivious. Joy stood on the other side of the bed and smiled, remembering who had done most of the talking for fifteen years. All things considered, it had at least been blissfully quiet since he'd been gone.

Interrupting a long, colorful yarn about why he didn't join the Navy—something about submarines routinely flooding when the heads belched up everything two hundred men flushed down them—Joy clapped her hands, looked at the clock, and said, "Look at the time." Smoothing her mother's sheet and jostling her back awake in the process, she told her she'd be back the next day. Quida Raye nodded and, after a sideways glance at Dick, went back to her nap.

"See you tomorrow, hon," Dick said, which answered Joy's most pressing question. He planned to stay at least a night. When he reached through the snarl of tubes to gingerly hug her, she saw one of her mother's bloated hands twitch in response.

"She's looking good," Joy announced in the elevator. "Definitely doing better." Dick, however, just kept punching the first-floor button. Even the Little River Bridge didn't faze him on the drive back to the station, where he picked up his hearse-camper, followed Joy to her house, parked, and with a wave, disappeared between the lushly padded seats.

Though Joy dreaded the prospect of spending time

with the parent she hadn't slept in the same house with since she was sixteen years old, her guest proved gratefully elusive. Coming upon his ex-wife in critical condition in a charity hospital's intensive care unit subdued the normally voluble Dick, threw him into a pensive frame of mind, took him off her hands. He not only stayed in his hearse-camper the rest of that night but the next three days, as well, emerging only for visits to JFK. Joy went to work or up the street to Boo-Boo's. And Dick stayed in his well-stocked wagon, watching a portable TV he proudly announced picked up all the local stations. After traveling to the hospital together during visiting hours, Joy would take him back, watch as he climbed like Dracula into his hearse, then head two doors down for the only solace at her disposal anymore.

"I feel sort of guilty," Boo-Boo said the second night, looking out the window at Dick's spooky black chariot parked in front of Joy's house. "Don't you think we ought to take him out or something? Show him a good time? After all, he came a long way just to be left alone in that, uh, contraption of his."

"Don't worry about Dick," Joy said, pulling him away from the window. "He's never been one to suffer in silence. If he wanted to do anything, believe me, he'd say something."

Just about the only time he spoke, however, was at her mother's bedside. Sensing a captive audience in the ICU, Dick became his boisterous old self again, regaling Quida Raye and everyone else within earshot with loud tales of one harebrained scheme after another.

"Remember when Joy wanted a horse, so I yanked the backseat out of our new convertible and crammed a pony back there? You wouldn't ride home with us, remember, 'cause that pony kept chewing on your hair?"

And, "Remember when I took Joy out for a snipe hunt, and she sat holding the bag in that field all night long 'cause she was scared a blame snipe was gonna get her if she moved?"

And, "Remember when Joy's little turtle, Turpy, was on his last leg, and I told her I'd take him to the vet and get him fixed up? Only I went to the pet store and bought her a new turtle instead? Remember how she took one look at that dern thing and screamed, '*You're not Turpy!*' "

He'd tell his stories, honking and hawing as if a sitcom was taping in a dingy white hospital on the Little River's banks. Dick laughed. The nurses and interns laughed. The other critical cases laughed. Quida Raye even rolled her blood-red eyes and grinned. Everyone clearly adored the new stand-up comedian of ICU.

"They say laughter's the best medicine," Tanya reminded her.

"Why don't you use some of his jokes for your show?" Boo-Boo suggested.

So Joy started taking notes as she and Dick huddled around her mother, who had begun sitting up, was responsive, alert, absorbed in the details of Dick's tall tales and Joy's upcoming appearances. According to the nurses, she would even have her respirator tube removed soon, which meant a move back to a regular room. Though her eyes remained red and her body was still retaining fluid, Quida Raye made more progress in those three days with Dick than she had in the last six months. Dick was shocked, but Joy was the wizened old soldier here. And this was one battlefield he knew nothing about. He had no idea of the dogfights she and her mother had been through, every one as touch-and-go as this one. As a result, Joy responded to her mother's improvements the way she always did. By egging her on, ticking off all the reasons she needed to get better.

"Remember, now," Joy said that Friday. "You've got to hurry up and get out so you can go to Kentucky." Across the bed, Dick craned his head to one side. "I've told Mother she can take one of the cars and go see Grandma and Granddaddy," she gaily explained. Dick craned his head to the other side.

"Also," she continued, getting her mother's attention again, "I've made an appointment with a dog groomer who claims she can make Radar look like a Shih Tzu for the first time in her life. Sugar Pie's going to get fixed up, too." The respirator tube bounced up and down, signaling a snort. "So you'd better get out soon, before they're both back to looking like shrubs with paws."

Later, when they passed JFK's sullen guard, Dick eyeballed him and marched toward the Wedgie, silent as he usually was when they were alone together. But, as Joy unlocked his door, he turned and said, "You're not really going to let her out on the highway, are you, honey? Even if she does get out of the hospital?"

"If you could have seen how much it tore her up when Grandma and Granddaddy said she couldn't come home again, you'd promise her just about anything, too. Besides, trust me, she'll be out of ICU before you leave for Alabama."

****

Saturday, May 10, 1986, Boo-Boo dropped off an extra blanket at JFK's early visitation while Joy took the dogs to the groomer. Boo-Boo had been instructed to tell her mother that she and Dick would be there at eleven o'clock sharp. And they might have been, too, had it not been for the truck.

Joy pulled into JFK's parking lot behind the big semi. Like all truck traffic headed in or out of Ferndale for decades, the driver had swung through the north side of town from the bypass and taken the big, four-lane bridge. That meant Dick and Joy, who had come from the south and the old Little River Bridge, had a clear shot to the gun shack. As if on cue, the guard looked up, saw the big rig inching toward him, and beamed as if his best friend in the world was behind the wheel.

"Shit fire!" Dick hollered. "Visitation's at eleven hundred hours. We're gonna be late."

Joy parked, and they huffed up to wait their turn as the truck driver and the guard chatted away. While Dick fumed and the minutes ticked past, Joy controlled her blood pressure by admiring the truck. She had never seen anything like it. With gold marker lights tracking along the steps, trim and grill, a scoop on the top, and everything else chrome plated—the stacks, the twin two-hundred-fifty-gallon tanks, even the mud flaps—the jonquil yellow eighteen-wheeler sparkled under the midday sun like the Milky Way fallen to earth. It occurred to Joy that not even her mother could have designed a gaudier cab. On the door, an airbrushed swirly script announced "White Lightnin'!" Joy was conducting a word search in the registration when Dick jabbed her in the side.

"Come on," he ordered.

Stricken, she saw he meant past the truck—and the guard—to the hospital. "Without clearance?"

"What's he gonna do?" Dick roared, leveling an ice-blue dare at JFK's sentry, who suddenly didn't seem in charge of much. "Shoot us? Man, I'd like to see the sumbitch try." Then he took off. By the time Joy caught up with him, he was well into a hiccupy rendition of "White Lightning." Neither of them knew the words, so they just kept bawling *"Wa-at Light-nin!"* all the way into the hospital. *"Wa-at Light-nin!"* they squalled, *"Wa-at Light-nin!"* People stared down halls and up the elevator, but on they sang, *"Wa-at Light-nin!"*

It took a minute or two to get hold of themselves outside the door to ICU. Joy hadn't laughed that much in months. Hadn't laughed that much with *Dick* her entire life. Suddenly, she was filled with shame for leaving him alone in that hearse-camper every night, for barely concealing the fact that she could hardly stand being in the same room with him for more than fifteen minutes. So what if he had routinely gotten tanked up and whipped her as a child. Joy Savoy looked into a pair of laughing old eyes—baby blues so much like Jessie's—and finally began forgiving the flawed man in front of her. No one knew better than Joy Savoy that no parent is perfect. Aside from her own immortal failings, her mother, with her mulish unpredictability, outlandish schemes, and maniacal concentration on the material over the emotional, certainly hadn't been perfect, either. That Dick had occasionally been as far off the mark as any man can be without getting arrested was no longer the point. Joy was big enough to defend herself now.

She could also be big enough to accept what was clearly a heartfelt apology and get on with her life.

Before she could do or say anything to reveal her newfound sense of inner harmony, Dick shoved the door open and into ICU they walked.

"Mother," Joy happily commanded, leaning over the rail. Quida Raye perked up, instantly alert. Smiling at Dick to see if he noticed the marked improvement, Joy said, "I see Boo-Boo brought you that extra blanket." She nodded and sat up, snatching her covers around to her liking. Always on the lookout for topics that brought out her spunky best, Joy knew Boo-Boo was perfect.

"While he was here, did he happen to mention anything about proposing anytime soon?" Her mother shook her head and rolled her eyes. "Of course, there's always the possibility he might come to his senses and realize no man in his right mind would want to live with *me* the rest of his life, isn't that right?" Her mother nodded vigorously, smoothing the sheet around her.

"Wouldn't that be something, honey?" Dick said. "Our little girl getting married. *Again*." As he honked and her mother turned companionably toward him, Joy knew she had two choices. She could watch the blinking, blipping heart monitor, blood pressure machine, and respirator while her mother and Dick stared at each other, possibly recalling the day twenty-seven years earlier when Father Number One exited and Father Number Two proposed. Or she could keep jabbering.

"Have you heard?" Joy continued. "They finally voted to keep the Little River Bridge open indefinitely." Her mother's head did a surprised little bob. "Shocked me, too, but some of Avalon's merchants managed to get it declared historic. And guess who was leading the charge? Your old buddy Abe, down at the pawn shop. They might do a few improvements on it, but Tanya's already said she's swimming the next time she comes to see you."

As Dick looked around the ICU, sizing up the audience for his next routine, Joy could tell he was ready for the opening act to wind down. "Speaking of Tanya and wide loads, I probably shouldn't tell you this, especially considering what *you'll* be having for lunch, mmm, let's see, glucose," they all snickered, two of them out loud, "but I'm taking Dick to the mall today so we can have an A&D Cafeteria feast, my favorite."

"Yep," he began, hearing his cue. "I'm craving the works, what they call a divine dish—fried chicken, mashed taters and gravy, green beans, corn on the cob, coleslaw, and biscuits. Just like you used to make, remember, honey? And don't forget dessert. I tell you what, I've never had banana pudding that could touch yours." Quida Raye took the compliment like she did all others—staring straight ahead, confident.

Years later, Joy often returned to this moment—her mother's smug smile, Dick's rare pause between thoughts—and imagined any number of happy outcomes connected to any collection of other words Dick might have uttered next. The possibilities were endless. Until he spoke again.

"Yep, I'd give my right arm for one of your Sunday dinners, honey. It just breaks my heart to think you won't ever be whippin' me up another one." Joy knew Dick was under the impression he had just given her mother another compliment, but she also knew what her mother had heard in his rueful words—that he didn't think she would live to cook again. It was a dare, and no one should have known better than Dick never to dare Quida Raye Perkins. Especially when it was wrapped around a craving for some of her home cooking.

Racing to beat the peeved expression already slipping across her gray face, Joy set the record straight. "What he *means* is he's leaving out first thing in the morning. I wasn't going to tell you that until tonight, but, well, there you have it."

"Right, right," Dick said, backtracking. "I've gotta go see Sergeant Major Vinson, honey. Our reunion's this weekend, and I don't want to miss it. But you can cook for me when I come back. Assuming you still want to, of course. If not, I suppose I can take you both to Joy's cafeteria. Because I *will* be back. And it won't be no ten or twelve years next time, either. Shoot, I wouldn't mind coming down to see the Natchitoches Christmas lights one of these years."

Great, Joy thought. Now she knew he was leaving and wouldn't be breaking his neck returning. The way he smiled and patted her hand somewhat condescendingly, Joy realized Dick thought all was well. But she also knew he was as wrong as he'd ever been. They might not have a trailer with purple carpet for him to take, but his pending departure appeared to be pulling something out from underneath her mother all the same. For a moment, she seemed to shrink there in cubicle number four, withering in her hospital gown and dashed hopes. What had she been thinking? That maybe he'd stay? Try again? Start over, with no bottle on his part and all bones on hers?

Joy's voice wobbled when she spoke again. "At least he'll get to see the new-and-improved Radar and Sugar Pie before he leaves. We're picking them up from the groomer's after we eat."

"Which reminds me of that dang old dog we used to have that nursed a whole litter of baby squirrels. Remember that, honey?"

By the time visitation ended and Dick's latest comedy routine had wrapped, Quida Raye was oddly content again. Probably, Joy told herself, because her ex-husband had kept raving about her culinary skills to anyone who'd listen.

"Let me tell you about her New Year's dinners," he told one orderly, who patiently listened as Dick described in detail the pork chops, collard greens, black-eyed peas, boiled potatoes, cornbread, and chocolate meringue pie, licking his lips all the while.

"We'll see you at six," Joy told her. Quida Raye nodded as Dick patted her foot on the way around the bed. Following him out, Joy turned one last time to see her mother watching them through the rails, her best smile wrapped around the respirator tube that was scheduled to be removed shortly. Joy waved. Quida Raye waved back. And in that fleeting moment, while Dick continued on to the elevator and the nurses went about their business, it was just her and her mother, the way it had pretty much always been.

When you get out of here, Joy silently swore, just wait and see what fun we're going to have for a change. With—or, better yet, *without*—Dick.

****

Though Joy had not planned on spending the rest of the afternoon at the mall with Dick, she was somewhat dismayed to realize they had nothing better to do. "Since Boo-Boo's stuck in meetings, you want to walk around some before we eat?"

"I guess so, honey," he said, voice curiously hollow.

Joy drove and drove, looking for a parking place, until she finally found one near the road. "What's going on?" she wondered, though she had her answer in the first window display they passed.

"Tomorrow's Mother's Day," Dick declared.

"Holy cow! You're right." What kind of daughter doesn't remember Mother's Day?

"It's a good thing we came here to eat, or else your mother would've known you forgot. What are you gonna get her?"

Not one idea came to mind. So she dragged Dick through the throngs from one end of that mall to the other. "There's one more department store we haven't been in," she finally suggested. "It's down near A&Ds."

Groaning, Dick trudged off again, pushing against the crush of shoppers. Joy tried to think of something to chat about that might ease the irritation of browsing for a Mother's Day gift in a mob scene, but all she came up with was, "Got a penny?"

He glanced over and Joy nodded at the big fountain in front of them. "Oh," he said, drawing up short. Digging in his pocket, he pulled out a nickel and handed it to her.

"You make a wish, too," she insisted. Acting like she'd told him to order his last meal, he shoved a hand back in a pocket, yanked out what looked like a quarter and unceremoniously plunked it into the gurgling water.

Determined to follow proper wish protocol herself, Joy turned around, put Jefferson heads up, closed her eyes, and sent her usual request up, up, up. Then, to make sure it would come true, she tossed the coin over her right shoulder, careful not to look back. Just in case she didn't get a hundred more years with Boo-Boo, it wouldn't be because she had jinxed a perfectly good wish. Figuring Dick needed a break from shopping, she sat down on the fountain's edge and attempted small talk.

"What did you wish for?" Telling wishes, of course, was the surest way to invalidate them, but, judging from the effort he had put into his, Joy figured he didn't stand to lose much.

"I wished I didn't have such a long drive ahead of me," he said.

"Really? You made that wish?" Dick was becoming downright cooperative in his golden years.

"No. I just dread the drive." Heaving a sigh, he eyed the hordes of shoppers shuffling around as if imagining them all in stalled vehicles between him and Alabama. "I've been thinking I might as well go ahead and get on the road, honey. With a couple more hours of daylight behind me, I might get to Sergeant Major Vinson's by nine or ten."

"Tonight?" she stammered. "*Now*? I thought you weren't leaving until the morning."

But, when Dick looked at her, she saw in his ice-blue eyes that he had already gone. All traces of that week's reminiscent sentimentality were now replaced by a chilling void she recognized only too well. What had triggered this? Had shopping for Mother's Day gifts reminded him what drudgery family life could frequently be? Or, more likely, had he simply grown tired of trying to be someone Joy only wished he was?

"But what about Mother? What about the six o'clock visitation?"

"You can tell her bye for me," he said, rattling the coins in his pockets.

I could also tell you to go straight to hell, which is what Quida Raye would most certainly say if that tube had indeed been removed. Her mind reeled. Great rivers of roiling condemnations rushed through her veins, joining the roar of the fountain spewing behind her. Oh, how easy it was to slip back into, if not hating the man, at least hating herself for getting duped again. She sat on the fountain's edge, glaring at Dick, wanting to hurt him as much as this would surely hurt her mother. What would Joy tell her? She had just gotten used to him again, had just started counting on him once more. And she was counting on seeing him one last time. Everyone deserved a last time.

"Can't you at least drop by the hospital before you go?"

Dick shook his head. "Not if I'm gonna beat the traffic," he said, jingling his change. She looked away, determined not to let him see the heat filling her eyes.

"If you're ready, honey, why don't you take me on back to my camper. Here's some money for lunch. Get Mother some flowers or something with the change."

Joy whipped her head around and saw he was holding out a twenty-dollar bill. Twenty dollars would buy several divine dishes. Flowers and a card for her mother. Half the dog grooming bill. Twenty dollars would go far in Joy Savoy's world.

She got up from the fountain's edge and took

Dick's money. Then, making sure Jackson was heads up, she closed her eyes, made a wish, and tossed the bill over her right shoulder. She didn't hear it flutter into the water behind her, but she knew it did because a couple of little boys jumped in after it and their mothers started hollering as Joy turned and stormed off.

"I wish you wouldn't have done that, honey," Dick said, hurrying to catch up with her.

"I wish I wouldn't have done a lot of things," Joy spat, marching on.

As difficult as it was to blitzkrieg their way through the crowded mall, they encountered even more congestion once they rounded the rock garden by Coco's Electronics. A solid wall of shoppers seemed to be shifting gears, sweeping Joy and Dick along until they were no longer stampeding toward Joy's car but were swerving off to the side instead, tugged along with everyone else whose sights were set on Coco's and the bank of TV screens in the window. Coming to a standstill, straining through the fire in her eyes to figure out what everyone was staring at, she saw twenty images of the local station's afternoon newswoman. The words "Breaking News" were stripped in over her head.

"...again, we have just received word that the Little River Bridge has collapsed after an eighteen-wheeler started across it from the Ferndale side. Although work continues at this hour on extracting the driver's body, authorities have confirmed the big rig, affiliated with the Atlanta-based trucking firm White Lightning, had been stolen minutes earlier from the delivery dock at John F. Kennedy Memorial Hospital. Reports are conflicting at this time, but authorities believe the driver may have been a female patient still wearing a hospital gown…"

No one will ever convince Joy Savoy that God doesn't tell us everything we need to know exactly when we need to know it. For the second time in her life, she heard Him loud and clear. Above the gasps in front of Coco's, He again said, "Run."

She didn't remember the drive. She didn't remember Dick. She would never, however, forget the rest.

"There she is," Vernon cried. And Boo-Boo carried her down to the water's edge.

Chapter 33
"Angel Flying Too Close to the Ground"

Late Saturday afternoon, once the divers packed up their gear and the detectives wrapped up their reports, Dick and Joy were finally left alone with Quida Raye. The room was cold. The lights were dim. The world was flat. Facing Dick across the table where her mother lay, Joy saw him reach for one of her swollen, still slightly damp hands, purple in every spot she had jerked a needle out. Murmuring softly, he seemed to be striking some old battlefield bargain.

"You go on, now," he was saying. "Don't worry about Joy Faye. She's old enough to take care of herself, and what she can't do, there's a fine man who'll do it for her. You just go."

Then, blue eyes glittering, he looked over at Joy. She thought for a moment he had gone mad. "Do you feel her?" he asked in a high, frightening voice. "She's up in the corner, looking down."

As a blanket of tiny needles raked down her back, Joy Savoy knew it was true. The recently departed spirit of her big-haired mother was softly *tap-tap-tapping* the ceiling, contrarily refusing to leave till she got one last look at the stringy-haired wreck below.

****

Later, she dropped Dick off at her house, looked at all the cars belonging to all the people who were inside waiting, and kept on going. Driving, driving, till she was in front of her mother's apartment complex. Rolling the Wedgie across the Barge-mobile's old oil stains, splattered like black tears across the pavement, she found the key by memory on her jangling ring.

Easing through the door and leaning against it till it quietly closed, she inhaled deeply, filling her lungs with stale cigarette smoke. Standing there with her eyes shut and the smell she would forever associate with her mother banging like a pinball through her brain, it seemed for a moment as if Quida Raye were back on the couch. Like she might be sitting cross-legged and content, jamming a spoon like a posthole digger through a tall glass of cornbread and buttermilk. Joy pictured the image so vividly, embraced the promise of it so fully, that she was momentarily dazed when she opened her eyes to pitch darkness. Flipping on a light, her heart clenched at the sight of her mother's fussy creations, the glittery craft projects she had hoped would make a home.

On she went into the room she dreaded most. Avoiding the unmade bed and Jessie's altar area, she opened the closet. There, in front of a year's supply of anti-aging potions, hung a blue ball gown. That sugary blue generally only seen on bakery cakes. Sweet, creamy blue. Baby blue.

It was still in the dry cleaner's bag. A note straight-pinned to the plastic read, "Joy Faye, this heres the one. Love, Mother."

****

Joy was almost back home before she remembered the dogs were still at the groomer's. And it was only then, once she turned around and was racing toward the

pet store, that she finally broke down. What were poor
Radar and Sugar Pie going to do now? The way she
wept, there seemed nothing more tragic than a pair of
motherless dogs.

The groomer met her at the door and said, "Lord,
child, I saw the news! You don't know me from Adam,
but I've always felt like your mama was a friend of
mine. It just breaks my heart to think we'll never hear
about her sawing up sofas or shooting mice or picking
pecans or…" She paused, incapable, Joy knew, of
saying the words "stealing trucks." Instead, she waved a
hand and managed, "Or driving some old jalopy that
sounded every bit as bad as mine."

****

Bess and Bubba came to the visitation Sunday and
brought the Barge-mobile. Also in attendance were
Joy's other former neighbors, the pecan thieves, several
grocery-store cashiers, a few of her mother's old hooker
friends, and, of course, Harvey and half of Pitts.

The funeral home did a fine job of spreading the
gown's generous chiffon ruffle across her mother's
distended arms. Only her folded, swollen hands
showed, and all the purple spots had been covered by
the same amber makeup that was under only a slightly
heavier dusting of blush than she normally wore. Her
hairdresser had come armed with two boxes of Moonlit
Brown and hadn't left until Quida Raye was her old,
bulb-headed self again. Tanya brought her a corsage
from Gran D.'s favorite florist. And, for a respectable
amount of time, Joy sat in the funeral home with
everyone else who had come to pay their respects to her
mother on Mother's Day.

Finally, she quietly told Tanya that she would call

406

her later, squeezed Boo-Boo's hand and said she'd see
him at the station, then went and sat behind the mic in
the production room's silence. Empty minutes ticked
past till she checked the Top 100. "Grandpa (Tell Me
'Bout the Good Ol' Days)" was number one. That got
her going. Soon, she had some semblance of a ragtag
broadcast taped to run Monday, the third anniversary of
the first mention of her mother on air.

Midway through, Boo-Boo came in, sat down, and
leaned back, letting the music wash over him. After Joy
flipped off the tape, she kept the records spinning,
reeling through the years with her best memories, still
tucked where they'd always been, in the whorls of those
old forty-fives. When "Lost in the Fifties Tonight"
began, she smiled, picturing the prettiest girl in
Tompkinsville, Kentucky. Saw her laying rubber in her
cherry-red '57 Chevy. Imagined her waving toodle-oo
over a bare, brown shoulder. Never looking back, eyes
on the road ahead. And what a road it surely was.

Because dying, come to find out, cut hours off
Quida Raye's route to Kentucky.

As Joy's grandmother later said in a solemn,
rickety whisper, her grandfather was inconsolable when
word came about the bridge. After sitting in his recliner
and sobbing for hours, he shambled into the bedroom,
slipped off his house shoes, and turned around to hang
up his robe. And that's when he saw them. His darling
daughter was standing by the foot of his bed. And his
giggling little great-granddaughter was hiding behind
her. After she got one last look at the parent whose pet
she had always been, Quida Raye reached for Jessie's
hand and simply vanished. To his dying day, Joy's
hellfire-and-brimstone Southern Baptist grandfather

remained so unstrung by his dead daughter's visit that he never spoke of her, or Jessie, again.

But Joy still can't imagine the spooky scene without grinning. Her grandparents should have known better than to tell Quida Raye Perkins she couldn't go home again.

****

Quida Raye also made it back to church that Monday. Joy watched her minister linger near the white-and-gold casket and, while his words escaped her, she remembered every song the organist played. "How Great Thou Art." "Old Rugged Cross." "Rock of Ages." "Amazing Grace."

Then Ruthie—unveiling yet another surprising talent—stood up and sang her heart out on a medley of some of Quida Raye's old favorites. "Uncloudy Day." "Will the Circle Be Unbroken." An aching rendition of "Across the Bridge." Then she paused a moment before beginning Joy's final request, "Angel Flying Too Close to the Ground."

As time stood still and every major life event waiting for Joy on down the line lost some of its sheen, Ruthie opened her mouth and began singing one of the saddest songs in all of country music. By the time she finished, there wasn't a dry eye in the church. Even the custodian waiting with his dustpan and broom out in the hall got choked up.

****

That night, Joy and Dick sat up talking for the first time in her life. Having delayed his departure out of sheer decency, Dick was finally leaving the next morning. And he had apparently decided to talk nonstop until then. While Joy might not have listened to much of what he said, lying on the couch with her head in Boo-Boo's lap, patiently waiting out Dick's rare attempt to do the right thing for once, she knew at last she didn't hate the man. Didn't love him, either, for sure. But there's a long road between the two and, in time, Joy knew she wouldn't mind meeting him somewhere in the middle again. If nothing else, she figured she could count on the measure of peace she might find in the rattle of his words. After all, Dick had lived with her mother long enough to sound a bit like her. The night after they buried her, Joy rode the sad, swaying train of his runaway thoughts until, around daybreak, he made an observation that resonated well.

"One thing's for sure, honey," he quietly said. "Your mother had six of the finest-looking pallbearers in the history of Morrow Parish. I can't think of anything that would have tickled her more. And I should know, as many men as I had to beat off her with a stick."

As the sun pinked the night, a coralline glow cast a creeping checkered shadow through the window screen behind the couch. It was going to be another blazing May day. The kind that traditionally found Quida Raye in a field somewhere with her mower, cutting a wide swath free of all rats, whatever their species.

Six of the finest-looking pallbearers in the history of Morrow Parish. Boo-Boo, WildDog, Vernon, Ray, Jimmy, and Tanya's dad from Missouri. Six good men from Joy's small world had swept her mother along on her last May morning, shown her to the turned-back bed alongside her precious girl. In failing to mold Joy after her image, no matter how much liberty she had taken with it for three solid years, her mother had inadvertently created her own final success. Joy had called. The men had come. And Quida Raye was tucked in one last time by six handsome princes while a withered old dethroned king looked on. Joy knew the Kentucky Cajun Queen wouldn't have had it any other way.

****

A week later, Joy returned to work and a box of cards Ruthie had collected from listeners. "I put the really sweet ones, the ones with letters or pictures, on top," she said. "The bottom bundles are the 'We heard and we're sorry' variety. Read them when you're up to it. By the way, my mom and dad and their whole congregation are praying for you."

"They've *been* praying for me for years," Joy replied, feeling nothing but gratitude.

Along with heartfelt sympathies, those condolence cards also encapsulated the entire gamut of theories regarding her mother's descent into the choppy, gray waters of the raging Little River. Most correspondents claimed she was a victim of the bridge, which should have been condemned years before. One or two suggested the bridge was a casualty of Quida Raye's. That it would have stood another hundred years if she hadn't managed to pop a big rig out of gear and roll downhill across it, exceeding its weight limit by just enough. Joy's favorite note, however, advanced a scenario both comforting and cunning as fan fiction. That writer proposed Joy's mother knew she was on her death bed anyway, so she stole her last truck and sacrificed herself in order to spare any of her daughter's listeners the same fate someday. After all, everyone had certainly come to expect a unique brand of problem solving on the part of Quida Raye Perkins.

No one—fans, friends, authorities—ever explained how she made it out of ICU. Or why the truck was left driverless, empty, and idling outside JFK's delivery dock, two hundred yards from the back gate of the Institute for the Criminally Insane. Or even where she was going that was so damn urgent that horrible May day.

Joy packed up all the clues and lies Quida Raye left behind and stored them in a hope chest bought with some of the $3,819 in Social Security underpayments that arrived that August. Next to a short stack of old embroidered linens and a starched set of pink party clothes went a big zip-top baggie filled with Quida Raye's purse and several half-eaten candy bars. In addition to a wallet bulging with Jessie's pictures and her own ID collection, the purse held three more items Joy hasn't looked at in years.

Two white-gold rings wrapped in a blank Abe's Pawn Shop slip.

The only thing missing was a grocery list, not that Quida Raye needed one any more than she needed recipes for the fried chicken supper Dick wouldn't shut up about that last day.

"Makes sense," Tanya allowed, the one time Joy connected those particular evidentiary dots. "All she needed was to get to Abe's. Then she would have had taxi money for the rest. I bet she thought she wouldn't even have been in much trouble for the truck, 'relocated' as it *should* have been just across the river, in full view of JFK. I can even hear the case she'd make for 'sprucing up' River Street with a twinkling runaway canary-yellow rig."

"Now that you put it like that," Joy sighed and said, "I guess that idea's about as crazy as all the rest."

Epilogue
"We Believe In Happy Endings"

Nashville, Tennessee, July 17, 2022

"Left with no answers, I soon stopped asking questions. Or even speaking more than was strictly necessary," Joy Savoy said, nearing the end of her retrospective. "With the heart of my show quite literally gone, I found I didn't have much of anything left to say that folks cared about hearing, or that I cared about mentioning. Sure, my engagement provided fun, fresh material, as did our quirky Halloween wedding at a haunted South Louisiana plantation. But those were random highs, flukes amid the frequency."

Smiling at the engineer, who was ready to call it a day, she said, "Luckily, what was becoming far more commonplace at KLME and every other country radio station on earth was an unprecedented demand to hear the hot, new sounds thundering out of Nashville and the West Coast. Almost as if some celestial program director was pulling a few strings, plucking new stars out of the firmament to give a certain DJ a break. The less I spoke, the higher my ratings climbed till, by the time Boo-Boo landed the job in California, I was barely speaking at all. On my last day as Poi-Son Communication's first syndicated DJ, I played ten in a row. Then I cued up the track that had ended every shift since 1980, 'Leaving Louisiana in the Broad Daylight,' and Boo-Boo and I did exactly that, wishing WildDog nothing but the best.

"During those early years in the San Joaquin Valley, I was content to sit in our hot little house on a parched brown hill, sifting through box after box of memories. Later, when I grew restless and mentioned maybe having Tanya move to California, too, Boo-Boo quickly came up with a different suggestion—I could spin records every now and then at a nearby VFW hall. As always, his idea was sheer inspiration. The occasional gig gave me a nice break from the kids while keeping me somewhat current with the music, an asset years later when invitations began trickling in to tape retrospectives like this one for satellite stations or streaming services.

"While I still love the old tearjerkers as much as ever, I've added some newer gems to the mix, like 'Chiseled in Stone' and 'How Can I Help You Say Goodbye,' not to mention the heartbreaker I've ended every show with since it came out, 'Go Rest High on That Mountain.' "

Joy Savoy adjusted her headphones and considered her various standards as well as her many expectations. The rare times she DJs anymore, she still watches the crowd filter in, looking for one particularly thin, exquisitely tanned two-stepper with a crease in her jeans sharp enough to carve a turkey on. She invariably gets compliments for her selections those nights. But little does anyone know—except the big man in back, supporting her still—that she's serenading a certain globe-haired woman who, as the drinks get stiffer and the smoke gets thicker, kicks off her shoes and starts making all the right moves across the sawdust of Joy's hardwood memories. Dancing, dancing, almost right back to her.

"Tanya, for whom country music groupiedom was gradually replaced by advanced degrees, thinks I have too much time on my hands. But she's still happy to do anything she can for Quida Raye. While that generally means taking my boxes of silk flowers out to the cemetery on Mother's Day and Christmas, it also includes keeping lines of random communication open, however dubious."

Checking the clock, Joy Savoy was pleased to be finishing on schedule, not to mention with just the kind of supernatural twist her fans had always enjoyed.

"When a black cat appeared and wound around my feet as Boo-Boo was slipping the ring on my finger that Halloween, Tanya decided it was my mother's spirit. 'As if she'd miss this!' Later, when I lost control of the Wedgie and spun around a busy two-lane road before hitting a power-pole-riddled ditch, unscratched, Tanya endorsed the odd sensation I had that my mother had been perched in the passenger seat. 'She was making sure nothing happened to her car. Or you,' she added, chuckling.

"Then there was the dream as real, decades later, as the old forty-fives I still shuffle through from time to time." Pausing as she did every time at this point in her story, mainly because she always got choked up, Joy cleared her throat and plowed on.

" 'Freud said dreams are wish fulfillment,' Tanya told me, 'but *I* say the fact that it was so lifelike and lasting is proof that it was more than a dream. It was a message from your mother.'

"Whatever it actually was, the dream's impact has shaped every country-music assignment I've accepted in three-plus decades. Not to mention the bulk of my waking hours.

"In the dream, I was at the hospital, talking to Mother's doctor. I was asking him questions that would haunt me forever. Like, would she have lived if I'd been a better daughter? Would love have saved her? Any compassion whatsoever? Then the phone rang, the doctor answered it, said, 'Yes, she's here,' and handed me the receiver.

" 'You always wanted me to call 'fore I showed up,' twanged a contrary, long-distance country voice. Even sound asleep, I knew the physical shock reverberating head to toe should have sent me bolt upright in bed. But I remained completely still, eyes squeezed shut, desperate to keep the connection alive.

" 'Well, hello!' I said in the dream. Then, quickly, sensing time was running out, 'How are you? *Where* are you?'

"The line grew staticky, but it sounded like Mother said something about ghosts or toasts or hosts. Even asleep, I knew I hadn't heard her clearly, so I concentrated on what she said next as if life itself depended on it. And, in a way, it did.

"As the call dissolved in a hiss of snaps and pops, three words beamed through the heavens as powerfully as the effect they have on me still.

" 'I love you,' Quida Raye Perkins told me for the first time ever." Blinking back tears and modulating her voice, Joy sighed and leaned toward the mic.

"Though I responded before my eyes fluttered open, I always worried that the line had already died.

So now, every time I tape a country retrospective or serenade two-steppers down at the VFW hall, I play the kind of good old country music my mother never could resist. Because, just as light travels endlessly through space and time, I have come to pray that strains of the best country music might, too.

"Then, at the end, I ask my fans, old and new, to pull out their phones and call their mothers—even if the women drive them out of their ever-loving minds.

"And I always close by telling them what I'm telling you now—'Good night and God bless. Remember, tell your mama you love her, and thanks for indulging me as I do the same.'

"Because, Mother, if you're listening—and I know you are since I just played all your favorite songs—I have something to say at last.

"I love you, too."

A word about the author...

Kathy Des Jardins owns a publications firm in metro Atlanta and is a member of the Atlanta Writers Club and Roswell Reads. A former newspaper reporter, columnist, and editor, she won her first journalism award for a country concert review. During the next decade, another category would dominate her nearly 100 national, regional, and state awards: humor writing. In addition to winning two Louisiana Press Association's Best Regular Columnist Awards, four Louisiana Press Women Sweepstakes Awards, and a first for humor articles from the National Federation of Press Women, she was honored by the Louisiana-Mississippi Associated Press Newspaper Contests and United Press International Newspapers of Louisiana, among other organizations. She has also received California Press Women's Outstanding Excellence Award and USTA Georgia's Media Excellence Award.

Mama Tried, her first novel, revisits her two earliest, and most winning, themes: tragicomedy set to classic country music.

In addition to appearing in *O, Georgia! A Collection of Georgia's Newest and Most Promising Writers*, she has written for several national and regional publications. Beginning in 2015, she also penned a book column for a monthly Atlanta magazine.

Kathy claims dual citizenship, having been born in Kentucky and raised in Louisiana, where she fleetingly attended Louisiana State University-Alexandria and Louisiana College. She and her husband live in Johns Creek, Georgia, and have three sons.

http://kathydesjardins.com